Max Connor is the pseudonym for bestselling and award-winning author Neil Lancaster. He served as a military policeman and worked for the Metropolitan Police as a detective, investigating serious crimes in the capital and beyond. As a covert policing specialist, he used all manner of techniques to investigate and disrupt major crime and criminals. He now lives in the Scottish Highlands and works as a broadcaster and commentator on true crime documentaries. He is an expert on two Sky Crime TV series, *Meet, Marry, Murder* and *Made for Murder*.

Writing as Neil Lancaster, he is the author of the DS Max Craigie books, which have been twice longlisted for the McIlvanney Prize for Best Scottish Crime Book of the Year.

Also by Max Connor (as Neil Lancaster)

Dead Man's Grave
The Blood Tide
The Night Watch
Blood Runs Cold
The Devil You Know
When Shadows Fall

No Mercy

MAX CONNOR

ONE PLACE. MANY STORIES

HQ
An imprint of HarperCollins*Publishers* Ltd
1 London Bridge Street
London SE1 9GF

www.harpercollins.co.uk

HarperCollins*Publishers*
Macken House, 39/40 Mayor Street Upper,
Dublin 1 D01 C9W8
This edition 2025

1
First published in Great Britain by HQ,
an imprint of HarperCollins*Publishers* Ltd 2025

ISBN: 978-0-00-875154-8

Printed and bound in the UK using 100% Renewable
Electricity by CPI Group (UK) Ltd

This book contains FSC™ certified paper and other controlled sources
to ensure responsible forest management.
For more information visit: www.harpercollins.co.uk/green

This book is dedicated with deep respect to those who have worn, or continue to wear, the green beret, and who embody the commando values they live by. Courage, determination, unselfishness and cheerfulness in the face of adversity.

Life is mostly froth and bubble,
Two things stand like stone,
Kindness in another's trouble,
Courage in your own.

Extract from 'Ye Wearie Wayfarer'
Adam Lindsay Gordon, 1866

Chapter 1

Sunday 14 November 2021

Frankie Chapman looked at himself in the mirror. His blazer was clean and fresh from the dry-cleaner's, his shirt blinding white, his trousers sharply creased and his shoes like mirrors. He adjusted the knot on his blue, yellow, green and red striped tie, the colours of the Royal Marines, then picked up his green beret and pulled it onto his head, which was covered in closely shorn silver hair, and adjusted it to the correct angle, the globe and laurel badge above his left eye.

His gaze dropped to his jacket. Two rows of polished medals, each one topped with a different-coloured ribbon. They glittered in the morning sun that blazed through the window of his modest semi-detached house in Sandridge, a small village just outside St Albans. He and his wife, Macey, had settled here just after he'd been medically retired from the Corps in 2008, and it had been a good family home for them.

The memories flared in his mind of all the places he'd served in to earn those medals, and then even more strongly of the comrades and friends he had lost in wars fought. The Falklands,

Iraq, Afghanistan, Sierra Leone, Kosovo, Yugoslavia; the memories were almost technicolour in intensity, but it all suddenly felt terribly pointless, and the medals looked like what they were: cheap bits of non-precious metal attached to colourful lengths of ribbon. Not special, not unique, and not telling the true story of those who didn't come home. Pinned on him by others who wrote the citations to make themselves look good.

He sighed deeply, his limbs tingling, as they always did when he was anxious. Frankie was a man who feared nothing and had faced death up close many times, but the thought of being the subject of others' intrigue was uncomfortable. He preferred life in the shadows nowadays.

He looked at his watch, a battered Omega he'd had for years, and realised that it was time to go. It was just a short drive to the memorial at the top of St Albans, but it'd be busy with people paying their respects.

He wasn't marching with all the other old soldiers from the local Legion; that wasn't his bag at all. He'd never been one for drill during his twenty-six years in the Corps, even when he was the RSM, so he wasn't about to start now. He'd stand quietly on his own as the veterans marched past and then stare straight ahead as the 'Last Post' was played. Afterwards, he'd go to the local pub and toast his oppos with a pint, then come home, where he'd return the medals to the shoebox under his bed until next year.

Macey had wanted him to have them properly mounted in a frame, but that wasn't Frankie's way. Every time he looked at them, he could see the faces of those who hadn't come home, and it would take him back to those places he'd rather forget. The Distinguished Conduct Medal from the Falklands, almost forty years ago, the numerous campaign medals from all the other theatres he'd fought in. The Conspicuous Gallantry Cross, the Mention in Despatches, long service and good conduct, United Nations. To him, they were stained and tarnished with the blood of those who hadn't returned. They were the heroes, and he had just got lucky.

'Well, they should be in a safe then. Worth a few bob, I reckon,' Macey would say. He'd never told her how much the medals were really worth; how much the expert had estimated, in any case. That would have shocked her to her core, being the daughter of a labourer.

He'd been tempted to sell them, to put some money away for their daughter, Josie, but Macey had gone mad at the mere suggestion. 'You earned them, Frankie, all those tours, all those countries and the years away from home. You damn well wear them with pride.' She was a small woman, but she was full of fire, and not to be trifled with.

He looked at the framed photograph of their wedding day that hung on the wall, and smiled at her voluminous dress. 'Like a bog roll cover,' she'd said as the years rolled by and the chic became the kitsch. The smile widened at the daft grin on his best man's face – 'Macca' Mackenzie, resplendent in his own uniform, never managed an appropriate facial expression, whatever the occasion – then he sighed deeply at the sight of Macey, so kind and beautiful, standing there looking at him with eyes full of love as he held her arm, dressed in his best No. 1 uniform, thirty-eight years ago.

The next photo was of a group of old bootnecks, all in the same blazers, berets and medals. The 11/06 club, so named after the date of the battle of Mount Harriet in 1982. Macca, Charlie Drake, Jacko and Neil Asquith, their old officer. Great guys, all of them.

Next to that was a photo of Josie, his strong, tough daughter, dressed in her climbing gear and standing under an imposing rock face, arms aloft, still wearing her harness. He looked with pride at her wide, toothy smile, lean, sinewy frame and long dark hair tied back in a ponytail. She wasn't big, just like her mum, but she was strong, and moreover, she was the most determined person he knew. He straightened another snap of Josie, this time arms outstretched in the middle of Wenceslas Square in Prague, where she had spent almost two years teaching English. A smile crossed his face as he took in the next photo: Josie on stage playing the part of Peter Pan in a pantomime, years ago. She'd always loved the stage, before her real passion, for the outdoors, had taken over, apart from occasional forays into am-dram, where she'd loved showing off her prowess at accents, impressions and dressing up.

Josie was a real chip off the old block, and was forever away on expeditions, climbing mountains, parachuting, mountain-biking or on some mad triathlon somewhere around the world. His chest swelled with pride as he thought about her achievements.

The phone began to ring on the sideboard, an old-fashioned bell type that always made him jump.

'Hello?'

'Hi, Frankie, it's Jenny. Are you coming in today?' The bright voice belonged to one of the staff at the care home where Macey now lived.

'I was going to later on, yes.'

'Macey's awfully upset, love. She had a terrible night, and I don't think she'll be able to rest until she's seen you. Will you come?'

Frankie sighed and closed his eyes. This had been happening more often of late. Macey's decline from early-onset Alzheimer's had been as shocking to watch as it had been cruel. He looked at his watch. Almost 10.15; he'd miss the 'Last Post'. His hand touched the metal of the Conspicuous Gallantry Cross, which was cold and smooth.

'I'm on my way,' he said.

'Thanks, love,' and Jenny hung up.

Frankie unpinned the clasp from the medal group and pulled them away from his blazer. Then he walked back through to the bedroom and, with some difficulty, dropped to his knees, one of which creaked alarmingly. He pulled the shoebox lined with tissue paper out from under the bed, placed the medals in it, replaced the lid and pushed it back out of sight.

Pulling up his trouser leg, exposing the smooth, dull metal

4

of his prosthetic limb, he made a minor adjustment to the knee joint and, leaning on the bedside table for support, eased himself back up. His stump ached and itched like a bastard, as it always did in the mornings, an ever-present reminder of the improvised explosive device in Helmand in 2008 that had cost him his career.

He loosened his tie, grabbed his keys and left the house, locking the door behind him. It was only a ten-minute walk to the Verulam Lodge nursing home, and he always chose to walk if he could, remembering a time when he wasn't sure he'd ever walk again. Hopefully he'd be able to settle Macey, and then go and pay his respects quietly a little later. It was sometimes better that way, anyway. His medals sometimes caused a bit of a stir with the military groupies who often stalked these occasions.

Attention that Frankie wanted to avoid.

Chapter 2

'You look smart, Doctor,' said Macey as Frankie walked into her small but comfortable room, eyeing him with a suspicious smile.

'Remembrance Sunday, love,' said Frankie, stooping to kiss her on the cheek where she sat in her high-backed chair.

'Oi, you cheeky bugger. I'm a married woman, you know. If my husband finds you kissing me, there'll be hell to pay, let me tell you. Used to be a sergeant major. You'd better watch out, as he'd be none too happy,' she said, her voice sharp and the once-captivating green eyes flat and full of confusion.

'Oh, sorry, Mrs Chapman, I didn't know. I'll be less familiar next time. How about a handshake?' Frankie extended his hand, which she took. Hers was small and dry, and the skin felt papery thin.

Macey stood only five feet tall in her stockinged feet. Her normally immaculate hair was thin and grey, and her once-ruddy cheeks were sunken and hollow now. Frankie's heart surged with love, only tainted by how his vibrant wife had become the husk she now was. Time passed inexorably, but it had treated his poor wife particularly cruelly. Dementia wasn't picky. He'd got lucky;

6

Macey hadn't. It was hard not to be bitter.

'More appropriate, isn't it? Not too much to ask for? Now, Doctor, what's wrong with me?'

'How'd you mean, Macey?'

'You know perfectly well what I mean. Why am I here, and when can I go home?' she said, her eyes querulous.

'Soon, hopefully.'

'I need to be with my Frankie. He's a lousy cook and he'll be losing weight. Can't have that, can we?'

'No, of course not. Would you like me to read to you?' said Frankie, pointing to the well-thumbed Danielle Steel novel that lay on the small table.

'Yes, that'd be wonderful, Doctor. For some reason I find reading such a chore nowadays. I keep telling the other doctors, but they never listen to me. But then no bugger listens to me.' She pursed her lips and wiped her mouth on the ever-present handkerchief clutched in her hand.

Frankie grabbed the book and sat on the bed. It always happened this way. She was initially mildly suspicious of him, but then she thawed. He'd learnt the lessons of trying to allow his wife a more contented journey with dementia, and that meant never correcting her. Doing so made her anxious and angry, and then things would just deteriorate. So he'd simply sit with her, or maybe they'd watch TV together, or chat if she wanted to, but they'd always, always read the first chapter of the Danielle Steel novel. Without fail, by the time he'd got to page fifteen, Macey would be asleep.

He opened the worn and creased cover of the book.

'What's this one called?' said Macey, looking at it over the top of her spectacles.

'It's called *A Perfect Stranger*. You read it on honeymoon in Majorca, remember?' said Frankie, looking deep into her green eyes.

And then briefly, like a snapshot in time, the clouds cleared from the sun and she smiled her beautiful smile. She extended her hand and rested it on Frankie's as it clutched the novel. 'Of course I remember, poppet. How could I possibly forget?'

Frankie smiled back and curled his fingers around his wife's hand. '*I'll* never forget, darling.'

'Well get on with it, then.' She closed her eyes, and in that moment, his beautiful, kind wife was back in the room.

He cleared his throat and began to read.

As always, Macey had fallen asleep quickly, peaceful and relaxed and breathing easily. Frankie looked at his watch. It was almost midday, and all the crowds and marchers would have gone from the memorial. He decided then that rather than get in the car, he'd go to the lychgate at St Leonard's Church close by. It was a lovely, peaceful place, and as it was a bright, chilly day, it'd be pleasant to spend a few moments there alone with his thoughts. He didn't like the huge, elaborate ceremonies, full of politicians, councillors and dignitaries, all present just to be seen. He really preferred to do his acts of remembrance in private, so this was perfect.

He adjusted the poppy in his lapel and picked up the pace as he crossed the road from the nursing home and walked towards the church.

The lychgate was a free-standing structure at the entrance to the churchyard, with a tiled roof and the names of fallen soldiers on slate plaques. A small red wreath had been left to the side of it, and half a dozen wooden crosses with poppies at the centre had been jammed into the grass. As always, Frankie felt the familiar tingle at the nape of his neck and a slight quickening of his breathing as he read the names. So many young men sent by politicians to foreign countries and their deaths. It was hard not to feel a little bitter.

He stood there for a few minutes, almost meditative, his mind full of a lifetime worth of images from his own experiences.

Memories of friends killed, blown up or dismembered by mines and IEDs. Such a waste. He began to feel tears well in his eyes, so he decided it was time to go. The Rose and Crown would be open, and a pint would be welcome. He plucked his poppy from his lapel and tucked it into a crevice in the rough brickwork, bowed his head for a moment, then strode off, his limp barely detectable to any onlookers.

The pub was almost empty, with just Bernie, one of the regulars, propping up the bar, a half-drunk pint in front of him.

'Afternoon, Frankie, what can I get you?' greeted Leo, the always smiling young barman.

'Usual, please, Leo. New ink?' Frankie nodded at the barman's forearm, which had a fresh-looking tattoo of chains snaking around it.

'Yeah, fairly new. How's Macey?' Leo asked as he pulled the pint.

'Just come from her now. Fair to middling is the best I can say, son.'

'Josie okay?'

'Aye, climbing in the Cairngorms right now, but she'll be back if you need babysitting.' Frankie attempted a smile. They'd known Leo and his family for years, and Josie had often looked after the barman when he was younger.

'I'd not mind, Frankie. She can drink more than me, and she knows more about rugby, so we'd have a cool night,' Leo said, grinning, as he deposited the pint on the bar.

'I'll tell her.'

'Give them both my best, yeah? Mum was asking after you all.'

Frankie gave a silent toast to all the faces currently swirling around his mind and drank his beer quickly. Bernie was starting to look like he might want a conversation and Frankie really wasn't in the mood, as even a brief chat with the old boy could stretch out interminably. He finished his pint and left, walking through the park and into his road, enjoying the warming rays of the weak early-winter sun.

When he arrived at the bottom of the cul-de-sac, he immediately saw that something was wrong. His front door was slightly ajar. He furrowed his brow. He'd locked up, of that he was sure. It was a pretty safe neighbourhood, but there had been some burglaries, so he was always careful.

But the door was definitely open, just a crack.

He looked around, his heart beginning to beat more urgently. Feeling for the phone in his pocket, he checked for signs of life at the houses either side of his, but both seemed quiet.

Cautiously he moved up the drive, where his Fiesta was parked, and eased towards the front door, straining to hear anything from within. He could see that there was no damage to the door, and he tried to remember if he'd double-locked it, but try as he might, he couldn't recall.

He pushed at it gently and it swung noiselessly inwards on smooth hinges. He poked his head inside. Everything in the front room looked as he'd left it. Immaculate. He breathed out. Maybe he had just neglected to shut the door properly. The lock wasn't the best, and sometimes if slammed, the door would bounce back open. That had happened once or twice in the past.

Then, out of nowhere, a figure appeared in the hall and stopped dead at the sight of Frankie standing at the door. He was in his thirties, skinny and scruffy, with a wild bird's nest of rust-coloured hair on top of a pale, spotty face. He clutched a shoebox in his hand. Frankie's shoebox. The box where his medals were stored.

Frankie felt rage surge in his chest at the sight of the intruder in his home, his fists curling tight. 'You made a big mistake coming to my house, son,' he snarled, his lips bared. Fight or flight was fully in operation, and Frankie only knew one way. He might have been the wrong side of sixty and only have one leg, but this bastard was soon going to realise he'd made a serious mistake.

The intruder didn't hesitate; he exploded towards Frankie and tried to barge past him. Frankie reached out and grabbed at the grimy collar of his denim jacket. The shoebox fell from his grip and hit the path, spilling open, the medals clattering free onto the concrete. Frankie snarled with naked aggression. The intruder, however, was stronger than he looked. There was a sudden tug-of-war as he struggled to escape Frankie's clutches, dragging him off the step and onto the path. Frankie stumbled, with the lack of flexibility in his prosthetic leg, but he kept a vice-like grip on the jacket collar and heaved backwards, towards the house. Quick as a flash, the intruder shrugged out of the jacket, like a reptile sloughing off its skin, and sprinted away, leaving the garment in Frankie's hands. All resistance suddenly having disappeared, Frankie overbalanced and fell backwards, hitting the hard ground like a falling sandbag, the back of his skull cracking on the door-step with a sickening thud.

Brightly coloured sparks burst behind his eyes like fireworks, and he felt warm wetness on his neck. He managed to turn his head, just as the thief dipped down, scooped the medals up and took off like a greyhound. His vision began to sparkle and swirl, and he reached a trembling hand towards the empty box, his mouth gaping, trying to suck in air. The last thing he saw was his neighbour's face looking on in shock, calling his name, before everything went black.

Chapter 3

Monday 15 November 2021

Josie Chapman felt as if someone had hollowed her chest out, such was the grief that gripped her as she perched next to her father, her green eyes full of tears. She held his hand, which was festooned with wires and monitors as he lay in the intensive care unit at Luton and Dunstable Hospital.

The tiredness she felt was bone-wearingly overwhelming. Twenty-four hours ago, she'd been leading a small group on Creag Dubh in the Cairngorm mountain range, on a charity-paid expedition she'd been running, teaching some kids to climb. A call from her parents' neighbour and dear friend, Liz, had shattered everything.

A call to the local police had revealed the terrible details. Dad had been badly injured during a burglary at the house, and his medals were gone. Leaving the group with her co-leader, she'd dived into her car and driven the ten hours back to Hertfordshire and straight to the hospital, where she'd been ever since.

Her dad was flat on his back, a breathing tube in his mouth and his eyelids taped down. Monitor leads snaked from his chest, which was covered in a patterned hospital gown.

Josie looked at her father's arm, once so thick and strong, now slim and wrinkled, the commando dagger tattoo a fading blue smudge on his forearm, the motto '*Per Mare Per Terram*' still visible through the fine mist of hairs. His head was swathed in bandages after the operation to release the pressure from a serious bleed on the brain. Things were initially thought to have gone well, but he was showing signs of a further bleed and his EEG scan was 'of concern', as the consultant had described it.

As tears began to flow from her eyes and down her cheeks, a shadow fell across her and she realised that she wasn't on her own.

She turned to see a smart middle-aged woman in a business suit, a lanyard around her neck holding a police identity card. The name on it was Detective Inspector Judith Kelly.

'Miss Chapman?' she said in a softly accented voice.

'Yes,' Josie replied, reaching for a tissue, which she used to dab at her tears.

'DI Kelly from the Hertfordshire and Bedfordshire major incident team. We're investigating the attack on your father. I'm so sorry this has happened.' The woman's voice was sincere, and her eyes were full of concern.

'Who did this?' said Josie, turning back to her father, the rasp of his breathing accentuated by the ventilator.

'We're doing all we can to find out, I promise. Your father ripped the burglar's jacket from him, and it's been submitted for DNA examination. We're hoping for results imminently. Did DC Johnson not say?'

'He said that things had been sent away, and he told me that Dad's neighbour, Liz, saw what happened through the window. The bastard pulled him over and he smashed his head.' Josie's voice was as hard as tempered steel, and her jaw was tight.

'Have the doctors said much?'

'I'm just waiting for someone to arrive. I was called urgently, and the nurse isn't saying much. I'm really worried he's going to die.' Fresh tears welled in Josie's eyes as she gripped her father's hand even tighter.

'They'll do everything possible for him.' The cop squeezed Josie's shoulder softly. Normally she'd have found this uncomfortable, but there was something about DI Kelly that was genuine and warm.

'Is the house a mess?' she asked, clearing her throat and wiping her eyes.

'Not at all. It seems the burglar only went into his bedroom. There was an empty shoebox where he fell outside the house. Does that mean anything to you?'

'A shoebox?'

'Yes. Was there something valuable inside it?'

Josie closed her eyes, realisation arriving. 'His medals. His bloody medals.'

'Medals?'

'Yes, Inspector. My father spent his life in the Royal Marines and fought all over the world. He was the bravest man anyone knew and his medal group was unique. DCM, CGC, Mention in Despatches and many more. We told him he should put them somewhere safe, but he wouldn't listen.'

'Were they valuable?'

'Very. He'd been offered a lot of money for them on a number of occasions, but Mum would never entertain the idea.' Josie massaged her temples, the pressure swirling in her head like a maelstrom.

DI Kelly's face softened. 'How is your mother?'

'She knows nothing. She has early-onset dementia and is in a home close to the house. No way can I tell her; she'd never be able to process this.'

There was a knock at the door, and a man wearing scrubs walked into the room, a stethoscope around his neck. His name badge read *Dr Khan* and his face was solemn.

'Doctor?' said Josie, her voice trailing off, her heart sinking.

His body language and expression told her that there was no good news to impart.

'Ms Chapman, we need to speak. Shall we go somewhere private?' He looked towards DI Kelly.

'Can Dad hear us?' said Josie, her voice wobbling.

'He's in an induced coma, so I can't be sure either way.'

'Then we should stay. He always wanted to hear news straight, good or bad. I want him to be aware of everything; it's his right.' She stroked her father's hand, tears falling from her cheeks and onto his sallow skin.

'Would you like me to leave, Josie?' said DI Kelly.

'No, please stay,' Josie said, her voice wobbling.

Dr Khan pulled up a chair, clasped his hands in front of him and sighed. 'The EEG and CT scans show that there has been a substantial subdural bleed. The operation did ease it for some time, but it seems there is another bleed that has put pressure on your father's brain stem. I'm sorry, but there appears to be very little we can do.'

The silence in the room was heavy and thick, only punctuated by the soft rasping from the ventilator.

'Unfortunately, our latest scans are showing coning, which means your father's brain is being forced through the small opening at the base of the skull. I'm sorry to say that there are no signs of electrical activity in that area, and all manual tests are not optimistic. That leads us to draw only one conclusion: that your father's brain stem has died. I have to tell you that I think we have come to the end of the road.' His voice was kind and calm, which was at odds with the medicalised language he used.

'So he's dying now?' said Josie, the colour draining from her face.

'The ventilator is keeping his tissue alive, but were that withdrawn, he would die. Again, I'm so sorry to be relaying this news.'

Josie looked at her father. Her indestructible hero. The man who had given everything for his country and his family, lying there pale, withered and tiny.

DI Kelly moved forward and put her arm around Josie's shoulders. 'I'm so sorry, Josie,' she said.

'Promise me you'll get the bastard who did this.'

'I promise. I'll do everything in my power to make him pay.'

Chapter 4

Tuesday 16 November 2021

Josie unlocked the front door of her childhood home and stepped inside, feeling numb. As the doctor had predicted, as soon as the life support had been withdrawn, Frank Chapman, her dear father, had simply slipped away, Josie clutching his hand and staring at his face. When the doctor had confirmed that he'd gone, she'd just nodded and left wordlessly, not knowing what to say or do. She'd gone home, to her small place in the centre of St Albans, and surprisingly had pretty much passed out on the sofa, waking hours later wondering where the hell she was.

She was devastated to realise that she hadn't been dreaming.

Her parents' living room was as it had been for years. Comfortable, clean, tidy and homely, still with the feminine edges that her dad hadn't knocked off even after her mother had moved to the nursing home. Beyond regular vacuuming and dusting, he'd just left it alone, in some forlorn hope that Macey would one day return.

Of course, she never would, and now neither would her dad. Josie was empty of tears, with none left to give, but she swallowed a golf ball as she realised that she was now effectively an orphan. She'd soon learnt the realities of dementia, in that you had to get used to watching your dear mother die a little more each day. A series of bereavements that would only worsen. She felt the emotions begin to bubble again, but forced them away. What would her dad have said?'

'No point dripping about it, love. Get on with it and move forwards. Always move forwards.'

Josie walked through the house, towards the kitchen diner at the back, a comfortable and airy space that her parents had had renovated a decade ago, just before Mum's decline began. Similar to the rest of the house, it was immaculate.

She knew where she had to look. Her dad, ever practical, had impressed it upon her. 'I've made all the arrangements, my girl. If I slip off this mortal coil before your mum, it's all in there.'

Josie went to the small unit in the corner of the room and slid open the top drawer. A plain white envelope was in there with just one word written in her dad's small, neat handwriting. *Josie.*

She went to a knife block on the work surface and with trembling hands slit the envelope open, pulled out the sheet of paper. Then she took a deep breath and began to read.

My darling Josie,

If you're reading this, then it looks like things have gone belly-up for me. Such is life (and death).

Sorry I didn't stick around as long as I'd hoped, but either something crap has befallen me, or the hangover from all the bloody injuries got too much for my old body.

Now, Josie, you'll know that I'm not one for overly elaborate things like a letter from beyond the grave, all far too showy for a man like me, but we always did them before we went to war, so this seems the best way.

Maybe we should have had this conversation before, but I'm not the greatest at heart-to-hearts, so this is the easiest way. For me at least.

You'll know how much the nursing home is costing, as despite all my years of service I've been paying for your mum's care costs ever since she went in. There's little to no chance that the council will ever pay them, and if they do, she'll almost certainly be moved to a much cheaper place, which I just can't let happen.

So here we go. It's all in legal speak in my will, but in short this is what should happen. Depending on how much time has elapsed, there should be enough savings to last for a while. I've not touched my compensation from after I got blown up, so there's still a decent sum there, all left to your mum in trust for you. After that, the only asset left is the house, and we both always wanted that to be kept for you to set you up for life. We've made good money on it, and there's no mortgage, so protect that money, Josie. This place has been good for us, so it can be good for you. A home base to come back to in between all your mad expeditions will be just what you need. I spent so much time away from home with the Corps that this place meant a lot to me when I retired. It can do the same for you.

It's in the will that it can't be sold while your mum is still with us, as I know what you're like. You were always contrary, but the house is our legacy to you. Live in it, or sell it to buy your next place, but not to fund Mum's care, okay?

Now this may be hard to swallow, and your mum always forbade me from ever doing it, but it's what I want. If the cash runs out, I want you to sell the medals. I had an expert (Mark Smith, nice bloke on the *Antiques Roadshow*) look at them a while back and he tells me that if they were to be sold, they'd make some serious cash as they're pretty unique. I know what you and Mum will think of this, but as far as I'm concerned, they're just things – people and being able to live your life is what matters. Whatever they make should be more than enough to keep your mum in a decent home for the rest of her days and any left is for you. That plus maybe chuck a few quid behind the bar at the Rose and Crown for whichever of the 11/06 club are left. No big military funeral. Just whichever of the old lot want to come. Dig a hole and sling me in the ground, love. Memories stay with you for ever, so no need for a big do that will cost a right packet. Maybe have the service at St Leonard's. I'll need every bit of help I can to get me past St Peter at the pearly gates, so a word from the nice vicar there might help.

Always know, Josie, that despite everything I've done in my life, the wars I fought in and all the medals that were pinned on my chest, you are my proudest achievement. Keep on grabbing life by the throat and squeezing every bit of fun out of it.

Love always,
Dad x

Chapter 5

Saturday 11 December 2021

It was a beautiful if chilly winter's day as the mourners stood in the small, shady graveyard next to the church.

Josie's Chapman's fingers went to the battered and scratched Omega that her dad had been wearing when he died. She'd had the strap adjusted so it would fit around her slim wrist; it still felt big and bulky, but it was comforting to the touch. She watched as her father's coffin was carried from the hearse by six of his former colleagues and friends from the marines, many of whom she recognised from her time at the bases they'd stayed on over the years. They were dressed in blue blazers and Corps ties, with medals on their chests that glittered in the weak sun. They lowered the coffin to the grass next to the yawning hole, stepped back as one, heads bowed, then turned in unison and marched a few steps away before joining the rest of the mourners. All low-key and respectful as silence descended on the graveyard, with just some birdsong and the whispering of the wind as it passed through the naked trees.

The previous four weeks had been hideous. A whirl of meetings with cops, solicitors, undertakers and extended family, and of course, many excruciating sessions trying to get her mother to understand. Josie still wasn't sure if her poor mum had any clue that the man she'd loved for over forty years was no longer with them.

She stared at the pale wood of the coffin, unable to process that her father was inside it, about to be lowered into the clay soil. Her eyes flicked to his treasured green beret, which was laid on the top of the coffin. She rested her hand on her mother's shoulder. Macey was in a wheelchair next to her, dressed in black with a chequered blanket over her knees. She stared directly ahead, but her eyes were flat, confused, and she was clearly not taking the events in at all.

Tears streamed down Josie's face, and she sobbed as her dear dad was lowered into the gaping hole in the ground. She knew that from that moment, nothing would ever be the same again. All her achievements as an athlete, a competitor, an explorer would mean less because the person she'd shared them with was gone. Everything felt so empty, and she wondered who would she celebrate with now.

One of the pallbearers approached, his face simultaneously full of kindness and sadness. She recognised him immediately.

'Macca, I'm so glad you came,' she said, throwing her arms around the short, wiry man. He had a worn, lined face and silver-grey hair, and wore a blazer with a crest on the breast pocket. In his hand was the familiar green beret, but unlike the other pallbearers, his blazer badge was the crossed oars and frog of the Special Boat Service, the SBS. The motto read, 'Not by strength, by guile'.

Macca had been a constant presence in her life for decades, being a long-term comrade of her father, and she'd grown up regularly visiting him and his family at their house in Poole. He was now divorced and living alone close by. Josie always felt like Macca was lonely. Having given everything to the SBS, there was nothing left for him. Despite being in his early sixties, he looked much younger.

'I'm so sorry, Josie. Your dad was a great man,' he said, his eyes damp and full of emotion. His voice was rich and sonorous, with a soft Scottish burr still detectable.

'Thank you,' was all she could manage to say as she buried her face in his broad chest, his double row of medals digging into her. Her dad had worked with Macca for years before Macca undertook the gruelling selection for the Special Forces, but they'd stayed in touch and seen each other as often as they could.

Macca turned to her mother and took hold of her hand. 'Hello, Macey love. It's me, Macca. I'm so sorry,' he said, his voice cracking.

'You shouldn't be holding my hand, you know. If my husband finds out, well, I don't know what he'd do. He's the jealous type, let me tell you,' Macey admonished him, pulling her hand away hastily and rearranging the chequered blanket that lay across her lap, shaking her head and rolling her eyes.

'Oh, I'm sorry, Macey love. I'll be more respectful, I promise.'

'That's better. A little decorum isn't too much to ask, is it?' Macey nodded in apparent satisfaction at her rebuke of her old friend.

'Of course not, love.'

'I don't like funerals – they make me sad,' she said, casting her eyes down.

'No one likes funerals, Mum, but it's a beautiful day, yes?' said Josie, looking at her pale, tiny mother, who was glancing from side to side at the mourners, many of whom were in uniform, or at least in blazers with crests on the pockets and green berets on their heads. The morning light sparkled on the rows of medals that adorned their chests.

'Are you coming to the pub?' Josie asked Macca, who was shifting uncomfortably from foot to foot.

'Definitely. All the boys from the 11/06 club want to pay their respects and raise a pint to old Chappers.'

'So who's died?' said Macey, her brow furrowed with confusion.

'We talked about this, Mum. It's Dad's funeral.' Josie's voice was soft and kind.

'Poor Dad. I miss him so much. Firm but fair, he was. Kindest man ever, although my mum was the real disciplinarian, let me tell you,' Macey said, dabbing at her eyes with a handkerchief.

Josie felt an overwhelming surge of love for her mum as she sat in the wheelchair, her eyes full of confusion. They'd agonised over whether she should attend, but her key worker felt it was for the best, and Josie had agreed.

They were a small family; both Frankie and Macey had been only children, and all the grandparents had long since passed away, so it had always just been the three of them. It never used to matter, as her parents were so formidable, and her dad's work had given them all the family they'd ever needed.

Her feelings of deep, dark sorrow were suddenly joined by something else even more palpable. Her mother might be confused, but Josie Chapman knew exactly what she wanted.

She wanted revenge.

Chapter 6

The remaining members of the 11/06 club had all gathered. Macca, whose full name was Gordon Mackenzie, sat opposite Pete 'Charlie' Drake, Jim 'Jacko' Jackson and Neil Asquith. They'd been thrown together during the Falklands conflict almost forty years ago, and though they'd gone their separate ways afterwards, they'd stayed in touch, and after retirement had ended up living close to each other. They were all in their early sixties now, apart from Jacko, who was a little younger.

In the last few years, they'd taken to meeting each 11 June to have a beer and remember the events of that day in the South Atlantic, and this was going to be their first meeting without Chappers being present. They sat in silence, pints of dark bitter in front of them, each with a traditional glass of port to the side. Four furled green berets sat on the chipped wooden table next to their drinks.

They all exchanged knowing looks, before Macca raised his glass of port. Despite the fact that Asquith had been the commissioned officer on that date all those years ago, Macca had become the unspoken leader. Asquith had remained in the Corps for a few years after the Falklands before leaving and moving into the business world, whereas Macca had gone on to have a glittering three-decade career in the elite Special Boat Service, rising to the rank of regimental sergeant major.

The other three raised their glasses too, and waited respectfully.

'Chappers,' was all Macca said.

Chapter 7

Friday 11 June 1982,
Mount Harriet, Falkland Islands

Corporal Frank 'Chappers' Chapman knew that tonight was going to be the longest night of his life when the tracer rounds from the Argentinian forces' machine guns began to crack over their heads as they made their last approach towards Mount Harriet. Any trace of the bone-wearing fatigue after many days yomping in filthy weather had been blown away by the adrenaline of the firework display that was going on over their heads right now.

The incoming bullets didn't sing like nightingales, buzz like bees or even hum like hummingbirds as war poets would have you believe. The report was a sharp crack as the supersonic slugs of hot metal broke the sound barrier above their heads.

It was supposed to be a 'snurgling', or covert, approach by Chappers' section, a recce at the base with the objective of drawing fire, but then Jacko, a nineteen-year-old cockney bootneck, trod on a mine. He was screaming in pain, in open ground, with bullets thumping into the soggy peat around him.

Chappers raised his head above the rock he'd dived behind.

'Medic!' he screamed at the top of his lungs, as the bullets began to dance around their position, a much deeper and heavier report that he recognised immediately. Shit, he thought, that was a .50. A heavy machine gun, designed to shred vehicles. It could decimate the whole troop, let alone their section. They needed to get back into some proper cover. Now. But they couldn't leave Jacko where he was. Chappers crawled along the dirt to the troop boss, Lieutenant Neil Asquith, who was sheltering in a depression in the tussocky grass and shaking with a mixture of cold and fear. Marine 'Charlie' Drake, the signaller, was next to him, eyes wide, his headset askew.

'Charlie, have you called for a CASEVAC?' said Chappers.

Charlie just shook his head and looked towards the troop commander.

'You've called the contact in?'

'Yeah, but everyone's in the shit, mate. We're on our own for now.' Charlie's face was grim, but he looked determined and resolute.

'Boss, we need to get Jacko into cover and get that machine gun silenced. It'll stop the whole advance and that'll leave J troop exposed,' said Chappers, his voice edged with hardness.

Asquith just sat there, still looking impossibly young despite the grime and camouflage cream. He seemed shell-shocked, his face ashen and his mouth agape. The twenty-year-old lieutenant was fresh out of Lympstone's young officer training programme, and this was the baptism of fire to end all baptisms of fire.

'Sir, we need to make a plan. There's a fifty-cal two hundred metres ahead, between us and the objective. We have to take it out or the timings are gonna be fucked.'

'Shit, what do we do, Chappers?' Asquith's hands trembled as he rubbed his face.

There was a pop, and a flare went up a few hundred yards away, momentarily bathing the mountain in a ghostly white light. The ground around them suddenly exploded with a long burst of automatic gunfire, and they all buried their heads in the soft, boggy peat. The light went out almost as quickly as it had arrived.

Chappers looked at the young officer. 'You have to lead these men is what you have to do, sir. We need to take out that fifty-cal, then we can assault the slope to the first ridge line.' His tone was sharper than it should have been when addressing a commissioned officer.

Asquith opened his mouth, his jaw quivering, but he didn't answer. He'd lost it. Chappers made a decision there and then.

'Heads up and into firing positions, boys,' he yelled, 'and when I shout, give me loads of covering fire. There's a fifty-cal two hundred to our front; watch my tracer for location.'

The lads from his half-section recce patrol all looked up and repositioned themselves, snuggling down into the soaking peat, SLRs pulled into their shoulders, ready to engage. Muscle memory of years of intensive training coming to the fore at exactly the right time.

Chappers ignored Jacko's screams, knowing that he couldn't get to him until that machine-gun crew had their heads firmly down. He reached into his combat jacket pocket, where he had three loose tracer rounds, each tipped with phosphorus, which would ignite when fired. Working the action of his SLR, he slotted a round into the chamber and slid the working parts forward.

He pulled the weapon in to his shoulder, his eyes fixed on the deep shadow of a cluster of rocks where he'd seen the flashes from the machine gun, and squeezed the trigger on the SLR. It bucked as the round streaked towards the firing point like a supersonic firework, bright in the dark.

'All seen?' he yelled as the machine gun sparked up again, too high, but getting lower as the gunner got his aim in.

'Seen,' came the reply from his lads.

'Okay, when I shout, I want as much lead as possible on that position while I grab Jacko,' he bellowed.

'Roger that,' came the reply.

Chappers closed up to Asquith. 'Boss, get in position and put down some fire, and fucking switch on. You need to grip this while I'm getting Jacko out.'

Asquith just nodded, but he began to move into a firing position, his jaw firming with renewed determination.

'NOW!' screamed Chappers, leaping to his feet and charging forward, zigzagging towards the still-screaming Jacko. Thunderous gunfire erupted from behind him as the boys laid down fire on the machine gun.

He didn't pause or flinch at the mud kicking up as the .50 still spat its murderous volley; he just pumped his legs until he reached Jacko. Grabbing him by the shoulder strap of his webbing, he dragged him along the bumpy turf, thankful now for all the hellish phys sessions on the bottom field at Lympstone and the regular training they performed. Fitness in battle was everything.

Clutching his SLR in one hand and towing Jacko with the other, he moved as fast as he could until he reached his half-section, where he ditched the still-grunting marine on the ground and quickly assessed his injury. The mine blast had shredded his boot, and blood was oozing through the gouged leather, but he wasn't going to die. 'You okay, Jacko?'

'I'm hanging out, mate, but it's still attached. I'll live,' said Jacko with a crooked smile, his cockney accent as wide as the Thames. This was typical Jacko. He was a disaster area in the troop, always in the shit, often late and invariably scruffy, but he was hard as nails, and never without a beaming grin that showed his broken teeth.

Chappers tossed a field dressing at him. 'You're lucky, mate, anti-personnel mine. I reckon it was buried too deep, or you'd be missing one of your boots, together with your foot.'

Jacko's ropy teeth almost shone in the flash of a flare. 'Yeah, I'm feeling really fucking lucky, you twat,' and he cackled loudly.

Chappers returned his grin. 'Stop dripping and get the dressing on. It's a flesh wound only. We're gonna be busy shutting that gun up.'

He went back to the section and clapped one of the senior guys on the shoulder. 'Macca, that gun has to come down. Get the rest of the lads in a position to give more fire.'

'Yes, mate. On it.' Macca moved away. He was a good man, a tough little Scot who'd been in the troop a few years. He was one of the best bootnecks Chappers had served with, and he knew he'd do the business.

Chappers moved back to Asquith, who was looking a little more together. A sudden shaft of moonlight emerged from behind the thick cloud and bathed his cam-cream-smeared face in white light. Chappers fixed him with a firm stare. 'Right, sir. Can you organise the guys and get ready to pour fire down on the gun?'

'Should we not withdraw and get Jacko to the RAP?' said Asquith, referring to the regimental aid post some five hundred metres to their rear.

'If we do, we open ourselves up to that gun. Proximity is the only thing making it hard for him to get an aim on us. If we withdraw, we'll be bang in his sights. I'm gonna flank left and move up fast and frag the bastards. Track me with the night sight, and when I'm within ten metres, call a ceasefire. I don't want to get shot by one of ours, okay?'

Asquith nodded, and hefted the bulky night sight that was around his neck on a bungee cord.

'Don't take your eyes off me while I outflank them, yeah?'

The lieutenant's jaw firmed up and his eyes hardened, the resolve visibly returning.

'You've got this, boss. Just think of it like the final exercise at the end of your training. We're all chinstrapped, our feet are fucked in these shit DMS boots and all that bloody yomping, but we're bootnecks. We do this for fun, yeah?' Chappers clapped his commander on the shoulder.

'Go for it, Chappers. We'll put a wall of fire down,' and Asquith even managed a wry grin.

'Are we all ready?' said Chappers.

31

There were nods all round, tired, filthy faces grim. They were bootnecks. They lived for this shit. 'Yeah, let's do it,' said Macca.

'Okay, on three, light the bastards up. One, two, three, now!'

Seven high-velocity rifles opened up at the machine gun's location in a thunderous cacophony of deafening fire.

Chappers leapt to his feet and sprinted left, his SLR clutched in both hands as he leapt from rock to rock, ascending the low slope that led to Mount Harriet. The machine gun had fallen silent as the occupant of the bunker took shelter from the withering fire. Suddenly there was a flash just yards in front of him, followed by a sudden violent impact to his side, like he'd been kicked. He grunted, but didn't stop, just kept heading to where he'd seen the flash coming from. A lone Argentine, American-style helmet on his head, was in a trench just five yards ahead, his face pasty white in the flashes from the gunfire. He had a rifle in his hand that was pointing straight at Chappers. Chappers raised his own rifle and pulled the trigger.

Nothing happened. Just a dry click. A stoppage. He didn't hesitate; he just unleashed a bloodcurdling cry and plunged his bayonet straight into the face of the young Argentinian soldier, twisting it with a further roar before withdrawing it and diving into the trench alongside the dying soldier, chest heaving and hands shaking with the adrenaline that was surging through his body.

Without even a sideways glance at the soldier next to him, he quickly cleared the stoppage on his SLR, then moved his hand to where he'd felt the impact. There was no pain, but there was a huge hole in his soaked water pouch. A smile somehow stretched across his face and he began to chuckle. Their training team had always impressed on them that their water bottle was a life-saver, but he doubted that they'd meant this way. He took a deep breath and counted silently to three, then leapt out of the trench and resumed his ascent towards the machine-gun bunker.

Taking a grenade from his webbing pouch, he dropped to a

half-crawl and eased up to the sandbagged wall of the bunker, which was about five feet in height. He pulled out the pin, stood up and threw the grenade over the wall before falling to his stomach and jamming his fingers into his ears. The machine gun began to pound again now that the fire from the section had stopped, but only a dozen rounds were fired before the grenade exploded with the familiar dull *crump*.

The machine gun fell silent, and the only sound in that moment was the wind that howled across the bleak, desolate landscape.

Chapter 8

Saturday 11 December 2021

'Chappers!' The 11/06 all sank the ruby-red liquid before returning the glasses to the table. Then they stared at each other, the tension tight and thick in the busy, buzzing pub.

'Charlie, have you heard anything on the cop grapevine about the bastard that did this?' said Macca, taking an exploratory sip of his pint.

Charlie looked left and right before speaking, as if checking for eavesdroppers, and shifted his bulk in his chair. He was a heavy-set man, with a bit of middle-age spread and slightly wobbling jowls. He'd left the Corps a few years after the Falklands and gone straight into the Metropolitan Police, where he'd risen to the rank of detective chief inspector, before transferring to the National Crime Agency for a few years until his recent retirement.

'I had a brief word with DI Kelly just before the funeral, but she's being cagey. She seems competent enough, and she's agreed to have another chat with me and Josie later. Fortunately, I have an ex-Met mate who transferred out to Hertfordshire and is on the team, and he gave me a bit more. I have to say, it's not looking great,' he said in his flat Home Counties accent as he scratched at his almost entirely bald scalp. He'd been struggling to hold on to his hair forty years ago, and now it had all but disappeared.

'Why? I thought they'd nicked the shite,' said Macca.

'They did. He's called Patrick Jarman, a scrote of a burglar with heaps of previous. A total junkie loser. They got a DNA profile from the jacket that Chappers ripped from him and nicked him as soon as the profile match came through. Fair play to them, they had him in custody within a few hours.'

'So what happened?'

'He no-commented the interview completely; just sat there and said nothing at all. They charged him with manslaughter and burglary, although they had to fight hard to get the manslaughter through the Crown Prosecution Service, and they aren't convinced it'll survive the process. It could easily get dropped if what the eyewitness said is accurate.'

'Why, what did they say?' said Asquith, his cultured accent notably different from those of the others.

Charlie shrugged and sighed. 'Basically, Jarman was trying to get away and ditched his jacket, which Chappers had hold of. Chappers staggered back, fell and cracked his head. If that's true, I'd say it's possible the CPS could drop it down to the burglary only, and go for maximum sentence possible, but . . .'

'But what?' said Macca, his voice low, staring straight at Charlie.

'He'll only serve half of whatever they give him. Maximum for burglary is fourteen, so if they drop the manslaughter, he's looking at seven max, and I'm not even that sure he'd get much more for manslaughter.'

Despite the hubbub of conversation in the room, it seemed that a silence had descended over their table.

'Seven years for killing Chappers?' said Macca, his voice low and menacing. Macca was one of the most decent men any of the group had served with, but it did not pay to upset him. Despite being in his mid sixties, he was still lean and whip-like, and by far the fittest of any of them.

'How about the gongs?' said Jacko.

'Apparently the only things that were stolen. No leads on their whereabouts,' said Charlie as he lifted his beer to take a swig.

'Stolen to order, then,' said Jacko, his firm voice indicating that this was a statement rather than a question.

'You think?' said Macca.

'Stands to reason.' Jacko raised his beer too and took a long swallow, swishing it around his mouth contemplatively.

'No other possible motive,' agreed Charlie. 'I mean, why would a junkie burglar want some red-hot and difficult-to-shift medals when there was plenty of readily nickable stuff in the house. There was a load of Macey's jewellery, including a really nice watch, not to mention the TV and some tech, all of which could have been pawned easily. Yet this bastard only takes a specialist item that you'd need inside knowledge and contacts to fence.'

'And this bloke didn't have that knowledge?' said Macca.

'No chance. His previous convictions are typical shithouse burglary stuff. Cash, TVs, computers and the like. All stuff he could knock out instantly for readies that he could then spend on skag.'

There was another long and heavy pause as they looked at each other, the sense of simmering rage beginning to spread like a virus.

'Jesus. That medal group was worth a fortune, and Chappers kept them under the bloody bed?' said Asquith incredulously. His eyebrows rose, neat and tidy like the rest of him.

'That was Chappers. He couldnae give a shit for anything like that. He hated having smoke blown up his arse, which is why he never went anywhere near the British Legion and big ceremonial parades after he retired. The bravest and most humble man I ever had the honour of serving with,' said Macca, his face hard.

'I even heard that his last medal was posted to him, as he couldn't be arsed going to fetch it from the CO,' said Charlie.

'But tens of thousands of pounds' worth of medals under the damned bed?' said Asquith, shaking his head.

'Where he always kept them. He once told me he wanted to flog them, for his girl and that, but Macey went ballistic. He even had them valued by a specialist I put him in touch with,' said Jacko, swigging from his pint.

'Who?'

'Geezer off *Antiques Roadshow*, has a place in London.'

'Is he legitimate?'

'Mate, he's as straight as they come. In any case, it's not like you can flog a valuable gong group and get anything for it. It'd be like trying to sell the *Mona Lisa*.'

'Never had you for an art connoisseur, Jacko. I thought you'd be all about armed robbery,' said Asquith.

'I never blagged nothing, mate, and I've not touched a shooter since leaving the Corps. I was a commercial burglar, far more skilled. I was always interested in anything I could turn into a pound note, and nicking from big businesses seemed a good option. Listen, honest medal collectors all use reputable dealers, auctions or personal sales on the internet. If you nicked a medal group, you couldn't display it, or even show it to anyone, or you'd get grassed up before you could say Victoria Cross.' Jacko ran his hand over his slicked-back hair, thick with product, then sniffed and cuffed at his straggly moustache.

'I thought you'd know about all the hooky medal dealers, being the dodgy geezer you are,' said Charlie.

'If there were any, I would. I know most of the approachable pawnbrokers in Hatton Garden from the old days when I was still grafting, but they like Rolexes, sparkles and gold. Hooky medals ain't worth shit unless a collector wants them and is willing to pay under the counter, and then they can never show them, or even talk about them.'

'Can't the police get the burglar to reveal where the medals went? Maybe I could offer a reward?' said Asquith.

'You'd do that?' said Macca, looking at his former troop commander.

'Yes, of course. It's not right that whoever facilitated these medals to be stolen gets to keep them.'

'How much are they worth?' said Macca.

'The expert told Chappers they would certainly hit six figures,' said Jacko.

'I wonder what sort of reward would spark interest? Maybe twenty K?' said Asquith.

Three sets of eyes turned to look at him, mouths agape and eyes wide.

'Twenty grand?' said Jacko eventually, his voice shocked.

'Do you think that could prompt interest?' said Asquith.

'Doubtful. Anyone who wants these medals wants them for their own sake and was willing to pay a no-mark to nick them. A reward wouldn't help, I'd say.'

'Nice offer, though, Neil. I know you've made a few quid since leaving, but that's generous,' said Macca.

'Fuck me, I knew you were a posh twat, but I didn't know you were that rich. I thought you were a security guard?' said Jacko, grinning.

'I'm no Bezos, but I was a partner in an international security and risk management company, and I sold my share a few years ago.' Asquith shrugged, and smiled almost shyly.

'So you're proper minted, then?' said Jacko, his eyes glinting as he smiled widely.

'Not rich enough to sort your teeth out.'

'We was too poor for a dentist in the East End,' said Jacko, playing up his already strong accent.

It was a typical exchange between the two men, who were at opposite ends of the class structure. Asquith was of middle-class stock, grammar school and a marines officer; Jacko came from the wrong side of the tracks and had left the Corps for a life of crime.

'Weren't you a successful bank robber for a while?' said Charlie.

'Never a bank robber, mate, but successful enough that you

never caught me when you were a DS on the Sweeney,' replied Jacko.

'But not successful enough to avoid getting nicked and ending up in the Scrubs for a ten-stretch, eh?'

'Bloody grassed up by an ex-guardsman, but I'm straight as an arrow now.' Jacko drained his pint and stood up. 'Another?'

'Yeah, right, straight,' said Charlie with a chuckle, waggling his glass.

'On my kids' lives, mate.' Jacko grinned.

'That's equivalent to a confession in villain-speak, right?' Charlie returned the smile.

'So the cops never found the wedge you nicked then, if you're buying the beers?' said Macca.

'That and the fact that I'm busting for a piss. I may as well go to the bar on the way.'

'Another piss? Are you a twelve-year-old boy?' said Charlie.

'Bursting. I'll bring the beers back. Who's the posh-looking MILF eyeballing us from the bar?' Jacko nodded at a smartly dressed middle-aged woman who was surveying them from the middle of a small knot of soldiers.

Macca raised his gaze, and his eyes flared wide open in sudden recognition. He lowered his head and muttered, 'Shit.' Normally unflappable, for once he looked nervous.

'Old flame?'

'Piss off, Jacko,' he muttered, his shoulders hunched, as if trying to make himself as small as possible.

Jacko sniggered. 'I'll leave you old goats to it before I burst,' he said, and moved away.

Charlie raised his eyebrows at his friend's reaction. 'What is it?'

'Nothing,' said Macca, still looking flustered.

'Bullshit, who've you seen?' Charlie craned his neck towards the bar. The woman was still staring at them, her eyes quizzical. She was immaculately dressed in a sober dark business suit, and her silver hair was elegantly styled in a collar-length bob. As they watched, she began to head towards their table, effortlessly negotiating the throng.

'Gordon?' she said in a confident voice as she arrived, the American accent as strong as it was unexpected.

Macca looked up, the discomfort on his face reminiscent of someone experiencing a sudden twinge of toothache.

'Hello, Laurel,' he said, as he stood to shake her immaculately manicured hand.

'It's so good to see you. How long's it been?' she said, her flawless teeth displayed in a wide smile. Her lips were a perfectly painted bow and her sparkling eyes surveyed Macca with humorous delight.

'Maybe twenty-five years?' he said, returning her smile but with none of her confidence.

'Jeez, that long. You look great, Gordon, lean and mean. Hardly aged at all,' she said, her hand reaching out and briefly brushing against his Corps tie. Her eyes twinkled with mischief as she swept a loose strand of hair from her face and tucked it behind her ear.

Macca cleared his throat, his face beginning to colour a little. 'Laurel, these are old comrades from the Corps, Neil and Charlie.' He nodded towards his grinning friends, who were both clearly enjoying the spectacle of his discomfort.

'Charmed, gentlemen,' said Laurel, nodding briefly before turning her attention back to Macca. 'It's so sad about Frankie – he was a great man.'

Macca just nodded. 'What brings you to the UK?' he asked, his voice catching nervously at the back of his throat.

'I'm at the embassy in London for a six-month project. I'd been meaning to look you up. I've never forgotten, you know,' she said, reaching out to touch his hand, which he quickly withdrew and raised to his mouth to stifle a fabricated cough. Laurel acted as if nothing had happened, and glanced at Charlie and Neil as she continued, to Macca's obvious discomfort. 'Gordon is too humble to say, but he saved my life in Maysan province many years ago.'

'Ach, none of that, Laurel. It was way too long ago, and anyway, it wasn't just me,' Macca protested.

'Oh, Mister Modest, as always. Now, how's your lovely wife – Barbara, no?' she said, her head cocked to one side, her eyes locked on Macca's.

The old commando shuffled his feet, almost like an errant schoolchild, and mumbled, 'We split a few years ago.'

'Oh, that's sad. Any kids?' she said, her face lighting up with obvious glee that didn't reflect her statement.

'No,' Macca almost whispered.

Her eyes flitted briefly to the door of the pub, where a dark-suited, well-built man was raising his eyebrows towards her and pointing at his watch. 'I'm so sorry, but I must run. I'm needed back at the embassy, but I couldn't let Frankie's funeral pass without paying my respects.'

'Aye, well. Lovely to see you, Laurel,' said Macca, relief almost visibly flooding his face.

'Yes, isn't it. We must meet for lunch. Or maybe dinner?' she said, her head cocked to one side.

'Aye, maybe. I've been a bit busy—' began Macca, but Laurel was quick to interrupt.

'I'll call you. I suspect I can find your number,' she said with a dazzling smile. She nodded to the others, then turned towards the door, leaving a trail of expensive-smelling perfume in her wake.

Macca stood there rooted to the spot, his face frozen. Neil and Charlie stared at him, both grinning.

'Who was the silver-haired temptress, then?' said Jacko as he deposited four fresh pints from a tray onto the table.

Charlie and Neil both had to stifle giggles as Jacko sat.

'What did I miss?' he asked.

'Some American from Macca's past flirting outrageously, and him acting like a scared twelve-year-old virgin who has just discovered that the babysitter fancies a bit of slap and tickle,' said Charlie, still laughing.

41

'She looked well classy. Out of your league, I'd say,' said Jacko, his eyes glinting.

'Piss off,' said Macca, sipping his pint, his red cheeks returning to their normal pale hue.

'Who is she?' asked Asquith, trying without success to hide his grin.

'She was a young CIA agent back in the day. Probably still CIA now, I guess.'

'Not so young, but still definitely totty, eh?' Charlie winked.

'A spook – blimey. How did you two meet, oh-so-sexy and desirable Mr Silver Fox dreamboat?' said Jacko in a truly terrible approximation of an American accent.

Macca sighed, and rubbed at his brow with a fingertip before answering, his voice full of weariness. 'Years ago, it was. She was meeting an agent from within the Marsh Arab militia in Maysan. I was attached to Frankie's team when we got bounced by some insurgents. Just a bit of a minor to-do, and she seems to think we saved her life. Load of nonsense. Now can we change the subject?'

'She's obviously bang up for it, geezer. You're totally in there. You should go for it, a smart bit of septic-tank spy action,' said Jacko using the cockney rhyming slang for 'Yank'.

'Get fucked,' said Macca.

'Mate, you're single; you can totally do it.'

'Still get fucked. As in get tae fuck, you cockney bastard. Case closed, line of questioning over. End of.' He nodded and picked up his pint again.

'So have you?' asked Jacko.

'Have I what?' said Macca, eyes narrowing.

'Given her one?'

He closed his eyes and banged his head softly against the table.

'How was your piss, Jacko?' said Asquith, stifling a grin and changing the subject.

'A saggy bladder, the bane of being old, eh?' said Jacko, winking as he sipped his pint.

'That and knackered knees,' said Charlie, slapping his leg with a theatrical wince.

'And lumbago,' added Asquith.

'What's lumbago, you posh git?' asked Jacko.

'Backache to you,' said Asquith.

There was more laughter, which turned to silence as it faded. The four men stared at each other. Something was passing between them. Something intangible. The hubbub in the pub receded into the background as Macca broke the impasse. He raised his glass. 'Chappers.'

All the others followed suit.

'I just wish we could do something about it,' said Macca.

'Ain't that the truth, but what? We're just four old codgers with failing bladders, dodgy knees and fucking lumbago, for the posh 'uns among us.' Jacko winked at Asquith, his teeth like malformed piano keys.

Asquith had opened his mouth to retort when a female voice stopped him.

'This looks suspiciously like you buggers are planning something,' said Josie, with a half-smile but sad eyes that were still red with tears. She had appeared out of nowhere, pushing Macey in her wheelchair. Her face was pale and wan, and she was dressed in a simple black dress showing her slim arms, which were corded with tight muscles.

'Just shooting the breeze, love. Are you off?' said Macca.

'Yes, I'm taking Mum back to the nursing home. She's tired.' She nodded down at Macey, whose eyes were closed, her head lolling to one side.

'So sorry again, Josie. Any word from the cops?' asked Macca.

Josie pulled a face. 'Sadly, they think it's unlikely we'll retrieve the medals. Without access to thumbscrews, Jarman won't give them up, and DI Kelly suspects they've gone to a collector, maybe overseas. We've arranged to meet tomorrow, and Charlie's kindly agreed to come so she doesn't try and give me any nonsense.'

'I'll not let them bullshit you, love,' said Charlie.

Josie smiled again, weakly. 'Dad left me a letter telling me to sell the medals to pay for Mum's care if it became necessary. Shame I won't have the opportunity now. He was always dismissive about the bloody things, but I suspect he cared more as he got older. Age does make you more nostalgic, right?'

'He was a cussed old bugger. Never had much time for the formalities of military life,' said Charlie.

Tears brimmed in Josie's eyes. 'He was the bravest and most honourable man I ever met, and now some bastard has the medals he earned with his blood, sweat and ultimately his leg.' She paused and looked at her mother, then shook her head, her eyes glistening. 'I have to go. Mum looks uncomfortable, and she'll be hard to settle if I don't get her back soon. Are you staying locally tonight?'

'Jacko's in a hotel, and the rest of us live close enough.'

'Come and see me before you leave, yeah? I'm moving into Dad's now. Nice to be closer to Mum.'

'We'll be in here for lunch tomorrow,' said Macca, standing up and hugging her warmly.

The 11/06 club watched her negotiate her mother out of the pub door, then they all sat again, a dark silence between the four former comrades as they stared at their near-empty pint glasses.

Macca's face darkened. 'So *is* there anything we can do about this?'

'What do you expect us to do, Macca? Most of us left the Corps decades ago, and even you, with your Special Forces career storming embassies, left ten years ago. We're just four old fossils living off past glories,' said Charlie, each word laced with a sigh of disappointment.

'Seriously? Nothing? We just let the bastard get away with it?' Macca's eyes were full of sadness, laced with a steely flash of anger.

There was a long, tense silence between the old friends before Jacko spoke.

'I dunno, but I do know one thing.' He paused, draining his beer, wiping his moustache and slamming his empty glass back on the table. 'I'm going for another slash, then I'm getting the beers in. If we can't do shit to get Chappers' medals back, we may as well get on the piss.'

Chapter 9

Sunday 12 December 2021

Josie Chapman eyed DI Kelly balefully as the detective sat returning her gaze. Charlie was sitting next to her, dressed smartly in a well-cut suit. He and Kelly had exchanged pleasantries at the outset of the meeting, working out all the mutual acquaintances they had in policing.

Josie and Charlie both sat stony-faced as DI Kelly gave a full and comprehensive report of the investigation to date. It seemed she'd decided to leave nothing out. Charlie had told her that he expected her to be candid, and that he'd know immediately if she was holding anything back. 'I've investigated more murders than she's had hot dinners, Jose. I won't let her give you any flannel,' he'd promised.

'Can I ask a genuine question?' he asked now, blinking in a bright shaft of early-morning sunlight that suddenly shone through the window.

'Of course.' Kelly shifted uncomfortably in her seat, as if expecting an interrogation.

Charlie nodded. 'Jarman is charged with manslaughter and

burglary, but the account from the neighbour seems to demonstrate at the very best a dangerous act as he simply shed his coat to get away. Will the manslaughter charge survive?'

Kelly screwed her face up uncertainly. 'I have to be honest, Charlie, early advice from counsel is that there is unlikely to be a realistic prospect of a conviction, and bearing in mind that Jarman has indicated a guilty plea to the burglary already, I can see that the CPS may take the simple option and just push for the harshest sentence for the burglary. Defence counsel has already alluded to the fact that he will be making an application to dismiss the manslaughter charge, and he's a powerful advocate. I'm not saying it will definitely happen, but I'm not ruling it out, either.'

'How long will he get for the burglary?' asked Josie, who was sitting low in her chair, her face pale and wan.

'Fourteen years is the maximum, but as he has indicated an immediate plea, he will have to be given credit for that.'

'How much?'

'Up to a third.'

'Less than ten bloody years?' Josie sat up in her chair, and her face began to flush with anger.

'Possibly.'

'So with time off for good behaviour and all that shit, how long will he actually serve?' Her voice was harsh and her eyes flashed accusatorially.

'Probably half whatever he is sentenced to. Look, I'm sorry, Josie. I have no control over what sentence he receives – you must realise that.'

'Potentially five years for causing my dad's death. Shit.' Josie slumped back in her chair, her arms dangling by her sides, the stuffing knocked out of her.

'Josie, love. It's not DI Kelly's fault. The sentencing guidelines are set by the government.' Charlie reached across and took her hand, which remained limp and cold in his.

'I know,' she said, her eyes moistening.

'What about the medals?' said Charlie, fixing the detective with a clear-eyed stare.

'He made no comment in interview, and it has formed no part of his defence team's submissions. There was no trace of them when we searched his property,' said Kelly, flicking through her decision log in front of her on the desk.

'Are you working on the supposition that they were stolen to order?'

'It's a line of enquiry, but we have no leads. It's possible he was disturbed and it was just the medals he managed to get hold of.' She shrugged.

'Genuinely?' said Charlie, his voice laced with incredulity.

'Well, no, I don't actually *think* that, but what I think isn't the issue here, is it? All that matters is what we can *prove.*'

'Anything on his phone? If they were stolen to order, there must be calls in and out, or possibly messages.'

'He had no phone, either on his person or at his premises, and we have no number on intelligence records for him. Look, Charlie. Not to put too fine a point on it, but Jarman is a bottom-of-the-pile, habit-feeding burglar, who steals so he can buy drugs. It's possible he realised how hot the medals were and tossed them away.' Kelly's brow furrowed, and it was clear that she wasn't convinced of this herself.

'Fucking hell. He spilt blood for those fucking medals,' Josie spat, feeling her face flush.

'You genuinely think that?' Charlie sounded sceptical as he squeezed Josie's hand.

Kelly shook her head. 'I don't. I think they're too valuable for that, but it doesn't change the fact of where we are. I've had officers touring pawn shops, and word has gone out to all our informants, but we have nothing. It's not like there's an easy market for stolen medals, as they're so immediately traceable and therefore not valuable to the average thief or fence. I'm sorry, but the reality is that if these were stolen to order, then Jarman had sufficient time to pass them on to whoever ordered their theft, and with such notable and high-value items, I'd not be surprised if they'd gone overseas to a private collector. I'm sorry, Josie, we'll do everything we can to try and locate them. We're liaising with Interpol, and the medals are on international watch lists and have been circulated widely in the antiques and militaria community, but you may have to come to terms with the fact that you might not see them again.'

The finality of Kelly's words hit Josie like a hammer blow. 'So the medals that my father risked his life to earn are gone. Sod this. Come on, Charlie. We're getting out of here.' She rose to her feet, but Charlie remained seated.

'Sit down, Jose. Judith is on our side.'

Josie hissed through gritted teeth.

A sudden silence descended on the room. 'She's understandably distressed, Judith,' said Charlie.

'Yes, I fucking am. Those medals were supposed to be sold to pay for my mum's care, and it's not like insurance is gonna pay out, bearing in mind Dad left them under his fucking bed.'

'I do understand, but you must realise we're doing what we can.'

'Whatever.' Josie sat back in her chair and folded her arms.

'Is this case a non-starter? Cop to cop?' said Charlie.

'Unless we get a whisper from a source, or some other intelligence steer, then probably. I hope no one connected is going to do anything daft, Charlie. I was at the funeral yesterday and saw you with your comrades. We may not have many leads, but we're best placed to recover those medals. We don't need anyone else knocking on doors or rattling cages.' Kelly looked hard at Charlie, feeling her antennae quivering. She'd watched the four of them chatting around the table in the pub, and despite their advanced age, there was a formidable quality to them all.

'What are you saying, DI Kelly?' said Charlie, eyes narrowing.

'We don't need civilian interference in a police investigation. I hope I'm being clear.' She held his gaze, unblinking.

Charlie paused for a full beat, which seemed like an age. Then he exhaled softly before answering. 'Crystal clear. We're just a group of old pals mourning their fallen comrade, nothing more.'

'Good, now look. I have a meeting with the CPS soon, so you're going to have to excuse me. My deputy, DS Mark Johnstone, will show you out.'

'I know Mark. We worked together in London,' said Charlie, brightening a little.

He nodded at Josie, and they both stood. Josie's insides were burning with rage and her mind swirled as she shook the detective's hand and they left the room.

As they walked through the CID office, a tall, beefy man approached, and Charlie grinned.

'Hello, Mark, long time no see.'

'Good to see you, man. How's retirement?' said the detective in a soft cockney accent.

'All good, though the missus is constantly giving me grief about the decorating.'

'And the kids?'

'Grown up and doing their own things now. What about you, how long before you retire?'

'Under a year. I'm counting the days, mate.'

Charlie turned to Josie. 'This is Mark Johnstone, an old mate from the Met. Mark, this is Josie Chapman.'

Josie shook hands with the man. He was in in his fifties, with a shock of grey hair and a slightly bovine expression that presented in his heavy-lidded, tired-looking eyes.

'Sorry for your loss, Josie, but pleased to meet you.' He smiled kindly.

'Thanks,' was all Josie could say, her mind still a maelstrom of colliding emotions.

'Your boss has just been giving us the low-down on the job,' Charlie told him.

'Yeah, nasty business. That shithead Jarman is locked up now, slam-dunk case and won't get bail, but I take it Judith explained the problems with the manslaughter?' Mark's eyes turned down at the corners.

'Yeah. I get it, but it's hard to take.'

'Sorry about that, but it is what it is. Listen, I have to run – the boss has a ton of work for me.' He nodded, and disappeared off to DI Kelly's office.

'You okay, Jose?' said Charlie.

'How long have you known me?' Josie turned to face him, and her eyes were steely hard. Charlie had seen that look on her face before. It meant she wasn't playing.

'Longer than I care to remember.'

'Then you know I'm not okay. In fact, I'm very fucking far from being okay. I want my dad's medals back, but it looks like the cops aren't going to help.'

Charlie opened his mouth, no doubt with some platitude, but Josie cut him off. 'Not interested, Charlie. I'm not bloody interested.' She turned, and headed off towards the exit, her shoulders square.

Chapter 10

The Rose and Crown was quiet, with just one other drinker present, an elderly man who was propping up the bar talking to Leo. The bartender nodded when the four of them walked in.

Macca looked at his comrades, knowing that the fact that he'd arrived at the wooden counter first meant he was buying.

'Four pints, please, Leo,' he said cheerfully.

'Coming up. I'll bring them over,' said the young man with a wide smile.

'One for Bernie here as well,' added Macca, nodding at the elderly man.

'How do you manage that?' said Charlie, once they were seated with their pints in front of them.

'What?'

'Well, as far as I know, you've not been in this pub before yesterday, and yet you know the name of the bartender and the old barfly there as well. You were always such a grumpy bastard in the Corps.'

'Was I?'

'Very. Total grouch, always dripping about something or other. Age must have mellowed you, you old goat,' said Charlie, sipping at his beer with an impish smile. His eyes were red and rheumy, evidence of a few more drinks the previous evening.

'Well, Chas, I spent some time on a HUMINT unit dealing with IRA snitches in Northern Ireland, so I learnt to appreciate the value of building bridges, unlike you dodgy Met coppers.'

'You mean covert human intelligence sources or informants, not HUMINT, bloody cabbage heads,' retorted Charlie.

'Fine, CHIS, then. How'd it go with the cop?'

'So-so. She gave chapter and verse, and it's as I suspected.' Charlie gave a summary of the meeting with DI Kelly.

'Shit, really not good. Scumbag gets out in five and they're admitting defeat on the medals?' said Macca.

'Seems that way. She also gave me a warning about us getting involved in the case.'

'Seriously?' said Macca.

'Yeah, just a word to the wise, like. She's not daft, that's for sure. Cops hate civilians interfering in investigations.'

'Screw her, she's full of shit, isn't she?' Macca's voice lost a little of its natural authority, almost as if he was doubting his own words.

'Are you asking me?' said Charlie.

'What?' Macca narrowed his eyes.

'*Are* we planning something?'

'Course not, we're just shooting the breeze.'

'I wish we could do something,' said Neil, his first words since entering the pub.

'Yeah, I agree,' said Jacko as he nursed his pint and stifled a yawn.

'Like what?' asked Macca.

Both men just shrugged.

'What about your copper mate, Charlie?'

'Mark's a decent man. Sound Old Bill, but he's dead straight, and if I tried to press him for more, he'd tell me to sod off. He retires soon; there's no way he'd risk his pension with DI Kelly sniffing around us.'

'Typical cozzer – no backbone,' said Macca.

'Bit harsh. He's a good bloke.'

'Aye, maybe. I'm just feeling so bloody powerless. Back in the day, I could deal with my frustrations with the day job, but now what? I spend the day on my allotment checking on my winter onions.' He shook his head and hissed between his teeth.

'Back up there, you have an allotment?' said Charlie, grinning.

'Aye, and?'

'The big, tough ex-SBS RSM tending to his cabbages.' He chuckled.

'Aren't you into baking bread?' said Macca by way of retort.

Charlie coloured a little. 'I'm partial to making a sourdough since lockdown. We all need to eat, don't we?'

'All right, you old codgers,' said Jacko. 'Back to the immediate issue of Chappers. We all feel it. It's bloody shit, and nothing would give me more pleasure than to rip that little fucker's spleen out, but he's banged up and ain't getting out of Bedford jail for a few years at least.'

'How d'you know that?' said Charlie, his brow furrowed as he stared at Jacko.

'A guess,' Jacko replied, but his eyes gave him away.

'Bullshit. How do you know?'

'Stands to reason it's Bedford, don't it?' said Macca, his face impassive.

'Not really. Could be Hemel Hempstead, or any of the London jails. St Albans Crown Court disperses remands all over.' Charlie's eyes narrowed as he stared at Jacko.

Jacko's eyes glinted. 'Okay, I asked about. He's in Bedford, on the remand wing.'

'How did you find that out so bloody quick?' said Macca.

'Friends in low places, boys. Just interested, that's all. Anyway, who's hungry?'

Chapter 11

Josie looked across the bar at the 11/06, heads down and conferring with serious expressions and cleared plates in front of them. She felt as tightly wound as a spring, the tension of the preceding days ratcheting up the pressure that had prompted her to come for a drink in the first place. Now, watching the 11/06 having a secret conflab felt like a punch in the guts. She almost growled until Leo's cheery voice dragged her away from her thoughts.

'Hi, Josie, what can I get you?'

'Oh, er, G&T, please, Leo. How long have those old buggers been in here?' She fixed her gaze on Macca's stern face as he addressed the other three in what looked like a serious conversation. The appearance was one of efficient briskness, and it was clear that they weren't discussing the weather, or football scores. Something prickled at her subconscious. It was a briefing, not a nice comradely chat. The tension went up a notch.

'About an hour. They've been deep in some sort of discussion, like four old lags planning a bank robbery,' said Leo with a chuckle as he handed over her drink.

'What makes you say that?' Josie turned to face the smiley young man. Leo's chirpy expression slipped a little at her expression.

'Just a feeling; that and the fact that they stop talking when I get too close. Despite the fact that they're all ancient, there's not one of them I'd want to get on the wrong side of.' He nodded admiringly at the four tough and grizzled-looking commandos.

'Hmm, yeah.' She continued to stare before turning back to the bartender. 'You'd never get on the wrong side of anyone, Leo, you're far too good-natured, but I take your point.'

Josie sipped her drink and appraised the four men with fresh eyes. Macca was short, wiry and fit, with buzzed grey hair, and he still looked tough. Asquith was lean and well dressed, in chinos and a sweater, but again, despite the receding steel-grey hair and a pair of spectacles, he had a quiet determination that was visible to the naked eye. Charlie was taller and broader and carried a little excess weight around his middle, but his firm jaw, almost bald pate and hard eyes gave him an air of menace. And Jacko, with his swept-back dyed hair, straggly moustache and teeth like old gravestones . . . well, Jacko looked like what he was. A career criminal. She'd met them all a number of times when they'd got together with her dad for the 11/06 reunions, and they were all good men, but she had to admit, Leo's flippant comment was accurate. They did look like a group you wouldn't want to get on the wrong side of.

'Anything to eat, Josie? They've all had burgers.'

'No, I'm good. I'd better go and say hello.'

She walked towards the four old soldiers, who were sitting with their heads close together, chatting in low tones. As she approached, she could see the look in Macca's eyes. She'd known him all her life, and this was a long way from his usual open, smiling expression. He looked angry, and he looked determined.

That was when she knew.

They *were* planning something. Or if they weren't, they bloody well should be. She squared her jaw as she reached the table, feeling the same surge of adrenaline in her chest that she felt when hanging off a two-hundred-metre cliff by her fingertips.

'What are you reprobates up to then?' she said without smiling, and plonked herself down on a spare chair.

Four sets of eyes turned to her, wide with alarm at the sudden intrusion.

'Josie, hen. I didn't see you come in. You've a drink?' said Macca, a forced smile on his face.

Josie held her glass up. 'I'm good, but you didn't answer my question.' She sat back and fixed him with a glare.

'Just shooting the breeze, you know. How's your mum?'

'She's tired, confused and emotional, Macca. Now stop avoiding my fucking question.'

'No idea what you're talking about, Josie,' said Charlie, but his eyes told the real story.

'Bullshit, Charlie. You old codgers must think I was bloody born yesterday, but I've known you for most of my life, and I know you're fucking planning something. Now you level with me, or I'm gonna lose my shit. *What* are you planning?' She felt a tickle running up her spine that she always felt when she was angry or emotional. She pursed her lips and could feel her cheeks reddening.

'Planning our next pint, love,' said Jacko, grinning.

'Good. Mine's a G&T, and while you're getting that, Macca is going to tell me what's going on.' Josie fixed her eyes directly on Macca and folded her arms, waiting. She'd learnt from her dad that sometimes saying nothing and letting the other person stew was the most effective way of getting an answer to your question.

'Right, I'm off for a slash, and then I'll get the beers in,' said Jacko.

'Yeah, I could do with one as well,' said Charlie.

'Think I'll join you; it's my round anyway,' Asquith chipped in, looking suddenly nervous. Three chairs slid back in unison, and the three ex-marines headed to the toilet.

Josie's gaze didn't leave Macca as she sat there appraising him coolly.

'You look just like your dad, Jose. Same eyes. When he was RSM, that was the treatment he gave his lads. Never shouted or screamed, just looked at them like you're looking at me now. You're a chip off the old block, girl.'

'Enough of the platitudes. I deserve to bloody well know.'

'Josie, I have no idea what you're talking about,' said Macca, but his eyes told another story.

'Bollocks, Macca. I was watching you lot from over at the bar. What is happening?'

'Seriously, love. Nothing. We've just had a hangover-curing burger, and now we're shooting the breeze.'

Josie pursed her lips. 'Well, why aren't you planning something, then? Because I know one thing for sure: if *you'd* died while your medals were being stolen, Dad would never have rested until he'd got them back.' Her cheeks were spotted with red blotches that reflected her harsh tone.

'Your dad didn't care about medals – you know that, Josie.'

'No, Macca. He didn't care about *his* medals, but he'd have put it all on the line for yours. Now what are we doing about it?'

'Doing about what?' said Jacko as he sat back down at the table, his eyes twinkling.

'Dad's medals. I'm saying we should be getting them back, as the police don't seem arsed.' Josie's face was impassive.

'But—' began Macca as Charlie and Asquith both sat down, eyes narrowed at the sharp exchange going on in front of them.

'But. Fucking. Nothing. Listen, boys. Those medals are out there somewhere, and since the police don't seem to give two bloody shits, I've made my decision. I'm getting them back one way or the other, either with you lot or without you.' She sat back in her chair and drained her drink.

'Another?' said Jacko.

Josie looked at the ex-criminal. 'Yes, I want another bloody gin. And I want you lot to help me. You're all ancient, knackered old gits, but when I was watching you from the bar, I came to one very firm conclusion.'

'Go on?' said Charlie, eyeing her with interest.

'You're still a formidable bunch of ancient, knackered old gits, and I wouldn't want you after me. You've all got complementary skills and experience. Together you're worth more than the sum of your slightly crocked parts, no offence.' Her face was flushing and her stomach roiled.

A long, almost thick silence enveloped the group, only broken when Jacko sniggered and spoke.

'I'm in,' he said, winking at Josie.

'Me too. I owe Chappers everything,' said Asquith, his face impassive, his eyes hard.

Charlie sighed. 'Jesus, this is madness, but I don't mind looking into it. I'm not *that* long retired.'

Macca stared at Josie with a serious expression. 'I don't want you anywhere near this, Josie. It could be dangerous, and you've no experience in this kind of caper.'

'Bullshit. I've attributes you buggers don't. I can be useful. I bloody need to *feel* useful, Macca, as I'm going mad here. I'm helping. Get used to it.' She sat back, a trickle of sweat running down her spine.

'But we're professionals—' Macca began.

Josie was having none of it. 'You're all living on past glories. You have skills and contacts, no doubt, but I have a few things you lot don't.'

'Like?' Macca raised his eyebrows.

'Youth for one. I'm also way tougher than any of you geriatrics. I was the second-placed female in last year's Marathon des Sables, I'm one of the UK's best free climbers, I've done over five hundred free-fall skydives, I'm mustard on a motorbike, and I'm a black belt in ju-jitsu. Dad trained me well, Macca. You know it.

59

I never played with dolls; I was camping in the woods, hunting, or climbing in Yosemite. You need me. I'm in.'

Macca opened his mouth to argue, but then closed it again as Josie raised her hand to silence him and fixed him with an unrelenting stare.

'Now I know I take the piss about you lot being old, but I also respect each and every one of you. You're still formidable bastards, but I've one further attribute none of you have and will almost certainly need.'

'Jesus, you really are a chip off the old block. What?'

'I'm a woman.'

Chapter 12

Monday 13 December 2021

Patrick Jarman barely looked up from his bed as the sounds of the prison coming to life began to seep into his cell. There was a rattle of keys at the door, and it swung open, the head of one of the more agreeable screws popping around the corner. 'Morning, girls,' he said, a wide smile on his meaty face.

Jarman's head was muzzy and sore, and every part of his body ached, as it always did after he'd smoked the heroin that had been sold to him by Jazzy, the huge, muscled and scary prisoner along the hallway who kept most of the cons in skag, puff and spice. No money had changed hands inside the prison, of course. Jarman's sister had paid two hundred quid to one of Jazzy's cohorts on the outside, and the small wrap of brown powder had been passed across on the landing yesterday afternoon. He'd intended that it would last him the week, but of course the obvious happened. He'd binged the lot in two nights, chasing the acrid, foul-smelling stuff on foil, much to the disgust of his cellmate, Clive. Not that Clive was of concern to Jarman, owing to the fact that he was a skinny little runt who had spent the week they'd been sharing sobbing in the top bunk, having been convicted of some kind of white-collar crime.

Jarman himself accepted jail as part of life, particularly the life he'd fallen into ever since he'd been grabbed by the skag. He'd be able to handle whatever stretch he was given, particularly as he knew there was a decent bit of wedge waiting for him when he got out. He yawned as he sat up, grimacing at the foul taste in his mouth and the swirling fog in his brain. Then he stood, sighing heavily, walked to the kettle in the corner of the room and switched it on, yawning again.

'Morning, Patrick, sounds like you slept like a baby,' came the thick, wet voice of Clive from the top bunk.

'Do I look like I want a conversation?' Patrick mumbled without looking at his cellmate. He went to the stainless-steel toilet and took a piss, trying to dampen down the feeling of nausea that was beginning to bubble in his gut. It always started like this. Cold turkey. First the nausea, then the sweats and the shivers, then, before you knew it, quaking, quivering pain. That was a few hours away yet, but it was coming, blue lights and sirens warning of its impending approach and the abject misery it would bring. He was going to need to score, and score soon, or life was about to get unpleasant. He looked at his cheap digital watch and was shocked to realise that his last hit had only been just over eight hours ago. Jesus, it was getting bad. He needed to slow down, or the money he'd got for the medals wouldn't last any time at all.

He washed his hands in the stainless-steel sink, then brushed his teeth, trying to scrub the foul taste in his mouth away. He hoped he could get a shower today, as his skin felt like it was covered in a thick layer of grease. He looked up at the safety mirror that was attached to the wall above the sink, taking in his sunken eyes, sallow skin and dank, dull hair. He looked awful, and his appearance wasn't helped by the fresh outcrop of spots around his mouth.

All of a sudden, the cell door banged open, revealing a

diminutive prisoner in his sixties called Lenny. Jarman had never really taken much notice of him during the couple of weeks that he'd been in jail, although he had observed that he was treated with a good deal of respect by other cons and staff. More alarmingly, he was with his padmate, Stevo, a much bigger and much younger shaven-headed hooligan from Luton.

'You, fuck off,' barked Lenny in a gruff cockney accent, pointing at Clive, who responded immediately, bounding out of his bunk barefoot and into the corridor. Stevo pushed the door closed.

Jarman looked at the elderly con, who wore a crisp shirt that revealed slim, wrinkly arms covered in the fading blue ink of prison tattoos. His head was covered in wispy strands of grey hair, and his chin bristled with stubble. But his eyes told a different story. They were small, piggy and cruel, and totally devoid of humour.

'Lenny—'

'Shut up and sit down,' interrupted Lenny just as the kettle began to boil. His voice made it clear that this was an instruction and not a request. Jarman sat.

'Kettle's boiled, Lenny. Fancy a cuppa?' said Stevo.

'Don't mind if I do, Stevo.'

'What's going on?' said Jarman, his voice wobbling, a tremor in his hands as he brushed his hair away from his face.

'Tea first,' replied Lenny as Stevo handed him a plastic cup filled with weak-looking black tea.

'No milk, Len,' said Stevo with a shrug.

'No milk? What kind of savage are you, Patrick?' Lenny wrinkled his nose. 'Fuck me, it stinks in here. Don't you ever bloody shower?'

'On the list for today—' began Jarman, but Lenny interrupted again.

'Don't give a fuck. I need something from you.' His voice was machine-gun fast in its delivery, the accent pure East End and edged with steel.

'Of course, Len,' stuttered Jarman.

'Of course, of course, you muppet. I need some information, and I need it fucking now,' said Lenny as he sipped the tea. He screwed his face up. 'This tea is fucking shit, what type of bags do you use?'

'PG Tips.'

'P-fucking-G Tips? You need to spend less on skag and more on tea, son. Now, pipe down and listen. I know why you're in this shithole, and frankly I don't like it. I don't like junkie scum like you killing old boys who fought for this country, capeesh?'

'Len, it was an accident— Ow!' Jarman cried out in pain as Lenny, with unexpected speed, slapped him hard on the top of the head.

'You little shit, that hurt my fucking hand.' Lenny massaged his palm, his face creased in a grimace.

'I'm sorry, Len.'

'Shut up, you shit-bag. I don't give a fuck about your apologies. You did what you did, so you owe what you owe. You need to make this fucking right. So, Patrick, old geezer, I'm gonna ask one question, and you're gonna answer it for me, okay?'

'But—'

'It was a fucking rhetorical question. Stevo, why don't people recognise when I'm asking a fucking rhetorical question, eh?' Lenny turned to his gorilla-like accomplice, his voice laden with sarcasm.

'No idea, Len. Thick bastards, eh?' Stevo stepped forward and viciously slapped Patrick round the face. His shovel-like hands were hard and callused, and it felt like a punch, the pain immense and vivid as Patrick's head rocked to the side and sparks flew behind his eyes.

'I'm learning that the beatings I used to dish out are a bit hard on the old bones,' Lenny went on, 'which is why I come with my associate here. He don't have arthritis, or gout, or piles, or any of the old-person shit that I have. Oh, I forgot to mention,

Patrick. Stevo here minds about the medals a great deal. Stevo is an ex-paratrooper, so he isn't happy about it at all and wants to hurt you badly, do you understand me?'

Patrick nodded mutely.

'See, the thing is, there used to be a code. No kids, and no old folk. You broke the fucking code, Jarman.' Lenny's eyes were flat and unfathomable behind his spectacles. 'Now, Stevo here's a patriot, and patriots don't like veterans getting hurt by scumbags like you. Isn't that right, Stevo?'

'Yes, fucking right, Len,' the gorilla growled, his eyes looking way too small for his muscular body.

Lenny paused for a moment to allow the comment to land before he followed up with the question, his face just inches from Jarman's. 'Who did you nick the medals for?'

'I don't kn—'

The black tea in the plastic cup had cooled a little, but it still burnt as it was thrown into Jarman's face. He cried out as the hot liquid splashed onto his chest, scalding the skin underneath the thin material of his T-shirt. Terror surged, and a scream crackled in his throat. Stevo's thick arms were wrapped around him, pinning him to the chair with incredible strength. He was trapped as completely as a rodent wrapped up by a boa constrictor.

Lenny stepped forward and pulled Jarman's boxer shorts down, exposing his bare thighs and shrivelled genitals. Jarman yelped, but Stevo just clamped his huge hand across his mouth, and he knew it was hopeless.

'These plastic cups are horrible, aren't they, me old cock sparrer,' said Lenny as he held the cup aloft, smiling. 'They just don't hold the heat, do they? Still, there's a solution to that, right?' He walked over to the kettle and switched it back on. Jarman stared at him, terror bubbling in his chest, his muffled cries pointless against the massive hand.

Wordlessly Lenny picked up the bubbling kettle and stood over him. 'Now this water is properly hot, Pat. Imagine what will happen to your tiny little todger if I empty it all over it, eh? One last chance. Are you gonna tell us who you passed the medals to?'

Jarman began to nod as fast as the hand over his mouth would let him, feeling his bowels loosen. The hand moved away.

'Jimmy Grigson. It was Jimmy Grigson.'

'Who's he?' hissed Lenny.

'He's a fence in north London, lives in Harlesden, I think. He's taken antiques off me in the past and passes them on to a dealer in London. Posh place, apparently, with overseas clients who can't get stuff they want any other way.' Jarman was babbling, his voice a harsh squeal.

'Who's the dealer?'

'I don't know, I promise. Please don't hurt me any more,' Jarman blubbed, fat tears streaming from his eyes and snot bubbling from his nose. Lenny lifted the kettle high and began to tip. Jarman screamed and thrashed against Stevo's grip. 'I don't know. I swear I don't. I've not been, but he says it's a swanky place in London. All I know is that the end client is a proper rich bloke, like a mega-millionaire. I just got paid to rob the place,' he squealed, his eyes wide like saucers.

'You better be telling us the truth, you little toerag.'

'It is the truth, I promise.'

Lenny nodded and looked at Stevo, who immediately relaxed his grip. He placed the kettle back down on the table. 'One thing, Pat. One word of this anywhere, and I'll fucking destroy you, do you understand?'

'Yeah, I'll not grass, Len,' Jarman said, his voice scratchy.

'I know I look like your friendly old grandpa, but I have friends in all the right places, and if I even suspect you've tipped the bastard off, I'll be back, do you understand me?' Lenny moved his head closer to Jarman, his voice a deep, sonorous growl.

'Yes—'

Jarman's reply was stopped by a punch that came from behind him. Massive, huge and agonising, it knocked him to the hard floor, on which he landed like a sandbag. When the velvety comfort of unconsciousness arrived, he almost welcomed it.

Chapter 13

Jacko's mind was whirring when the call from Lenny ended. He placed his mobile down on the scuffed Formica-topped table in the cheap hotel room in St Albans, sat back in the scruffy armchair and sipped at the cup of tea he'd just made. He looked at his watch and saw that he'd need to get a move on. He was due to meet the others soon. After Josie had thrown the cat among the pigeons, they'd all gone their separate ways to mull the idea over for a while before getting together again later to discuss what they could all bring to the party. Jacko knew what he could bring that the others couldn't. Access to a world they knew nothing about. He grinned, feeling excitement in his chest. A chance to pay back Chappers for saving his life on that bleak hill in the South Atlantic forty years ago. A chance to be not just a lowlife villain, but someone who could make a difference to a worthy cause.

The others would be impressed. Just a few hours had passed, and he already had a name, and so they had somewhere to start. A name, and the fact that a posh antiques dealer in London had taken the medals off Grigson for a swanky collector. It wasn't much, but it was certainly a start.

Jimmy Grigson. He'd heard the name, but he couldn't put his finger on where from. He'd spent most of his time since leaving the marines in Ealing, which wasn't that far from Harlesden, but as he hadn't been involved in low-level thievery, he'd had no need of a mid-level fence. Anything he'd ever nicked had been nicked to order, be it computer chips, antiques or quality jewellery.

Jacko had left the Corps in the late 1980s, once the medics had realised that his foot was never going to fully recover enough for him to continue as a marine. It was ninety per cent there, but that was no use in the toughest of military units. Also, he'd had far too many close shaves with authority, which probably made the decision to cast him out easier. He knew he was a good soldier in wartime, but in peacetime he was lousy. He wasn't good with rules, and he enjoyed a pint far too much to be on time for turn-to in the mornings. That plus the constant guard duties, shite exercises and Northern Ireland deployments had all been too much. So he'd wrapped his bangers in, as the saying went, and headed out into the big wide world, leaving behind him the only job he'd ever had.

It was something of a shock to learn that opportunities for a soldier with a gammy foot and a poor disciplinary record were limited to say the least. A whole line of shit cash-in-hand jobs hadn't helped his feelings of self-worth, but then one day everything changed. He met an ex-Grenadier Guardsman who'd been heaved out after decking his sergeant but who had the benefit of a load of criminal contacts. It was the early 2000s, when people were realising just how valuable and sought-after high-value computer chips were, and the manufacturers couldn't keep up with demand. His new contact had a plan, but didn't want to use traditional thieves to help him out.

'They're no use, Jacko. The Old Bill know all about them, and they're sloppy as anything. It's child's-play stuff, mate. Nip into the bank, a word in the shell-like of the security guards, if you get my drift, then up to the server room. Rip out the servers with the chips and piss off. I can get eighty per cent of the value of the chips, so we're talking serious wedge here. Are you in?'

Well of course Jacko was in. So he became a burglar, and after a few jobs in banks and a couple of universities, he'd made some proper money and was living a good life in Ruislip with a girl called Sally and their daughter. Later he got involved in some burglaries in Hatton Garden, and a couple of art galleries that netted plenty of dough. But then his Grenadier Guard mate got nicked and did a deal with the cops, and they put an undercover cop on Jacko who was so bloody good that Jacko stitched himself right up. He ended up getting ten years for aggravated burglary, of which he served almost six, and came out to nothing. Sally had gone back to her mum in Liverpool, and his daughter, Jess, was now grown up and at university and wanted nothing to do with him.

His mind returned to the name Lenny had given him. Jimmy Grigson. He still couldn't work out where he knew it from. Another name popped into his head, and he made a decision. They needed a break, and he wasn't getting it sitting in a shit hotel nursing a mild hangover. He picked up his phone and dialled.

A rough London voice answered. 'Hello?'

'Errol, mate. It's Jacko.'

'Jacko, you bastard. How ya been, me old Bacardi? Not spoken for bloody ages. Staying outta the bucket?' Errol Strickland's voice was deep, velvety and resonant, with a distant trace of Caribbean blended with full-throated cockney. He used more rhyming slang than anyone Jacko had ever met: 'Bacardi' for 'Bacardi Breezer', or 'geezer'; and 'bucket' for 'bucket and pail', or 'jail'.

'Thankfully, mate. Listen, I've had a whisper about some business and I could do with someone able to offload something interesting. Someone put a name in the frame from your manor. Jim Gregson, you heard of 'im?' Jacko's own cockney drawl strengthened a little. Errol was a retired blagger he had served

70

time with. Before he retired, he had specialised in jewellery shops and watches, and knew everyone in the north-west London area. He now was basically a criminal concierge who took a fee for introducing villains to each other.

'Grigson, not Gregson, mate. Yeah, I know him. Decent fence, with plenty of contacts all over. Specialises in quality tom, antwacky stuff and kettles. Links in with lots of jewellers in Hatton Garden, posh antique dealers in Mayfair and the like. Can't stand the snooty bastards myself, but Jimmy has all the names, even if he does keep them close to his George Best.'

Jacko stifled a smile. Luckily, having spent plenty of time with Errol, he could translate: 'tom' was jewellery, 'antwacky' was antiques, and 'kettle' was watches, while 'George Best' was rhyming slang for 'chest'.

'Where's he live?'

'He's got a nice drum right by Roundwood Park. You need an intro?'

'Maybe.'

'What you looking to knock out?'

'Some medals. Might be valuable. Is that Jimmy's bag?'

'If it's shiny and worth a few shekels, then yes, he'll know the right people.'

'Can you sort an intro?'

'Course I can. I'm sat on me 'aris right now, just 'ad me Jimmy Hendrix out, but I'll be up and about in a couple of days.' From which Jacko gathered that Errol had recently had his appendix out.

'That'd be great. This geezer is kosher, yeah?' he said.

'Diamond Bacardi, yeah. What type of medals are we talking about here?'

'Not over the blower, mate. Sensitive, yeah?'

'You know me, chap. I'm like James Bond with a secret. Griggo's no muppet; he only takes decent-quality gear and he pays top dollar for the right stuff. He's careful as anything, doesn't touch drugs, stays out of Old Bill's way, barely drinks, and has only one vice as far as I know.'

'What's that?'

'Birds. He loves a blonde. Married a few times, but always gets caught shagging about. Costs him a fortune in divorces, the daft bastard. Let me know when you want an intro, and we'll have a meet in the battle cruiser near me. I take it there's a drink in it for me?'

'I'm sure I could come up with something. I'll bell you later. Be lucky.'

'Later, potato.'

Jacko hung up, his mind spinning with possibilities. It seemed he could easily get an introduction to Grigson, but what then? They could hardly put the thumbscrews on him and make him lead them to the medals.

He shook his head and picked up his phone, which had just buzzed on the table like a demented mosquito. It was Macca.

'Jacko, you coming to Josie's?' he said by way of greeting.

'Yeah, just sorting my shit out.'

'The others are on the way and we all need to chat. You still up for what we talked about?'

'Damn straight, mate. In fact, I've news on that front that I'll tell you about when we're all together. I've put the feelers out.'

'Shite, that was quick. You don't piss about, Jacko.'

'No time to lose, Macca. I've a mate who knows a mate who knows a mate – you know how it is. I'll see you in the pub in twenty.' Jacko hung up and sat back, a grin spreading across his face.

It was really happening. They were gonna do this, and he had given them their first lead.

It was on.

Chapter 14

The 11/06 were sitting around the breakfast bar at Chappers' home in Sandridge, holding mugs of coffee.

'Who wants to go first?' said Macca.

Jacko stood and went to the coffee pot to replenish his mug. 'I have intel,' he said, stroking his raggedy moustache.

'What, already?' said Charlie.

'Us Cockneys don't mess about, geezer. I had a word via a contact, and something was whispered into Patrick Jarman's shell-like, you know, suggesting that he should consider being helpful. Wonders will never cease, he spilt the beans.' Jacko sat back down, smiling, showing his broken and uneven teeth, his eyes sparkling.

'Well, go on then,' said Asquith, who was looking fresher than the others and was dressed in a crisp shirt and chinos.

Jacko repeated the information that had been relayed to him by Lenny, and the subsequent conversation with Errol.

'I hesitate to ask, Jacko, but how did your pal elicit this intelligence from Jarman?'

'Violently, I hope,' said Josie with an expressionless face.

'Really?' said Macca.

'Yes, really. The bastard.'

Jacko sniggered before continuing. 'Let's just say that Lenny can be persuasive. He looks like your favourite uncle, but he has a way with words that can be very motivating. I was behind the door with him in the Scrubs, and I got him out of a little bother one day with a belligerent bugger, so he feels he owes me.'

'Wasn't that risky, him talking on a prison phone?' said Asquith.

'Ah, mate. You may be rich, but you don't know shit about prisons, do you? We spoke on WhatsApp voice call.'

'What, he has a phone in jail?' Asquith sounded incredulous.

'Bugger me, you've lived a sheltered life, Neil. Any decent villain will have access to a phone when he's behind the door. How do you think things get sorted?' Jacko grinned and thumped Asquith on the arm good-naturedly.

Asquith just shook his head.

'I vaguely remember Jimmy Grigson from when I was the intel DI at Kilburn,' said Charlie. 'He dealt mostly in good-quality jewellery and watches from burglars and smash-and-grabbers. A smart bloke, and well connected. I can see it that Jarman would hand Chappers' medals to Grigson, but I can't see Grigson knowing how to offload a serious medal group himself. That's a real specialism. There must be another link in the chain. No suggestions on who that could be?'

'Jarman doesn't know, and I'm as confident as I can be that he would have spilt if he did. Lenny was being quite motivational when he asked the question.'

'Care to elaborate?' said Macca.

'Threatened to scald his meat and two veg with boiling water.'

No one said anything, but there were a couple of sharp intakes of breath before Josie's voice pierced the silence. 'No more than the shit-head deserves.'

'Do we pin Grigson in a corner and read him his horoscope?' asked Macca.

Charlie shook his head. 'I think that's unwise. He's an old-school pro, and he'll either just grass us to the cops or go straight to his client, and then we're buggered. We need a covert strategy, and to think of this like a police investigation, but with one big benefit.'

'Which is?' said Macca.

'We don't need to stick to the rules, and Jacko here has just given us a great big opportunity,' said Charlie, a smile stretching across his face.

'I'm fucking brilliant, ain't I?' Jacko grinned, his teeth like tombstones.

'Care to elaborate for those of us who haven't either been cops or been nicked repeatedly?' Neil said, looking a little confused.

'Put it this way, if I was still a DCI running this officially, I'd be delighted if you were my informant, Jacko.'

'I never grassed, cozzer, but this ain't grassing. This is doing the right thing. I'm up for it.'

'Up for what? Can someone explain? Neil looked confused.

Jacko sniggered. 'Grigson is a decent-quality fence. I have a bit of a rep in that world as a burglar who can get his hands on some nice gear, so it's obvious, right?'

There was a long pause, and they all looked at each other in turn, a mix of confusion and realisation in the air.

'Jacko, it sounds like you're suggesting an undercover operation,' said Macca.

'I didn't think of it like that, but I guess I am. Ironic, eh?' Jacko chuckled.

'Just a bit.'

'Advantage is I don't have to act the part. I've met fences loads of times when I've offloaded hooky gear. I just have to be myself – piece of piss.'

'Didn't you get stung by an undercover cop?' said Macca.

'Yeah, that Grenadier bastard introduced me to a cop when he did the deal with the police. Cost me almost six years of my life, that, but it worked. It worked a treat, boys.'

'Are you blaming the cop?' said Charlie, eyebrows raised and a half-smile on his craggy face.

'Nah. Cop was a decent sort, just doing his job. Grenadier was a dirty no-good grass, though.'

Asquith looked confused. 'What are we suggesting here?'

'Isn't it obvious?' said Charlie.

'Not to me.'

'Grigson is a fence. So let's go undercover and Jacko can flog him some dodgy gear. We meet him, we get his car reg, we get his phone number and we get him. Who knows what opportunities will arise. Jacko has a route to him via the middleman he knows. Way I see it, we have to make our own luck. In the meantime, Neil can get his old firm doing the open-source intelligence analysis to give us everything we can get on Grigson.'

'You know enough of the right sort of people, I imagine, Jacko,' said Macca.

'You mean the wrong sort of people. I do, and I've a suggestion.' Jacko stood up suddenly.

'What?' they all said at the same time.

'I'm busting for a piss. When I get back, I'll tell you.'

Chapter 15

The Green Man pub in Harlesden was not what Jacko was expecting. He'd been there a few times many years ago and it had been a typical north London boozer, with scuffed floors, chipped tables and revolting food. The place had been totally renovated and was now a bustling bar and Portuguese restaurant full of hip young things and smart professionals eating piri-piri chicken, tapas and what looked suspiciously like octopus. He shuddered and wondered what had happened to scampi and chips in a basket, which had been the classy choice of food when he was younger.

He swept his eyes around the bar, seeing but not reacting to Neil Asquith sitting in the far corner reading a newspaper, an empty plate in front of him and a beer at his elbow.

'Blimey, this place has changed, Errol,' he said, eyeing the glass in front of him, which was only one small step away from being a wine glass, with overly fizzy-looking ice-cold beer in it.

'What, no claret on the floor, shitty khazis, and angry-looking white men in Arsenal shirts looking to kick seven shades of shit out of me for being black? I ain't complaining, Jacko. Anyway, here's mud in your eye.' Errol raised his Guinness and they chinked glasses.

Errol was a small, compact and grizzled-looking man. He was smartly dressed in a suit, with a crisp shirt and a tightly knotted tie. He wore gold rings on every finger and a gold hoop in his left ear. For as long as Jacko had known him, he'd always made it clear that he lived for the halcyon days of crime and criminals, and felt that when 'grafting' you should dress appropriately.

'So, how's business been?' said Jacko. He'd made an effort to dress a little smarter himself, but his shapeless chinos, scuffed trainers and baggy polo shirt really didn't compare with Errol's slick look.

'Judging by your standard of schmutter, my friend, I'm doing better than you.' Errol pointed a gold-clad finger in Jacko's general direction before sipping at his Guinness and nodding appreciatively. 'Decent pint. So, Griggo is on his way and I've given him a bit of background on you, which hopefully will distract from your scruffy-arsed appearance.'

'You're a cheeky bastard. I take it he's asked around about me?'

'I imagine he has. He wanted your name and anyone you'd worked with, so I told him about your touch of bad luck with a dirty grassing bastard that cost you a ten-stretch. Look out, he's just coming in now.' Errol nodded at the door.

Grigson was tanned, early middle-aged and heavily built, with short, neatly styled hair. He was immaculately dressed in a grey three-piece suit and carried a small oxblood attaché case. He looked across the bar and nodded as he saw Errol, walking over with a seemingly effortless grace. 'Errol,' he said, with a charmless smile as both men stood.

'Jim, this is Jacko, geezer I was telling you about.' Errol jerked a thumb in Jacko's direction.

'Pleased to meet you, Jacko.' Grigson extended a hand, and they shook. His grip was firm yet not crushing, with no trial of strength.

'Get you a beer, Jim?' said Errol.

'Yeah, Estrella, ta.' Grigson sat down on the chair opposite Jacko, appraising him through frameless spectacles.

Jacko's attention turned to the phone in the fence's hand. A sizeable iPhone encased in the red and white colours of Arsenal.

'Gunners man?' he said.

'Always, mate. You?'

'Hammers.'

'I'm tempted to get up and leave right now, but West Ham are tanking in the league, so I'll not bother.' Grigson grinned, but there was steel behind the twinkling eyes. His accent was educated London.

'As this is business, mate, I won't be drawn on you Gooners.' Jacko returned his grin.

'Errol has vouched for you,' Grigson said without preamble, fixing Jacko with a gaze that could have been described as either inquisitive or suspicious.

'He's a good guy,' said Jacko with a shrug.

'I've also asked about. Some people I trust have good things to say about you. Kept your mouth shut even after getting properly grassed on and copping a ten-stretch.'

'I'm no grass. I also hear good things about you, like you can handle unusual items that others maybe can't?'

'Possibly. What are we talking about?' Grigson accepted the beer that Errol handed him. Errol nodded and left them alone, sitting on a bar stool close enough to watch but not to hear. Jacko was relieved that he'd not closed in on Neil's location, and the ex-officer still seemed relaxed from his position behind the copy of *The Times*.

'Well, the kind of thing that isn't easy to sell onwards and could be described as niche? Anyway, cheers, good to meet you.' They chinked glasses.

'Look, I'll be frank, Jacko. I'm here because of Errol, but the way you look isn't filling me with confidence. I don't take stupid risks, and I only work with quality people.' Grigson almost sneered, and Jacko felt his hackles begin to rise.

'How I dress isn't really the issue, is it? You come in here dressed like a toff and looking down your nose at me, so if you don't want what I'm offering, I can just as easily piss off and go elsewhere, but your clients will miss out. Imagine they get what they want from someone else, eh? What will that do to your rep?' Jacko's eyes blazed and he jutted a finger at the man with genuine anger. On another day, he'd have thrown his beer all over the snidey bastard, or lamped him, big as he was.

A grin stretched across Grigson's face, showing blindingly white capped teeth. 'All right, chill out, Jacko. I was just having a bit of fun. So what do you have access to?'

Jacko sighed and sat back in his chair, his elbows on the arms as he appraised Grigson.

'You know I'm ex-military, right?'

'I heard. It was a fellow soldier who snitched on you.'

'Yeah. Well, my background has left me with a particular set of opportunities among my old colleagues to obtain some, shall we say, memorabilia.' He nodded, almost to himself, before continuing. 'Memorabilia that may be of value if you know collectors who would be interested, particularly if they ain't so bothered about provenance but are concerned with authenticity. I guarantee that anything you get from me will be totally genuine. No fugazi from Jacko, mate.'

'Your information is accurate, Jacko. I do have customers on my books who are liberal when it comes to where their latest purchases come from. What type of memorabilia are we talking about?'

'Well, for instance, special-edition prestige watches, only available for sale to members of the Special Forces. How's that for starters? Some of them are worth six figures.' Jacko was careful not to jump straight in with medals. He was just opening the door and hoping that Grigson would walk through.

'Nice, they're hard to find, so I'm interested. How about medal groups? I have some collectors who are always on the lookout for interesting or unique bravery awards. Sad types who like to bathe in others' reflected glory, eh, but what can you do?' Grigson shrugged.

Jacko had to squeeze the back of his hand till it hurt to stop a smile stretching across his face. Not only had Grigson sniffed at the bait, he'd stuffed it right in his gob and was hooked. 'Let's see then. Say I was able to lay my hands on a group of medals, such as highly sought-after gongs for bravery, would clients be bothered if they were a little "warm"?' He mimed quotation marks.

'Some would, some wouldn't. Most soldiers, or families of dead soldiers, are reluctant to sell their medals, so if they can be somehow persuaded, or you manage to acquire them by other means, I'm confident I can secure a decent price for them. Not auction valuation prices, of course, as I'm sure you'll appreciate, owing to the slightly high temperature of said gongs.'

'I think I understand you, Jim. You'll not be able to get things like this from anyone else, I can assure you. If it's medal groups you want, I could lay my hands on something special at short notice. As in a once-in-a-lifetime group, worth six figures. But your client would have to be aware that they could never be shown, shared or boasted about.'

There was a long silence between the men.

'I do have a client who is particularly skilled at locating buyers for this type of gear. One in particular is like a magpie. He has expensive taste and won't take no for an answer if certain items are not for sale. He's apparently unconcerned as to how they are located, as long as he ends up possessing them. When do you anticipate getting hold of such items?'

'Soon. Just so I know, what other types of desirable yet unattainable items are your clients looking for?'

Grigson shrugged. 'My contact is always on the lookout for medal groups. One of his client's ambitions is to possess a VC, but I suspect that's a stretch.'

'I should fucking coco, mate. Almost all of those are in museums or bank vaults. How about if I could get my hands on the next best thing? Something very *special*.' Jacko winked, wondering whether the reference to Special Forces would be picked up.

'Let's just say that I'm sure I can provide you with an outlet for such items and leave it at that.' Grigson grinned, his teeth reflecting in the harsh light.

Jacko nodded and drained his beer. 'I'll keep my eyes and ears open, then.'

'Excellent, let's stay in touch. Here's my direct number.' Grigson passed over a slip of paper.

'I hope your client has deep pockets, Jimmy.'

'*His* clients have deeper pockets than you can imagine.'

'Then I'll be in touch.' Jacko stood up, nodded at Errol and left.

Chapter 16

'So whoever this bastard collector is, he wants more medals?' said Macca, once Jacko had finished recounting the meeting with Grigson.

'Definitely. I made it pretty plain that any medals I passed on would be red fucking hot, and Grigson didn't even flinch. I'd say we have our man,' said Jacko.

'Am I taking it that Grigson is a middleman, then, who feeds the next link in the chain?' said Asquith, sipping his coffee.

'No way would someone who's able to afford the sort of shit he's collecting want to deal with a lowlife criminal. Grigson is just passing the gear on to the next man, who's likely to be someone straight, on the face of it at least. That gives the end user plausible deniability in case the cozzers come calling. I did get the impression that there is one big client, but I also got the impression that Grigson doesn't know who that is.'

'It's brilliant work, Jacko, but where do we go from here?' said Macca.

They were all sitting once again in the spacious kitchen at

Chappers' home in Sandridge. Josie was busying herself at the coffee machine, and soon everyone was clutching steaming mugs as the late-evening sun was casting dappled shade pierced by the sinking sun through doors that looked onto the well-tended garden.

'One of my old analysts is working up the open-source intelligence available on Grigson, including the phone number he gave Jacko and the car I followed him to after he left the pub,' said Asquith. 'I'm promised a summary imminently, which will give us something to go on.'

'I never had you for a surveillance operator, Neil.' Charlie chuckled. 'Good work, by the way. I was able to get the car checked out via a close mate in an intelligence unit who tacked it onto a bulk check. A blue Mercedes C Class registered to James Grigson at an address on Longstone Avenue in Harlesden. He's had it since new. I had a drive-by and it's a well-kept place on an up-and-coming street.'

'Nice work, Charlie. What type of doors, and did the locks look decent?' said Macca.

'What, you thinking of breaking in?' said Josie, her eyebrows raised in surprise.

'Let's say I'm not ruling it out. I did extensive lock-picking courses during my days on the Det in the Province,' said Macca, referring to his time in 14 Intelligence Company in Northern Ireland, who carried out long-term covert operations against the paramilitaries.

'Hard to tell, Macca. I'll do a leaflet drop on the street later today and get you some photos,' said Charlie.

'What will breaking in achieve? I mean, what would we be looking for?' said Josie.

'Not sure, love. Just thinking ahead,' said Macca.

Josie frowned, her face colouring. 'Listen, I know I'm much younger than you lot, but can we ease up on the "loves"? It's not 1975, and women don't just sit at home waiting for hubby any more, you know.'

Macca opened his mouth to argue, but then closed it again, looking sheepish.

Charlie looked at Josie. 'So we know who the fence is, but we don't know who he gave the medals to and where they went after that. Computers and phones may be our best options.' He spoke slowly, almost as if lecturing a reluctant school kid.

Josie's eyes hardened. 'Charlie, been working with computers most of my life, and I've used GPS devices and tech at the bloody North Pole. A little less patronising would be nice, okay?'

There was an uncomfortable silence in the kitchen, only broken when Charlie cleared his throat and muttered, 'Sorry. Dinosaur moment.'

Josie just shook her head.

'No chance of phone data via your sources, Charlie?' said Jacko.

Charlie just shook his head.

'So, we have nothing. Shit, this is difficult,' said Macca, shaking his head.

'I wouldn't say that, Macca,' said Asquith.

'What?'

He held his phone up. 'Early report from my open-source intel analyst contact. Plenty of data already from the car, the phone number, address and the like, plus associated links that my man has uncovered.' He smiled widely as he studied the screen.

Josie tutted, audibly, her cheeks flushed in frustration. 'I'm surprised any of you lot got anything done, ever. We're all over the bloody place here and need some structure before we can decide what's next. What do we have in the report, Neil?'

'Confirmation of Grigson's address, vehicle details, social media and apps, bank accounts. An absolute gold mine. My man uses tools that can detect IP addresses, networks, open ports, webcams and basically anything that's connected to the internet. He also uses people search engines like Pipl and ThatsThem. We may not need to break in if we can activate a camera in Grigson's house, or on his TV or laptop.'

'I understood about one bleeding word in ten there, mate,' said Jacko.

'I suspect that technical expertise is not what you're bringing to this particular party, Jacko.'

'Speed could be of the essence in case the medals end up somewhere that would be really difficult to operate in, like Russia, for instance. I'm betting they're still in the UK at the moment,' said Charlie.

'How can you be sure?' asked Josie.

'Anyone knowingly handling something so hot would probably keep them under wraps for a while. The theft has hit the newspapers, so they'll lay up for a bit until the trail goes cold.'

'I agree with the cozzer, which is something I don't often say,' said Jacko. 'Always good to let the heat die down before moving shit.'

'Anything obvious in the report that we can use straight away?' asked Macca.

Asquith squinted at his phone. 'It looks like he's going through a divorce, according to filed court records.'

'Divorce? Errol said he was a right shagger, so that's not surprising. He's a slimy bastard as well as being a bloody Gooner.' Jacko almost scowled.

'Gooner? He's an Arsenal fan? Does he live alone?' Josie asked.

'Looks like it,' said Asquith.

'Tinder?'

'What's Tinder?'

'Oh, Jesus. Tinder, the dating app. Does he have it?'

'What, you've never heard of Tinder?' said Macca.

'I've been married thirty-eight years, so no, I've never heard of Tinder.' Asquith shrugged. 'And even if I had, you've met my wife and know exactly how scary she is. How do *you* know about it?'

'I've had a few dates since getting divorced. A lean, mean and attractive man like myself is a catch.' Macca chuckled.

'The lovely septic-tank spook would certainly agree.' Jacko smirked, his eyes glinting mischievously. Macca held his middle finger up in response.

'Any tales to tell?' said Charlie.

'None that I'm telling you buggers.'

'Couldn't get it up, I bet,' said Jacko.

'Ran out of Viagra,' added Asquith.

'They were put off by his walking stick,' said Charlie.

'Listen, you cheeky ba—' began Macca.

Josie interrupted. 'Guys, shush, you're all wittering on and it's doing my head in. I've an idea. Neil, is his Tinder app live?'

Asquith looked at his handset again. 'Yes, looks like it. IP address puts it at his address, and the account is active and being paid for.'

'How old is he?'

'Forty.'

'Show me his picture?'

Asquith swiped on his phone and held it up so that Josie could see.

'Is that his Tinder profile pic?'

'Yes.'

Josie looked at the photo. Grigson was well built, with thick, carefully styled brown hair, and was expensively dressed in a crisp shirt, pale blue chinos and deck shoes with no socks. He was holding some kind of elaborate cocktail and smiling widely, showing blindingly white teeth in a deeply tanned face.

'Ugh, lounge lizard. What's the bio say?'

'Josie, what are you thinking here?' said Macca.

'Neil?' said Josie, ignoring Macca.

'"Generous thirty-five-year-old male, solvent, adventurous, seeks sex-bomb younger ladies for no-strings fun." Jesus, if he came anywhere near my daughter, I'd smash the oily bastard,' said Asquith, scowling.

'Aye, he needs filling in,' agreed Macca, puffing his cheeks out.

'Guys, while you lot are being protective boomers, we could be missing a perfect opportunity here,' said Josie, her brow furrowing with thought.

There was a long pause in the room, before Macca spoke, his Scottish brogue deepening. 'Over my dead bloody body, young lady.'

'Macca, I hate to say this, but you're not the RSM any more, and certainly not the boss of me. This is a solid gold opportunity. Also, can I point out that if you call me "young lady" again, you're going to be wearing this cup of coffee.' She smiled, but the steel behind it was evident.

'Josie, no. I'll not allow it; your father would turn in his grave. You can't go on a date with this creature.'

'Look, Macca, this is my business and Frankie was my dad. We won't get a better opportunity. Neil, you said you had people who could do technical stuff, right?'

Asquith looked confused. 'Well, yes. One of the responsibilities of the company is protection and examination of companies' IT assets before they deploy to hostile environments.'

Josie gave a knowing smile, and they all leant in to listen as she announced, 'I've got a plan.'

Chapter 17

Tuesday 14 December 2021

Josie checked her appearance in a shop window as she approached the gastropub in Queen's Park where she'd arranged to meet Grigson. She'd had to rush out and buy an outfit in a swanky boutique in St Albans, as her own selection of clothes consisted of mainly jeans or sports- and mountain-wear and she was playing a wholly different role here. A short fitted dress, nude stiletto heels and a denim jacket. She adjusted the long blonde wig and blinked, the green-tinted contact lenses still feeling a little odd. She thought she looked faintly ridiculous, but all the lads had mumbled that she looked great, clearly embarrassed at having to appraise her dressed in that fashion, particularly as they'd all known her since childhood.

Her Tinder profile with the nickname 'GoonerGal' had been speedily created, with a fairly anonymous profile photo that made it clear she was decent-looking and slender, but from enough of a distance to make her not immediately recognisable.

She'd swiped on Grigson's profile and he'd messaged her with almost indecent haste. There'd been a bit of flirty back-and-forth, during which she'd had to avail herself of her acting skills. She'd been involved in amateur dramatics for years, and playing the role of a girl on a blind date was far more comfortable than actually *being* a girl on a blind date.

According to her profile, she was Janet, twenty-nine years old and from Enfield, a football fan and call-centre employee who liked 'dancing, drum and bass, and holidays', looking to meet a 'nice, generous and solvent man who's kind to animals'. She'd felt faintly sick when creating the profile, and even sicker when engaging with Grigson, but she'd held her nose and done it.

In reality, none of this was natural to Josie. She wasn't great at dating in any way, shape or form, and had only had one serious relationship in her thirty years, which had ended last year. Morrison was a nice guy, who worked in IT, but he had got sick of her being away for months on end on climbing expeditions, marathon training or solo treks to the North Pole. She wasn't so bothered. She had so many other things she wanted to achieve that didn't involve men.

She reached into her bag, pulled out a small hip flask filled with vodka and took a swig, screwing up her face at the taste of the harsh liquor. She swished it around her mouth, her gums burning, and spat it out on the pavement. Then she took a deep breath and pushed the door open.

The place was warm and convivial, and only about half full. It was all scrubbed wood and Scandi-chic decor. She saw him straight away, sitting alone at a table looking at his phone in its Arsenal case. She staggered a little in her heels as she headed towards him.

Grigson looked up and beamed a huge smile, his stupid teeth glinting. Josie groaned inwardly. He was dressed in overly tight jeans and a slim-fit shirt, and was so far from the type of man she was attracted to it was almost remarkable. Jolting herself into performance mode, she changed her gait, softening her limbs and letting her jaw sag, and began to totter over, stifling a hiccup. He watched with a lecherous leer as she approached.

'Jimmy?' she slurred, giggling as he stood. She threw her arms around his neck and hugged him, breathing vodka-laced breath all over him. His nose wrinkled, but the glint in his eye was undiminished. Releasing him, she wobbled towards the table, hiccuping again as she almost fell onto the chair opposite.

'Janet, lovely to meet you. Are you okay?' said Jimmy, looking at her with an expression that was part alarm, part lust. Her pissed act was clearly having the desired effect.

'Not gonna lie, Jimbo, I've had a few.' She giggled, and stifled a burp, closing one of her eyes as she picked up the menu, clearly trying to focus on the small print.

'Would you like another?' he asked, his voice deep and tinged with north London tones.

'Yesh please,' she said, pulling the menu close to her face and then moving it away as though trying to focus. 'This menu is both too big and too blimming shmall, fuck sake,' she said, raising her voice and staring at the barman, her face transforming from smiley to angry in a heartbeat. She couldn't help but notice the guy shooting a look at Grigson that said firmly, 'Keep her under control, mate.' Grigson squirmed. Josie giggled.

'Er, what shall I get you?'

'Prosecco, perrrleassse,' she said, hiccuping again.

'Sure you don't want something soft?'

'No way. Sorry, I had a few with a girlfriend, but I'm feeling very nice and relaxed now, babes.' She winked drunkenly. 'Ooh, look, we have the same phone case. Arsenal, Arsenal, Arsenal!' She picked up his phone and held it next to hers before placing both phones back down on the table and sitting back in her chair.

'I'll get your drink,' said Grigson, heading to the bar. It was only a few steps away, and despite the soft hubbub in the pub, Josie could hear every word of the exchange.

'Prosecco and another pint, mate, please.'

'Is she okay?' the barman asked.

'She's fine,' said Jimmy, sounding a little too eager. He obviously wasn't in any way put off by her state of inebriation, and Josie felt herself chill a little. Clearly a total scumbag, who felt that he was now on a promise.

'You okay?' said Grigson as he sat down, placing the drink in front of her.

'Fine,' she said, removing all the excitement and vivacity from her voice and slurring even more. She knocked her glass as she picked it up, slopping some on the table. She lifted it to her lips and shuddered.

'I need to go to the loo,' she said, standing up abruptly. Her chair clattered to the floor and she stumbled off in the direction of the ladies'.

Chapter 18

Josie staggered into the corridor that led to the toilets, straightening up as soon as she was out of sight of the bar. She looked at Grigson's phone, which she'd lifted from the table when he was at the bar, having left her own phone in its place.

Quickening her pace, she dived into the disabled toilet and locked the door. Her recce earlier had identified this place as perfect, the toilet having a window that opened to the rear of the pub. Now she grabbed the handle and opened it as far as it would go, which was just about four inches.

'All okay?' said Neil Asquith's voice from the other side of the gap.

'Yes, but I don't have long before he realises it's my phone on the table and comes looking for me.'

She passed Grigson's phone through the crack, then moved to the mirror and pulled out a make-up wipe, beginning to scrub at her heavy foundation, eyeliner and lipstick. She turned on the tap and splashed water on her face, making sure that her mascara ran and smudged.

'It won't take much longer,' Asquith said. 'It's downloading now and there doesn't seem to be much on it. I suspect it's new. I hear you're putting on a fine performance. Did you clock Macca in the corner of the pub?'

'I didn't notice him, which is a good thing. Grigson won't get lively; he seems almost scared, and I've just made myself look like I've been puking.'

'Okay, it's done. Phone's coming through now. We'll see you in the next street along, like we practised, yeah?'

'Yeah, see you in a bit. Oh, and text Macca and tell him to watch my next performance. I'm gonna make the pervy bastard squirm.'

She took the phone as it appeared through the window, then had a quick look at herself in the mirror. With her pale face and smudged mascara, she looked totally different from when she'd entered the loo. She pasted on a hangdog, sick-looking expression and set off back towards the bar. Pushing heavily at the door, she followed it inwards, staggering. 'Whoops,' she slurred as she stumbled towards Grigson, who was turning to watch her. He had her phone in his hand, and his face wore a mix of alarm and irritation at the sudden deterioration in her appearance.

'Are you okay?' he asked as she approached the table unsteadily and plopped heavily down on a chair with a grunt.

'Think I'm a bit pished,' she slurred.

'No shit. You've got my phone,' he said, holding the identically covered handset aloft.

'Oops, silly me,' she said, letting her jaw quiver a little. She spent thirty seconds rummaging through her bag before pulling out his phone and handing it over with a half-smile that didn't reach her rheumy eyes. Grigson opened the screen with his fingerprint and checked it before tucking the phone away in his pocket.

He looked at her searchingly, and Josie could see the cogs turning in his brain but also the lecherous desire in his eyes. She shuddered, and this time it wasn't an act. She knew then that he'd happily take her even in the state he believed she was in. His next words made that clear. Jimmy Grigson clearly didn't give a shit how pissed his date was. 'Want to come back to mine? I'm not far away,' he said suggestively.

'Maybe not. I'm a bit drunk and I feel a bit ick, babes. Another time?' she said.

He sighed, his disappointment obvious, then nodded and shrugged.

Josie let her face fall a little further and cupped her hand over her mouth. 'I need to go,' she slurred, and rocketed to her feet, suddenly animated. Stumbling forward, she jarred the table, knocking his beer glass over and depositing the contents into his lap.

'Jesus,' he bellowed, leaping up and wiping frantically at his trousers.

'I'm sorry, I'm sorry,' she said, lunging forward with a napkin, only to send her Prosecco flying into him.

'Bloody hell,' hissed Grigson.

'I'm going, I'm going. I'm shorry, so shorry.' She grabbed her jacket from the back of the chair and dashed towards the door, almost falling into a staring group of drinkers at the bar.

Shoving the door open, she staggered out into the cool night air, picking up her pace as she did, a grin spreading across her face as she headed to where Neil and Macca would be waiting for her. She knew she'd nailed it; all Grigson would remember was the pissed bird, and no way would he give the fact that she'd had access to his phone another thought. He was such a lech, she was confident he'd agree to another date, particularly if he thought he was on a promise. She felt mildly nauseous at the prospect, but it was all part of the game.

Her skin was prickling with the excitement. It was such a buzz, she thought as she headed to the rendezvous point.

Chapter 19

'Did it work?' said Josie as she climbed into Neil's mammoth Audi SUV that had pulled to the side of the road just around the corner from the pub. She pulled off her wig and shook out her own deep brown tresses, then blinked rapidly as she carefully took out the green contact lenses.

'Yep, full download of the whole bloody phone. It's a hell of a bit of kit, and so simple a moron could use it. It makes me regret paying the bloke so much when I was running the company.' Asquith held up a plain-looking metallic box.

'I have to say, my girl, if you ever give up all your adventure stuff, you've a career as an actress,' said Macca from the driver's seat.

Irritation flashed in her stomach. 'Girl? Come on, Macca. We've talked about this. I know you've known me all my bloody life, but I'm not ten any more.'

'Sorry, Jose.' He sounded genuinely contrite.

'No worries. It's all the am-dram I've done; I knew it would come in handy one day. Where are Charlie and Jacko?'

'At Jacko's flat in Camden,' Neil replied. 'We'll go there, and then I'll upload the contents of this onto my laptop and we can have a look. My man put a load of e-discovery software on it, so it should be child's play to interrogate. Hopefully we'll get a lead.'

'You were watching, Macca. Do you think he twigged?' said Josie, wiping the remains of the smudged make-up from her face.

'No chance. He only realised you'd taken his phone just before you came back. That was some transformation, from hot chick to scary pissed bag-lady in a few minutes.' Macca chuckled.

'Just a quick bit of make-up removal and a case of the staggers. It was fun.'

'It certainly looked it. You were bloody convincing, and he'll be thinking he had a lucky escape.' Macca put his foot down, and the big car roared as it headed east away from Kilburn.

'The dirty perv was still up for it. Even after I came back looking like I'd been decorating the toilet bowl, he was asking me to come back to his.' She shuddered.

At that moment, her phone buzzed. It was a message from Grigson on the dating app. *Hope you're okay. We should try again soon.* Josie chuckled. 'He's just messaged me. He's up for a second date. He must be desperate.'

'Fucker's a predator. I'd like ten minutes alone with him,' snarled Macca, his eyes flashing at her in the rear-view mirror.

'Nice to have as an option, in case we need more from him, but he's an oily creep, that's for sure. How far to Jacko's place?'

'Fifteen to twenty minutes.'

'Brilliant, I can't wait to tell the others. We're making progress, lads. We're getting closer.'

Chapter 20

Jacko's flat wasn't what Josie had expected, bearing in mind his slightly straggly and shambolic appearance.

A modest two-bedroom apartment in a modern block on Regis Road in the centre of Kentish Town, it was tastefully furnished and immaculately clean, with a well-stocked galley kitchen and modern appliances.

'Jacko, I'm flabbergasted,' she said.

'Why?' asked Jacko as he frothed some milk with the steam wand on his expensive-looking Sage coffee machine.

'I expected your place to be like an overly ripe student pad, and yet here we are with tasteful cushions, posh coffee, pleasing art and even some potpourri!' Josie accepted the latte that Jacko handed her with a proud smile. '*And* you've done a tree in the frothy milk. What's going on? Is there a secret woman in here?'

'Cheeky mare. I just like to keep a nice place. I bought this gaff for a song when I had a couple of nice scores. It's the pension scheme,' said Jacko, wiping down the shiny composite surface with a cloth.

'Well, my flabber is gasted. Good coffee, by the way.'

Jacko just shook his head, suppressing a smile, and looked at Asquith, Macca and Charlie. 'Beer?'

'Now you're talking,' said Macca, flopping down on a leather sofa.

'How come I didn't get offered a beer? This is just bloody sexist,' said Josie.

'Because you asked for a coffee as soon as you came in,' Jacko pointed out.

'I didn't know beer was on the menu,' she said.

'You want a beer then?'

'Yes, I want a bloody beer. I'm gagging after pretending to be pissed.'

Jacko returned to the fridge with a big sigh and pulled out a fistful of Budweisers, which he handed around before presenting Josie's in the style of a sommelier at a posh restaurant, proffered across his forearm. 'Madam?'

Josie smiled and accepted the beer, taking a big swig.

'Boys, I have to say that massive kudos is due to Josie here. Her performance in that pub was worthy of an Oscar. She totally threw that slimy leech off his stride, and he won't suspect a bloody thing.' Macca nodded in admiration.

There was a brief round of applause from the others in the room.

'You should have seen my performance as Mary in the nativity play when I was at primary school.' Josie smiled widely and took another swig of her beer.

'Success, then?' asked Charlie.

'Aye, a full download of the phone,' said Macca. 'The matching phone cases was a stroke of genius – well noticed, Jacko. He didn't suspect a thing.'

'I'm just putting the data onto the computer now, and I'll run it through some e-discovery software that my old analyst sent. It should make it easy to search with keywords, so I'll email it to all of you.' Asquith was sitting at the breakfast bar, tapping away at a Mac.

'Much on it?' said Charlie.

'Enough. Lots of call data. It'll take a bit of sorting. Look, here's his social media selfie,' said Asquith, turning the Mac to display a photo on the screen. They all looked at the beefy features, sharp haircut and perfect teeth of Jimmy Grigson.

'Looks a right smarmy cockwomble, don't he,' said Jacko.

'As eloquent as you are accurate, mate. Can I have a look, Neil? I spent a lot of time interpreting phone downloads in my former life,' said Charlie, moving to Asquith's shoulder.

'Be my guest.' Asquith pulled back from the laptop and Charlie slipped his spectacles on and moved in front of the machine.

'His Bluetooth menu only shows the Merc, and some devices in his home. Nothing obvious from that.'

He swept and clicked using the trackpad until he brought up a spreadsheet.

'WhatsApp was always my favourite place to look to start with. I had a dedicated officer to interrogate phones on any murder enquiry. Let's see if the basic approach works.' He pressed control and F together and a search box appeared. He typed in 'medal*' and pressed the return key.

No matches

He searched for 'antique*'.

No matches

'Chapman*'

No matches

'Frank*'

No matches

'Sandridge*'

No matches

He frowned and tapped at the keys again: 'DCM*'.

No matches.

'Does the software search for deleted messages?' he asked,

looking over his glasses at Asquith.

'Erm, not gonna lie, I'm familiar with the reports, but the actual interpreting and technical stuff was done by other people.'

'Can I see?' asked Josie.

'Do you have any experience of mobile data interrogation?' said Asquith.

'No, but I've been around computers all my life, and I basically live on a phone and a tablet when I'm away. I probably know more than you old dinosaurs.' She edged Charlie out of the way and clicked and swiped on the trackpad, her face fixed in a mask of concentration.

Asquith cleared his throat. 'Look, Josie, this isn't something to mess about with. It needs an expert—'

'Done. You just needed to check the box marked "recover",' Josie interrupted, smiling widely.

'Ah.' Asquith looked crestfallen.

Charlie, Macca and Jacko all burst out laughing.

'Boom, touchdown, knockout,' crowed Jacko, wiping beer from his chin.

'So despite being an ex-commissioned officer, you need a thirty-year-old to show you how to work a computer,' said Macca, a big smile on his face.

'Well I didn't see anyone else trying,' said Asquith sheepishly.

'Never mind that. Check this out,' said Charlie. He swivelled the computer around so Macca and Jacko could see.

A screen grab appeared: a semi-detached house with a large conifer tree on the lawn.

It was Chappers' house.

A hush descended on the room, the only sound the hum from the large refrigerator.

'And this.' Charlie pressed a key and the image changed to another screen grab, this time a map of Sandridge, the property highlighted with a crudely drawn arrow.

'Bastard,' said Josie quietly.

'Aye. Was that in a message?' asked Macca.

'Looks like it. I've the number here, sent the day before the burglary.'

'What else is there?'

'Lots. Lots of deleted messages. Neil, can you get this to someone who knows how to deal with the data properly? We need to see if we can overlay it with GPS data, web searches, photos taken and similar. I want this proved to a standard that a court would accept before we act. I want to be able to establish who Jarman handed the medals to, and where they went after that, and the phones will give us that. It's all in here.'

'Why?' asked Jacko. 'For the cops? I mean, who gives a shit?'

'Me,' said Charlie. 'I care. We can't go to the cops, as they've already shown they've no leads. We're breaking all the rules to track the medals, and any evidence we've obtained so far is completely inadmissible. We get the evidence so we're sure, then we have right on our side.'

Asquith nodded in agreement. 'We're not criminals, Jacko. The data on the phone proves we're in the right place, doing the right things.'

Josie suddenly looked up from the laptop, her expression a mix of triumph and anger. 'You're right, the cops can't do anything, but we can, and we will. Look.' She tapped at the screen. 'This photo was sent to Grigson about an hour after the burglary, and he then forwarded it a few minutes later to a number in his phone listed as "GH".'

The photo was pin-sharp and showed a pale, grimy-looking hand holding a group of medals they all recognised. The Conspicuous Gallantry Cross, the DCM, the Iraq medal with its Mention in Despatches oak leaf, the multiple campaign medals and the US Bronze Star. Chappers' medals.

Josie swiped on the track pad, and there was another photograph, of the rear of the CGC. The inscription was clear: *WO F Chapman P0542727.*

Chapter 21

Wednesday 15 December 2021

'Are you sure about this, Macca? It's your medal group and you earned them. It's really risky, and I'd never forgive myself if you lost your medals as well,' said Josie as she sat in the kitchen looking at the medal group on the table. The morning sun was shining through the bifold doors, and the team all looked tired and jaded after just a few hours' sleep.

'Best option we have. Who else has a group like this to dangle as bait, eh? You never know, we may get the opportunity just by showing them to the next link in the chain.' Macca picked up the medals and ran his hands across them.

'You were such a brave boy, Macca.' Jacko giggled, and Macca flipped a middle finger at him.

'Are you willing to let them out of your sight?' said Asquith.

'They're just bits of metal and ribbons, mate. If this works, we'll get them back along with Chappers' medals, and anyway, I'm not sure I even want them if I can't get his back as well. It wouldn't feel right.'

'But they're your legacy, Macca,' insisted Josie.

'Look, I'm sixty-two. I'm divorced, and I have no kids. I spent my whole life on operations around the globe doing bad shit for the government, so what do I care, eh?' Macca's voice was almost matter-of-fact.

'Well you could sell them then. Must be worth a fortune,' said Jacko.

'A hundred K was the insurance estimate.'

'What the actual fuck?' said Jacko.

'Hands off, you thieving cockney bastard,' said Macca with a wide grin.

'Not thinking of me, mate. Thinking of your bank account.'

'I don't need the money. My years on the circuit after leaving the SBS paid off my mortgage, and what else do I do? I don't like cars, posh restaurants are weird, I hate holidays – apart from climbing Munros in Scotland, which is free – and I'm partial to growing organic veg. I've nothing to spend the money on, so I'd rather we used them to try to get Chappers' medals back for Macey and Josie.' His voice was dry and firm and his jaw was set. They all knew enough about Macca to know that once his mind was made up, there was no arguing with him.

'Okay, so we set the trap. What do you have, Neil?' said Macca.

'I narrowed parameters, with Josie's help. It turns out she has a much better grasp of this type of thing than I do. The GPS data is really helpful, I have to say. We already know that Grigson received the message with the photos of the medals attached shortly after the burglary, and we're assuming it was from Jarman, yes?'

There were nods around the room.

'GPS for Grigson's phone remains static around Kilburn and Harlesden until three days after the burglary, when it makes a journey, having called the number listed in his phone as GH.' He paused to sip from his coffee cup.

'And?' said Jacko.

'The GPS signal travels west for almost forty minutes, then settles in Mayfair.' Asquith pointed at a map on his laptop screen with a blue line tracing the route.

'Bloody hell. Any villain really should leave their phone at home, right?' said Jacko.

'Indeed, and it gets more interesting. From what I can see, he goes into JustPark in Arlington Street.'

'Shit, it can be that precise?' said Macca.

'Yep.'

'How can you tell?'

'He used Apple Pay to pay for his stay there. Bloody eye-wateringly expensive for two hours. It's all recorded here.'

'Phones really are just spies in your pocket,' said Macca, shaking his head. 'Where did he go after that?'

'He walked for ten minutes and went into the Chesterfield Hotel, where he stayed for an hour, spending thirty-one quid in there.'

'Still Mayfair?' said Jacko.

'Yeah, Mayfair. What of it?' said Asquith.

'Errol mentioned that Grigson had a snidey antique dealer in Mayfair. Top-end posh geezer who would take hot antiques and shit like that. Grigson isn't a typical villain really. I think he could operate in both worlds, even though he's an arsehole,' said Jacko with a chuckle.

'He's much worse than just an arsehole. He's a predatory oily bastard.' Josie almost grimaced as she said the words.

'That's as may be, but we're no further forward, are we?' said Asquith. 'The open-source data doesn't help with the phone number for the mysterious dealer, who we're assuming is "GH", so I'm imagining it's a burner phone he only uses for talking to reprobates like Grigson, or Jacko.'

'I actually resent that remark, you judgemental bastard,' said Jacko.

'Yeah, right. So six years in prison and access to the under-world, including having a serving prisoner battered, makes you practically a vicar, then?' said Asquith, shaking his head slightly and stifling a grin.

'Fair point, well made.' Jacko shrugged, and showed his teeth in a wolfish grin.

'So, we dangle my medals as bait to flush him out into the open, and once he has them, we hope he takes us to GH, right?' said Macca.

There were nods all round the room.

'Let's do it then,' said Josie. 'Make the call, Jacko.'

Jacko looked at Macca, who nodded. 'Go for it.'

Jacko picked up his phone from the kitchen island and dialled. It rang for ten full rings before Grigson answered.

'Hello?'

'Hello, Jimmy, it's Jacko Jackson. How ya doing?'

'Doing good, Jacko. What can I do for you?'

'Well, remember what we were talking about the other day?'

'Of course.' The sounds in the background made it clear that Grigson was in a car.

'Well, I've something that may be of interest.'

'I'm listening,' said Grigson, his voice tight with anticipation.

'A shit-hot medal group. The recipient was SBS, and there are some serious gongs on it for bravery.' Jacko winked at Macca.

'That sounds interesting. Special Forces medal groups always attract a premium. Which gallantry awards?'

'All of them, mate. One of the best groups I've seen.' The grin on Jacko's face was wide and full of crooked teeth.

'Can you send a photo? My client will want to see them first before offering on them.'

'I'll send it now. One thing, though.' Jacko hesitated.

'Spit it out,' said Grigson, irritation detectable in his voice.

'Be aware that your client isn't the only customer showing interest in these, so he needs to get a wriggle on. Man's got bills to pay.'

'Send me a picture.'

'On its way.' Jacko hung up.

'Short and sweet,' said Macca.

'Bastard's playing it cool, but he's nibbling. Pass me the box,' said Jacko.

Macca handed over the wooden medal box and Jacko opened it. They all paused to admire the group: the Military Medal, the Military Cross and various campaign medals. They were magnificent yet understated, the embodiment of one man's life in the most elite military outfit in the world.

'You sure about this, Macca?' said Jacko.

'Of course.' Macca's face was impassive.

Jacko took a quick snap of the medals and sent it straight to Grigson.

The reply was immediate.

I need to see these ASAP. Call me.

'He's bitten like a bastard, wants to see them right away,' said Jacko, looking up from his phone.

'Good. No time to lose,' said Macca.

'I'll get on it now.' Jacko stepped out into the garden, raising his phone to his ear.

'Depending on when the meet is, I've a suggestion for a bit of intel-gathering,' said Charlie.

'Go on,' said Macca.

'Maybe a bit of a poke-about in Mayfair could be of some value. Appeal to someone's good nature, rattle a few cages. Old-school policing style. We know that the bastard's in Mayfair. We get a face, a name, we've got a proper starting point.'

'Sounds like a useful idea,' said Asquith.

Macca nodded. 'Good call. Let's just see what Jacko says first.'

'Josie, obviously we need to keep you well away from Grigson now,' said Charlie.

'I was pretty well disguised, though.' Josie looked crestfallen.

'I know, but it's just not worth it. If you come face to face, he may well twig, and that'd be disastrous. You've proved your worth already, but we don't want to take unnecessary risks.'

'Yeah, I guess.' Josie sat back in her chair and sighed.

'Come along with me to Mayfair. I could do with a wing man.'

'I prefer "wing person", but okay, why not,' she said, immediately brightening, almost bouncing with energy.

'One thing.'

'What?'

'Dress like a cop.'

'What, a smart suit, notebook and badge?' she said, her smile widening at the possibility of more acting.

'No, a cheap, ill-fitting suit with a kebab stain, and a general air of lassitude, defeat and despondency. Come on, let's get on with it. It'll take a while to get to Mayfair, and I'd like to spend some time at home tonight. Mrs Drake is getting slightly irritated at my absences.'

'I'll just go and change. Give me five minutes.' Josie bounded off with as much as enthusiasm as Tigger.

'Blimey, she's loving this shit, ain't she?' said Jacko as he re-entered the room.

'This is just her latest fix as a total adrenaline junkie, I'd say. She really is a chip off the old block. News?' asked Macca.

'Ten hundred tomorrow at the café in Roundwood Park, by the entrance on Harlesden Road.'

'His suggestion or yours?'

'Mine. Plenty of opportunities there for concealment and he's bound to park in the little close by the entrance – always plenty of space there. I don't reckon he'll want to hold on to red-hot medals for long, so maybe he'll make a trip to Mayfair afterwards.'

'Can I see the medals again?' asked Asquith.

Jacko flipped the box to him and Asquith turned it over in his hands. It was about the size of a piece of A4 paper and made of what looked like polished walnut. He opened the clasp, revealing the double row of medals inlaid in green baize. 'Amazing group, Macca.'

Macca just shrugged in response.

'I'm staying in my London flat tonight – which reminds me, I must call my wife to tell her. Can I keep hold of these and put them in my safe? No disrespect, Jacko, but Kentish Town has a burglary problem.'

'You've a flat in London? I thought you had a big posh place in Bedfordshire?' said Jacko.

'I do. That's the family home, but I have a pied-à-terre in Hampstead.' Asquith's gaze flickered downwards, almost in embarrassment.

'A pee what?' Jacko's eyes twinkled with amusement.

'Jacko, I know you like to play it dim, but I happen to know you got an A in your English A level, so don't play the thicko with me.'

'How the hell did you know about that?' Jacko looked flabbergasted, and not a little embarrassed.

'I know it was a long time ago, but I was once your commanding officer, with access to your file. Your A-level results struck me as odd then, and they still do now.'

Macca grinned. 'We all thought you were totally solid, and now we learn you're a brainbox. What other A levels do you have?'

'Maths and physics, but I've forgotten it all.' Jacko's discomfort was clear.

'It's okay, mate,' said Asquith. 'Your secret cleverness is safe with us, and I won't mention that I noticed *The Great Gatsby*, *Atonement* and one or two Hilary Mantel novels on your shelf.'

'All right, I like reading. You said you were going for a slash, and now I learn that you were sneaking about my flat looking at my books, like a suspicious parent searching for porn in their kids' bedrooms. Invasion of privacy, I tell you. Now can we all shut up and get to the point? You want to look after the medals, Neil?'

'Yes, safer at mine.' Asquith nodded.

'Fine by me. I'll just need them back in plenty of time for the meet. Where shall we RV?'

'Your flat? I'd like to see some more of your bookshelf,' said

Josie, who'd reappeared in the kitchen pinning her hair into a bun. She had changed into a drab trouser suit with a plain blouse and scuffed flat shoes.

'Blimey, Josie,' Jacko exclaimed. 'You really should consider a career treading the boards. You're a spit for a weary, scruffy and washed-up cozzer.'

'This is actually my best, and only, suit,' she said, scowling.

'Oops, sorry. Anyway, tomorrow morning, Chez Jacko at eight. I'll have the coffee and bacon on. I just need a piss, then I'll crack on.'

Chapter 22

The Chesterfield Hotel was just as Charlie had expected it. Slap-bang in the middle of Mayfair – that most salubrious area of central London – it had a grand facade with a maroon canopy, and wrought-iron railings with an impressive floral display. A Union flag and a White Ensign fluttered alongside each other, directly above where the top-hatted doorman stood, hands behind his back.

'Blimey, this place is seriously posh,' said Josie as they loitered on the opposite side of the street.

'All of Mayfair is. Here, take this.' He handed over a blue lanyard emblazoned with the words 'Metropolitan Police', although the holder where the ID badge would have been slotted into was empty.

'Charlie?'

'Just put it around your neck and tuck the card-holder inside your jacket. Make sure the police logo is visible. We need to do a bit of blagging here,' said Charlie, reaching into his pocket.

'What about you?' asked Josie.

'It's possible that when I handed my warrant card in, I kept hold of the case and badge. I wanted it as a souvenir for my grandson, but it just stayed in my briefcase and I'd forgotten all about it.' He showed her the battered leather case with a silver police crest and a Braille panel underneath. Inside the clear plastic portion where the ID card should have been was what suspiciously looked like a gym membership card bearing Charlie's photograph.

'Jesus, Charlie. You're gonna get us nicked for impersonating police officers,' said Josie, eyes wide.

Charlie shook his head. 'Nah, we'll be fine. I made a call first, so they're expecting DS Dray and DC Shufflebottom to view some CCTV for a covert enquiry. Just be confident and look like you belong.'

'What?' said Josie, her face incredulous.

'CCTV for a covert enquiry.'

'No. Not that. I'm not being called DC Shufflebottom. That's a shit name.'

'It's memorable. They won't question it, as they'll be worried you'll think they're taking the piss. Plus if the cops come sniffing later, all they'll remember is your name. Perfect tactics.' Charlie grinned.

'You're a nasty man, Charlie Drake. Or should I call you DS Dray?'

'Aye, close enough, eh?'

'I hate to think what strokes you pulled when serving.' Josie shook her head.

They crossed the road, and the doorman nodded at them and opened the lacquered door, which opened into a grand and opulent reception. The floor was highly polished black and white marble and a large, ornate chandelier dominated the space. Leather chairs and sofas were dotted around. A solitary receptionist smiled as they approached the dark wooden counter.

'Good afternoon and welcome to the Chesterfield. How may I be of service?' He was a good-looking, immaculately dressed man

112

in his thirties, and his accented English was flawless.

'Hi, are you Piotr?' said Charlie, holding out the wallet with the crest showing. The receptionist barely glanced at it.

'Yes, that's me. DS Dray, I assume?' He smiled again, showing teeth so white and even they could only be veneers.

'Thanks for seeing us at such short notice, Piotr. As I mentioned, it's a slightly delicate situation that we're trying to sort with the minimum of fuss. A guest of yours either lost or possibly had his wallet stolen from his coat when he was having breakfast here a few days ago. We are investigating the possibility that the incident may have been caught by the CCTV in the lobby or dining room.' Charlie's own smile was warm and genuine and yet at the same time radiated a determined sternness. He was clearly someone used to being in charge.

'Delicate how, may I ask?' said Piotr, his brow furrowed in confusion.

'Delicate in that the guest is reluctant to admit to his wife that he was here, and really could do with this being kept on the down-low, if you know what I mean?' Charlie raised his eyebrows knowingly.

Just as Charlie had hoped, realisation dawned on Piotr. The down-low. On the QT. Discreet. The watchwords of a select group of hotels where confidentiality could be assured. 'Ah, I think I understand, DS Dray. The client wishes to get his property back no questions asked, eh?

'Indeed, so it would be hugely helpful if we could view the CCTV, just to rule out any foul play.'

'Of course, please come through.' Piotr was clearly a fan of spy films. He looked left to right conspiratorially, then nodded to the door beside the long counter. 'The monitoring station is just in here.'

They were shown into a small anteroom at the back of the reception, where there were four large flat screens, all subdivided into four separate camera views. The images were pin-sharp, showing the lobby, a close-up of the reception counter, the street outside, the dining room and the hotel corridors.

'What date and time are you looking for?'

Charlie told him, and when the receptionist entered the digits into the keyboard, the views on the monitors all changed to the historic images.

'Can you go forward at double speed?' Charlie took out his glasses and settled them on his nose as he leant forward to look at the grid of images.

'Yes, sir,' said Piotr, expertly tapping at the keys with the flourish of a concert pianist.

Charlie focused hard as the images shifted, the hotel staff and guests coming and going at an almost comical speed akin to an old silent movie.

'Hold it there,' he said all of a sudden, as a long-haired Asian woman arrived through the door and headed towards the reception desk. Piotr tapped a key and the image froze.

Keeping his phone low, Charlie pressed the last-number-dialled key, and a phone began to ring back on the reception desk.

'Excuse me while I answer that,' Piotr said. 'My manager often tests phone-answering speed, and he gets most irritated if I take too long.'

'No problem. Take your time, mate.'

'What are you doing?' Josie hissed when Piotr had disappeared. 'I'm no expert, but this thirty-something attractive woman isn't our man.'

'I know. But look on the street outside. Two fellas have just met.' Charlie pressed a key, and the screen covering the pavement outside filled the screen. 'Is he busy on the desk?' he whispered to Josie. She frowned and poked her head around the door.

'With a guest.'

He tapped at the computer keyboard again, and the hotel entrance appeared on the screen, two men walking through the huge black door. She immediately recognised Jimmy Grigson, alongside a well-fleshed man with a mane of golden hair wearing a beautifully tailored tweed suit. Charlie raised his phone and took three snaps of the image, at different distances, then returned the display to the grid view and spun the footage on, just as Piotr returned.

'Sorry about that. Whoever it was hung up. I hope it wasn't my boss,' he added with a grimace.

'Not to worry. Nothing of use on the CCTV, so it looks like our complainant may have made a mistake. He was a little the worse for wear.' Charlie shrugged.

'Sorry I couldn't be more help,' said Piotr. He'd clearly enjoyed the distraction from his normal day's work.

'No, it's a good result. Means we can close this down and give our victim advice about caring for his property.'

'Glad to have been of service.' The receptionist gave a half-bow as he ushered them from the room.

'Bingo, we've a face for the next link in the chain. Let's tell the others,' said Charlie as they walked back into the chilly air, his stride brisk and shoulders squared. Slowing his step, he opened WhatsApp and attached the shot he'd taken of the tweed-clad man, then forwarded it to the group. *This is the man who met Grigson. Anyone recognise?*

A response came back from Macca almost immediately. *That's a no for me and Neil. He looks like a posh boy in that shit suit.*

Charlie's fingers flashed on the phone's keys. *Jacko, you know all the snidey antiques dealers, right?*

Three dots appeared as Jacko typed. When the response came, it was just one word: *Nah.*

'Boys don't know him. Come on, let's get going. Busy day tomorrow.'

'You're enjoying this, aren't you?' said Josie, almost having to jog to keep up with the ex-detective, who was whistling tunelessly as they crossed the road.

'Best I've felt since I retired, my girl. We're making progress, and we have a photo of the dealer. We're on track to get your dad's medals back.'

Chapter 23

Thursday 16 December 2021

Jacko zipped his parka up, shivering against the chill as he walked into the crescent in front of Roundwood Park. It was a stunning morning and the area was buzzing with dog walkers and young mums taking their kids to the park. The perfect place for a quiet meet. He grinned, a sense of anticipation in his gut. This was his world, so he didn't even need to play a part. He was a thief, even though he'd effectively retired, and thieves always needed an outlet for their wares. He'd had countless meets like this in the past, selling what he'd stolen from whatever premises he'd broken into. Never homes, though. That was sacrosanct to Jacko. He was a thief, but he had morals, and breaking into someone's home was against his ethos.

As he rounded the crescent towards the café, he clocked Grigson's Mercedes parked close to one of the meters. There was a surly-looking warden eyeing the car. Jacko sensed an opportunity to ingratiate himself a little further. He pulled out his phone and composed a message to Grigson.

There in 5. Warden's ticketing cars. Are you parked by the gates?

The reply came back immediately. *Yes, Blue C Class Merc.*

Jacko grinned. *I'll chuck some money in the meter and fuck him off.*

Thanks, I'll get you a coffee.

He sidled up to the warden. 'Hang on, mate, I'm just feeding the meter now,' he said, stuffing a pound coin into the slot. The warden shrugged and moved on. Jacko pulled the ticket out and stuck it to the car window. It'd probably get nicked, but at least the warden was dealt with, and Grigson would have him pegged as a stand-up guy. He whistled tunelessly as he headed into the park and towards the café.

As he pushed the door open and stepped inside, he immediately spotted Grigson sitting at a table, two mugs in front of him. Grigson rose as Jacko approached, and they shook hands.

'Morning, fella. Cheers for the coffee, must go for a piss before I sit down. Give me a minute.' Jacko headed off to the small unisex toilet at the back of the café, relieved himself, washed his hands and then pulled his phone from his pocket. *I'm in. He's here. About to negotiate.* He looked at himself in the mirror, ruffled his straggly hair and returned to the café, plopping himself down opposite Grigson.

'Lovely morning.' He took a sip from his coffee and smacked his lips.

'Could be worse. You have them?' said Grigson.

'Certainly do. Want a squint?' Jacko took another sip and nodded appreciatively. 'Nice coffee.'

'I definitely want a squint. Why d'you think I'm here?'

Jacko reached into the inside of his parka on the back of his chair, pulled out the wooden box and passed it to Grigson under the table.

Grigson's eyes flicked down, and there was a click as he opened the box. 'This is some kind of group, Jacko. Dare I ask what RSM Mackenzie will think of you being in possession of them?'

'I suspect he'd be none too chuffed, but then he doesn't even

118

know they ain't where he left them yet, so there's plenty of time to move them on before they get too scorchio.'

'Good to know. How much do you want for them? Bearing in mind their temperature will affect their value.'

'Open to offers, mate, but bear in mind that these could easily make high six figures if they hit auction.'

'I don't doubt it, but this isn't an auction, is it?' Grigson snapped the box shut and looked up.

'I'm assuming you want to get them checked out by your man first, yeah?' Jacko sat back in his chair and stroked his moustache.

'Of course. I can't guarantee a price, but he'll know what they're worth, even with their somewhat unconventional provenance. How long do I have?'

'Not long. I have other interested parties, but Errol assures me you play with a straight bat.'

'I only need twenty-four hours. If my man and his client are satisfied, we can get whatever price we agree to you immediately. I take it you're a cash man?' Grigson raised his eyebrows.

'We'll I ain't taking a cheque, and I've still not got my head around crypto, so yeah, spondoolies will be fine.'

Grigson looked at Jacko with renewed interest. 'Excellent. Spondoolies it is. Give me until this time tomorrow.'

Chapter 24

Josie was hardly out of breath as she jogged through Roundwood Park dressed in running tights, a waterproof top and a beanie pulled low over her brow. Running was of little difficulty to her, having done it almost all her life, ever since her dad first took her out when she was barely out of nappies. She was a gifted marathon runner but had never been quite good enough to make it at the top level, so she had turned her attention to ultra-marathons. She found that she could manage a really decent pace for mile after mile, and was soon participating in and winning fifty-mile-plus races. The climax of these achievements was her placing in the brutal Marathon des Sables: 156 miles over six days in the Sahara Desert.

So a morning jog in a suburban park was nothing, even if fitness wasn't the goal this morning.

'They're both still in the café, Josie. Go for it,' came the voice in her AirPods. She was on an open line to Macca, who was sitting on a bench a hundred metres from the café.

'Roger that,' said Josie as she headed towards the wrought-iron gates without a trace of laboured breathing.

'Road's also clear; no one near the car. Blue Merc twenty metres past the entrance,' said Charlie, who was also on the call.

'Roger that as well,' said Josie.

'Nice use of radio procedure. Your old man taught you well.' Charlie sounded impressed.

'Coming from an old signaller, I take that as a compliment, even if your last experience with military radios would have been two bean tins connected with string.'

'Oh ha ha, you cheeky whippersnapper,' said Charlie in a sarcasm-laden voice.

Josie jogged out of the park and turned towards the sparklingly clean Mercedes saloon that was parked on the opposite pavement.

'Still clear?' she whispered, barely moving her lips as she approached the car.

'As a bell,' said Charlie.

She slowed her pace as she came alongside the car and knelt as if to fix a shoelace. Without hesitation, she pulled a small magnetic black box from her bum bag.

'Josie, you need to get a wriggle on,' said Macca. 'He's out of the café.'

'Shit. Can Jacko slow him down?' She pressed the activation switch hard for three seconds, as she'd been told to do.

'We're not in contact, and we can't call him. Just get it on or abandon it. We can do it another time,' said Charlie, his voice calm.

'How long do I have?'

'Two minutes, no more.'

'Hold on.' Fumbling with the device, she looked at the wheel arch. It was totally different from the one she'd practised on. 'Dammit,' she muttered. The space between the tyre and the arch was much tighter owing to lowered suspension and low-profile tyres. She pulled up the sleeve of her jacket and pushed her hand into the gap, but it was still too tight. She couldn't reach through towards the preferred site to snap the tracker in place.

'Josie?' said Charlie, sounding anxious.

'It's tight as a gnat's chuff between the wheel arch and the tyre.'

'Abort. Just abort,' he said, his voice urgent.

She looked down at her bum bag, about to put the tracker back and get out of there. As she opened the bag wider, she saw the blue stick, about the size and shape of a roll-on deodorant, and her mind flared. Like many distance runners, she suffered from chafing, and her Body Glide stick made all the difference.

'How long?

'One minute. God's sake, get out of there, girl.'

Even with the situation as it was, Josie felt a sudden flash of anger at being called 'girl' yet again. She'd bloody show them, she thought as she grabbed the tube, removed the lid and quickly applied a thick layer of the viscous gunge to each side of her arm. Then she grabbed the tracker and tried again. This time her arm squeezed through the gap and she forced it towards the suspension strut. There was a soft clunk as the magnets attached, just behind the shock absorber on the exposed blue metal.

She withdrew her arm, with a grunt of pain as the tyre scratched the soft underside, wiped the excess lube from the wheel arch and tyre and stood up.

'They're seconds away, get out of there now,' said Charlie, his voice shot through with stress.

'All done, no panic,' said Josie, setting off at a brisk pace towards the street where they'd agreed to meet, a smile forming on her lips and her heart pounding in her chest. And it wasn't because of the strenuous exercise.

This was a buzz that skydiving couldn't touch.

Chapter 25

'Good work, Josie. You've a gift for this stuff. You should've become a cop,' said Asquith as Josie dived into the back of the Audi. He had an iPad on his lap with a map application open, a pulsing blue dot in the centre.

'Yeah, top work,' said Macca, putting the car in gear and fixing her with an approving stare in the rear-view mirror.

'Not bad for a girl, eh?' said Josie with a touch of snark in her voice. 'Is it working?'

'Yep. Nice and strong, great job.' Asquith raised a small hand-held radio and spoke into it. 'He's on the move, heading towards Harlesden Road.'

'Roger that. I've just scooped up Jacko and we'll shadow you. Call us up if you need us to take eyeball.' Charlie's voice crackled over the handset.

'Eyeball?' said Asquith to Macca, one eyebrow raised.

'Cop surveillance talk. They get touchy about using the correct terms. "Eyeball" if they have eyes on a subject, "visual" if it's on an unmanned car or a door where someone's gone in. I wouldn't worry about it. I did some urban surveillance with the Met on counter-terror stuff, and they're good. We just need to stay close enough.'

'Are we following him, then?' said Josie.

'We certainly are,' said Macca. 'We can hold back and watch on the tracker and then close up when he stops. We want to tail him to his destination, as that's clearly where the dealer is.'

'When was this decision made?' Josie prickled.

'Recently, but it was always an option.' Macca looked confused.

'Maybe keep me in the loop, eh? I'm part of this job too, you know.'

'Right turn onto Donnington Road, Charlie,' said Asquith into the handset.

Macca nodded. 'Understood, sorry, but can we have this out later? It's all happening now.'

'Just bloody include me, okay?'

'Fine.' He shook his head slightly.

'Received,' replied Charlie. 'We're close by and following. No visuals until he stops, we'll rely on the tracker. Good work by the way, Josie.'

'Tell him thanks,' said Josie, pulling on a pair of jeans over her running tights and jamming a Nike baseball cap on her chestnut hair.

Asquith relayed the message.

'You're cut out for this malarkey, my girl,' said Macca, nodding approvingly.

'Less of the girl, Macca. I'm thirty, for goodness' sake,' she said, but there was no anger on her face.

'Sorry, but my point stands. You really do take after your old man. I never once saw him flapping, whatever the drama he was in.'

'Panic never makes things better, does it?' Josie settled down into the back seat of the car, pulled out a compact mirror and began applying make-up.

'He's heading towards the A40, I'd say, which is the natural route towards Mayfair and Bond Street,' said Asquith, watching the iPad intently.

'Makes sense.' Macca nodded. 'Where's all the antiques shops in London, eh?'

'He's picking up speed and has just turned right onto the Harrow Road towards central London.'

They continued through the busy London streets, Asquith calling out landmarks and road names for another thirty minutes before the blue blob halted.

'We've got a definite stop. Albemarle Street, just outside the King's Head pub,' he said, his voice urgent.

'How far away is Charlie?' said Macca, accelerating.

'Charlie, how far away?' said Asquith into the radio.

'We're close by. We anticipated Mayfair and took a shortcut. Hold up, I'll get out and get an eyeball on him.'

There was a pause, and Josie could imagine Charlie diving out of the car and rushing to where the Mercedes had stopped.

Two minutes later, there was a buzzing in the front of the car, and Asquith picked up his phone. 'Charlie?'

'I have him. He's just feeding a meter opposite the pub, leather bag in his hand. Not aware, and he seems totally relaxed . . . He's heading back towards the Merc and is putting the ticket in the windscreen. Door's now shut and he's locked the car.'

'Shop must be close by; he won't want to be too far away with a hundred grand's worth of medals in a bag. Any antiques shop nearby?' said Macca as he pulled to the kerb.

'Yeah, one fifty yards down the road. Hunter Antiques and Militaria, looks posh from what I can see,' said Asquith, zooming in on the map.

'What next?' said Josie.

'Wait and see. If he goes into a premises, we're another step forward, so we just wait,' said Macca, switching the engine off.

There was a full minute's silence before Charlie's voice came out of the crackly speaker on Asquith's phone. 'Right, he's off, heading north on Albemarle Street, still carrying the bag. I'm following at a distance.'

'Come on, you bastard. Go home to Papa,' muttered Macca, drumming his fingers on the steering wheel.

'Ten metres. Five metres, and he's in, in, in and into the doorway. He's ringing a bell at the door of Hunter Antiques and Militaria, and someone's coming to answer.' There was another brief pause.

'Why did he say "in" three times?' asked Josie.

'Surveillance cop thing. They're not too bright, so saying it three times ensures it goes in,' said Macca, his voice tight.

'Door open, large-framed man, tweed suit, swept-back blonde hair.'

'Sounds familiar,' said Josie.

'That's a confirmation. It's the guy he met at the Chesterfield. We have our man, boys and girls. We have the dealer.'

Chapter 26

Macca, Asquith and Josie were sitting in the Audi a few streets away from the antiques shop, all clutching disposable cups of coffee, when Macca's phone rang. It was Charlie.

'Grigson's out, heading back towards the car.'

'Can you follow him?' said Macca.

'Well I'm having a pleasant coffee in the hotel just up from the shop, and I've a lovely view to his car. No need to follow him now, is there, unless he still has the medals?'

'Is he carrying anything new?'

'No, just the same leather bag. He's bringing his phone out now, and dialling. Jacko, are you ready for this? I've a suspicion you may be about to get a phone call, and probably a bit richer,' said Charlie.

'I'm listening, and as if by magic, my phone is ringing. It's Grigson. I'll put the phone on speaker so you can listen,' said Jacko over the radio, and the chiming dial tone could be heard on the handset that Macca was clutching.

Jacko left the radio mic open. 'Jimbo, I'm hoping you're calling me with good news.'

'Yeah, nice little result, mate. He's made a tidy offer.'

'How much?'

'Seventeen. He played hardball, but that's a decent wedge, bearing in mind the provenance.'

'Bleedin' robdog. I want twenty, minimum.'

'Be reasonable, Jacko. They're red hot, and if he says no, what you gonna do?'

'I've other interested parties.'

'Yeah, right,' said Grigson, and the sarcasm in his voice was obvious.

'Straight up. Twenty bags or I walk.' Jacko's voice was firm and resolute.

There was an audible sigh that caused static to reverberate down the tinny speakers. 'Okay, I'll speak to him, but I'll leave him to stew for half an hour. I could do with a beer anyway, and there's a pub a minute away.'

'Good call. You know these toffs, mate. If he's willing to pay seventeen, he's willing to pay twenty. Call me when it's done, and we can meet. I need this dosh pronto.'

'Fine, I'll let you know.' The phone beeped as Grigson hung up.

'Jacko, are you sure about this?' said Macca into the radio.

'Dead sure. If I accepted the first offer, he'd get suspicious, and he'll be screwing me over anyway by giving the dealer a higher price. He's no muppet, hence now going to the boozer to let the toffee-nosed bastard sweat. Trust me, fellas, this is my world and I know how to deal with fences.'

'Can you get Grigson to introduce you to the dealer? That could offer up all sorts of opportunities,' said Macca.

'No chance. Any decent fence wouldn't want me within a mile of his people. He'd be worried I'd go direct next time and cut him out. And he'd be right, because I would,' said Jacko firmly.

'So what do we do now?'

'We wait. We'll get the deal, and we have the opportunity to move this job on.'

'Okay, let's find somewhere to park up, and we'll go and have a coffee in the hotel. At the very least we now know where my medals are. That means Chappers' medals are either in that shop or they've been moved, and we have a lead to work on. We need to progress to the next phase of the operation, and for that we need fresh intel.'

'Such as?' said Josie from the back of the car, her voice registering some confusion.

'Well, we need to find out where this Hunter lives, what car he drives and what opportunities there are to gather new evidence. Neil, can your man start on that?'

'Sure thing, he's waiting for a call. There'll be accounts online, as the shop will inevitably be a limited company, and I'm sure there's lots more to find. It shouldn't be difficult to trace a car and a phone; it'll just take a bit of time.'

'Surely we could be doing something while we wait,' said Josie.

'Aye, to be honest, I could do with popping into a chemist,' said Macca, wincing.

'Why? You okay?' asked Josie, a touch of concern on her face.

'All this sitting down in cars, I'm not used to it.'

Asquith chuckled.

'What's so funny?' Josie said.

'His piles are playing him up,' he said, trying to keep a straight face.

'Thanks for that, Neil.' Macca shook his head, a flush of embarrassment on his face.

'Oh you poor old sod,' said Josie, suppressing a smile.

'It's not bloody funny. Things are bloody sore as a bastard, and I told you in bloody confidence, Captain Asquith.' Macca glared at Asquith.

'Sorry, Macca, but Josie's practically family, right?'

'Aye, as long as that bloody ned Jacko doesn't find out. Right, enough about my sore ringpiece. What can we do now?' said

Macca, desperately trying to move the conversation on.

'Such as?' said Asquith.

'Well, he's right there,' said Josie. 'Literally a couple of streets away, and he's in a shop with the medals. I've a suggestion.'

'Your suggestions make me nervous, lassie,' said Macca.

'This is a good one. Are there any charity shops around here?'

'It's Mayfair, Josie. They refer to them as "vintage" and charge more than most full-priced shops,' said Asquith.

'I take it that Mrs Asquith likes a vintage shop?' said Josie.

'She certainly does. She recently assured me that three hundred pounds was reasonable for a ten-year-old blouse because it said "Hermès" on the label.'

'Blimey, I only spend that sort of money on Arctic clothing. Okay, well let's go and find a proper charity shop, quickly.'

'What are you thinking?' said Macca, looking at her in the rear-view mirror.

'Just an idea. Come on, I look like an unsuccessful third division footballer's wife after the gym. I need to smarten up a bit.'

'If you're thinking what I'm thinking you're thinking, lass, you can forget it. You were up close and personal with Grigson just a couple of days ago.' Macca looked like a concerned father.

'And like I reminded you before, you're not the RSM any more, and this is an opportunity. Neil, do you have the kit we talked about from your mate?'

'Yeah, I've a whole selection of stuff, but it's not tested and I'm not even sure how it all works,' said Asquith.

'Josie, I'm not happy about this. I always promised your dad that I'd see you came to no harm if anything happened to him, and—'

'Macca, I love you, but this is my dad's medals we're talking about, and yours too now. We need a break, and we need a lead, and it won't happen by pissing about sitting in this car. Grigson will be going back into that shop soon, and from there, Hunter will be making arrangements to move your medals on.'

'If Grigson sees you, he'll recognise you.'

'No he won't.'

'How can you be so sure?'

'Because men like him are stupid, and he won't see me anyway. He was just looking at my tits and legs, not my face, and was thinking with his dick, not his head. He'll never recognise me, I guarantee it. You lot can't know what it's like being a woman, dealing with lowlifes like him. I bloody well do, because I've been dealing with it since I was fourteen. Call Jacko and get him to buy us another fifteen minutes before Grigson goes back to the shop. Then lend me your aviators, Macca, and let's find that charity shop, fast.'

Macca sighed. 'As long as I can find a chemist, it's a deal.'

Chapter 27

Josie took a deep breath as she walked along the Mayfair pavement towards Hunter Antiques and Militaria, feeling a fizz of excitement in her belly. She paused at a shop window where there was a full-length mirror and took in her reflection.

She was wearing a long, stylish camel-coloured woollen coat, tightly belted, displaying her narrow waist, a traditional Russian fur hat, which she knew to be called an ushanka, with the earflaps lowered, and large dark sunglasses. She looked like a typical boho rich Russian, living for spending her husband's money. The coat and hat had been speedily purchased from a nearby vintage shop at an eye-watering price, courtesy of Neil's Amex. She almost giggled at the thought, as it reminded her of the quick changes she was once required to undertake for an improvised sketch as part of her university theatre group's activities during rag week.

She took a deep, cleansing breath and carried on walking towards the shop, not hesitating when she arrived but confidently pushing the door open, her face full of bored arrogance. An old-fashioned bell rang, announcing her presence.

Giles Hunter looked up from his desk, where he was admiring Macca's medals in their presentation box. On seeing Josie, he snapped the case shut hurriedly and slotted it into a drawer.

'Can I help you, madam?' he asked, with a wide smile that was a curious mix of irritation and leering lechery. He obviously liked what he saw.

'Hallo, I look for present for hasbind,' she said in a thick Eastern European accent, swivelling her gaze left and right with disdain.

Hunter looked at her with renewed interest. 'Of course, madam, please do come in,' he said, standing up and half-bowing.

'Tank you,' she said, sweeping into the shop with an arrogant flourish.

'Now, what type of thing are you looking for, madam?' Hunter clasped his hands together in a toadying, oily fashion.

'He like traditional Russian art. He love *ikona*, but so hard find now.' Her accent was thick, and her words were delivered in the peremptory fashion of the seriously brusque and extremely wealthy.

'An icon? Well, your husband has good taste, madam. I do have a couple just over here.' He wafted his hand at a small painted board on which there was a gilded mother and child. 'This is a lovely example of an orthodox icon, or *ikona*, as you more correctly describe it, madam. It was painted sometime around 1890 and is of Our Lady of Vladimir. Stunning in the gold, don't you think?'

'Yes, very nicely, but something more colourful?' Josie checked her watch, paying little attention to him, affecting disinterest.

'Well, there is this.' He pointed at a much smaller icon next to it that depicted the Crucifixion in reds and silvers. It was garish and hideous.

'No. I don't like. Very ugly.' She shook her head decisively and scowled, dimples forming in her cheeks as she pursed her heavily painted lips. She began to wander around the shop, pausing to look at an ornate bronze-gilt clock on an eye-level shelf. 'This verra nice – what it?' she said.

'Excellent taste, madam. This is a French mantel clock by Vincenti, made in 1860, very desirable, and bound to appreciate.' He waved his hand languidly at the hideous timepiece.

'How much for it?' she said, looking at her fingernails, which were unfortunately short and unpainted. She made a mental note to get some stick-on nails for future deployments.

'Eighteen hundred pounds. A good price, madam.'

'Too much. What can do?' She yawned, appearing bored at the prospect of a negotiation.

Hunter exhaled softly, clearly trying not to show the irritation he was obviously feeling. 'Just let me look at the markets for a moment on my computer and see if I can make any adjustment. Can I offer you a coffee?' He pointed to a machine behind his desk.

'Espresso,' she said, walking to the desk and sitting down with a heavy sigh.

Hunter placed a small cup underneath the spout of the machine, pushed in a pod and pressed the button. Josie pulled out her phone and stared at it, crossing her legs. This caused the coat flaps to open, revealing way more stockinged leg than she'd normally feel comfortable displaying, but she was already fully in character. The bored, rich Russian wife.

'Your coffee.' He set the cup and saucer down next to her and sat down behind the desk.

She just nodded and continued looking at her phone, without a trace of a smile.

Hunter tapped some keys, and Josie lowered her phone and sat forward to get a view of the computer. He quickly minimised the browser page, fumbling with the mouse, his eyes fixed on the screen. Such was his agitation that he didn't see her hand slide to the underside of his desk.

'I can go no lower than seventeen hundred pounds.'

'One tousand. Cash, now.' She picked up her phone and began to scroll again.

'Madam, I can't possibly go that low. I'd make a loss, and this is a highly desirable item.'

She scowled, baring her teeth, then picked up the espresso cup and sipped at it. 'What this shit?' she spat.

'I assure you—' Hunter began, but Josie shot to her feet.

'No good. You disrespectful me. Bad coffee and bad price. Bye, Mister Shit Antique Shop. I go to proper place.' She turned on her heel, and swept towards the door, not slowing down as she passed Jimmy Grigson, who was just entering the shop, looking at her with interest but no flash of recognition.

As she strode off down the pavement, she tried desperately to stop the smile that was forming on her face, the adrenaline coursing through her veins.

'Goddammit, this is a total drug,' she muttered to herself, lips barely moving, as she headed back to the car.

Chapter 28

'Jesus, girl. You've gonads the size of Grantown,' said Macca, turning in his seat to look at Josie, who was pulling off her furry hat.

'Has it worked?' she asked, her face animated with excitement.

'Yes, clear as a bloody bell. Neil, that is a seriously good piece of kit. Listening devices have obviously improved since I last used them in Ireland. Exactly what type of security stuff did your firm do?' said Macca, looking at Asquith, who was studying the iPad and fiddling with the controls on an open app. There was a light hiss of static, and then a stifled cough and the sound of a chair scraping on a wooden floor.

'Corporate espionage is a thing, so having access to easily deployable listening devices was occasionally of use, and they've got better since I retired. The one Josie planted is the latest state-of-the-art type. Where did you put it?'

'Under his desk. He was so put out by the angry, aloof Russian act that he was always on the back foot.'

'Sure he didn't clock you?' asked Macca.

'Not a chance.'

'CCTV?'

'From what I can see, a crappy old black-and-white system that only covers the door so he can see who's buzzing. Even if there are internal cameras, all he'd see is me leaning forward, and why would he want to look at that? I was just a rude customer.' Josie grinned proudly.

'Well, you've a career ahead of you as an actor, or possibly a spook. You had me convinced, and I know you of old. Accent was bang on.' Macca chuckled.

'I'm flattered. More importantly, Macca, how's your bum-hole?'

He glared at her via the rear-view mirror as Asquith struggled to stifle a giggle. 'Soothed. Now can we move on?'

'What did Hunter say to Grigson?' Josie asked.

'Deal done, and Grigson's ripping off Jacko. Skimmed two and a half grand off the top, and got a nice fee as well.'

'Has he been in touch with Jacko? Don't look, by the way. I'm getting these horrible stockings off.' She began to reach under her coat.

Both men's heads snapped forward, looking pointedly out of the windscreen.

'Aye, called as soon as he came out. They're meeting back at the café. Jacko and Charlie are on their way there now.'

'What's next with Grigson?' said Josie, raising her backside up and pulling on her jeans under the coat.

'Nothing. Leave him for now. He'll get his comeuppance, I'm sure. We're now totally focused on Hunter. He has my medals, and possibly your dad's as well, if he's been sitting on them to let the dust settle. Let's just wait and see what happens, but we've an advantage that we didn't have half an hour ago. Good work.'

'Blimey, praise from the notoriously difficult-to-please RSM.'

'Apart from your rude jokes about my poor bahoochie issues, I'm impressed, and so should you be, my girl.' Macca nodded into the mirror, his eyes full of admiration.

The familiar tones of a mobile being dialled were suddenly audible on the iPad.

'Sounds like he's making a call,' said Asquith.

There was a pause, and the sound of a stifled yawn.

'Danilo, it's Giles Hunter, how are you?'

Silence.

'Good, good to hear. Anyway, excellent news. The items I promised the General are now safely in my possession. When would he like them?'

Another silence.

'Yes, both groups. They're magnificent, Danilo. The General will be delighted, I assure you. Two of the most notable groups from recent conflicts.'

A faint ticking came out of the speakers.

'That soon? . . . Yes, of course I can, I just need a little time to get the two groups together. The first set were hot, so I have them safely away from the shop. The others are ready to go.'

'The bastard,' muttered Josie.

'Shh.' Macca held his finger to his lips.

'Well, that's extremely kind of him, and of course I can come tomorrow. Will you handle the flight arrangements? . . . Oh, that's generous. Please extend my gratitude, and I'd be delighted to come to dinner and stay overnight at the castle. How exciting. I look forward to your email, Danilo, goodbye.'

There was a click, and an immediate chuckle came out of the speakers.

A sudden hush descended on the car.

'He's got both groups and he's flying tomorrow to deliver them,' said Josie in a hoarse whisper.

'Aye. They're within range, hen. We need to be ready.'

'Flying from where to where, though?'

'Neil, we need to trace where he lives. We also need to identify a car for the bastard and get a tracker on it, and we need this bug monitored constantly for any changes of plan. Once Jacko and Charlie have got the cash from Grigson, we'll get together and make a plan. Charlie will have loads of experience of dealing with fast-time surveillance jobs like this.'

There was a rustle over the speakers, and then Hunter's voice rang out again.

'Hi, can I book a cab tomorrow morning for an airport run?'

All three of them held their breath.

'Great, pickup at six a.m. from 21 Archery Close, W2, name of Giles Hunter. I'll need a quick stop-off en route to pick something up, okay? . . . Thanks.' There was a click and a further rustle, and then the bug went quiet.

'Well, that was fortunate,' said Asquith. 'We were due a break on this job. We've a start point tomorrow, and hopefully he'll have both sets of medals on him. We could take him out on his bloody doorstep.'

'I don't think we can be too hasty,' said Macca. 'You heard him. A stop-off en route.'

'We know for certain that he has your medals,' said Asquith.

'But Dad's are somewhere else,' added Josie.

Macca nodded. 'We need to follow him. As soon as he picks those medals up, we strike. We can't let him get on a damn plane – that's for sure. Let's get everyone together; we've a surveillance operation to plan.'

'But a general, and in a fucking castle? Who the hell is Hunter selling these medals to?' said Neil, mouth agape.

'No need to worry about that right now. Thanks to Josie, we know he's flying tomorrow, and at some point before he gets on that plane, he'll have both groups of medals in his possession. We stick to him like shit to a blanket, and when he picks up Chappers' group, we take the bastard out. It's game on, people. We're getting those medals back.'

Chapter 29

Friday 17 December 2021

'That's a standby, standby, standby, everyone, we've a vehicle pulling up outside Hunter's address now. Looks like a cab, a dark blue Ford Galaxy, and he's bang on time.' Charlie's voice was calm and collected as he spoke into the small radio handset.

'Standing by nearby,' said Macca, equally calmly.

Silence descended in the car as Charlie and Jacko watched the front of Hunter's house. 'Come on, you shithouse,' muttered Jacko.

'Patience is a surveillance officer's best quality, Jacko. He'll move, and we'll be ready,' said Charlie, not taking his eyes off the door.

They were parked at the far end of Archery Close, just thirty metres away from Hunter's house, tucked behind a white van. Macca, Neil and Josie were waiting on Connaught Street, at the other end. One way in and one way out; it was almost the perfect location for a pickup, thought Charlie. The only downside was that they had just the two cars, whereas in his days as a surveillance cop on an active team, there might be as many as twelve cops, all trained and ready to go. They'd need to be careful, and on the ball for every second. He was just happy that it was early and the streets weren't too busy.

There was a shaft of light from the door as it was opened, and the bulky form of Hunter appeared, yawning extravagantly.

'Okay, front door is open, and that's a confirmation. Subject is leaving the house, locking up and heading to the cab . . . in the cab and it's moving off, moving off, away from our location. For info, he's wearing a tweed jacket and flat cap and is carrying a leather case. Get ready to move, Macca.'

'Ahead and waiting,' said Macca.

'And he's off, off, off, heading towards your location.'

'Roger that,' said Macca, calmness personified.

Charlie gunned the engine and engaged the gears. 'I'll let the cab get out of the close before I move.'

'I can see why I never bloody saw a surveillance team,' said Jacko. 'You bastards are careful.'

'You have to know where to look, mate. Right, let's do this.'

As the cab turned out of the close, Charlie set off steadily and headed towards the main streets, which were still barely coming to life. There were just a few early delivery vans about, and a smattering of commuters.

'Okay, we have eyeball. He's immediately right, right, right, onto Connaught Square, and there's an indication and he's onto George Street, with an immediate left onto Seymour Street,' said Macca over the radio.

'He's going for the A40. Why's he taking that route? Surely he'd go down to the A4; that's straight to Heathrow,' said Charlie as he negotiated the dark streets.

'He said he was doing a stop-off, didn't he. We'd best stick to the bastard. He could be going anywhere.'

Charlie nodded, but his brow was furrowed in thought.

Within a couple of minutes, they were behind Asquith's Audi, heading west on the A40, the light traffic meaning that they made good progress. After about ten minutes, Macca's voice came on the radio.

'Time to switch, Charlie, we've been behind him for long enough. We'll head off at Hanger Lane Gyratory, do a circuit and rejoin immediately once you've taken over the eyeball, just in case he's watching out of the back window. He may be a bit jumpy with the medals on board.'

'All received.' Charlie pulled closer to the Audi as they approached the large roundabout at Hanger Lane. Asquith indicated right and disappeared from view as he went to do a full circuit of the roundabout.

'Okay, confirming we have the eyeball, speed forty, no cars for cover, no signs of awareness from the driver and Hunter isn't looking back at all.' Charlie's delivery was cool and unhurried.

A further ten minutes later, the cab indicated as they approached the Polish War Memorial junction.

'Right, he's leaving the A40, heading off at the war memorial,' said Charlie.

'Roger that,' said Macca.

The cab skirted around the roundabout and then gave an indication.

'He's heading to West End Lane, right by the war memorial now, and we have another indication, and immediate off-side, and he's turning. He's into the service road by the memorial. He's gonna stop, everyone, standby, standby. We could have a meet.' Charlie could see a solitary car, a small Volvo saloon, parked in the far recesses of the service road. The cab skirted all the way in and stopped just twenty metres from the car. Its lights went out.

'Charlie?' said Jacko, his voice tight.

'What?'

'Cozzers, right behind us.'

Charlie glanced in the mirror just as a big liveried BMW swung into the service road and pulled over thirty metres from the cab.

'Shit. We've cops on the plot,' he said. He pulled over to the side of West End Road and into a concealed entrance to a large property, and extinguished his lights.

'Ah, bollocks,' said Jacko. 'they're about to do the handover now. What do we do, Charlie?'

'We sit tight. That's a traffic patrol car, mate. They won't be looking to give them a tug, I bet. They'll probably be knackered and just want to park up for the last half an hour of their shift. We wait, let them do the handover and carry on the follow. Can you see what the minicab is doing?'

'It's parked up right in front of the memorial, and the small Beemer is at the far end in the dark. Christ, I'm busting for a piss, as well.'

'You're always busting for a piss. Tie a knot in it.'

Jacko shifted in his seat, and there was a grunt from under his backside. A sudden fetid smell filled the car.

'Jesus, you stinking, honking bastard,' said Charlie, lowering the window, his face twisted in disgust.

Jacko cackled. 'Sorry, mate. Kebab last night.'

'I'd forgotten we used to call you "foul bowel" back in the day. Totally justified. It's like a rat has crawled up your arse and died.'

'Charlie?' said Jacko after a long pause.

'Yeah?'

'He's got the nicked medals, right?'

'He'll have both sets once they've handed over, yeah.'

'Why don't we just let the cops find them? And I say this as someone with no great love for the cozzers – no offence, like.'

'None taken, but it's a bad idea, mate. We're making a big assumption that he'll have both sets, and the ones we know for certain he does have are the medals you flogged him yesterday. He could easily claim that he paid a fair price for them and had no idea they were nicked. And the issue is that they *weren't* nicked. They're Macca's, and he passed them over as bait. Even if Chappers' medals are in that car, he could just claim that he bought them in good faith, and we could be in for years of legal back-and-forth of property restitution. I know from experience that shit like that can go on for ever.'

'What? That's bullshit; they're Chappers' medals.'

'I know, but if that posh bastard Hunter could persuade a court that he did buy them in good faith, which a smarmy bastard like him with an expensive lawyer might be able to, it could even be that we'd never get them back. He is a militaria dealer, after all, and he'll know the score.'

'Shit.'

'Another problem, Jacko.'

'What?'

'You. You're hardly a paragon of virtue, and you're the main source of all the evidence, with your unsanctioned and possibly inadmissible undercover antics. I suspect the CPS wouldn't even call you, given that you're a convicted thief.'

Suddenly the cop car burst into life, its blue strobe lights flashing as it pulled away from the service road.

'Cops must have an emergency shout. We're good to go. Call the others up, Jacko. We'll strike as soon as they're here and take the bastards out.'

Jacko began to bark into the radio handset as Charlie gunned the engine.

'Three minutes away,' said Asquith over the radio.

'That's too long. If they move, we'll follow, but we need both cars to box them in here. We can't get into a chase; that'll end up in damn disaster and we'll all get nicked. We'll have to stick with him and wait for the opportunity. Once he gets to Heathrow, he'll have to get through the terminal, and we can interdict then.'

The minicab was moving slowly towards the Volvo. As it pulled up alongside, a shadowy hand extended out of the car's window.

'There's the handover,' said Jacko. 'Package has been handed to Hunter now. Repeat, he has both sets.'

'Two minutes away,' came the shout from Asquith.

The minicab barely stopped; it just continued around the

service road and turned left onto West End Road.

'Where's he going? I thought he was getting a flight?' said Jacko. 'Eh?

'Heathrow's the other way, mate. He's got the medals, yet he's heading towards Ruislip.'

'Shit, I don't know. I'm gonna follow. Where are the others?' Charlie pulled out and began to follow the minicab.

'Where are you, Neil?' Jacko spoke urgently into the radio. 'Hunter has turned left and is heading towards Ruislip.'

There was a brief pause before Asquith replied, his voice tight and full of stress. 'RAF Northolt. They're heading to RAF Northolt. He must be getting on a private jet. Shit, if they get in there, we can't follow. Stop them now.'

'Fuck, of course. Northolt isn't just an RAF base, it's a VIP airfield.' Charlie floored the accelerator, and the engine roared as the car sped up, but the minicab was driving fast as well, and before they could close the gap, it had indicated and turned through a set of gates.

Charlie stamped on the brakes and eased right back.

'We can't follow them in there. It's an RAF base protected by armed guards. We'll have to let them go. Shit, shit, shit!' he bellowed.

'What? No way. Get in there Charlie,' said Jacko.

'What's happening?' came Asquith's urgent voice over the radio. 'They've gone into RAF Northolt,' said Jacko.

Macca's voice came on the radio, calm, yet full of immediacy. 'Don't pursue, repeat, don't pursue. I've flown from there before and you can't just pitch up. Abort, abort.'

They were too late anyway. As they pulled up outside, they could see the minicab parked up in a floodlit area and Hunter heading to the reception centre. A white-capped RAF policeman was leaning down, talking to the driver, clipboard in hand, pistol in a white holster at his hip. A camouflage-clad guard stood by the gate, cradling an SA80 assault rifle.

As they sat there outside the gate, Hunter came out of the reception building clutching some kind of pass and got back into the cab, which headed off into the recesses of the base.

He was gone.

The medals were gone.

Chapter 30

Macca, Asquith, Charlie, Jacko and Josie sat in silence in a nearby café. There was a general fug of malaise among them as they looked into the mugs they were clutching. Only Asquith was in any way animated, laptop open on the rickety table, tapping away industriously, his tongue poking out of the corner of his mouth.

Macca took a deep pull on his tea, then slammed the mug down on the table, which rattled alarmingly, slopping liquid onto the Formica top. 'I should have bloody realised they were flying from Northolt as soon as the handover happened at the Polish War Memorial. Should have been obvious, for Christ's sake. We used to regularly fly to Northern Ireland from the bloody place back in the SBS days, even if the entrance was on the A40 back then. Shit.'

'I thought his route was a bit odd,' Charlie said. 'Mayfair to Heathrow it would be more natural to hit the M4, but you weren't to know. Neil, can your man work out which flights have departed, and to where?'

Asquith didn't seem to hear; he was still staring hard at the screen of his Mac, his glasses a little askew. He was tapping at the keys with urgency, his body tense with concentration.

'Neil?' repeated Charlie.

'Sorry, what?' said Asquith.

'Bloody hell, pay attention, man. Are you tracking flights?' said Charlie.

'I asked my man to have a look, but he's emailed to say that there are nine flights out in the next few hours. All private jets.'

'That's not a lot of use, then. Any idea on destinations?'

'In hand, but he's not that hopeful. Some are diplomats and the like, so the destinations aren't on the normal lists.' Asquith's eyes were dragged back to the screen, and he continued tapping away.

'Shit,' said Macca, rubbing at his furrowed brow.

'What, that's it from your famed intelligence contacts?' said Josie, irritation in her voice.

'Eh?' said Asquith, looking up again.

'Neil, for fuck's sake, we need a lead and you're the one with access to analysts and data. Where has the bastard gone?' Macca looked at his former boss, his eyes wide with anger.

'Well, he was still in the terminal on the south side of the airfield, but now it appears he's taxiing, ready for take-off.' Asquith looked up at his teammates, who were all wide-eyed and staring at him with astonishment. A grin spread across the former officer's face.

'How the shagging hell can you know that?' said Jacko.

'Because I planted a GPS tracker in Macca's medal box.'

Asquith swivelled the laptop around to display the screen, which had a map application open. A blue blob pulsed in the middle.

'Gathering speed now, so looks like it's all happening.' He appeared totally delighted with himself. 'Taking off right now, I'd say.'

They all watched as the blob headed off over the green strip of road, which was the A40.

Then it disappeared.

It just vanished, and the map page was just that. A simple Google map page with nothing else on it.

Chapter 31

'Er, Neil. Where's it gone?' said Josie, her voice uncertain.

'Yeah, what's happened?' echoed Macca.

Asquith began to swipe and click. 'I'm trying to find it again, but it should still be working.' His jaw was tight and his face had coloured.

'Neil?' said Charlie, his voice low.

'Give me a minute,' Asquith said, his eyes hard.

'It's cool, pal. Massive BZ for getting the tracker on in the first place, but now would maybe be a good time to get the signal back.'

'I've tried to re-initialise it, but it must be something on board the aircraft. Maybe a dampening field, or maybe the signal can't get out of the aircraft now it's on board. I'm not sure. I'm no expert.' He swiped and clicked again before sitting back with a muttered 'Bollocks.'

Macca sighed and put his hand on Asquith's shoulder. 'Nae bother, Neil. Hopefully it'll come back on when they land and the box is outside the aircraft. We just have to be patient.

Josie huffed. 'For how bloody long? It's like someone giving you your favourite toy for Christmas and then nicking it straight back.'

Macca ignored her. 'Where did you get the tracker from? Can whoever supplied it to you get it back online?'

Asquith looked a little embarrassed. 'I don't know, but I'll ask. It was secured in a real rush by my ex-employee, and his contact wasn't sure it would work inside an aircraft or whether it would be picked up by a scanner. I didn't want to use it unless we needed to, as my man could only give me a fifty-fifty guesstimate of the prospect of it working, bearing in mind the shielding that had to go into the box to make it undetectable.'

'Neil, I know that back in the day you were the boss, but now you're just one of us, right?' said Macca.

'I'm aware of that, yes.'

'So why the hell didn't you tell us you were doing it?'

'A number of reasons. Mainly because I wasn't sure it would work, and I didn't know what effect the X-ray machine would have on it if he was going by air. I had to let it get through security first, and then wake the device up remotely, which is what I've been doing on the laptop.'

'Yeah, but Macca's question stands,' said Jacko. 'Why the shagging hell didn't you share this information with us? I handed it over to him all confident, not knowing that there was a bug in there. Shit, imagine he'd found it?'

Asquith smiled nervously. 'That's why I didn't tell you. Look, guys, I know it was a little irregular, but I thought it was worth the risk. The tracker is state-of-the-art, tiny battery, minimal circuitry, and it would just appear on X-ray as a blob the size of a fifty-pence piece.'

'Still a shagging liberty not telling me, particularly now the fucker isn't working.' Jacko puffed out his cheeks in exasperation.

'That's as may be, but it's still there, and it may still give us an advantage if we can get it working again once the plane lands. We don't need the route the plane is taking; we just need the destination. Neil, get on to your man and see if there's anything he can suggest.'

Asquith nodded. 'Look, there's something else . . .'

'What?' said Macca.

'We all owed Chappers everything, right?'

'Aye.'

'Well, I always felt I owed him more. He saved me that day in that honking weather on the side of Harriet. I'd lost the plot, I was crapping my bloody self and I had no idea what to do next. Chappers dragged me back to reality and told me straight how I needed to behave. He told me that I had to lead, and to stop pissing about. He was only a corporal, but he had the guts to tell his troop commander to sort his shit out, and it bloody worked.'

A heavy silence descended among the group, before Jacko chuckled. 'He was a hoofing bloke for sure, but don't think you've the monopoly on gratitude. He dragged me out of a bloody minefield after I'd had my foot shredded.'

'Yeah, we all owe him equally, Neil, so stop feeling sorry for yourself. Without him fragging that fifty-cal, we'd have all been bloody filled full of lead, so don't go giving it the "I'm so bloody threaders" line,' said Charlie, a smile spreading across his face.

'And don't keep shit from us. We're a team, and we all have skills that bring the good stuff to the party, but we keep each other in the loop, okay?' added Macca.

'Right, Neil, you make the calls and see what your techy geek can do. Meanwhile, we just have to wait. Any suggestions?' said Charlie.

'Anyone fancy a bacon banjo?' suggested Jacko.

There were enthusiastic nods all round the table, the mood having gone from depressed to buzzing and excited in a heartbeat.

'And as you've fucked up, Captain Asquith, you can buy them.'

'I've fucked up? How?'

'Not telling us of your shit-hot idea. And there's the fact that you're rich, whereas I'm just a poor reformed inmate, guvna.' Jacko waved to the unsmiling woman behind the counter. 'Five bacon baps, please, love.'

Asquith just shook his head, a half-smile on his face, picked up his phone and left the café.

'Jacko, you've got twenty grand tucked away somewhere from the sale of my bloody medals,' said Macca.

'Safe as houses under my bed, mate.'

'So not safe at all, then.'

'It'll be fine. Stop dripping.' Jacko chuckled.

Asquith was back within two minutes, and by the look on his face, they could tell that the news wasn't good.

'No dice. My tech man isn't that techy, it seems. He's great at buying the kit, but not so hot at remotely mending it.'

'What, no idea at all?' said Charlie.

'Well, beyond turning it off and on again, which I've already tried.'

'Shit,' said Macca.

'What are we gonna do?' asked Josie.

'We're gonna eat our bacon banjos, and then we're gonna go to my place. I need to grab my old diary to get a phone number.'

'Who're you going to call?' said Asquith.

'Someone who knows someone who knows more than anyone else in the world about bugs and trackers.'

'And can you trust him?' asked Charlie.

'Her. Yes, I trust her, but I bloody wish I didn't have to call her.'

Chapter 32

The private jet eased smoothly onto the tarmac and was soon taxiing to a remote pan at the far edges of the airport, where a sleek-looking blue and white helicopter sat.

'We really are going to the castle by helicopter?' said Hunter incredulously, feeling a knot of excitement in his stomach.

'Yes. Compliments of the General. He want medals quick, I think. Come, no time to waste,' said Danilo, unbuckling his seat belt.

'Does the General own it?'

'Yes, a Bell 222. Cost a small fortune, but he like it. He bought recently, as his Bentley and Rolls-Royce struggle with the bumpy track, and he doesn't like the Land Rover so much, all too uncomfortable for him. Easy for him to travel, and he like you, so you get nice ride.' Danilo's voice was full of scorn; he clearly didn't approve of Hunter being given such treatment. Hunter wondered if he cared, and soon realised that he didn't. As long as the General approved of him, he didn't care what some ex-grunt from a crap Slovakian Army unit thought.

'Lucky me,' he said.

Danilo's face remained blank, showing no reaction to Hunter's words. 'Get your bag; we go straight away. Pilot is waiting for us.'

The steps to the aircraft were lowered and Hunter followed Danilo into the icy-cold wind that was whipping in from the east, his suit carrier over his shoulder and small leather bag in his hand. He fumbled with his wool coat, trying to secure the buttons against the suggestion of a light rain that was beginning to fall from the lead-grey sky. Danilo looked at him with flat eyes.

Hunter tried to suppress his almost childlike levels of excitement. First a private jet, and now a privately owned helicopter. He couldn't help but feel that he really had arrived. A grey-uniformed pilot with a salt-and-pepper beard and dead eyes wordlessly opened the door, and waved a hand indicating that they should get in. The name badge on his overalls simply said 'Havel'.

There was no safety brief, no introductions and no ceremony. Hunter had to admit that it felt just like being ushered into a minicab by a bored driver who couldn't wait for his shift to be over, and his excitement was soon replaced by a gnawing discomfort. Both Danilo and the pilot looked ex-military, tough and nasty, with eyes that had seen many terrible things. Despite his own brief service in the Scots Guards, Hunter had seen no action beyond a few tours of duty at Buckingham Palace, and he suddenly felt a little less worthy.

Within a few minutes, he was strapped into his seat with a headset clamped over his ears. The engine note increased to a roar, and in no time at all the helicopter was airborne and heading south, hugging the coastline. The grey North Sea stretched out to the east, seemingly for ever, crested with waves and the monolithic oil rigs dotted around in the distance.

'Flight time is just fifteen minutes, so don't get too settled,' came Havel's voice over the headset.

Hunter relaxed into the sleek leather of the seat and stared out of the window at the damp grey scenery. To his right he could see large chessboard fields on either side of the long, snaking A92, the road on which he normally travelled in a Land Rover on the half-hour journey.

Fifteen minutes later, the pilot spoke again. 'Prepare for landing. In case of emergencies, put head between legs and kiss your butt goodbye.' His slightly alarming instruction was given without even a trace of humour.

Hunter looked out of the rain-spotted side window as the helicopter banked out over the now distinctly rough sea as it headed to its landing point. Glancing down, he saw their destination. He'd always been impressed when he'd arrived at the castle in the past by road, but coming in from the air was a different experience altogether, and he almost felt the breath being ripped from his body. It was staggering.

Stonehaven Castle. The fourteenth-century fortified home of the Keith clan, which had been totally renovated and restored by its current occupant. Once a total wreck and little more than a collection of Scottish stones, it was now a luxurious home for its mysterious billionaire owner.

It sat hunkered down against the unrelenting wind, perched on top of a hundred-and-fifty-foot-high grassy rock, surrounded on three sides by the crashing North Sea. The four-acre outcrop was only connected to the mainland by a short, narrow causeway, at the end of which was an ancient-looking gatehouse arch set into the solid granite, with a raised portcullis through which all arrivals had to pass. It was almost the perfect defensive stronghold, and would once have been defended by the Jacobites against the marauding redcoats.

What at first sight appeared to be a random collection of ancient low-rise stone buildings surrounding a larger single-storey construction was in fact a vast property, at least seventy per cent of which was underground, dug into the soft peat or blasted into the hard granite superstructure of the island. The focal point was a huge glass window and balcony set into the cliff face overlooking the sea. Small stone turrets jutted upwards from each end of the main house, with ramparts and, pretentiously, a flag on which the General's crest was represented. It was an oddly juxtaposed mix of ancient history and state-of-the art modernity, staggeringly beautiful and yet simultaneously monstrously ugly.

Hunter wondered how the hell the General had managed to obtain the necessary permissions to build and develop the main house into the palatial dwelling it now was. The sight of the still semi-ruined tower building to the east of the outcrop suggested that some compromises had been made.

The helicopter eased down, its engine note changing as it hovered over the sea, the sun bouncing off the large expanse of glass in the cliff side. Despite the pilot's somewhat rough appearance, he was clearly a skilled operator, which Hunter was thankful for. As they touched down on the circular pad, he released his seat belt and grabbed his scratched and worn leather attaché case, a knot of nerves forming in his stomach.

He was almost here, in the seat and home of the new laird of Stonehaven Castle. General Marek Bruzek.

Chapter 33

When Macca had said 'we're gonna go to my place', the team had all imagined that he meant his cottage in Markyate, the anonymous village where he had lived since his divorce a few years ago. They didn't realise that he actually meant a small shed in the middle of an allotment patch half a mile away. They were sitting on a hotchpotch of vegetable crates, an old stool and sacks of fertiliser. Strings of onions, garlic and chillis dangled from the ceiling, and spotless tools were neatly hung on hooks on the rustic wooden walls. They all clutched tin mugs of weak black tea that he'd quickly rustled up within a few minutes by boiling a battered kettle on a rickety camping gas stove.

'Christ, I had no idea you were like Monty Don,' said Charlie, referring to the TV gardening expert, as he sipped his tea.

'Man needs a hobby. It's nice and peaceful here, and look. My sprouts are ready if anyone wants some,' said Macca, pointing out of the window to a neat row of brassicas. He picked up a penknife from a potting table covered in plastic pots, markers, garden string and other horticultural paraphernalia.

'Not with my ropy bowels, and probably best not with your Chalfonts, mate,' said Jacko. The cockney rhyming slang was short for Chalfont St Giles, to rhyme with 'piles'.

Macca glared at Asquith and Josie in turn. 'That information was in confidence, you buggers.'

'Ah, come on, Macca. Sharing is caring,' said Asquith, chuckling.

'Piss off.'

All the others burst out laughing, loud enough that the Perspex windows in the shed rattled.

'You load of scumbags. They're sore, and I could do without your hilarity.' Macca's face was hard, but his eyes twinkled in amusement.

'Not enough fibre, geezer, but you have my sympathies. Arse grapes are 'orrible.'

'If you're eating sprouts, Jacko, I'm not sharing a car with you any more. I'd need a canary in a cage,' said Charlie, wiping at his moist eyes.

'Anyway, enough laughing at my afflictions and Jacko's bogging bowels. I need to get something.' Macca pointed at the rough wooden floor, which was covered in tatami matting. Josie moved to one side, and he lifted up a corner of the mat. Using his penknife, he prised up a loose floorboard and pulled out a plastic-bagged A5 notebook. He leafed through it until he found what he was looking for, then reached under the boards again and pulled out another bag containing an ancient-looking Nokia phone and a dog-eared passport, together with a single credit card.

'You've got a grab-and-go bag?' said Jacko.

'I kept hold of my alternate passport when I left the Corps. I even managed to get it renewed a few years ago, when I did a wee bit of a freelance for HMG. You never know when a man might need to give it legs.'

'Blimey, you're just like a spy, Macca,' said Josie, with no trace of sarcasm.

159

'Just old-fashioned tradecraft.' He tapped the open notebook, powered up the Nokia and dialled. 'If you'll excuse me, I best do this outside. She may be a bit shy. Neil, pass me the iPad.'

'Who's "she"? That Laurel MILF you were behaving like a naughty schoolboy in front of at the wake?' teased Jacko.

Macca said nothing, just flicked a two-fingered salute and left the shed, slamming the door behind him.

'It's definitely her he's calling. Top-level Yank spook. If anyone can trace a rogue plane, it's her. I hope he's up for whatever she wants in return.' Jacko sniggered.

The four of them sat there watching as Macca strolled head down, looking at his sprouts, as he spoke on the phone. The expression on his face betrayed the fact that it was not a totally comfortable exchange. He held the phone between his ear and shoulder as he swiped at the iPad, then nodded and turned back to the shed.

'So?' said Asquith as Macca entered.

'She wants to meet. She thinks she can help but doesn't want to speak over the phone.'

'Nice one. So where's the date?' said Charlie, a smile creeping onto his face.

Macca flashed a glare at him. 'It's not a date. I'm meeting her in London as soon as I can get there.'

Charlie looked at his watch. 'So a lunch date, then?'

'It's not a bloody date.'

'Sounds like a date to me. Whereabouts?'

'Vauxhall Park. Close to the embassy.' Macca averted his gaze and looked at the iPad.

'A picnic lunch? How romantic, particularly as it's such a beautiful day. You'd best stop for flowers,' said Josie, deadpan.

Macca's stare was flinty. 'You can wheesht as well, young lady.'

'She's a handsome woman, Macca. You could do worse.'

'Right, piss off, the lot of you. Charlie, can you give me a lift there? I don't want to risk public transport.'

'Why not me?' said Jacko.

'With Charlie's description of your flatulence issue, I'd rather not. I suggest we all meet in a couple of hours at your place. Let's go, Charlie.'

Chapter 34

Marek Bruzek was in his wood-panelled library, which was lined from floor to ceiling with tomes of various ages and types, all beautifully catalogued, as he always insisted on.

Stifling a yawn, he stretched his legs out in front of him and reclined in his reading chair, placing the leather-bound copy of *Catcher in the Rye* down on the table. The soft sounds of Beethoven wafted out of unseen speakers, and he took a sip from a heavy crystal glass, savouring the warmth of the old Macallan whisky. He frowned at the faint sound of the helicopter. The library was his sanctuary, and he hated it when anything or anyone intruded upon his peace without his authority.

He stood up, ignoring the groaning from his knees, and walked across to the floor-to-ceiling windows that looked out over the endless expanse of the North Sea, the rivulets of rain trickling down proving the only impediment to the enormous vista. The helicopter swung briefly into view, its altitude dipping as it descended to land on the pad just a few metres above where he was standing. He was thankful for the heavy soundproofing that he'd insisted on when the castle was being renovated and the new subterranean modern home hacked out of the harsh landscape.

The helicopter was essential to his life at Stonehaven Castle. The only vehicle access was a precarious causeway, just big enough for one sturdy off-road vehicle, leading to the rocky outcrop that jutted from the Aberdeenshire coast and into the North Sea. The expense really didn't bother him. It was not like money was a concern to Marek Bruzek.

There was a soft knock at the door and Danilo appeared, his scarred shaved head shining in the light. The powerfully built man was Bruzek's personal assistant and bodyguard, and a former member of the Slovakian Special Forces.

'Morag Smith and Giles Hunter have arrived, General,' he said in his heavily accented English. Bruzek insisted that his staff all spoke in English when he was in residence in the castle; it just seemed appropriate to him. He employed a few locals in domestic roles, to stay popular with the community, and he paid them well, but his small security team were all Slovaks. He trusted Slovak soldiers particularly, as Danilo personally vetted them and they were all from his old unit, the 5th Special Forces Regiment.

'Did Morag come on the helicopter as well?'

'Train. She doesn't like to fly, so I pick her up from station in Land Rover.'

'Poor woman in that terrible bumpy car. They have the items?'

'Yes, sir. Just as you ordered. Who first?'

'Give me a moment, and then send Morag through.' Danilo disappeared, and Bruzek stood and checked his appearance in the full-length mirror, noting the cut of his Harris tweed, which he habitually wore when in residence in his Scottish hideaway. He nodded approvingly at the beautifully tailored suit, which had been more than worth the seven thousand pounds he'd paid to have it made by Gieves & Hawkes in Savile Row.

Morag stepped into the room, smiling widely. She was a softly spoken, birdlike woman, with a halo of grey hair and spectacles that were always on a chain. She ran a specialist bookshop in Edinburgh that sourced and sold rare first editions, and would travel to the castle whenever she managed to find something Bruzek had been on the lookout for. He regularly scoured the auction houses for the books he was seeking, and would bid online, or send one of his representatives if in-person bidding was required.

He didn't like to leave Stonehaven Castle unless he was travelling to his home in Dubai, where he went if he wanted to escape the Scottish weather. He'd come to spend more and more time here, and while not a recluse, he rarely left the place, preferring to receive guests at occasional lavish parties. It wasn't like he was short of accommodation for them, in the guest wing and a number of small lodges created from the ancient stone and dotted around the outcrop.

'Morag, my dear, what delights do you bring me?' he said in his high-pitched Slovakian-accented voice, a broad smile on his round, shiny face. His thinning dyed-black hair was scraped back and plastered to his scalp with oil. He stepped forward and embraced her lightly and awkwardly, his limbs stiff and face fixed.

'Good morning, General Bruzek, I have two beautiful books you asked me to locate for you.'

'Capital, capital!' He clapped his hands, his face alive like a child on Christmas morning.

'I was very excited with this find, General. A first edition of *Harry Potter and the Philosopher's Stone*, by Joanne Rowling. The provenance is perfect.'

'J. K. Rowling?' he said, his brow furrowed and eyes confused.

'Not in this case, General. The first print run of five hundred credits Joanne Rowling as the author on the title page, as opposed to J. K. Very few copies survive, as at least three hundred went to schools. It's a wonderful find.'

'And expensive, no doubt.'

'Well, yes. It's not signed, so just sixty thousand pounds, but

164

it will only appreciate.'

She proffered the book, but he waved it away. 'I really want signed, keep looking.'

'Of course, General.'

'What else?' he said.

'Another wonderful find. A first edition of *The Tale of Peter Rabbit*, first published in 1901. One of only two hundred and fifty copies, terribly rare again.'

He nodded in approval. 'Any information on *The Hobbit* we've been looking for?' he said, sitting back in his leather-buttoned chesterfield chair.

'Very hard to find, I'm afraid. My ear is close to the ground and I have some feelers out. You do realise that the last copy at auction sold for well over a hundred thousand pounds?'

'I do. Thank you, Morag, leave the books on the side, and shelve and catalogue them a little later. Are you staying here tonight?'

'Yes, General. It was kind of you to offer.'

'Well then, I'll see you at dinner. Now if you'll excuse me?' He folded his arms, indicating that the meeting was over.

Morag smiled, clearly used to his brusque manner. 'Enjoy the books.' She turned and left.

Danilo poked his head around the door. 'Shall I show Hunter in?'

Bruzek nodded, sipping his whisky, his interest in both the books and Morag already gone.

The door opened wider and a tall, large-framed man entered. He was immaculately dressed in a dark tweed suit with a knitted tie and highly polished brogues. He was in his early fifties, and had a mane of blonde hair that was swept backwards. His blue eyes sparkled in the dim light and he smiled widely, showing even white teeth.

'General,' he said, bowing his head slightly.

'Giles, how good to see you, my dear friend. How was the flight?' Bruzek clasped his visitor's proffered hand in both of his,

his eyes shining. Giles was different to Morag. He was closer to being an equal, as he had served as a captain in the Scots Guards looking after the Queen, and of course, he was a man. Bruzek had little interest in or regard for women. He enjoyed an attractive young woman, but only as a companion.

'The flight was perfect as always, General. It was generous of you to send your plane to collect me from London.' Giles's voice was redolent with the tones of the English public school system, mixed with a trace of Scots.

'My pleasure. I wouldn't have you on the dreadful commercial flights that travel to Aberdeen, particularly carrying such valuable cargo. You have them, I take it?' Bruzek said, his eyes shining with gleeful anticipation.

'Of course, General.' He reached into his leather attaché case and pulled out a plain velvet-covered box about the size of an A4 piece of paper. There was a gold crest embossed on the lid, a globe and laurel wreath, topped with a crown and a lion. Directly under the crown was the word 'GIBRALTAR' and underneath the globe, 'PER MARE PER TERRAM'.

The badge of the Royal Marines.

'Why Gibraltar on the badge?' said Bruzek, his face alive with excitement, like a child about to open a longed-for gift.

'It refers to the recapture of the island in 1704 by a force of Anglo-Dutch Marines and the later defence of the territory during a nine-month siege while outnumbered by the Franco-Spanish. Terribly brave soldiers, General. I had the box created especially for you.'

'Indeed, indeed. Such history, Giles.' Bruzek flipped open the clasp and lifted the lid, gasping at the polished double row of medals set into a tailor-made recess in the velvet within. His mouth gaped open and his eyes shone.

'Without doubt this is one of the more notable groups of medals awarded to a British soldier this century, General. Distinguished Conduct Medal from the Falkland Islands conflict in 1982,

Mention in Despatches oak leaf on the Iraq medal, Conspicuous Gallantry Cross for Afghanistan, and highly unusually, a Bronze Star from the USA. And of course, the campaign medals from Kosovo, Sierra Leone, Northern Ireland and others.'

'They are perfect, Giles. When I read of them and this soldier's exploits, I just had to have them. Well done, well done indeed. I'll transfer the fee immediately.' Bruzek caressed the sparkling medals reverentially, then picked them up and stared at them. Turning them over, he read the inscription on the CGC with its silver cross pattée and white ribbon with a crimson stripe. He noted the name on the back: WO F Chapman P0542727. 'Beautiful. A brave man, Giles.'

'I'm delighted you're happy, General. And here is the other group. Not quite the level of Sergeant Major Chapman's medals, but still very notable.'

He passed a wooden box across to Bruzek, who noted that it was embossed with the badge of the Special Forces. 'Special Boat Service?' he said.

'Yes, General. The most elite of soldiers. Another really notable group to add to your collection.'

'Sergeant Major Mackenzie is also a very brave man. Do we have citations?'

'Indeed, General. They're all catalogued in here.' Giles handed over a manila file.

'Thank you, Giles. My medal collection means more to me than anything else. You're still on the lookout for more groups with similar gravitas, I hope?'

Hunter nodded eagerly. 'My ear is permanently to the ground, General. I think I know your tastes.'

'Any word on a Victoria Cross?'

'Almost impossible. Nearly all are in museums, regimental collections or kept in bank vaults.'

Bruzek's face fell. 'A shame. My pockets are deep for such items. You're a good man, Giles. I'll see you at dinner. Now I must prepare.' He nodded and turned away.

Hunter left the room silently.

'Petra is here, General,' said Danilo, who had appeared as if by magic.

Bruzek smiled. 'Yes, why not. I have some time.' The smile turned into a leer, his lips thin and lizard-like.

'I must say, she's being somewhat difficult, sir.'

'How so?' His face darkened and the leer vanished.

'She wants to go home and is being rather petulant.'

'Show her in,' said Bruzek coldly.

Danilo nodded and left the room. A moment later, a petite and very pretty young woman entered, her heavy make-up failing to disguise her sullen expression. She wore a tiny skirt that left most of her slim bare legs exposed and a skinny-fit vest top. Her dark hair was piled on top of her head and secured with a scrunchie. She looked no more than eighteen.

'Petra, my dear, why no smile for me, eh?' Bruzek moved close to the girl and stroked her cheek with the back of his finger.

She averted her eyes as she spoke, her voice carrying a sharp edge. 'I don't feel happy, General.'

'Oh my darling. This is not what I expect from my companions. I give you nice food, beautiful clothes and a warm home, and this is how you repay me?'

'I have my period,' she said, gazing at her Converse sneakers.

Bruzek sighed, his heart sinking at the unwelcome news. 'Well why didn't you tell Danilo, eh?' He raised his hand from his cheek and stroked her hair, almost tenderly. She flinched at his touch, but didn't look up.

'Would you rather rejoin the unfortunates?' he said, his voice almost like that of a disappointed teacher.

Petra's head jolted upwards, and her eyes met Bruzek's. 'No . . . please, General,' she stammered, her expression full of fear.

'Maybe I send you away in my helicopter, then?' He stared at her, his small eyes dark and featureless.

A solitary tear carved a path down her porcelain cheek, but she didn't answer.

Bruzek sighed again and nodded. 'Go back to your room and send Renata. I'll see you again soon, when perhaps you'll be a little more appreciative.' He turned away from her, all interest suddenly gone. She was dirty.

As soon as the door shut, he went to one of the large bookcases and pressed a hidden button. There was a click, and the bookcase popped away from the wall, swinging out on smooth hinges, apparently almost weightless. Behind was a stout-looking wooden door, with metal struts giving it the appearance of a chessboard and a small keypad at the centre. He keyed in a six-digit code, then pressed his thumb to a glass pad, and the door opened to reveal a small oak-panelled room with an expensive-looking swivel armchair in the centre of the polished wooden floor. The far wall was covered in green baize and lined with multiple groups of medals, glinting in the overhead light. Bruzek took the medals from the velvet-covered box that Giles had brought and slotted them into an empty space, fixing them in place with the pin at the rear of the group. Then he stroked the wooden box containing the second group and flicked it open, laying it down on a table to the side.

Sinking into the swivel chair, he sighed contentedly at the display. So many stories, so much bravery and so much to admire. If only he'd had the opportunity to fight, maybe his own medals would be there, but he had been too busy serving the communist regime until the Velvet Revolution changed everything. His honorary rank had been gifted to him by General Secretary of Czechoslovakia Gustáv Husák before the fall of communism, and he'd been grateful, but he was forever unsatisfied.

The break-up of Czechoslovakia had presented opportunities that he was quick to exploit. He used his acquired wealth to start up an investment company and was soon lending vast sums to many of the new businesses. When he'd sold his company ten years ago, it netted him so much money, he decided that it was now time to relax and build Stonehaven Castle. He had a deep and abiding love for Scotland, probably because of his ancestry. His maternal grandfather had been a Scottish engineer, who'd got his grandmother pregnant while working in Czechoslovakia. When Bruzek had first visited Scotland, many years ago, he felt like he had come home.

These days, he was happy and satisfied, but as always, he wanted to acquire beautiful things. He wanted things that had meaning and history, things that money couldn't buy.

He sat back in the chair and swivelled it towards the left-hand wall, smiling as he saw the painting there. His pride and joy. *Storm on the Sea of Galilee* by Rembrandt. It had been stolen in 1990 from a museum in Boston, and he'd bought it via one of his agents for a song when the thieves, who'd been sitting on it for years, decided it was far too hot to handle. He didn't care how hot it was. He wanted it, so he had to have it, and it didn't bother him even slightly that he was the only one who could enjoy it.

He swivelled his chair another ninety degrees and began to admire the exquisite brushwork of the next painting. Another Rembrandt, *Landscape with Cottages*, stolen in 1972 from the Montreal Museum of Fine Arts.

The next wall held the stunning *Madeleine Leaning on Her Elbow with Flowers in Her Hair*, by Renoir. He didn't care a jot that this had also been stolen, from a private residence in Houston, Texas. He'd have been willing to buy it, but the stupid American had told his agent it wasn't for sale. Bruzek couldn't accept that. He never took no for an answer. He knew he was like a magpie, and frankly, he didn't care. No one told General Marek Bruzek what he could or could not possess.

His last swivel took in the final painting. The masterful *View of Auvers-sur-Oise*, by Cézanne, which he'd coveted for many years. Thankfully Giles knew just the people to get the job done, and it had been acquired for him when it was liberated from the

Ashmolean Museum on New Year's Day in 2000.

He chuckled as he looked at his wonderful treasures. All said to be out of his reach by those born into wealth.

Bruzek hadn't been born into wealth; he'd been born into abject poverty in a rural village in Bratislava. But he was a fighter, and he was smart.

He always got what he wanted.

Chapter 35

Vauxhall Park was thankfully quiet when Charlie dropped Macca outside one of the side entrances. He zipped up his puffa jacket against the afternoon chill and strode briskly through the gates and into the centre of the smallish park. He'd been here a couple of times in the past when on covert jobs that necessitated meetings with American spooks. The park was a favoured location, being not too far from the embassy, and that mix of busy enough to not stand out but not too busy to be indiscreet.

He made his way to the bench that Laurel Freeman had specified, a hundred metres in from the gate on Fentiman Road. It was perfect, being not too close to the café, nor to any of the other attractions, such as the play park or model village. A dull, unremarkable bench in an unremarkable London park.

Macca shivered as the chill bit into his exposed skin, cursing the outdoor meeting and yet thankful that the temperature would hopefully keep it brief. He sat on the bench, feeling the cold metal through his jeans, and looked at his watch. Similar to all ex-military, he was a stickler for being on time, the product of having it drilled into him from teenage years that in the marines, if you weren't five minutes early, you were late.

As usual, he didn't see her arrive. She just seemed to appear next to him on the bench before planting a soft kiss on his cheek. He tried his best not to wince at the touch, but he almost certainly failed.

'Gordon, so lovely to see you. I'd hug you as well, but we should at least try and be discreet, eh?' Her smile was wide and typically American, with a dazzling display of white teeth.

Macca turned to face her, seeing his own face reflected in the large-framed sunglasses she wore. She was smartly dressed in a long wool coat, dark jeans and books. Her hair was covered with an embroidered woollen hat.

'Hello, Laurel,' he said, feeling a knot of nerves in his stomach. He always felt this way around her, and he wasn't sure why. She was never anything but pleasant, but she also radiated something else.

Power. She was a natural leader, and despite her sunny and ebullient nature, she knew how to take the lead in all situations. She was most certainly someone used to getting her own way.

'Thanks for saying you'd help us,' said Macca.

'I'm not sure that's exactly what I said. I said I'd listen to you, and you were being very mysterious on the phone. So I'm here, and I'm listening. Maybe it's best you tell me what's on your mind and what you want from me.' She removed her sunglasses and fixed Macca with that stare he'd experienced many times before. Deep, searching, enquiring, intelligent, a little cynical, and intimidating. Seriously intimidating. A stare that had taken her to the senior levels of the world's biggest intelligence agency. A stare that had been used against Islamic terrorists, Russian dissidents, North Korean defectors and corrupt senators. A stare that could gaze into the very centre of your soul – not that Macca believed such a thing existed.

Ex-Regimental Sergeant Major Gordon Mackenzie, formerly of the Special Boat Service, was a tough cookie who had operated at the very top end of the Special Forces.

But he needed Laurel's help, so he told her.

He told her everything.

When he'd finished talking, she paused a moment, her eyes flicking up to the branches of the tree above the bench.

'You have the iPad with you?' she said.

'Aye, in my bag.'

Without a word, she raised a hand, pulled off her hat and laid it down on the bench beside her. Macca knew what this was. It was tradecraft. 'Pass it to me,' she said, glancing to her left. Out of nowhere, a jogger appeared, dressed in typical winter running gear. She held up the iPad, and without pausing, the jogger took it and tucked it under his arm, continuing to the exit and out onto the street.

Macca had seen CIA agents in action before, but he was still impressed at the slickness of the handover.

'Nice,' he said, a smile turning up the corners of his mouth.

'I've a man waiting. If the tracker can be located or woken, he's the person to do it. Shouldn't take long.' She reached out and put her gloved hand on his. 'I was so sad about Frank. If we can trace the bastards who enabled this, I want them punished, and the medals back. It was selfless of you to use yours as bait. I see there's still life in the old dog yet.' She chuckled, and squeezed his hand.

'Nae bother. We want them back for Josie and her mum. We'll do whatever it takes. We're grateful for your help, Laurel.' He pulled his hand out from under hers and stifled a nervous cough.

'I can't help with anything operational. No boots on the ground, nothing like that – you understand that?'

'Aye, of course. If we can locate the medals, we'll handle the rest, whatever it is.'

'I have faith in you, Gordon.' Her eyes sparkled, and she brushed her neat hair away from her face. 'Now, enough of this. Lunch.' She dug down into her leather bag and produced two brown paper parcels, handing one to Macca along with a bottle of mineral water. 'There's the best sandwich shop just around the corner from the embassy. Pulled pork okay?' she said, grinning.

'Aye,' said Macca, stuttering slightly and feeling his cheeks colour.

Laurel took her gloves off and unwrapped her sandwich. 'It's so nice to see you after so many years. I've never forgotten what you did for me. I want to repay you, firstly by helping out with the medals, but more importantly, once this is all sorted, there's something else I want.' She paused and fixed him with that gaze once again.

'Aye, whatever,' said Macca as he took a bite from his own sandwich. Predictably, it was delicious. 'Great sandwich,' he said through a mouthful.

'Dinner at the Ivy. Just us two, my treat, no excuses.'

He gave what he hoped was a convincing smile, but as his insides boiled with embarrassment, he was acutely aware that it could be presenting quite differently. 'Aye, that'd be grand,' he said, his voice wobbling just a touch.

Macca hurried out of the park, his breath forming clouds in the cold air, retracing his steps to where Charlie had said he'd wait. He'd managed to extricate himself from Laurel after another fifteen minutes' small talk, most of which had come from the CIA agent. He still felt the bite of nerves in his stomach that he had always experienced when dealing with her. He found her latent power both reassuring and a little uncomfortable.

'Nice lunch?' said Charlie as Macca opened the door and sat in the passenger seat.

'She scares the shit out of me, that woman, but she's got her best man on the tracker. Hopefully he can sort it. All we need to do is wait.' Macca sat back and yawned.

'No we don't,' said Charlie, starting the car.

'What?' Macca's head snapped round.

'We don't need to wait. Some random bloke in running gear tapped on the window just before you got here and handed it over. It's fixed, apparently. Said it's all good now. Some unintelligible bollocks about a rotating GPS handshake malfunction. Just needed a hard reboot and a reconfiguration of the APN and SIM settings, and aligning with the correct satellite frequency or some such shite. Anyway, look.' He passed the iPad over, a map displayed on the screen.

Macca took the tablet and zoomed in on the blue pulsing dot. When he switched to the satellite view, a craggy green outcrop appeared, surrounded on three sides by sea and apparently only accessible by a causeway.

Recognition surged in his chest. 'Stonehaven Castle in Aberdeenshire. Shit, I went there as a boy once. It was just a pile of stones, as I recall. Huge great cliffs on all three sides, almost the perfect fortress to defend. Let's get to Jacko's. The others need to see this, but it looks like it's game on.'

He held out his fist, and Charlie bumped his gently against it.

Chapter 36

The 11/06 were clustered around the iPad on the breakfast bar in Jacko's flat. Everyone was clutching a bottle of beer, and the sense of relief in the room was palpable. They were back in the race.

'That place looks almost impregnable,' said Asquith as he zoomed in tight on the outcrop.

'What the hell is Hunter doing in an ancient ruined castle in Aberdeenshire?' said Macca, massaging his temples with his fingers.

'Christ, I've been there as well,' said Josie, 'when Dad was serving with 45 Commando at Arbroath. I remember it being pretty wild and windy, and as Macca says, just a pile of crumbling stones. What are the medals doing there?'

Asquith's face came alive with realisation. 'I read about it somewhere not that long ago. It's no longer an old ruin. It made the national papers, as I recall. Let me find the news story.' He reached into his bag and pulled out his laptop, leaving the iPad on its stand. Opening the Mac, he tapped at the keys, his face rapt with concentration. 'Here it is. Some crazy Slovakian plutocrat bought the place a few years ago and defied all logic by somehow getting permission to build on it.' He swivelled the computer around for the others to read.

Aberdeenshire residents reacted with fury at the decision to grant a development licence to restore elements of the ruins of Stonehaven Castle on the stunning Aberdeenshire coastline. Billionaire recluse businessman Marek Bruzek, who amassed his fortune in the former Czechoslovakia, had approval granted to restore the tower building, gatehouse and many of the historic dykes to their original state. He was also granted permission to build a new state-of-the-art eco-home, much of which will be underground and will not impact upon the site. Mr Bruzek's representative spoke with reporters. 'Mr Bruzek plans to invest many millions of his own money in bringing Stonehaven Castle back to life. He will ensure that the historic buildings are secured for future generations, while generating significant employment opportunities for the local community. His deposition to the planning committee guarantees that he will allow regular periods of access to visitors, who will continue to learn of the fascinating history of Stonehaven. He is working with Professor Ewan Henderson from Aberdeen University, who will advise on bringing the castle, tower buildings and historic gatehouse back to life. We feel that his desire to build a modest home on the site is a fair compromise, and the committee agreed that the plans demonstrate that it will have minimal impact on the site.'

'What do you make of that?' asked Josie.

'It sounds incredible,' said Macca. 'How the hell did he get permission to build a house on that place? It dates back centuries.'

'The real question is, who is Marek Bruzek?' said Charlie.

'I'm just looking now. I'll have it properly researched, but from what I can see, he's a Slovakian businessman who it seems did very well out of the so-called "velvet divorce" when Czechoslovakia was divided up in 1993. He headed a successful investment business, and as well as getting control of a number of previously government-controlled industries for a modest sum, namely some steel factories, and invested heavily in the burgeoning property market. Seems like he sold a number of businesses some years back and made himself very rich. *Forbes* estimates four to five billion net wealth.'

'Hence private jets and helicopters. How about the General thing?' said Charlie.

'Honorary rank as a reward for his work for the communist regime, from what I can see. Here's a photo of him.' Asquith swivelled the laptop around again.

They all looked at the slight man with slicked-back hair so glossy and dark that it had to be dyed. His wide smile was full of blindingly white teeth and his skin was stretched taut across his forehead, without a trace of lines or wrinkles. He was standing next to a statuesque blonde in a tiny dress who was significantly taller and decades younger than him, and was dressed in a well-tailored military uniform with a row of medals that glittered on his narrow chest. His eyes were small and dark and displayed nothing. It was almost like someone had assembled his face for an old-style police photofit, but had got the eyes from a different species.

'Creepy little wank-stain, isn't he?' said Jacko, his lip curling.

'I was trying to come up with a suitable description, but I can't improve on that,' said Josie with a chuckle.

'That's A-level English for you. What's next?' asked Jacko.

'Same as before. Treat it like a police operation, but without the rules. The difference now is that we have a location and we have a suspect. I'd say Bruzek is our man. Look at how he dealt with the planning issues; it seems he's not someone used to hearing the word "no". We make sure the medals are there, and then we go in and get them.' Charlie's face was hard as he looked at the photo of the Slovak.

'Police operations are a bit different, Charlie,' Asquith pointed out. 'They have infrastructure, resources and access to intelligence, and they have the law on their side. All we have is four decrepit old codgers who used to be soldiers planning something highly illegal.'

'Excuse me? Am I suddenly bloody invisible?' said Josie, her cheeks pink.

'Sorry, of course, we'd be nowhere without you, Josie.' Asquith looked momentarily embarrassed.

'How long will the battery on the tracker last for?' she asked.

'If I slow the pings down to one an hour, then up to two weeks. It's only just gone on, so that keeps us going until after Christmas. Blimey, Christmas is only a week away. Can we get this done before then?'

'I used to do this for a living in the SBS. I've planned high-value target operations all over the world, and I know they start with two things. Research and reconnaissance. We need to get up there, and we need eyes on. Is everyone up for it?' said Macca, his expression flinty.

'Damn right,' said Jacko, immediately.

'You know I am,' added Josie.

'I'll need to speak to the wife, but of course I'm there,' said Charlie.

'When?' asked Asquith.

'When what?' said Macca.

'Travelling up north.'

'Soon. We don't know if the medals are going to remain there, do we?'

'We still need this researching properly, Macca. I can head to my old office; I'd rather do this in person, as I'm asking a big favour of my ex-partner. My suggestion is that we take a couple of days to prepare before we rush off up to Aberdeen. I'll also need to speak to Mrs Asquith, but nothing will stop me coming.' Asquith slammed his laptop shut.

'Okay, twenty-four hours to get ready, and then we head north. I'll look into logistics. We'll need a vehicle, preferably off-road and not traceable back to any of us. Who can sort that?'

'Well, as I have twenty-odd grand of bunce tucked away from selling your medals, I'll deal with the vehicle,' offered Jacko. 'Are we worried if it's mildly iffy? If we want a reasonable four-by-four that can fit us and our kit inside and not break down, twenty's not a lot.'

'Depends on *how* iffy. We can't afford to get lifted in a hooky car,' said Macca.

'I'm talking about quality stuff here. And we won't need to worry about registering it. If we go to a legit dealer and try and wedge out twenty bags for a car, we run the risk of attracting the attention of Charlie's old mob.'

'That's a good point, Macca. Cash purchases for cars are fraught with money-laundering risks. If we're crossing lines, I'd rather we were in a totally untraceable vehicle, much as it pains me to agree with a dodgy geezer like Jacko.' Charlie punched Jacko lightly on the shoulder.

'Cheeky bloody cozzer.'

Macca stifled a chuckle. 'Charlie, can you pull in any favours from your old police contacts for intel on Bruzek?'

'It's hard and it's risky, but leave it with me and I'll see what I can do.'

'Fair enough. I'll sort out some logistics and equipment. I still know plenty of people in the private military contractor game. Neil, if we need a bit of extra operating capital, is there anything you have that we could avail ourselves of?'

'I'm sure I can help. What are we talking about?'

'Anything useful for a potential assault on a castle on a cliff that I can't provide.'

'Sure, let me know. I've a business operations account that I left dormant. There's a decent amount of liquidity in that.'

'How much?' Jacko's eyes lit up.

'Enough.'

'And you're willing to make it available to us?' said Charlie.

'Of course. A bit of money doesn't go halfway to repaying the debt I owe that man.' Asquith stood and picked up his Mac, his face firm but with a trace of a tremor in his voice.

'We all owe him; that's why we're here.' Macca nodded, his jaw set. A statement, not a question.

There was a long pause in the room.

'Thanks, guys,' said Josie, after a full thirty seconds.

Another silence descended, only broken when Asquith cleared his throat, his voice now businesslike once again. 'Well I'll be heading off to get this research under way. Knowledge is power, and we need all we can get.' He nodded and left.

'He's a good man, right. For a Rupert, I mean,' said Jacko, using the pejorative often deployed by enlisted ranks to describe officers.

'Yeah, I'd say. So Jacko, you'll find us a decent-sized seven-seater with off-road ability? Discovery, or maybe a Land Cruiser?'

'I'm on it. How about IDs?'

'Meaning?' said Macca.

'Well, we're doing shit that ain't overly legal, I imagine.' Jacko folded his arms and leant against the breakfast bar. 'We need to be ready for any eventualities.'

'Okay, get passport-type photos of everyone emailed to me double-quick and I'll see what I can do. I'll head off now as well. I've a few geezers I know who may be able to help out with a bit of this and that.'

'Mind if I hang about here for a bit?' Charlie looked at his watch, and then to the large TV that was mounted on the wall.

'Why? The missus not want you home?'

'Not exactly. There's something I want to watch on telly.'

'No football on, is there?' said Jacko.

'Nah, *Bake Off*,' said Charlie, his eyes low.

'What?'

'*Great British Bake Off*. It's the final tonight, and I've not missed an episode.'

Jacko cackled. 'Christ, we all fought the Argies in 1982, and now we have Macca and his allotment and you with your Mary Berry malarkey.'

'I just like baking. I'll bring you all my lemon drizzle next time we meet up.'

'Now you're talking. Just slam the flat door closed when you go.'

'What should I do?' said Josie to Macca.

'Not much you can do, love. Take it easy, I'd say. It's gonna be busy once we get going.'

'Jesus, Macca. I've been slogging my guts out on this job, and you're still going with the patronising "love"? Am I part of this fucking team or what?' Josie's voice carried an edge of steel, and her eyes were flint-hard.

Macca opened his mouth to retort, before closing it again. 'Sorry. You've more than proved yourself so far. Can you keep monitoring the listening device in the antiques shop in case Hunter comes back? He may let something slip. It's voice-activated, right?'

'Yeah, Neil reckons the battery should last for ages in standby mode, and it's supposed to be good for a full week of solid recording. It's recording direct onto the app, which I've got access to, so I can go back and check for any activity.'

'Excellent. You never know what the bugger might say, and we need every advantage.'

'You know I *can* do something else at the same time. I'm a woman, remember, and I can multitask, unlike you lot. Anything else?' Josie's eyes shone with excitement.

'Open to suggestions,' said Macca.

'I could do some prodding around on a computer and get a good look at the maps and Google Earth photos. I'm a climber, and that castle is surrounded by cliffs. I can make a list of any climbing kit we might need.'

'Good call, crack on with that.' Macca nodded. 'Right. Let's go, and remember, guys. Stay low, move fast.'

Chapter 37

Josie yawned as she let herself into the house in Sandridge, shivering in the chill air. She went to the thermostat and flicked the heating on, hearing the familiar and welcome sound of the boiler sparking into life. A gnawing feeling began to grip at her belly, and she frowned, trying to locate its source. Then it hit her. She was hungry. This often happened, and probably accounted for her overly lean runner's physique. Her stomach growled alarmingly, and she headed straight through to the kitchen and opened the fridge.

Sighing deeply, she stared at the contents, which weren't inspiring. A block of cheese with a suggestion of blue spots on it sat next to a dry-looking chorizo sausage that had seen better days. In the door section were two eggs, both of which, remarkably, were edible, if the printed date on the shell was accurate.

A smile stretched across her face. More than enough to make a tasty meal.

Within a few moments, the chorizo was chopped up and sizzling in a frying pan, to be followed by the eggs, some frozen peas and a handful of grated cheese, and soon an omelette was on its way.

She went to the wine fridge set into the granite-topped island

and pulled out a bottle of Pinot Grigio, thankful for her dad's appreciation of a nice glass of white. Despite being an ex-marine, he was only a modest drinker, although he was always happy to spend a decent amount on a nicer wine. 'A tenner minimum, love. Anything else just doesn't hit the mark,' he'd always said.

She poured herself a large glass and inhaled. It was fresh and clean-smelling – perfect for her omelette. She tipped the egg, chorizo and cheese mix onto a plate and carried it over to the small sofa in the kitchen diner. Taking a sip of the wine, she opened up her iPad and navigated to the listening device still secreted under the desk at Hunter Antiques. She clicked the tab marked activations. *None found.*

She ate a forkful of her omelette and nodded in satisfaction: it was salty and tasty. Then she opened a search engine and typed, *Stonehaven Castle.*

A long list of results filled the screen, many from tourist sites, many around the planning issues, but nothing that made her sit up and look hard. She needed some good images of the castle so that she could assess the cliffs that protected it from the sea. She also made a mental note to look on the climbing forums for any tips and suggestions.

Josie had loved climbing ever since her father had taken her as a child. Chappers had been a mountain leader in the marines, having completed the legendarily tough eight-month course, much of which was carried out in Norway. For decades he'd taught marines how to climb, to navigate and to survive in Arctic environments, and there was nothing he didn't know about the subject, all of which he'd passed on to his daughter. Cliffs and sheer rock faces were in Josie's blood, and with her sinewy, greyhound-like physique and immense strength, she was a formidable climber. She'd been competing for many years, and had won almost every accolade possible on some of the most challenging faces in the world. She had climbed in Yosemite Park, Madagascar, Canada and throughout Europe. There was no rock face she felt would defeat her, and certainly not a sandstone pile in Scotland.

She navigated to Instagram and searched again for Stonehaven Castle. There was one account called 'Scottish Castles from the Air'. She clicked on this and saw that it was a series of drone clips of various castles across Scotland.

She scrolled down the feed until she found a thumbnail marked 'Stonehaven, wipeout!!!' Clicking on this, she watched the pin-sharp footage from what was obviously a high-quality drone. The clip was marked 'DJI Mavic flyby, Stonehaven'. Josie had used drones to record some of her climbs in the past, and she knew that the DJI Mavic was a top bit of kit, with a large zoom, 4K imagery and active tracking technology.

The drone swept in from the side of the coastline to the edge of the outcrop and went out over the sea, approaching the cliffs, which were tall, rutted and sheer. The shining glass of a huge window glittered on the cliff face, stark and sleek and totally out of place. Just how the hell had they managed to dig down into the rock and install a huge great window? she wondered.

She estimated that the cliffs were close to a hundred and fifty feet in height. They were comprised of old red sandstone conglomerate, and judging by the fall at the foot, they weren't that stable. Even looking at them via the medium of the drone, though, she was confident that she could scale them without a problem. She knew that Macca had been a proficient climber from his time in the SBS, but he was over sixty now, and no doubt ravaged by injuries, as almost all career soldiers were. She had no idea about the others. They were all pretty fit-looking, but they were around Macca's age. Could they get up that cliff? They'd probably be able to abseil down it, but scaling that sort of height with arthritic knees and damaged shoulders? They would need a bit of help, and they'd need some practice.

She'd have to get hold of plenty of rope, harnesses, camming devices and karabiners if they were to negotiate that cliff. She frowned, something niggling in her subconscious. A bit of kit she'd heard about. She navigated to a YouTube video and sat watching it for about three minutes, her excitement rising quickly. Then she went to the email app and quickly composed a message to the others.

Guys. List of climbing kit to procure before we go.
1. Five climbing harnesses, Petzl or Black Diamond for preference.
2. Climbing shoes for all. Make irrelevant. I'm size 5.
3. Rope. Shit-loads. Cliff is 150 feet.
4. Lots of karabiners.
5. Spring-loaded climbing cams, (Black Diamond Camalot), a decent number and varying sizes, including enough for practices.
6. Chalk bag and chalk.
7. Helmets for all, any make. I'm size small.
8. Belay anchor, belay devices.
9. Quickdraws and climbing nuts.
10. Big one. Atlas Powered Ascender APA-5.
Macca, I'm relying on your old mountain-leader nous to make sure we have everything for a 150-foot ascent.
    J

She pressed send, and listened for the familiar *whoosh* before she returned to the Instagram feed and continued to watch the video of the castle. She couldn't help but be impressed by its restoration, as the drone swept up the cliffs and over the collection of low stone structures and towers and the discreet single-storey main building. It went into a hover and began to pan around the spectacular outcrop. And then the screen went totally blank. Josie's brow furrowed.

She looked at the video description from the uploader, who had commented: *Drone blasted out of sky by angry man. Live stream.*

There was lots of shocked-emoji faces and questions, and it

seemed clear that someone on the ground had taken exception to the presence of the drone and responded with drastic action. One of the comments asked if the police had been informed, and the response was perhaps telling: *I tried, but the cops weren't interested. Basically told me I had no rights flying above private property, and suggested I'd just crashed it, as there were no guns registered at the place. I reckon someone rich has the police in their pockets.*

It seemed that the occupants of Stonehaven Castle were not averse to going to great lengths to protect their privacy.

Josie returned to the search results on Instagram and continued to scroll through mentions of the castle. One result was from an account called 'Scotia Catering'. She clicked on the post, which was titled 'Stonehaven Grand Ballroom Community Christmas Reception'. It was dated almost a year ago.

The series of photographs were clearly of a drinks reception at the castle. The photos had all been taken in a huge stone-walled ballroom with lavish chandeliers and impressive tapestries and frescoes. The opulent room was packed with revellers dressed in their finery, all quaffing champagne and gorging on plates of delicious-looking canapés.

Stonehaven Castle thanking the local community for all their support was emblazoned on a large banner suspended across the ancient-looking joists.

A smiling waitress held aloft a huge silver platter adorned with prawns on cocktail sticks. She was surrounded by hungry-looking locals, and her black apron had a logo on the chest that read *Scotia Catering*.

Josie's fingers flashed across the keys, and she smiled at the results on the screen.

She picked up her phone and dialled.

'Josie, my girl. What you up to?' said Jacko.

'Jacko, where are you?'

'In the boozer near my gaff, why?'

'I need something and I need it fast. I'm coming to find you.'

Chapter 38

Asquith let himself into his flat on a quiet street in Hampstead and yawned as he kicked off his shoes on the tiled floor. He hung his coat on the stand in the corner before slipping his feet into his favourite tweed carpet slippers.

He ignored the blinking light on the phone in the hall, in the same way that he had been ignoring the numerous calls from his wife, who was at their country home in rural Bedfordshire. He resolved that he'd bite that bullet and call her soon, a task he was not looking forward to, as he suspected that she would be a little testy, to say the least, about the amount of time he'd spent away from home.

He walked through to the kitchen, flicking the lights on as he did, and switched on the kettle, desperate for a cup of tea. Then he pulled out his Mac and flipped it open, navigating to the research document that Nigel, the analyst, had put together. It was astounding how much detail he had managed to uncover in a short amount of time, and Neil could see why he was paid as much as he was. There were building plans, energy performance data, electrical diagrams and lots of other technical details.

He'd just spent a couple of hours with Nigel in the London offices of Legacy Risk Management, the company he had founded with his business partner thirty years ago.

After leaving the marines in the late 1980s, Asquith had joined the Foreign Office, working in Sudan and Congo, but he'd found the job frustrating and decided that being part of a huge government organisation just wasn't for him. So he started Legacy with an FO colleague, Michael Jeffries, who had been a major in the Intelligence Corps. The company had grown rapidly, and soon they were one of the go-to security and risk management specialists for many major corporations who operated in hostile environments, particularly as the Gulf conflicts began to bite. They were soon advising NGOs and many other organisations, and had also developed advanced intelligence systems to provide up-to-date information and risk factors of operational theatres. They had diversified into advising companies and providing business reassurance on security and counter-intelligence systems to prevent industrial espionage. Soon they had two hundred contractors operating in twenty-eight countries, and a whole team of analysts who led the way in the burgeoning market of data protection and risk management.

This new world of private intelligence was suddenly a growth industry, and they'd got in early. The company grew rapidly, and soon he and Michael were having to deal with becoming comparatively wealthy very quickly. Beverley, his wife, took to it immediately, buying the large country pile in Bedfordshire, and then the London flat. Expensive cars, prestige watches and extensive wardrobes soon followed, none of which really interested Asquith. He had not grown up in privilege. His family was solid lower middle class, and he'd gone to a grammar school, where he had done only moderately well, but his love of sport and physical activity had made him a good fit for the marines. It had been something of a shock when, straight after his training, he was sent to the Falklands.

His eyes moved to the photograph on the wall of his troop not long after the battle of Mount Harriet. He was standing next to Chappers, who had one of his hands on his shoulder, a big grin on his filthy face. Asquith's heart lurched at the sight of his old friend and mentor. He'd been the troop commander that day in 1982, but he knew for sure that he wouldn't have got through any of it had it not been for the steadying influence of Chappers. He was honest enough to know that he had lost it that day. He was only just twenty, fresh out of training, and he'd needed his section corporal to show him what it was to lead men in battle.

He opened the document that had recently been emailed to him and scanned the basic information about Bruzek, much of which he'd already had sight of. Many of the details were opaque, but it did seem like Bruzek had profited after the so-called 'velvet divorce' of the Czech Republic and Slovakia in 1992.

There did not seem to be an obvious source to his wealth, but he certainly had many fingers in many pies. Heavy investment in businesses, and property and the purchase of state-owned steel businesses, all of which he sold for an undisclosed, but rumoured massive sum of money.

Asquith looked with distaste at the photograph of the man in full military uniform with a colourful group of medal ribbons on his chest. He'd sold a number of businesses and factories and his enormous property portfolio in the early 2000s, and invested much of the proceeds in the booming UK property market, buying up large, decrepit industrial units up and down the country and renovating them into luxury apartments. He then diversified into office blocks, and very soon he was one of the leading property magnates across many northern English cities, where he quickly benefited from the overheating market. It seemed that whatever he touched turned to solid gold.

He purchased Stonehaven Castle in 2012, and at that point he was seen by the local community as a saviour, as the causeway was crumbling and dangerous, meaning that access to the outcrop was soon banned on safety grounds. He immediately invested heavily, and employed local firms to repair the causeway and open the ancient castle to visitors once again. He then spent millions more shoring up the sea defences and making the crumbling buildings safe.

It all changed with his application to develop the outcrop, restore many of the outbuildings and build a modern subterranean home. There was some degree of push-back from some in the locality, and injunctions were sought by a pressure group, but the application went through with only mild difficulties. There were suggestions of money changing hands and planning committee members being bought off, but nothing could be proved. The support of the Professor of History at Aberdeen University was key, and the promise of employment and regular open days was also significant. A slick presentation by a swanky London media relations team persuaded the planning committee that the best chance Stonehaven Castle had of surviving for future generations was with Bruzek's money behind it.

Once planning was agreed and a construction warrant issued, building started immediately, and within two years, Bruzek had moved in, together with numerous staff. The property was now astounding. A long, low structure made of local stone with turrets at each end on the footprint of where the castle would have once stood. Many of the outbuildings had been restored and were apparently guest or staff accommodation.

It seemed that Bruzek allowed the public into certain parts of the development on the regular open days, or at the receptions for civic dignitaries that took place in the grand ballroom. There were a number of photographs of him at these receptions shaking hands with important-looking local people, including a very senior policeman, military officers and a distinguished-looking man wearing a chain of office around his neck. Clearly he wanted it known that he was connected in all the right places.

Asquith gave a low whistle, thinking of the difficulty he himself had had just getting planning permission to put a small extension on the back of his Bedfordshire home. It was clear that Bruzek was an expert in exerting pressure on decision-makers. However, perhaps most telling was the fact that there was not a single photograph of the newly built underground parts of the house.

Asquith was about to flick to the next page of the report when he heard a key in the door. Almost as if electrocuted, he slammed the computer shut just as Beverley stomped into the kitchen hand in hand with Allegra, their six-year-old granddaughter. She flashed a look of pure venom at him, but said nothing.

'Grandpa!' squealed the delighted little girl as she leapt into Asquith's arms, burying her face against his neck in glee. She smelt of shampoo, popcorn and that indescribable essence of Allegra. He breathed it in like fine wine.

'Hello, my best girl.' He kissed her on the top of her head.

'Granny took me to the panto,' she said, her eyes shining with excitement and her face full of sunshine. Allegra was the apple of Asquith's eye, and she very much returned the sentiment, much to Beverley's chagrin.

'Oh no she didn't,' chimed Asquith as he stroked her straw-berry-blonde hair.

Allegra frowned. 'Yes she did. Tell him, Granny.' Her voice was a touch haughty at her grandpa's insolence.

'Oh no you didn't,' repeated Asquith, grinning widely, his voice an octave higher than previously.

'Grandpa is teasing you, darling. It's like in the panto.' Beverley's own voice was shot through with shades of lemon juice and vinegar.

A huge grin split Allegra's face, showing gappy teeth. 'Grandpa, you're so naughty,' she giggled.

Beverley marched over and took her hand. 'Come on, darling, would you like to watch some TV?' Her eyes flashed querulously at Asquith.

'Ooh, yes please. Mummy never lets me watch TV this late.'

'Our secret, sweetie. I'll make you some cocoa as well.'

Allegra squealed with joy and skipped off with Beverley. Asquith's belly churned with anxiety. His wife was no shy and retiring type, and he knew what was coming when she returned to the kitchen.

'Darling—' he began as she appeared in the doorway.

'Don't you bloody "darling" me. Where the hell have you been?' she demanded, her pale cheeks spotted red with anger. She pulled her furry hat from her head and shook out her neatly bobbed red hair before fixing him with the icy stare he knew only too well. They'd been married a long time, and he truly loved her, but she was fiery and ferocious if she thought she was being deceived.

'I didn't know you were using the flat.'

'That's not answering my question. I told you last week I was taking Allegra to the pantomime, but you never bloody listen. So what *have* you been doing?'

'Just a little bit of work.'

'Nonsense. You quit three years ago and haven't done a thing since.'

'But I—'

'Don't even try lying to me, Neil. Are you having an affair?' She glared at him, arms folded and her foot tapping.

'Bev, that's ridiculous. Look, I'm here on my own, with my laptop, and about to make a cup of tea. I've been working.'

Her face softened a little and she pulled out one of the bar stools and sat next to him.

'You haven't been answering my calls, you've not been home, and it's only because you'd forgotten I was using the flat tonight that I even caught up with you. Ever since Frankie died you've been absent, even when we've been in the same bloody room. What the hell is going on?'

'It's complicated.'

She stood and went to the fridge and took out a bottle of

wine. After pouring it into two glasses, she handed one to Neil.

'Try me.' She held her glass up, and they chinked and drank. There was a long pause, only disturbed by the whirring of the fridge.

'It's to do with Chappers.'

'Chappers? But surely the burglar was caught?'

'There's more to it than that.'

'I'm listening.' She leant forward and propped her chin on her steepled fingers.

'It's his medals.'

'What about them? The scumbag sold them on, so what can you do?' Her eyes narrowed.

'We've got a lead on where they are.'

'So? Tell the police.'

'That won't work. They're not interested, and anyway, they wouldn't be able to get a warrant.'

'Why not?'

'Because we got the evidence by slightly unconventional means.'

'We? Who's we?'

'Just the others, you know. Macca, Jacko and Charlie.'

Beverley shook her head in exasperation. 'Neil, you left the marines thirty-odd year ago. You're not the police. Is this some load of old nonsense that you and the 11/06 have come up with?'

Asquith shrugged.

'What the hell are you going to do? You're all old sods now. You've a terrible back and high blood pressure, and you've got a damn family. You're not to go running about storming buildings. I forbid it.' She sipped angrily at her wine.

'I have to try something. Josie deserves to get her father's medals back. We have to do something if the police won't.'

'Is it just you four old duffers involved in this farce?'

'Josie wants to be part of it too; she's the one losing out here. Macey's nursing home fees are massive, and the medals were her insurance policy.' Asquith sipped his wine, the condensation making his fingers wet. It was cool and soothing.

'God, you're deluded! And bloody Jacko? He's a sodding criminal. You used to run a multimillion-pound business and now you're consorting with thieves and hoodlums.' Beverley slammed her glass down, and the contents slopped onto the granite. Her green eyes fixed him with the hardest of stares, and Asquith knew that he would have to sell her a line she would accept or she'd never let it go.

'Look, all we're trying to do is locate the medals, then we'll present the evidence to the police once we have enough for them to use and they can get them back, okay?'

Beverley's eyes narrowed, looking for an indication that he was lying. Asquith kept his face totally impassive, knowing that any tic, movement or scratch would be interpreted as a sign of deceit.

'Are you staying here tonight?' she said.

'Are you?'

She looked at her watch. 'It's almost nine, so yes. I want to get Allegra to bed pronto. You can come home to Bedfordshire tomorrow.'

'Maybe. We may have a lead that means I have to travel at short notice.'

'Travel where?'

He hesitated. 'Not sure,' he stumbled.

'Neil?' she said, her eyes narrowing even more.

'Honestly, I don't know, but I have to do this, Bev. I owe Chappers everything. He stopped me from failing my men all those years ago and saved my life. I can't forget that, and I can't let the 11/06 down.'

Beverley exhaled and rolled her eyes. Neil knew that she could read him like a book. 'Can I talk you out of it?'

He shook his head. 'Sorry, love. Just give me until Christmas to do what we have to do.'

'More wine?' She proffered the bottle.

'Sure.' He pushed his glass forward and she refilled it.

'Well, you'd best be back and normal for bloody Christmas. Edward and Juliet are coming with all of theirs, and I've a huge turkey that I ordered from Jephson's.'

'I'll be there.'

'You'd better be. If I find out you're lying, Neil Asquith, I'll remove your testicles with a rusty spoon with jagged edges. Clear?' Beverley smiled, but her eyes were hard.

Neil gulped his wine, feeling his cheeks flush. 'Clear.'

Chapter 39

Saturday 18 December 2021

'So, what experience do you have, Miss McLeish?' said the bald man who had introduced himself as Grigor. His Polish-accented voice carried a trace of Scots. He sat back in his chair, which creaked arthritically, and studied the driving licence and single sheet of paper that had been presented by the young woman in front of him. *Scotia Catering* was emblazoned on the front of his polo shirt.

They were sitting in the drab office of a small unit on an industrial estate in Spurryhillock, on the outskirts of Stonehaven. The walls were stained and scuffed and the windows were almost opaque with dust. An ancient-looking calendar advertising catering equipment was affixed to the wall, adding to the tired decor.

'Lots of bar work, some event catering,' said Mary McLeish, brushing a stray strand of red hair behind her ear.

'References look okay, but there's a bit of a gap from last year to now?' He peered over the top of his glasses, the harsh overhead light reflecting in his shiny scalp.

'Travelling.'

'Anywhere nice?'

'Not really.' Her accent was educated, but with a soft Scottish burr.

'Okay, well we're really short of staff, so can you start immediately? Brexit makes keeping staff so bloody hard. They all piss off back to Poland now.' He sniggered.

'Aye, I can start immediately.'

'Where you staying?'

'Airbnb in town.'

'What bring you to Stonehaven?' He sat forward, suddenly more alert.

'Relationship breakdown. I needed to get away and be somewhere else for a while. Here seemed as good a place as any, and I like the sea air. Plus, I hear that the famous Stonehaven fireball festival at Hogmanay is worth seeing.' She pursed her lips, signalling that she didn't want this line of questioning to continue.

'I have room at my place if you want?' he said, a slight leer on his stubbly face.

'I'm good.'

'You sure? Cheaper than Airbnb.'

'Positive, and I've already paid for a week,' she added, staring at her unmanicured nails with disinterest.

'Suit yourself, if you have coin to waste, eh. So, you want the job?'

'Aye, what's it entail?'

'Mostly setting up and running Christmas parties, some in Aberdeen, some in Stonehaven. We have a real big one coming up at Stonehaven Castle. You hear about it?'

'I saw the sign, but I've not heard much. I'm from Arbroath.'

'Huge clifftop place owned by a Slovak billionaire on the site of an ancient castle. He has to have three parties a year to keep stupid locals happy. Christmas one is the biggest. It's in three days. Tell me you can do it. It pays well.' His eyes almost radiated desperation.

'How much?'

'Twelve pounds an hour. Better than average. It'll be set-up the day before, getting the ballroom ready, and then bringing booze and canapés in. Then the next evening it's from five till finish. Just walk around looking pretty with trays of champagne and nibbles. All local bigwigs go – chief constable, provost, councillors – and everyone gets very excited.'

'Fine.'

'Okay, meet me here at twelve, Tuesday, and we go in minibus with others to set up ready for the event on Wednesday, okay?'

'Can't I take my own car?' she said, brow furrowing.

'No, the owner doesn't let private cars on the castle grounds. It's only accessible by funny road in sea, and no car park on rock. We go in minibus.'

'I'll be ready,' she said, her eyes flat with boredom. Clearly catering contracting wasn't her life's dream.

'Okay, nice to have you on board, Mary. Don't be late.' He nodded dismissively and lowered his gaze back to his pile of invoices.

Mary stood and walked out of the office into the icy morning air. Her car, an ageing Ford Fiesta, was parked nearby, and she stood beside it breathing steadily, her gut fizzing with excitement.

Josie Chapman was getting used to playing other characters. She chuckled, thinking that the boys were either going to be pissed off at her or very impressed. She didn't care which. The advert for catering staff had been an opportunity, so she'd grabbed it with both hands.

As she stood there, her phone rang. She looked at the screen and felt her stomach flip when she saw it was DI Kelly. Reflexively she answered the call.

'Hi, Josie, it sounds windy where you are.'

'It is a bit blowy. What can I do for you?'

'I've got an update, and it's not good news, I'm afraid. Defence counsel have made representations that the manslaughter charge should be discontinued, and prosecution counsel, Mr Lownie, has conceded that there isn't a reasonable prospect of a conviction, so the CPS have made the decision that they will offer no evidence at the pre-trial preparation hearing. I'm so sorry.'

There was a long pause, only broken by the buffeting of the wind that swirled around her.

'Josie?'

'Yeah, I heard you. Is there anything we can do to appeal the decision?' Josie felt numb. Just burglary. Her dad's life worth only a few measly years in jail for that scumbag Jarman.

'Well, we have the right to review it, but I fear it would be doomed to failure.' DI Kelly's voice was sympathetic.

'Okay, forget it then. When is he likely to be sentenced?'

'He'll probably enter a plea at the pre-trial and preparation hearing, and then the judge will order a pre-sentence report from probation. Again, I'm sorry, Josie. Are you at home? I could come and see you.'

Josie felt a sudden grip of fear, and a realisation that she probably shouldn't have answered the call. She didn't want Kelly knowing she was in Scotland. 'No need. I'm with a friend in St Albans. I'll see you at the next hearing. Look, I have to go, thanks for calling me.' She hung up and exhaled before climbing into the car, her stomach alive with butterflies.

Her phone pinged in her pocket. She pulled it out and saw it was a message from Macca on the team WhatsApp: *Josie, where the hell are you?* She scrolled up and saw a succession of messages from the others all asking the same question, and she sniggered at the thought of the confusion. After seeing the photos on Instagram from Scotia Catering, it had been really simple. A quick look at their website made it clear that they were hiring, and within a few minutes, she had an appointment for an interview. She'd told Jacko that she needed the fake driving licence he'd procured for hiring some climbing equipment, and as he was half pissed, he didn't question this. Then she'd borrowed a friend's car and made the nine-hour trip north.

She smiled as she started the engine and drove out of the estate towards her Airbnb, calling Macca as she went.

'Jesus, girl. We were getting worried.'

'I've been busy.'

'What do you mean? Everyone's here and you're on loud-speaker, by the way. Where exactly are you?' said Macca, his normally light Scottish drawl deepening.

'Stonehaven.'

'What, Stonehaven as in right next to Stonehaven Castle?'

'Yep.'

'Why are you up there?'

Josie told them about the job. There was a long pause on the line, followed by a long exhalation.

'Hold on. You've managed to get yourself a bloody job at Stonehaven Castle?' said Macca.

'Seems like it.' Josie felt a smile creep onto her face. She suddenly felt a swell of pride.

'I should be pissed off with you for going behind our backs, but it's bloody brilliant work, so I can't.'

'It just kind of happened, so I wanted to do it before anyone got a chance to talk me out of it.'

'Josie, is this phone registered to you?' said Charlie, his voice tight.

'Yes, why?' Josie was puzzled.

'Okay, listen carefully, this is important. Leave the phone switched on, but don't make any other calls after this one, especially not to any of us. They can't know we're travelling to Scotland, hence we're going to leave our registered phones down here and use burners.'

'But I've just spoken to DI Kelly. She called to tell me about the CPS dropping the manslaughter charge.'

There was a pause on the line before Charlie spoke again. 'Did you tell her you were in Scotland?'

'No, should I have done?'

'It doesn't really matter. You need a cover story as to why you've gone up there in case she asks, so think of a good reason. Maybe you wanted to get away for some quiet time and you didn't tell her because you wanted to be left alone, something like that.'

'I told her that I was in St Albans. Have I messed up?' she said, tension in her voice.

'No, but we just need to have answers in case.'

'Okay, understood, sorry.'

'Don't fret about it. Buy a burner phone and SIM with cash from somewhere and then send me a WhatsApp to my usual number from it, not a text, okay? Cops can't intercept WhatsApp, and it just shows as data, rather than calls. We're all moving to burners when we travel north, so I'll message you, and we'll use new phones to communicate.

'Understood.'

'Make sure you install the tracker app for the medal box and the listening device app for the antiques shop so you can keep monitoring them. All comms on those secure phones after you've moved over.' Charlie's voice was soft and full of understanding.

'I'm sorry, I just didn't think. I was so excited I'd got the job and was going to get access to the castle. It's not like you lot include me in your decision-making, is it? Anyway, you'd have tried to talk me out of it.' Josie felt her cheeks grow hot.

There was a long silence on the line, and she prepared herself for the inevitable bollocking.

It didn't come. Instead, Macca just sounded impressed.

'It's fine, it's a brilliant move. Did you use your own car?'

'No, mine's old and knackered and I didn't fancy risking it. I borrowed one off a friend.'

'That's great. You're a marvel, Josie. We'd have had no chance at this, but now you're going to be able to properly recce the castle. How's your Scottish accent?'

'Aye, pal, I've a wee job at Stonehaven Castle starting the day after tomorrow. I've an Airbnb rented, a nice place big enough for all of us. I'll send the details by WhatsApp.' She had slipped almost effortlessly into a soft Scottish accent.

'Nae bad, hen,' said Macca, sounding surprised.

'Dinnae ken whit you're blethering about, pal. Three years in school in Arbroath. Get yersels up here, and dinnae spare the horses. We've a heist to plan.'

Chapter 40

'Jesus, that girl has more balls than the rest of us put together, but she's not one for team ethos. Why the hell didn't she bloody tell us?' said Macca.

'She's reckless, but she's got talent. I'm thankful she didn't use her own car,' said Charlie.

'Impetuousness of youth. She's more resourceful than any of us old duffers, right?' Macca shook his head in admiration. 'It's just possible that we could succeed on this job, and if we do, then most of the credit will be hers. She got us Grigson's phone, she got the bug in Hunter's place, and now she's got into the castle.'

They all nodded in agreement.

'I did wonder why she called me while I was in the boozer, wanting the snide driving licence I'd procured,' Jacko said. 'I didn't totally believe her story about hiring equipment, but I was too pissed to care. By the way I have all yours here.' He pulled an envelope out of his pocket, and dropped it on the breakfast bar in his kitchen.

'You never told us you gave her the fake licence.'

'I was shit-faced. Slipped my mind.'

'Blimey, Jacko. These are bloody good,' said Charlie, looking at the fake cards.

'Coming from an ex-DCI, I'll take that as a compliment. They were a grand each, but we don't want to be travelling on our own deets, do we?'

'Definitely not. I want no record of us going to Scotland.' Charlie held his new licence up to the light, and nodded, clearly impressed.

Jacko nodded in agreement. 'I must point out, boys, that simple possession of these is enough to get you lifted and charged with a pretty serious offence, so don't keep them anywhere obvious, and don't produce them unless there's a very good reason. They link to real people, even if they do happen to be dead, so if the cops check on DVLA, they'll find genuine driver records. Just remember the names.'

'I'm not having this,' said Asquith, his voice full of outrage.

'Why, what's up?' said Jacko, trying to keep a smile from breaking out.

'My name on this bloody licence.' Asquith slammed it down on the counter-top.

'Sorry, mate, I don't remember yours,' Jacko said, unable to disguise a chuckle.

'Piss off, you knew what you were doing. I can't use this. Hugo Smellie?'

There was sudden uproarious laughter in the kitchen.

'Posh bloke's name, innit. No way could I carry that off, but you can. Wasn't there a Para officer called Smellie in the Falklands?'

'Aye, there was. A decent officer, and a fine name, Neil. It suits you,' said Macca, grinning.

'Definitely look like a Hugo,' Charlie said, tears running down his cheeks.

'All right, all right. Safe to say I'm not doing any of the bloody driving. Now can we get on? Have you all had a chance to look at the research document I sent you?'

'Yeah, it's brilliant. I wish I'd had an analyst of that quality working for me when I was on the NCA,' said Charlie. 'Lots to look into, but Bruzek is a right shady bastard and I'm not happy about the level of contacts he clearly has. Did you clock the chummy photos of him and the chief constable of Police Scotland, not to mention the local sheriff, provost and Christ knows who else? One thing's for sure, anything official done by the local cops would leak.' He shook his head in exasperation.

'Jacko, did you get a car?' asked Macca.

'I did better than that. I figured we don't want to be all mob-handed in one vehicle, so I got two for flexibility. A Toyota Hilux with a nice big load area in case we need to carry lots of shit, and also a rather dull Volvo XC60, though it's sound as a pound.'

'You managed to procure two cars with twenty grand?' said Asquith, eyes wide with surprise.

'Well, it's just possible that they're a mite iffy, but they've been expertly rung. It would take a proper vehicle examiner to tell they'd been cloned.'

'Cloned? What do you mean?'

'I keep forgetting that you muggy straights don't understand my world. Cloned is just a hooky car that's been given a makeover to look like an identical model. Switched plates and fiddled frame numbers and it's all good. The only time you'll get grief is if you start pinging lots of speed cameras, and then the genuine plate owner will start getting a bit antsy when tickets keep coming. That's when Old Bill get told that there's a cloned car roving around Scotland, despite the real car never having left Surbiton.'

'Jacko, we can't afford to get nicked in hooky cars. How long have they been laid up for?' said Charlie.

'Long enough for the insurance to pay out, so the original owners ain't interested. My mate is one of the best ringers out there, boys. If we ever get stopped, we're just on holiday from Surbiton going fishing in Scotland.'

'What, you mean they were genuinely stolen from Surbiton?' said Asquith, his face registering discomfort at the conversation.

'Yep. Both nicked six months ago, and holed up in a lock-up while they had their IDs changed. Safe as houses.'

'Jesus. Why can't we just use regular cars?' asked Asquith.

'Too much of a paper trail. We've no idea what we'll have to do to get these medals back, and we could end up causing a bit of grief that might attract the attention of the local constabulary. We need to leave no trace whatsoever that we've been in Scotland. So no cars attributable to us, and our personal phones have to stay home. All understand?' said Charlie.

'Bev will not be happy about that,' said Asquith.

'Neither will Alice,' said Charlie, massaging his temples. 'She's been pissed at me all week for hanging out with you buggers too much, and I still haven't told her I'm going away for a few days. She'll go radio rental.'

'Problem with you married boys. Too much baggage. Me and Macca can just drop everything and go, whereas you two with your ball and chains get all sorts of grief.' Jacko sniggered, his eyes glinting with mischief.

'Oh, I dunno. Macca has his Yank spook bird,' said Charlie.

Macca just shook his head and changed the subject. 'So, we all have all the kit we discussed?'

They all nodded.

'And Josie's climbing gear?'

'Yes, and don't bloody ask how much it cost,' said Asquith.

'I won't. I've made some calls to old contacts, and some specialist equipment is ready for us to collect as soon as we're ready.'

'Is that going to cost me as well?'

'No, a loan. No charge unless we break it, but if Jacko is involved, that's a significant risk, right?'

'Hey, I resent that remark,' protested Jacko with false indignation.

'Anything else?' asked Macca.

'I know we don't want to talk about it, but I'm gonna say it anyway,' said Jacko. 'Guns?'

A thick silence descended on the room. Just that one word reinforced what they were all thinking. They were getting into something big, with high stakes, and possibly extremely dangerous. They all looked at each other in turn, the serious, hard faces of men who'd seen combat, had seen friends and comrades die.

'What do we all think? I can get some easy enough from my old PMC contacts,' said Macca.

'No guns. We go into that castle tooled up with shooters and the cops get hold of us, they'll throw away the key. I don't mind taking a risk, but going in armed takes this to a level I'm not comfortable with.' Charlie's voice was low and determined.

'Agreed,' said Asquith.

'What if *they* have guns?' said Jacko.

'I don't think they will,' said Macca. 'Neil's intelligence package only has one regular bodyguard identified, who seems more of a PA to me, despite the fact that he's ex-Slovakian Special Forces. We can't plan this raid until we see it for ourselves. Josie has worked a miracle by getting access to the castle, and hopefully that will give us a big advantage, but the whole ethos of this task has to be to get in and out without being seen, yeah?'

'What if Josie sees shooters? Does that change things?' said Jacko quietly.

'Change things how?' said Macca.

'Do we still do the job?'

'As far as I'm concerned, yes. How about you two?' He looked at Asquith and Charlie in turn.

Charlie sighed and ran his hands over his bald head in frustration. 'Shit, this is hard, boys. I was a cop for thirty years, and now we're talking about an armed raid on a bloody castle. You know what they'd do to an ex-cop in jail, right?'

'I'm still in.' Asquith's voice was low and even, but shot through with determination.

'Genuinely?' said Jacko.

'Chappers saved me on Harriet. Without him, I'm not sure I'd have survived. I won't let him down again. I'm in, whatever it takes. I'll go in there and shoot every bastard who gets in my way if necessary, and I'm willing to die trying.'

The familiar silence was tense and uncomfortable as the four old soldiers sat deep in thought.

'Charlie, how about this,' said Macca eventually. 'We travel up, do the recce and see what live intelligence Josie comes up with. If it looks clear of guns, we do the job without, but if we see there are shooters on site, we re-evaluate.'

Charlie drummed his fingers on the work surface, his eyes fixed on his hands as he breathed in and out, deeply.

'Okay, fine. We recce the site and plan the operation like we would as bootnecks and then decide what's next in the light of that.'

'So you're still in?' said Jacko.

'I'm still in.'

'Good, saves me referring to you as REMF Charlie Drake, then.' His serious face broke into a broad, chipped-toothed smile. REMF was military speak for 'rear-echelon mother-fucker'.

Chuckles began in the room, soon developing into full-throated laughs.

'We're all good then?' said Macca, slapping the work surface with his open palm.

'Roger that,' they said in unison.

'Right then, we say our last goodbyes to the significant others, make sure all the cover stories are in place for the fishing trip, and hit the road turbo early tomorrow morning.'

Chapter 41

Sunday 19 December 2021

Josie laced up her Asics trainers, pulled on a pair of thin gloves and jammed her AirPods into her ears. She selected the Cure on the music app on her new cheap smartphone she'd bought earlier and stepped out into the strong breeze being whipped in from the North Sea. Still looking at the phone, she opened the GPS tracker app that Neil had shared with them all. A blue blob pulsed on the map just south of her location. She zoomed in tight on the signal and switched to satellite view. Stonehaven Castle was visible, the long main building, outbuildings and ruined walls. The blue marker was slap-bang in the centre of the main house. She minimised the map and tucked the phone away in her pocket. It was a little bulkier than her iPhone, which was currently in a box in the post office in Stonehaven, waiting to head south to the house in Sandridge.

She'd rented a four-bedroom farmhouse from Airbnb on the outskirts of Stonehaven. It was perfect, as it was self-check-in, with the key in a small lock box, meaning there was no need to meet the host. It was also warm and cosy, with a decent Wi-Fi signal.

She checked her fitness tracker and set off at a brisk pace, her breath escaping in clouds of vapour as she felt the familiar warmth flood into her body. She headed away from the town and followed the cliff trail, which stretched ahead up the steep incline hugging the coastline. The weather was bright and clear, but there were bruise-coloured clouds amassing on the horizon, and it looked like the weather was about to turn, in the way it often did on this northern corner of Scotland.

Josie felt the stresses begin to leach from her body. She found running cathartic. The tougher and more brutal the distance and terrain, the more she relished the burn in her legs, the heaving chest and the feeling of elation as she punished her teak-tough body.

As she ran, a large red sandstone monument came into view. It looked very much like an old Doric temple, with eight stone pillars mounted on high blocks with a pinkish hue. It was huge and almost intimidating, and she slowed to a stop, her breath immediately returning to normal. As she ascended the steps to a wrought-iron gate, she realised that it was a war memorial. She pushed the gate open and stepped inside, looking around her. Inscribed on the lintel above her head were the words: *One by one death challenged them. One by one they smiled in his grim visage and refused to be dismayed.* A light grey memorial stone in the centre of the monument bore the names of the fallen. Wreaths of poppies had been laid at its foot.

As she stared at the words again, she felt her chest tighten and the familiar lump in her throat arrive, as it always did at war memorials. Tears began to prick her eyes at the thought of her brave, kind dad, his life cut short to satisfy some rich man's desire to possess. She cuffed the tears away, then turned and descended the steps.

It only took her twelve minutes to cover the two miles to the castle, and as she ascended the final steep gradient, she stopped dead at the view that met her.

Stonehaven Castle was perched on a flat expanse of green turf, which looked oddly out of place sitting over a hundred feet above the sparkling North Sea, supported by sheer sandstone cliffs. She stood there breathing hard, taking in the narrow causeway built on a crumbling strip of land that was the only thing connecting the outcrop to the mainland.

She looked down to the base of the cliff, where a small pebbly beach was visible now that the tide was at its lowest. Pulling out her phone, she navigated to the tide app, and using the location function realised that she probably didn't have long before the sea was lapping against the rock face. She replaced her phone in her pocket and set off down the steep incline towards the sea.

It only took ten minutes before she hit the pale sand of the deserted beach and began to jog towards the towering cliff three hundred metres away. As she approached, she viewed the rock face with a climber's eye. She estimated that the cliff was at least fifty metres in height, and the surface looked to be solid enough for a climber of her ability, but would be tricky for the others.

As she looked out towards the sea, she saw that the gentle waves were lapping closer, but this was an unmissable opportunity. She pulled out her phone and took some snaps of the cliff face, and some closer ones of the rock's make-up.

Tucking her phone back into her pocket, she walked along the edge of the cliff, studying it with a professional eye. She reached out and touched the surface, feeling the cool, rough texture of the ancient sandstone. It felt familiar and comforting. About two feet above her was a good-looking finger-hold. She was confident she could deal with it, but was less sure about her comrades, who were all bigger, heavier, older and a lot more broken than she was.

She leapt up, reaching her arm out and snapping her four fingers into the crevice in the rock. They caught immediately, and she pulled herself up, reaching with her free hand and finding a perfect crack that she could grab onto. Her trainer-clad feet scrabbled for purchase.

She released her grip on the rock and fell back softly to the sand.

She could climb that rock face without much difficulty – of that she was sure. If she was grading the route to the top, she'd estimate it to be 'difficult' on the adjectival scale. She'd need a decent length of good rope and at least eight spring-loaded camming devices for safety, but it certainly wasn't an insurmountable climb. No problem for her as an elite climber, but probably impossible for the others. Even if Macca had been adequate in his time, he was now over sixty, with arthritis in his wrists, a dicky shoulder and a suspect knee – not that he'd ever admit to it.

Her phone buzzed in her pocket and, pulling it out, she saw that it was an activation on the listening device that she'd planted in the antiques shop. He heart fluttered a little. It seemed Hunter was back home. She opened the app and pressed play on the icon.

Initially there was just the sound of the door opening and someone coughing, before a phone ringtone was audible.

'Hi, Danilo . . . Yes, I'm back now. Please do extend my thanks to the General for his hospitality. I had a marvellous time.'

There was a pause as Hunter listened.

'Dubai? When?'

Another pause.

'Well, yes, of course I understand he wants his collection cata-logued and then transported appropriately, but surely it doesn't have to be me?' He sighed heavily. 'Ten thousand pounds? I guess that changes things. Okay, let me make a note . . . fly to Aberdeen on the twenty-third at midday, and then we all fly together to Dubai at ten a.m. Christmas Eve. Well, I had no plans and it'll be a lovely holiday, I'm sure. I've heard that the General's Dubai home is something else.'

Jodie looked up from the phone, her face flushing. Christmas Eve?

She dialled Macca's new number.

'Josie?'

'Macca, where are you guys?'

215

'On our way up, why?'

'We have a problem, and we need to accelerate the plan.' Josie described what she'd just heard over the listening device.

'We need to do this job on the twenty-third latest, then. When do you start at the castle?' said Macca.

'Tuesday at twelve, and then back the following day for the reception.'

'Too risky to do it with heaps of civilians about; too many witnesses and more chance of collateral. We need the castle as quiet as it can be. So we do it the day after the event, or at the latest the day after that, which will be the twenty-second. At least you'll have had some time to get the lie of the land. Fuck, that's tight.'

'We can do it. We *have* to do it. Once they've gone to Dubai, they're gone for ever.'

Chapter 42

Marek Bruzek sat in the library in his leather chesterfield and took a deep, satisfying draw on his Cuban cigar, letting the rich, fragrant smoke trail from his nostrils. Despite the fact that it was mid afternoon, he was still dressed in his pyjamas and wore a silk dressing gown and a pair of bespoke slippers with a low heel and lifts inside that gave him an extra inch in height. He stood and walked across the oak floor towards the full-length windows, against which torrential rain was lashing, propelled by a fierce wind sweeping in from the sea. He looked down at the frothing slate-grey water topped with foam as it smashed into the cliffs a hundred and fifty feet below.

He loved being at the castle with all his heart, but the winters could be long and the days so short that he sometimes longed for some sunshine. He was used to the harsh climate, but his wealth meant he could escape any time he chose, which he'd made the decision to do upon seeing the weather this morning. And to think that it had looked like being a beautiful day when he'd woken, only for the clouds to rush to obliterate the weak sun.

His home in Dubai was palatial, and he could spend Christmas with beautiful young women by his pool, where the temperature would be a very pleasant mid twenties rather than the close-to-zero that it was here.

There was a gentle tap at the door, and the huge form of Danilo appeared, casually dressed in gym gear, his forehead spotted with sweat. 'General,' he said, bowing his head deferentially.

'Arrangements made?'

'Yes. Hunter is returning on the twenty-third and will catalogue and package the medals in preparation for moving them. Havel is filing a flight plan, and we'll depart for Dubai the following morning, as you ordered.'

'Have you contacted Samir?' Bruzek took another long pull on his cigar and turned back to the window.

'Yes. He is getting the house ready and has arranged for Michel from LaFond to cook for you and the guests on Christmas Day.'

Bruzek smiled at the prospect of having one of the best chefs in Dubai prepare his Christmas lunch. 'Excellent. Wine?'

'Michel is liaising with his sommelier and will email his suggestions to accompany the menu. Their cellar is extensive. He also has asked if you would like any Slovakian dishes. He thinks he can accommodate.'

'No. No peasant food. His best French menu.' Bruzek's face was hard. He hadn't escaped poverty in Slovakia only to now consume sausage meat, fish stew and potato salad.

'As you wish.'

'Have dinner invitations gone out?'

Danilo chuckled. 'Thankfully, the fact that most of your guests don't celebrate Christmas means that everyone's available, including General Hammad, who has just returned to Dubai.'

'I should think so, bearing in mind the contribution I made to his recent political campaign fund. Have you told him of the medal collection?'

'I think that's why he agreed to come. I'm told that his own

218

collection is quite something, and I think he wants to compare.'

'Pah, his collection will pale into insignificance next to mine, that is for sure, particularly with my latest additions. The fool will weep when he sees what I have. I'll have Giles explain the significance of them, just to ram it home.' A smile stretched across Bruzek's face, his thin lips parting to reveal his blindingly white perfect teeth.

'You still want to take all the girls?' There was something in Danilo's tone, and a trace of a frown crossed the General's face.

'I know that look. A problem?' He craned his neck to look up at the giant of a man.

'It's Petra – she doesn't want to go. She's become difficult, to say the least, and it's making the other girls restless.'

Bruzek felt a flush of anger rise and his cheeks redden, but beyond that he gave no outward sign of the fury he felt. He never showed anger, preferring actions over words. Petra was from a slum in Slovakia and had been brought to Scotland to be one of his companions. She and two other girls lived in the luxurious guest accommodation in one of the outbuildings that had been completely renovated, and were at his beck and call whenever he felt the urge for female company.

His voice remained even, its high pitch at odds with the look on his face. 'That's unacceptable, Danilo. The silly girl was living in poverty in Slovakia. I have given her a life of luxury, and that is how she repays me? I hope you explained this to her?'

'I did. The others are excited to escape the weather, but Petra is becoming more trouble than she's worth. Maybe we should send her back to the slum for Christmas?' Danilo raised his eyebrows questioningly.

Bruzek sucked on his cigar again and turned to stare out of the window once more, his eyes drawn to the rain lashing against the glass and running down in lazy rivulets onto the rocks below. Beautiful as that damn girl was, she had been so petulant since arriving three months ago. She'd been attentive at first, but was always asking for a little more: trips outside the castle confines, access to a cell phone, and even money for 'services rendered'. She was very young and very beautiful, with long dark hair, a slim waist and large breasts, but she was also unenthusiastic and discourteous, and looked at him with quiet contempt.

Bruzek never got attached to women; they were just products to be acquired, utilised and then discarded when of no further use. They provided a service, in the same way that a tradesman did. If a tradesman's service was no longer effective, then one would dispense with him. He made his decision there and then.

'Send her back to Slovakia. She's just going to corrupt the others. She can be replaced easily enough. Is there a flight today?'

'I've already checked. There's one this evening. I can book her on it and get her out of here immediately. Can I use the helicopter? Time is tight.'

'Make it so. I've had enough of that stupid little girl. And have Renata brought to me. I could use some pleasant company.'

'Yes, sir.' Danilo gave a half-bow and left the room.

Bruzek looked at his watch, a Patek Philippe, and saw that it was just after three. A small whisky would be welcome. He walked over to the drinks trolley, selected what he always described as his 'daytime whisky', a 1970 Macallan Speymalt, and poured a generous measure, inhaling the sherry-cask-aged spirit and detecting all the fruity notes that his dealer had described to him: raisins, pomegranate, sweet tobacco and many other complex aromas and flavours. The bottle had cost almost seven thousand pounds, which was what made it his daytime tipple. On more auspicious occasions, he might avail himself of the very rare 1928 Macallan Anniversary Malt, which lived in the strongroom along with the other valuables. He only drank it occasionally, as it had cost not far short of three hundred thousand pounds, which was in itself a good bit cheaper than the 1926, of which he had two bottles. He had vowed to open one of those once he'd sourced another bottle to complete his collection. They would have cost almost a million each if he'd paid full price for them, which he hadn't. He chuckled at the thought of the rare malts alongside his medals, paintings, prestige antique shotguns and millions of pounds' worth of watches.

All frippery, all simple possessions with a value that could feed thousands of hungry Slovakians. But they were his, and he loved them all. He loved beauty and perfection in all its forms. To possess beauty was to become beauty.

Chapter 43

Petra Garborova was sitting in an armchair in the lounge of the barn, painting her nails. She was dressed in her lounge pants and a hoodie, and her hair was piled up on her head and secured with a scrunchie.

Renata was watching TV, stretched out on a squashy sofa wearing her gym gear. She was a petite eighteen-year-old from Luník IX, a poor province that had been built to house the Roma population. She was strikingly attractive, very slim, with long dark hair that was tied back in a ponytail, and iridescent blue eyes.

They both flinched as the door flew open and the huge form of Danilo entered the room. His hoodie was spotted with raindrops and his scarred bald head glistened in the overhead lights.

'Renata, General Bruzek wants to see you, now,' he barked, his voice deep and gruff as he spoke to her in Slovakian. None of the girls spoke English; they were kept away from all visitors apart from a select trusted few.

'What, dressed like this?' she said, her eyes wide with alarm.

'You look fine. Go now, but take a coat, it's raining.' He pointed at the door, his eyes hard as flint.

'I don't want to go. I'm tired and I'm sore after yesterday.' Despite the beautiful shape and colour of her eyes, they were flat and almost lifeless. Her face was pale and wan, and she trembled.

'It matters not what you want, my girl. You go now, or you know what happens, eh?' growled Danilo.

Renata stood up quickly and crammed her feet into her trainers, brushing her hair back with her shaking fingers and moving to the mirror to check her make-up.

'Quick, don't keep him waiting. You know how he gets when he waits, eh?'

She quickly applied scarlet lipstick to her full lips. 'I'm going, I'm going, I'm sorry, Danilo,' she said, a catch in her throat as she grabbed a grey wool coat from the hook by the door and disappeared outside.

'Poor little Renata. It won't be long before she's as repulsed as I was,' said Petra, her eyes dead and her face pale.

'Shut up and get your things. You're leaving us, right now.'

'What?' she said, sitting upright, her face suddenly alive.

'Yes, hurry up. I have your passport and a ticket. You're on a plane back to Bratislava.'

'Really?' she said, almost in a squeal, a huge smile spreading over her beautiful face.

'You're too much trouble, girl. Hurry, flight in two hours from Aberdeen.'

'But there are no flights from Aberdeen to Slovakia.' Her face was suddenly puzzled.

'Change at Luton. Look, stop messing about. You wanted to go home, you're going home now. Get packed and be ready for the helicopter in ten minutes.'

'Helicopter!' she exclaimed.

'I'd have made you walk, but obviously the General is rewarding all those blow jobs. Now, stop repeating everything I say and just get your shit together, or the deal's off.' He threw her passport and tickets on the coffee table, turned on his heel and left the room.

Petra stood there, heart beating like a drum. She was going home. After the nightmare of the last few months, she was going home. No more having to fuck that hideous little man, no more being forced to sleep with his guests, she was going home. She ran to her room and began to pack, breaking out into a song as she did.

Petra looked excitedly out of the window as the helicopter ascended away from the small circular tarmac pad and rose into the darkening slate-grey sky. It had stopped raining, and she was able to get a good view of the castle disappearing below, the lights twinkling from the windows where she'd been compelled to sleep with Bruzek and his friends. She wrinkled her nose in disgust at some of the things she'd had to do. There had been no trace of the 'great job opportunities' she'd been promised by Bruzek's agent, a stout, matronly woman called Iveta. Instead she had become an old man's plaything, as had Renata and the other girls at the castle. They were just trappings of his extreme wealth. He was disgusting, and she was glad that she'd never have to see him again.

She felt a surge of elation and grinned widely as she extended her middle finger and shouted, 'Screw you to hell and back, Bruzek. You've a tiny cock and terrible breath.' She was thankful for the deafening din of the helicopter, as Danilo wouldn't tolerate any insults directed against his boss. He was such a suck-up, the pussy.

'Flight time fifteen minutes, so don't get comfortable,' said the pilot over the intercom, his voice crackly in her ears.

The aircraft gathered speed as it swept over the darkening mass of the sea, the waves topped with white foam. Petra felt elated about the prospect of going back to Bratislava. Her mother would probably be cross with her, as she hadn't been able to send any money home – which was unsurprising bearing in mind that no one had bothered to pay her anything. She had been well fed and given nice clothes, but the castle was a prison. A luxurious one, yet still a gilded cage. But no more. She was going home.

'You look happy, girl,' came Danilo's crackly voice over the intercom. He was looking at her with a half-smile from his seat directly next to hers.

'For the first time in three months. I was tricked, Danilo. You know this.'

'The General gets what he wants,' he said, shrugging.

'Well, no more. I'll never come back to the UK, and none of you will ever see me again,' she said, her voice hard.

'That is the first sensible thing you've said today, little one.' He sniggered, his small, piggy eyes blank and unfathomable and the smile on his face unpleasant. Petra felt an icy hand grip her stomach.

Before she could react, Danilo had reached underneath the seat and grabbed her ankle. She felt something hard encircle it, followed by a metallic click. She looked down at her trainer-clad feet and saw that a shackle had been attached from which a thin chain snaked away under the seat. She screamed, but the noise was drowned out by the roaring engine of the helicopter.

He reached across her and slid the helicopter door open, allowing a blast of icy air to rush inside. His face was a blank mask, his eyes empty as he looked at her.

'No, please!' she screamed, terror now gripping her like a vice, the blood in her veins suddenly frozen.

She began to flail her arms, hitting out at the huge bodyguard, but it was fruitless. He gave no indication that he could even feel the feeble blows. She screamed again as he unclipped her seat belt then picked up a black cast-iron kettlebell from under the seat and tossed it out of the helicopter. There was a pause of a microsecond before the chain pulled tight and jerked her forcefully and painfully towards the open door. She gripped onto the seat, screeching, her acrylic fingernails tearing off as Danilo prised her hands away. She felt the headphones being ripped from her head as she was dragged towards the door, and the harder she tried to resist, the more futile it became. She was going to die; she knew it right then. It was over.

Then it happened. As she grabbed hold of the seat leg, Danilo's boot loomed, kicking her straight in the face. Her head exploded in a sea of pain, and there was a burst of stars in her eyes as darkness began to arrive.

Then she was falling, arms windmilling, the rushing wind sucking all the air from her body. In a sudden flash, she realised that she didn't care any more. She had died the day she arrived at Stonehaven Castle. Her identity had been snuffed out when they took her passport. She was nobody.

And then there was nothing.

No pain, no fear, just blankness. She welcomed it.

Chapter 44

'You have all the kit I emailed about?' Josie had rushed out to meet the two vehicles that had pulled up outside the Airbnb: a large Toyota and a more modest Volvo. The farmhouse was a substantial single-storey building with a large stone-built barn at the end of a long, sweeping drive. It was surrounded on all sides by conifer trees, and the air was icy cold in the deep shade cast by the foliage.

'Hello, Josie. Yes, we had a lovely trip up, thank you very much, traffic not too bad, thanks for asking. Is the kettle on? It's bloody Harry von Ice Pigs up here, and I could murder a hot wet,' said Jacko, stretching his back as he jumped out of the car grinning sarcastically.

'Sorry. Hello, everyone, and yes, the kettle is on. Come on inside, it's Baltic out here.'

'The bright red hair suits you. Very striking,' said Macca as he pulled a heavy-looking bag out of the car.

'Makes sense to have something people will remember about me that I can easily change.'

'Sensible. We've said it before, you're a natural at this game. Nice gaff, by the way,' added Jacko, lugging in a large holdall, his face straining at the weight of the thing.

'Yeah, it's not bad. Plenty of choice at this time of year. I hope Neil will pick up the tab, though. It's gonna wipe out my credit card. Is that my kit?'

'Yep. Speaking of dosh, you should have seen Asquith's face when we told him how much the powered ascender cost.'

'I almost bloody fell over. It's a good job I built a successful company from scratch rather than robbing people, eh, Jacko?'

'Never robbed anyone, mate. Forget the tea. You got any beer, Jose? I could strangle one. It's been a long bastard drive.'

'Aye, a beer would be welcome. Jacko, can you put the cars in the barn? Makes sense to keep them out of sight, eh?'

'On it. I'll have a piss while I'm at it,' said Jacko, almost skipping out of the house.

'Too much info,' said Macca with a grin.

'He seems happy,' said Josie.

'Yeah, he's been getting progressively more excited the closer we got, which may account for how many pisses he made us stop for, and also the rampant flatulence,' said Charlie, who had come into the cottage also lugging a heavy-looking rucksack.

Macca grinned. 'Curse of being a more mature gentleman. We had to put up with you dripping about the state of your bad foot, Charlie, and Neil was constantly going on about his lumbago. Any food in here?'

'Yep. I've made a pot of range stew, using my dad's recipe.'

'Smells nice,' said Asquith. 'I remember Chappers' range stew; it was always pretty tasty.'

Jacko joined them in the huge kitchen, which was all scrubbed wood, uneven tiles, and copper pans hung up on the low beams. A crock-pot bubbled away on the island, filling the room with a rich, meaty aroma.

'All done, both vehicles away and ready to rock, with full tanks of gas. Mr SBS here made us fill them up down the road. Shite little place where they only took cash. Bugger me, that stew smells essence.' Jacko lifted the lid and sniffed.

'Correction, where they only took *my* cash. I saw no one else offering to pay,' said Asquith, sitting down at the kitchen table and rubbing his hands together.

'All good, though,' said Macca. 'Any time we can pay in cash, we should. The smaller the footprint we leave up here, the better. And on the subject of footprints, Jose, you've not been using your phone?' He looked at her over a pair of wire-framed spectacles.

'No, I left it switched on and popped it in the post, snail mail. I thought that would be confusing if the cops decided to trace it.' She paused and glanced at Charlie. 'I hope that was a good idea?'

'Bloody genius idea, girl. In fact, why the hell didn't I think to suggest it?' He shook his head in admiration.

'Because you were a cop, not a villain, mate. Come on, let's eat. I'm bloody Hank Marvin,' Jacko said, sitting at the table.

'Oh yeah, on the police front, I meant to say that I got a message from an old mate on the NCA. I asked him to share anything known about Bruzek.'

'And?' said Macca.

'Sod all. Just a couple of Interpol enquiries about two young girls reported missing from their homes in Slovakia. There was a suggestion from their families that they were working at a castle in Scotland. Local cops went around and visited Stonehaven along with a couple of others, but there was no trace of them ever having been there and everyone denied all knowledge. Probably a dead end, but it doesn't feel to me like a thorough job was done.'

'Does it impact on what we're doing?' said Asquith.

'No, but it stinks a bit. Trafficking is rife for modern slavery and sexual exploitation in parts of Scotland, and the fact that the cops went away happy and wrote it off seems slack, to say the least. Just thinking back to the cosy photos of Bruzek with senior cops, it all feels a little odd, but at the same time it's not our problem, is it? Anyway, cheers.' Charlie raised his beer bottle.

Within a few minutes, the four ex-marines and Josie were tucking into big bowls of stew, together with crusty bread and bottled beers. They ate silently, each of them alone with their thoughts.

When they had all finished, Macca sat forward in his chair and steepled his fingers in front of him. 'Okay, ideas, plans and timelines? All suggestions welcome.'

'Can I start?' said Asquith, reaching into his bag and pulling out his laptop.

'Go ahead.'

He opened the laptop and tapped on the keys. 'There's basically nothing available on Bruzek, nor on the castle, beyond all the planning kerfuffle, much of which is unavailable on the web. His finances are opaque, to say the least, and the analyst can't access any blueprints or anything about the castle's construction, energy usage or internet access.'

'So bugger all, then?' said Macca.

'Unfortunately, yes. We'll essentially be going in blind. There are photographs of the main hall and ballroom, and plenty of the exterior, but as to what happens underground, nada.'

'Shit.'

'That's what I thought. He clearly values his privacy a great deal.'

'The bastard. So back to the old way of the mark, one human eyeball, eh?' Macca sighed.

'Indeed.' Asquith leant back in his chair and cracked his knuckles.

'Josie, what have you seen?' asked Macca.

'I've recced the cliffs. They're a tough climb for most, but I could easily ascend them quickly. No disrespect, guys, but none of you could.'

'Hold up. I was a mountain leader. I trained in Norway on cliffs and ice climbs. I reckon I could give it a lash,' said Macca, his face flushing a little with indignation.

'Sorry, Macca. I've climbed with you before, and that was ten years ago. You wouldn't have been able to scale it then, and certainly not now with your dicky back and knees, and your piles.'

'Cheeky mare.'

'Just being honest. Anyway, I've a plan for that, and we can put in some practice tomorrow. I've identified a suitable cliff that's broadly similar. I'll get you all up there.'

'No chance of accessing the place in a more conventional way?' asked Asquith.

'I'll know for sure once I've done my first shift at the castle. After that, I'm back again the next day and I can consolidate. You never know what opportunities will arise.'

'You've shown that you're resourceful, but don't get reckless,' warned Macca.

'I won't. No one wants this job to succeed more than me, I can assure you.'

'How about power supply? The castle's pretty big and I doubt it could be totally off-grid.' Macca looked at Asquith.

'Definitely connected to the National Grid. It was part of the planning process, as they didn't want unsightly overhead lines going in. It's fed by a substation a short hop away, and the cable is under the causeway. All in the plans.'

'Backup?'

'Can't be sure, but there is a mention of generators. They wanted solar and wind, but that was turned down at planning committee stage. I suspect it's just grid with diesel generator backup in case of cuts.'

Macca nodded at this and made a note on a small waterproof pad.

'Well, it's two p.m. now. We have an hour's light left. How far away is the castle?' asked Charlie.

'Fifteen minutes.'

'Then let's go and have a look. I'd like a good gander with my own two eyes before the sun goes down. Then we'll come back here and study all the material Neil has gathered, and start to come up with options. One thing's for sure, we're gonna have to have a detailed look to ascertain security, guard movements, vehicle access and any other shite we'd get from a close-target recce.'

'Sounds like the old days: wet and cold on the side of a bleak hill. Almost like being back at Harriet,' said Asquith with a wry smile.

'That was in 1982, though. A quick look now, and then we plan a recce for when Josie is on site serving prawn cocktail canapés,' said Macca.

'And tomorrow?'

'Tomorrow, I'm in charge, and I'm teaching you geriatrics how to get up a cliff face without dying. Cheers, fellas.' Josie raised her beer bottle, and they all chinked.

Chapter 45

Monday 20 December 2021

Asquith was standing on a bleak beach at the foot of a large cliff, staring at the phone that was clutched in his hand. The wind was whipping in from the grey mass of the North Sea fifty metres away. He squinted at the display, narrowing his eyes against the breeze. It was his Ring doorbell app, which Bev had insisted they get, but she clearly wasn't answering it. The image of a smartly dressed woman and a beefy middle-aged man filled the screen. He tried to shut the app down, but pressed the wrong button.

'Hello?' came a tinny-sounding female voice from the speaker.

'Who's this?' said Neil.

'Mr Asquith?' The woman's voice was clear and well spoken as she looked directly at the camera on the doorbell.

'Yes, who are you?'

'My name is Detective Inspector Kelly from Hertfordshire Police. I'm investigating the death of your friend Frank Chapman. Can I have a word with you, please?'

'Sorry, I'm not at home. Out of town right now.' He winced, noting Macca glaring at him.

'Can I ask where, Mr Asquith?' She looked at her colleague and grimaced.

'I'm away on business.'

'When will you be returning?'

'I can't say for sure, DI Kelly. I'll call you when I get back.'

'I don't have a contact number for you, Mr Asquith.' There was an edge to the DI's voice.

'Sorry, my reception is poor. If you leave a card through the door, I'll call you when I'm back.' Asquith shut the app down, his stomach churning.

'Please don't tell me you just answered the phone?' said Charlie, who was securing a climbing harness around his ample waist.

'It wasn't a phone call. It was the doorbell at the Hampstead flat. I accidentally answered it. Shit, have I caused a problem?' Asquith's face was pale and his eyes wide.

'Should be okay. Those bells use your Wi-Fi and send it to your burner. She won't be able to do anything with that. Shows the buggers are on to us, though.'

'Why are they wasting time with us rather than looking for Chappers' medals?' Macca looked up from uncoiling a length of rope.

'She's a bloody busybody, that's why. Blatant careerist who takes exception to any suggestion of anyone trying to do their bloody job for them. We wouldn't bloody need to if they'd done what they're paid to. I tell you, the police are going down the pan. It was way better in my day.' Charlie shook his head.

'What, fit-ups and planting evidence?' said Jacko.

'Piss off, keyboard-teeth. Could these harnesses be any bloody tighter?' Charlie struggled with the adjustment clips.

'You've been eating too much of your missus's pies, tubby.'

'Get stuffed, Jacko.'

'Enough bants, troops. Does this change anything?' said Macca, securing his own harness.

'What, Charlie being a lard-arse?' Jacko grinned.

Charlie aimed a slap at him. 'Ha ha. Not as far as I'm concerned. We just have to stay off the radar and give ourselves plausible deniability. What Kelly suspects is irrelevant; it's only if she can prove things that we have a problem. We carry on, but we stay sharp, yeah?'

'Yeah, stay off your blower, Neil. Christ, she's like a bastard mountain goat, that girl, look at her go.' Jacko pointed up the sheer rock face, the rough and pitted red sandstone soaring over thirty metres up into the ice-blue sky.

'Shit, she's only tying in every ten metres or so. I'd be shitting myself, and I wasn't a half-bad climber in my day,' said Macca, shaking his head in admiration as he fed the rope that was attached to Josie's harness through the belay device clipped to his own. 'I can hardly keep up with the belaying, she's so bloody quick.'

'Slack,' came Josie's tinny voice through the radio Jacko was holding, which Macca knew meant she wanted more rope. He eased more through the device, and Josie continued up.

'Spoken like a true nostalgic old git. Your broken body wouldn't get you up there, but look at her go, she's a bloody machine. I'm half expecting her to start shooting webs,' said Charlie, chuckling.

'Her old man was a tremendous climber as well when he was a mountain leader, and you can see where she gets her whippet-like physique from. Chappers was a skinny wee mannie. I reckon she weighs about the same as one of your legs, Charlie.'

'Tension,' came the command through the walkie-talkie, meaning that Josie wanted to rest. Macca pulled the rope in tight and planted his feet securely, then nodded at Jacko.

'Gotcha,' Jacko said into the handset.

Josie leant back on the rope and took a breather, the tension being held by the cam she'd just put into the rock. She shook her hands out in turn before reaching around to her chalk bag to dust them.

'On belay.' Her voice was steady and showed no trace of the enormous effort that was required to scale the rock. Macca nodded to Jacko.

'Belay on,' said Jacko.

Josie set off again up the face with almost balletic ease. Within ten minutes, she'd reached the top and disappeared from sight. The walkie-talkie crackled. 'Off belay. That was a piece of piss, lads. Let the rope go, Macca, I've staked it in up here.'

Macca unclipped the rope from the belay and let it hang loose. Jacko spoke into the walkie-talkie. 'Rope clear.'

The rope began to whip like an angry snake as Josie pulled it up over the sandstone rock face. It slid through the karabiners before disappearing over the edge of the cliff. A few moments later, her voice crackled out of the tinny speaker again. 'Watch out at the bottom, rope coming down.' She tossed it over and it played out down the rock face, loose and unfettered, landing with a thump. 'Right, abseiling down now.'

'Here she comes again,' said Jacko, looking up as Josie appeared, her backside jutting out as she lowered herself into the void. She edged out until her feet found the solid rock of the cliff face, then pushed herself off and began to descend, zigzagging to each of the cams in turn, removing them and clipping them onto her harness.

They all stood watching her graceful traversing of the cliff, admiring her expertise.

'Are we really gonna have to do this?' Jacko asked with a grimace.

'Yes, Jacko,' said Macca. 'There's a good chance we'll have to climb that cliff to get to Stonehaven, and if we do, we'll need this practice if you're not to plummet to your death.'

'Thanks, that makes me feel a lot better.'

'Not scared of heights, are you, Jacko?' said Charlie with a chuckle.

'No.' Jacko looked indignant.

'As I recall, you struggled on the Tarzan assault course on the commando tests.'

'Piss off. That was over forty years ago, and anyway, I was faster than *you*, Tubby Drake.'

'Tubby?' said Charlie, his expression perplexed.

'That's what the rest of the training troop called you, until all the phys took the lard off you.'

'Okay, enough banter, boys,' said Macca. 'Let's do some cliff ascent practice, and then we're away. I want to be ready for later, as we need to properly recce the castle.'

'Are we talking about an all-nighter?' asked Jacko.

'Who knows, but we need to assess what security is there. I hope you packed all the kit.'

'All back at the cottage.

Within five minutes, Josie had landed, soft as a feather on the turf, a big smile on her face.

'Didn't want to leave the cams in as they cost a fortune, and you've spent enough on my kit, Neil.' She grinned as she whipped the rope from her figure-8 descender.

'Very thoughtful, but it's not like I can return them, is it?' said Asquith.

'I know, but I can make use of them, and I'm poor.'

'You're welcome.'

'Right, boys, I've done all the hard work; now it's your turn,' she said with a puckish smile.

Macca was looking at the ominous pile of kit at the bottom of the cliff face with a touch of anxiety. He'd climbed a fair bit in the SBS, as a mountain leader, but it wasn't his speciality, and he was nowhere near Josie's ability. He was more about canoes and free-falling. His wrist was throbbing already, and his backside was still sore. The thought of straining as he climbed up the sheer face wasn't attractive. He was thinking of voicing his concerns when his phone buzzed in his pocket. He didn't recognise the number.

'Hello?' he said with some suspicion.

'Gordon, how are you?' came a strong American voice. He felt his buttocks clench, and for once it wasn't his aching haemorrhoids to blame.

'Laurel?'

'Of course. How many other American women do you know?'

'Might I ask how you got this number? I only activated it yesterday,' he said, watching with interest as Josie hooked Jacko up to some complex piece of climbing equipment he'd never seen used before.

'Not difficult, darling. In fact, very easy. You need to up your tradecraft game. Now, I see you're close by Stonehaven Castle, seat of the newly appointed laird, Mr Bruzek?'

'You know about that, then?'

'You don't sound surprised.' The amusement in her voice was obvious.

'I'm not.'

'Well, of course we take interest in things such as this. When I saw where your tracker was, I couldn't help but dig a little. Would you be surprised to learn that the US Government has a passing interest in General Bruzek's activities?'

'What, a Slovakian billionaire with questionable sources of income? Can't say I am surprised, hen.' He immediately regretted using the term of endearment.

She chuckled softly. 'Oh honey, it's just so sweet being called that. Yes, very questionable sources of income, some of which he uses to support causes that aren't necessarily conducive to good order in the US. Seems to lend his backing to some undesirable types who are being a little troublesome. We also have concerns about trafficking intelligence that has been flagged up to us. All in all, he's not a very nice man, Gordon. Now, before I say anything else, I'm assuming I can't talk you out of whatever you're planning?'

'You assume right,' Macca said firmly.

'I suspected as much. I'm wondering if you fancy a little quid pro quo, then, bearing in mind I imagine you are considering some type of heist.'

'I'm listening.'

'I'm willing to share intelligence material on the castle, plus if you need any resources, I may be able to assist. No personnel, you understand. Just blueprints, satellite imagery and all the intelligence we have that may make your task easier.'

'And the quid pro quo?'

'Well, assuming that you get in okay, we'd very much like it if you could liberate any technology you might find. Phones, laptops, iPads. Just get whatever you can. We'll make sure to get some Faraday bags for you. How does that sound?'

'Reasonable to me,' said Macca.

'Swell. I'll be in touch very soon, but Gordon, you must promise me you'll take care. I'd hate it if anything happened to you.' Her voice was as soft as pouring cream.

'We'll be grand.'

'I'm serious. Bruzek keeps well away from violence, but he is protected, and I'd hate to miss our romantic dinner by way of you being dead.'

'I'll do my best, Laurel.'

'Great. Speak soon.' The three beeps in his ear told her that she had gone.

He looked across at the cliff, where Jacko was now suspended about five metres up the rock face. There was a sudden tangle of limbs and a yell before he was abruptly upended, his feet scrabbling for purchase as his helmeted head bounced against the sandstone. Macca began to laugh at the sight of his old comrade upside down, feeling a surge of energy at the thought of new leads and new opportunities heading their way from the mysterious Laurel Freeman. He jogged back over to the others, still chuckling, as Jacko yelled, 'Get me daan off this stupid fuckin' cliff.'

Chapter 46

Jacko grimaced as the icy wind whipped across the landscape, picking up moisture from the slate-grey sea, which was choppy and crested with white foam as it crashed against the rocks below them. His foot ached in his scratched and worn boots, the legacy of the mine strike all those years ago. He knew he'd been lucky that day, the mine being buried too deep and the worst of the blast going down into the peat, which saved his foot. It had never been the same since, though.

They were high up in the hills above Stonehaven Castle, which sat stark and jarring against the green of the outcrop. The attempts to rebuild the castle in keeping with its history hadn't been entirely successful, and it looked far too new among the ruins of the numerous outbuildings. The adjacent long, low, barn-like building was more sympathetic. It looked like an old agricultural shed, although the trail of smoke being whipped away from the chimney by the wind told of a cosier space. The lights illuminated the gloom as the low winter sun, hidden by the deep grey clouds, began to sink towards the horizon. Another barn sat, dark and inert, next to the main barn. There was no light emitting from the windows, and no smoke coming from the chimney. It just looked like an old livestock shed.

'This takes me back, Charlie, and not in a nostalgic way either. It was shit being out in crappy cold weather in the Eighties, and it's still shit forty years later,' he said, pulling his camouflaged cap lower on his head and zipping his windproof smock up to his neck.

'Aye, been a long time. Come on, let's get this hide dug before it starts pissing down. We've only thirty minutes' light left,' said Charlie as he pulled out the collapsible shovel secured to his rucksack.

Jacko nodded and they both set to work scraping back the turf alongside the collection of craggy granite boulders before removing the layer of topsoil, which they tossed behind the biggest of the boulders, to form a slight depression in the soggy peat. Jacko then pulled out a folded groundsheet and spread it across the expanse of exposed earth.

'That'll keep the wet out,' said Charlie as he stretched a larger camouflaged tarpaulin over the top and Jacko began to secure the edges with tent pegs. Charlie then produced a collapsible set of flexible poles, which he snapped together and used to lift the end of the tarpaulin, making a rudimentary tent with an open front affording a good view of the landscape down to the castle.

'Right, turf it up, and then we're in and getting the kit set up,' said Charlie, picking up a strip of the turf they'd removed and laying it carefully across the tarpaulin.

'Fucking hell, it's suddenly 1981 again on Woodbury Common, only difference being we haven't got that sadistic bastard Corporal Nevison screaming at us to do it faster.'

Charlie guffawed at the memory of the hellish basic training they'd shared all those years ago in Devon. 'Yeah, and the shit would always make sure we were piss-wet through before we got into our bivvy, remember that?'

'How could I forget. Somehow they were good times, though,

although that may be the passage of time.'

'It must be, because they were shit, cold and we never got any bloody sleep.'

'Made men of us, though, eh?'

'Maybe. Who knows? That looks pretty good, I'd say.' Charlie nodded, surveying the hide, which was now all but invisible. 'A bit of scrim on the open end and we're good to go.' He pulled some rough-cut hessian from his bag and used it almost like a curtain in front of the opening, and in the gloom, it blended completely into the scraggy grass.

'You never lose it, do you?' said Jacko.

'You never had it, geezer. Come on, let's get the camera set up.' Charlie flicked open a black vulcanised Pelican case with shoulder straps. A complex-looking khaki-coloured camera was nestled inside, the brand name 'Infiniti' embossed in matte black on the centre console. It comprised what appeared to be two cameras, one resembling a pared-back CCTV unit, one more like a huge torch. It looked sleek, tough and very expensive.

'I hope you were listening when Macca gave us the briefing,' said Jacko. 'I found myself losing interest.'

'Fortunately I was, and as it's designed for squaddies to use, it should be bombproof. It had better work, as it was a heavy bastard to lug.'

'Yeah, I'd have volunteered, but my dicky foot's playing up, you know, after stepping on a mine and all that. Not that I ever complain,' said Jacko with a grimace.

'You constantly drip about it, you old goat. Come on, let's get it set up and tested, and then we can back off somewhere warm.'

'Good idea, but I'd like to point out that I carried the battery, which was heavy enough for a disabled hero like me.'

'Disabled? Ten stitches and a broken toe, and your foot was right as rain, you malingering sod. I was more injured when I had a vasectomy twenty years ago.'

'No doubt because your tiny bollocks only needed a tiny hole,'

Jacko guffawed.

'Brilliant, Jacko. Small genital jokes. Genius.' Charlie removed the camera system from the box and fixed it to a solid-looking metal baseplate. It slid home with a reassuring clunk.

'I never knew you was a Jaffa?' Jacko looked at him with one eyebrow raised.

'Jaffa?' said Charlie as he carried the unit to the hide and slotted it in under the tarpaulin, settling it into the earth.

'Yeah, as in seedless.' Jacko threw his head back and cackled.

'Oldies are the goodies, eh? Pass us the battery.' Charlie shook his head, a smile playing around his lips.

Jacko handed over a battery the size of a shoebox, encased in rubberised material, together with a waterproofed lead. Charlie slotted the connector into the port at the rear of the camera unit and screwed it into place. He then attached the lead to the battery and tucked it in behind the camera unit. He checked the positioning of the unit, then depressed a rubberised switch, holding it in place for a full ten seconds.

The camera woke up with a faint whirring as the lens began to focus. Jacko nodded, then pulled out his phone and dialled. 'Macca, it's on.'

'I can see, mate,' Macca replied. 'Working a treat, and remote access is online. In fact, you should be getting the feed on your phones now. I've allowed access to all of us. Picture's shit-hot and I've not even started playing with it. Zoom function is off the dial. Look at your screen.'

Jacko switched to the app that Macca had installed on his burner phone earlier on. An image of Stonehaven Castle filled the small screen in startling detail. Then the camera began to zoom in, focusing on the front of the main building. He could almost see the grain of the heavy wood of the double door.

The camera made a smooth whirring noise and panned left just a few degrees to show the gatehouse. It was clearly made of ancient stone, with a pitched tiled roof. A bored-looking guard sat in a small guardhouse to the side. The camera zoomed in further and locked in on the face of the man. He had a hard-looking brow and Slav features, and his buzz cut completed his military bearing. He wore a plain black jacket and had a lanyard around his neck with some type of card at the end of it.

Jacko raised his phone back to his ear. 'Shit-the-bed, mate. That is bloody amazing. I wish we'd had these bastards in Northern Ireland back in the day. Would have saved all that time sat freezing your knackers off in some bush in a peat bog somewhere in Crossmaglen.'

'Hoofing bit of kit, right? Okay, get it properly cammed up and then get the hell out of there. I don't want any of us on that hill and we all need some rest. We'll be needing to bring our A game tomorrow when Josie goes in.'

'Sure you're happy to leave it here? I've a feeling it might be expensive.'

'You'd be right, but it's not mine, and the boy that lent it to me owes me lots of favours. Just make sure your concealment is good, and we'll be back to change the battery in twelve hours. There won't be anyone up there during the night. It's the middle of nowhere.'

'How will it cope in the dark?' asked Jacko.

'So you weren't listening in the briefing, then?'

'I may have drifted off a little.'

'Watch the screen,' said Macca, the smugness detectable in his voice.

Jacko lowered the phone and maximised the camera app. The view of the castle reappeared. Suddenly the picture flared and the screen went much darker, to a grey, monochromatic view. The camera panned back to the house, where a ghostly figure was leaving the front door, face, head and hands glowing almost white. The figure walked towards a dark shape and climbed on board. It lit up and began to move forward, its centre mass getting progressively lighter. It was a man on a quad bike, the thermal

244

imaging function on the camera locking onto the heat signature of the bike's engine and the warmth of the body riding it. The camera tracked the quad as it did a full circuit of the outcrop, zooming in tight, then out to a wide view. The chimney on the outbuilding glowed white, and all the windows in the castle shone stark against the black of the early-evening gloom.

'Thermal imaging too. Shit, this thing really must be worth a packet,' said Charlie, giving a low whistle.

'Yep. Infrared, also with full thermal capacity, although that will reduce battery life. What do you make of the quad circuit?' said Macca.

'Security rounds?'

'I agree. We have just over twenty-four now to get any security patterns established so we can work out the plan. Right, you two get back here. I want to do a full briefing with where we are now so we're all on the same page, okay?'

'Roger that. On our way.' Jacko hung up.

Charlie began to tear off clumps of grass, tucking them in underneath the camera and mixing them in with the hessian scrim. He quickly checked on his phone that the camera's view wasn't compromised, then looked at Jacko in the fading light. 'Happy?'

'Yeah, mate. We're doing this, ain't we?'

'Damn right. We're getting Chappers' medals back.'

Chapter 47

Tuesday 21 December 2021

'Jesus, girl, you scrub up well. You look essence,' said Macca, looking up from the iPad screen as Josie appeared in the kitchen of the farmhouse.

'Thanks, I think. Just keeping options open. You never know when a bit of well-placed flirting will be needed, so – uncomfortable as it makes me – I thought I'd make a bit of an effort.' Her usually subtle make-up had been far more liberally applied, with smoky eyes and lips forming a perfect red bow. She wore skinny jeans and a tight-fitting top that showed off her athletic physique.

'You'll certainly attract male attention,' said Macca, and his face told of immediate awkwardness at what he'd said. 'Sorry, is that a weird thing for me to say?'

Josie grimaced. 'Really? Too much?' For someone more used to outdoor wear, dressing to impress men was a little unsettling.

'Look like you're off to a nightclub. Probably a smart idea, but don't get yourself in any daft situations, eh?'

'It'll be fine. Anyone pushes their luck, they'll find themselves with a shattered wrist. Where are the others?' she asked, pouring herself a coffee from a drip machine.

'Charlie and Jacko have gone up the hill to change the battery on the camera but will be back any minute, and Neil is on the phone to his researcher for updates. He also has a man who is getting us accurate weather forecasts.'

As if on cue, Charlie and Jacko burst through the front door, bringing a blast of cold air with them. Asquith followed them into the kitchen, his laptop under his arm. 'Any coffee left?' He looked at Josie and his eyes widened. 'Goodness, Josie, you look amazing.'

'Blimey, doing my hair and wearing a bit of make-up and you'd think I had two heads,' she said, smiling.

He stopped, his mouth frozen open, his face riven with concern at what he'd just said. 'Sorry, was that inappropriate?'

'Why?' Josie looked confused.

'Well, one never knows if one's going to get cancelled nowadays.'

'You're okay.' She chuckled.

'I'm glad you're all back,' Macca said. 'I want to do a full set of orders.'

'Military orders, like the old days?' asked Charlie.

'Something like that. We've all been farting around doing our own stuff, so I want to make sure everyone knows everything. We can't finalise the plan until Josie's done the close-target recce, but she's in there on her own, so we need to be all over this.' Macca looked grim.

Within minutes, the whole team was sitting around the table, each nursing a hot drink.

Macca looked at them in turn. 'Right, this may seem like overkill, but I'll do it in the old military style, SMEAC, right?'

'SMEAC?' Josie looked confused.

'Yep, military acronym. Situation, mission, execution, admin and logistics, command and signal.'

'Okay, I guess.' She shrugged.

'Right. Situation as I see it. We can be almost certain that the medals are somewhere in that castle, or at least we know that *my* medal box is in there, as the bug Neil planted is still hitting a satellite. How tight can you get its location, Neil?'

'It's on the far western side of the building, which from the plans you shared seems to be the master suite. We're assuming that's Bruzek's quarters?'

'Has to be. How about security?' Macca turned to Jacko.

'Not a lot, and very predictable. Helicopter arrived early this morning, and only one vehicle has come and gone, a long-wheel-base Land Rover. I think the causeway is a little precarious for normal vehicles, hence the regular use of the helicopter. Nice being an oligarch, eh? Popping out in your Bell 222 for a pint of milk and a loaf.'

'How about the quad patrol?'

'On the hour, a circuit of the outcrop, and then after midnight the man on the gatehouse took over. I think they lowered the portcullis and went down to just one security man, who'd leave the gatehouse and do a round every hour on the hour. I guess they don't worry too much about anyone coming up a massive great cliff.'

'So, our mission today is to support Josie as she deploys undercover into the castle on a close-target recce to ascertain layout, security, physical features and access to the various parts of the castle in order that we can plan for a final assault to recover the medals. Understand?'

Everyone nodded.

'Communications?' said Macca.

Neil raised his hand. 'Josie is wearing a covert earpiece, linked to her watch, which is 5G enabled, so we'll be able to hear what she's doing and communicate with her as best we can. The watch also has a camera function and it will be live-streaming back here so we can see what's going on. We've tested the kit, and it's working fine.'

'You happy, Josie?' said Macca.

'Yeah, it's simple. The earpiece is discreet and covered by my hair.'

'Emergency extraction code phrase in case things come on top?' said Macca.

'Harriet?' suggested Josie.

'Seems appropriate to me.' He smiled wryly.

'As long as you come running if I shout it.'

'We'll be there within a few minutes. Jacko and Charlie will be close by. But hopefully you won't need us. Just keep your wits about you, and for God's sake don't do anything impetuous or daft. This is just you getting the layout, security, locks and the like. Once you've got that all squared away, we plan properly for the assault and retrieval, okay?'

'Don't fret. It's just the preparation today. Setting up tables and getting the champagne, glasses and canapés in place ready for the event. Tedious stuff, but it's useful for me to get eyes on the prize.'

'Nice one,' said Asquith. 'We'll be listening and watching all the time. Anything you need to show us, just hold the watch up and it'll stream to us. It's not the highest pixel count, but it's definitely better than nothing. You remember the tones?'

'All is good, Neil, I've practised with it and I know what I'm doing. Two tones for yes, one for no. No one will care about me. I'm just a waitress, remember.' Josie shrugged.

'Did you get the intel document I sent you?' Macca asked Neil.

'Yes. Where the hell did you get that from? My man couldn't find anything.'

'Never reveal an intel source,' said Macca.

'The American?'

He held his fingers to his lips.

'Payment in kind to come, I assume?'

'Don't you bloody start; I've enough with Jacko digging me out for that. Let's just say she's going to want her pound of flesh at some point in the future.'

Asquith sniggered and adopted a deep, booming voice. 'The court awards it, and the law doth give it. Most rightful judge.'

249

Macca looked confused. 'What the fuck are you blethering about?'

Asquith frowned. '*The Merchant of Venice*?'

'Who?'

'Shakespeare?' His face fell, just a touch.

'No idea what you're on about, pal. I stopped paying attention at school in about 1972, and the only merchant I knew was at the fish market in Leith.'

Asquith cleared his throat with obvious embarrassment. 'Well, whatever. Your document is dynamite stuff. There are detailed drawings here of the place, including building services, internet IP, electrics diagram and energy performance certificate, so we have a good source of intel to be looking at now. From what I can see, there is only one official point of entry: across the causeway and through the stone gate arch. The rest of the place is protected by the natural features of the cliffs. There's also a heap of intel on Bruzek himself: suspected sources of wealth, distribution, and lots of photographs. Whoever put this together knows their stuff.'

'Any law-enforcement activity?' asked Macca.

'Not much. Although there was a further missing person report that was linked to the castle a year ago. Slovak girl last seen there having come across for a working holiday. Apparently left the castle late one day and didn't return, and never arrived back in Slovakia. No resolution, but her parents made a bit of a fuss and there was some Facebook activity. I couldn't get to the bottom of it, though.'

'Trafficking?' wondered Macca.

'Not clear, but something to bear in mind, particularly after what Charlie learnt from his NCA source.'

'How about the weather and general conditions?'

'Yeah, that's looking decent, unusually for this time of year. Cold and clear, lows of zero, with no moon and little wind. Also, low tide is in the early hours for the next couple of days, which may dictate timelines.'

Macca nodded, his brow furrowing as he turned it all over in his mind.

'I'd better go – minibus leaves soon,' said Josie, looking at her watch and standing up.

Macca placed his big, rough hand on her forearm and looked at her, his normally hard eyes softening. 'Be careful, love. I know you're not a kid, and I know you've proved yourself more than anyone could have reasonably imagined, but you're just one person, and you're not indestructible. Any bad shite happens in there, just get out fast.'

There was a pause, then Josie smiled widely. 'Don't fret, Grandpa. I'll be fine. Remember who my dad was.'

Chapter 48

The other Scotia staff were only just friendly enough, but not exactly sparkling conversationalists. Josie had studied her colleagues as they got on the minibus that was parked outside the industrial unit in Spurryhillock. It seemed like the van had been somewhat beefed up, with bigger wheels, rustic-looking tyres, probably to deal with the rough roads. Apart from Grigor, who still oozed an oily attempt at charm, there was Marta, who was also Polish and who seemed to know him well, chatting away to him in Polish. Being fluent in Czech after her two years in Prague, Josie could understand a small amount of what they said, Czech and Polish both being East Slavic languages, but they just seemed to be moaning about money.

Leanne and Kirsty, both very pretty, well-made-up girls, sounded like locals and gossiped between themselves, occasionally shooting Josie dirty looks. There was also Jamie, a stocky, good-looking guy with a Glaswegian accent, who seemed pleasant and smiley but just sat at the back of the minibus staring at his phone.

The tiny earpiece tucked deep in her ear crackled. 'Josie, raise your watch for a test,' came Asquith's voice.

She theatrically held it up to look at the time, and then swept

252

it around the inside of the minibus before dropping it down to her waist again.

'Yep, all good. It's hardly 4K, but we can see, and we can hear audio as well. Remember, you'll need to change the earpiece batteries after six hours, as I showed you,' said Asquith.

Josie pressed the small button on the side of the watch twice, and two short beeps sounded in her ear. The code for yes.

'Two tones. Be careful, and we'll keep monitoring.'

She smiled at the thought of the four tough old marines sitting in the cottage listening in. It was comforting, even if she knew that in reality she was on her own, and if any dramas unfolded, she'd have to deal with them. Something deep inside her told her that she really should be nervous, but all she felt was a frisson of excitement and anticipation at the prospect.

'So, you ready for day's hard work, eh, Mary?' said Grigor from the driver's seat, his dark eyes catching hers in the rear-view mirror.

'I can't wait,' said Josie, with just a touch of sarcasm, as she rolled her eyes.

'Ha. You have to work hard. Mr Bruzek's people don't like lazy girls, but they like pretty girls.' His smile was more of a leer. 'This is why I employ you.' He guffawed, his mouth open wide, showing an absence of back teeth.

'Aye, we're pure flattered, man,' said Leanne, her accent as harsh and cutting as a rusted razor. It was clear that she wasn't buying Grigor's bullshit either.

Josie shook her head, then cast her eyes down at her phone to compose a message to the WhatsApp group. *This is gonna be a long shift. Grigor is a sex pest.*

A reply came back immediately from Macca. *Remember, no breaking bones or choking him out* 😉

Josie stifled a chuckle, and suddenly her flutter of nerves dissipated into more useful steely resolve. The fact that Grigor was a lecherous bastard could possibly be turned to her advantage.

The rest of the journey was undertaken in silence, other than Grigor and Marta talking to each other in Polish, mostly about Josie and the other girls, it seemed. Jamie kept his head down, and Grigor certainly didn't mention him.

They soon rounded a sharp bend where the landscape fell away to the sea, and Stonehaven Castle lay before them. Josie had to admit that it was a magnificent sight, as the lush green grass gave way to the steep descent to the flat-calm sea, with the outcrop jutting up ahead. The reddish hue of the sandstone contrasted starkly with the water, which had been painted blue by the low winter sun that was throwing out milky white light from a pale blue sky.

'Holy shit,' she said, feeling a genuine surge of awe. She'd seen the castle from lower down when she'd recced the cliff but hadn't appreciated the sheer scale or the staggering beauty of the place.

'First time you see the castle, eh?' said Grigor, eyeing her with a smirk.

'Yes. It's not what I expected. How on earth did he get permission to build a home on the site?'

'Mr Bruzek has many friends, and very much money. He makes the greasy wheels, no?' He guffawed again, and the noise was rattly and full of phlegm.

A long, winding single-track road led to the causeway, which stretched out a hundred metres towards the gatehouse, a large edifice with a steep tiled roof and a portcullis that looked to be as old as the stone it sat in the middle of.

The causeway was made of modern-looking material that had been used to fortify the thin strip of land and make a rudimentary road. It sloped steeply away on both sides to a sandy beach a hundred feet below. The only thing preventing vehicles from falling over the edge was a galvanised-steel barrier, the kind of thing that would normally be seen at the side of a motorway.

'I bet this isn't fun to drive in bad weather,' said Josie.

'Aye, bloody hell. Imagine flying off the side of that. You'd be fucked,' said Jamie, the first words he'd spoken, in a broad Aberdeenshire accent.

'It's why I have beefed-up van, so I can drive places like this. Mr Bruzek likes it for private. Why he uses helicopter.'

'Shite, just how rich is the bastard?' said Jamie, his mouth gaping as they left the road and drove onto the causeway.

'Richer than you can believe. Now, we're going in, so we start work now. No swear, no stare, and just do your job, yes?'

'Aye, you got it. Look at this bloody place,' said the suddenly chatty Jamie, staring wide-eyed out of the window.

The minibus negotiated the smooth tarmac of the causeway and halted in front of the gatehouse, the wrought-iron portcullis closed in front of them, an ancient impregnable barrier to incomers.

'Is this the only route into the place?' said Josie.

'Yeah, unless Mr Bruzek allow you in helicopter or you climb big cliff. Why he like it, defend all raiders against him,' Grigor said, chuckling to himself.

With a squeal, the rust-stained metal grid began to rise into the roof above the gatehouse, and a short, stocky man with Slav features and spiky hair ambled out and headed towards the van. He looked tough and uncompromising, and was dressed in black cargo pants and a black and white combat-patterned jacket. He wore dark sunglasses and was clutching a clipboard, and there was a blank white plastic card around his neck on a blue lanyard. Josie extended her wrist and held her watch up, giving a view of the gatehouse.

'Shite. I bet that portcullis weighs a ton,' said Macca in her earpiece.

Grigor lowered his window as the man approached. 'Teodor, my friend, how are you?' he said cheerily.

'Grigor, my man. I hope you bring enough food for us?' Teodor replied, grinning widely.

'Of course. Has the champagne delivery arrived?'

'This morning. Much champagne – locals will be very happy, eh?'

'We good to go in?'

'Hold up, who's in the van?'

'Me, Marta, Leanne, Kirsty, Jamie and a new girl, Mary. All should be on the list I sent in with scans of ID.'

Teodor studied his clipboard and nodded with satisfaction. 'In you go. Park outside main house. Danilo will meet you there and give you briefing and security access passes.' He nodded and returned to the gatehouse, where there was a glazed door within the small access tunnel.

Grigor put the van in gear and moved off, passing through the dark interior of the gatehouse and emerging into the sunshine in a vast courtyard. At the edge of it was a long, low building, which looked agricultural but had a sound roof, solid stonework and a wisp of smoke emitting from a chimney. Lights twinkled at the windows, and a young woman's face appeared, her dark hair stark against the artificial light.

The courtyard was a mix of lush grass and stone cobbles, occasionally punctuated by a pile of ancient-looking stones or the skeleton of a half-ruined building. Five hundred metres away, at the far edge of the outcrop, sat Stonehaven Castle itself. At each end of the sweeping stone building was a large stone tower topped by ramparts, the far-right one bearing a gently fluttering flag on a white pole.

It somehow managed to be both beautiful and brutally ugly at the same time. It was as if someone had tried to design a large, modern home that would sit harmoniously among the ancient buildings. Once again, Josie couldn't help but wonder just how the hell Bruzek got the necessary permission to build in such a fashion.

The van circumnavigated the courtyard and pulled up outside the castle's vast oak door. A huge shaven-headed man with a hard, scowling face stood there, his hand raised in greeting.

'Who's the gorilla?' said Josie.

'Mind your mouth, girl. That's Danilo, Mr Bruzek's personal

assistant. I don't advise making him angry; he has short temper,' Grigor said, and Josie could detect genuine fear in his voice.

'I'll mind my manners then,' she said, looking at her watch theatrically, giving the boys back at the cottage the first view of Bruzek's home and the huge beast that was his bodyguard.

The earpiece crackled. 'Intelligence is that Danilo's not a very nice man, Josie. Take a lot of care around him.'

The bodyguard stared at the van with dark, emotionless eyes, and she shuddered involuntarily. There was nothing in those deep-set eyes, but she knew without a doubt that this was a man who had seen and done terrible things.

Chapter 49

The catering team filed off the minibus and stood outside the castle door, where Danilo handed out white plastic cards on red lanyards. 'These allow you into vestibule, then into ballroom and kitchen, but nowhere else. And lose your card means lose your bonus.' He glared at them, his head like a block of granite, with the flat eyes looking way too small.

The vestibule was as grand as Josie had expected, with gleaming marble flooring and plain whitewashed walls, on which there were grand-looking paintings on every inch of exposed plaster. Old Masters competed with Scottish landscapes and a massive painting of a stag. The ballroom was vast, with a huge swathe of parquet flooring that shone in the light from three enormous crystal chandeliers. The roof was a work of art in itself. Josie knew very little about construction or joinery, but even she could appreciate the level of workmanship that had gone into the beams and joists that supported the slates above in a criss-cross pattern. The walls were elaborately decorated with beautifully painted frescoes of Scottish scenes, including a depiction of the Battle of Culloden, while an intricate tapestry reminiscent of the Bayeux Tapestry covered the rear wall, the backdrop to an ancient and solid-looking wooden throne set upon a low stage clad in a wine-red carpet. The whole place reeked of excess.

An elderly professorial-looking gentleman with white hair clapped his hands. 'Okay, everyone gather round while I brief you on the features in the room.' He sat on the elaborate wooden chair and the staff stood in front of him. 'I'm Professor Ewan Henderson. I advised General Bruzek on the restoration project and assisted in the finishing touches that you see on the walls and ceilings. As well as serving drinks and canapés, you'll be required to talk to the guests about the ballroom.' His eyes glinted as they flickered among the six Scotia employees, all of whom were now wearing black aprons with the company logo on the front.

Josie looked at Grigor, who shrugged and raised his eyes to the ceiling.

'What the hell is all this shite about?' she whispered to Leanne.

'Load of pish. Just nod and smile. He does this for all the events. Most of the guests don't give a monkey's. They just want to get blootered on free champagne and eat daft canapés because they think it makes them look sophisticated, like.' Leanne's eyes were flat and full of boredom; she had clearly heard the briefing a number of times before.

'I'll just give you a few basic facts so you can sound knowledge-able.. The General is obliged to do these events to maintain his excellent reputation with the community.' The professor grinned widely.

'Teeth like a medieval graveyard, eh?' whispered Leanne, and Josie had to fight to keep a smile from breaking out on her face.

'Now then, I'm sitting on one of only two painstakingly researched replicas of an ancient Pictish warrior throne, which would have dated back almost a thousand years. It's identical to the one that currently sits at the Glenmorangie distillery, and was re-created to show how advanced the early Scots were. It was likely inspired by the carvings of a pair of thrones depicted on the cross slab in Fowlis Wester in Perthshire. Note the clan symbols etched into it, and the classic shape. The original would no doubt have been the seat of a bloodthirsty warrior king, thrones being important symbols of power back in the eleventh century. All happy?' He cast his eyes over the group, all of whom nodded with faux interest.

'Excellent. Now follow me while I talk to you about the wonderful tapestry, and then we'll discuss the beautiful frescoes on the walls.' He clapped his hands again, and leapt to his feet with surprising vigour for a man of his advanced years.

There was a commotion at the far end of the ballroom, and everyone fell silent and turned to the source of the noise. Danilo, the hulking man-mountain, entered the room, his eyes sweeping from left to right as if looking for enemies, his fists balled and his massive shoulders squared.

'Look at this walloper, walkin' as if he's a bloody roll of invisible carpet under each bloody arm, eh?' said Leanne with a grin.

Danilo nodded to the professor, then turned to the door, hands behind his back.

Josie instantly recognised General Marek Bruzek from the photographs she'd seen, as he swept into the room, his Cuban-heeled brogues making a clip-clopping noise as the hard heels struck the parquet floor. He wore well-tailored corduroy trousers and a cashmere sweater, under which was a checked shirt with a tightly knotted knitted tie. Josie had to stifle a smile. He looked like a British military officer dressed in mufti. She remembered her father taking the piss out of officers for whom this exact get-up was almost a second uniform.

Danilo fell into step alongside Bruzek as he walked briskly towards the group. When he reached them, he turned and looked at the bodyguard.

Danilo cleared his throat. 'Pay attention,' he growled.

Everyone turned to face him, a curious sense of anticipation in the echoey ballroom.

'My name is Danilo. I'm the assistant to General Bruzek, laird of Stonehaven Castle, who is host for tomorrow's event.' He paused and made a half-bow to Bruzek, who inclined his head, a vulpine smile extending across his pale pudgy cheeks. Not one trace of the smile even touched his dark, deep-set eyes. 'Listen carefully to Professor Henderson. He is expert in the art and architecture, and it will be most helpful if you are knowledgeable about these things. Grigor, who is serving for VIP reception in General's quarters?'

Grigor was standing ramrod straight, hands behind his back, at the front of the group. 'Miss Fraser. My most experienced staff member.' He nodded at Leanne, who looked startled.

Bruzek turned to her and stared at her for a full fifteen seconds, taking in her knee-length skirt, nylon-clad legs and black patent high-heeled shoes. His lips stretched across his teeth in an unpleasant smile.

'You must be most discreet and efficient,' Danilo continued, glancing at Leanne. 'The General is receiving a number of important guests in his quarters at eight p.m. sharp, so I will need you to be immediately available to serve drinks and canapés. Speak to me once finished with Professor Henderson, and I will give you key card and brief you on protocol. After that, you bring a sample of canapés and champagne down to General's quarters, okay?'

Leanne just stood there, seemingly uncertain whether to respond.

'Answer, Leanne,' barked Grigor.

She flinched, her eyes wide with sudden fear. 'Aye,' she said, her voice almost inaudible.

'*Je hlúpa?*' said Bruzek in a curiously high-pitched voice, looking at Danilo with raised eyebrows.

Danilo just shrugged.

Josie's Slovak wasn't as fluent as her Czech, but the similarities between the languages meant that she understood well enough that Bruzek had told Danilo to make sure that Leanne wasn't stupid.

Bruzek looked at each of them in turn, the light from the chandeliers glinting in his hair oil. He paused before nodding at Danilo.

'This very important evening for General, and you are representing him. Bad service reflects badly, and I cannot allow this. A good night's work from all of you will attract a bonus, so pay attention to Professor Henderson.' Danilo turned to Bruzek, who spun on his heel and marched back out of the ballroom with the bodyguard in his wake.

A heavy silence descended on the room until Henderson broke it. 'Shall we continue?'

The professor spent the next thirty minutes giving overviews on the history of the other pieces of art around the ballroom. The rest of the Scotia staff were yawning and eye-rolling, but Josie found herself engaged with the castle's connection to the Stuart dynasty, which had prompted Bruzek to insist on the Culloden fresco.

She watched with interest as Leanne went to speak to Danilo, who towered above her as he gave her instructions of some kind. He then held out his massive hand, in which was a blue lanyard, which she swapped for her red one.

'Okay, people,' said Grigor. 'We've a lot of work to do here. We need to unload canapés from van, organise all the glasses, set up the tables and make sure everything is in perfect order for tomorrow. You heard the General, do a good job and we all get bonus; do a bad job, we go home a little poorer. Leanne, you ready for General?'

'Aye, as long as the pervy bastard keeps his hands off my arse. Gave me a right feel-up last time,' Leanne said, scowling.

'Okay, okay. Let's get on. Kirsty and Jamie, you unpack champagne glasses, polish and get on trays in the back room. Mary, unpack canapés and put on baking trays ready to go. Leanne, go to the kitchen, where the chef has heated the General's canapes. Get them on a platter, and then Danilo will escort you down. Come on now, we work hard for a few hours, then we go home. A long day tomorrow.'

Josie looked at her watch, performing a 180 degree as she did. The earpiece crackled. 'Nice place, Josie. The door passes are a pain in the arse, but we should be able to get through, even if I have to blow the bloody doors off,' said Macca, a smile in his voice at his bad Michael Caine impression.

'Come on, chip-chop,' said Grigor, clapping his hands together.

Josie set off outside whistling a tune from *The Italian Job*, a spring in her step and low-key adrenaline coursing through her veins. She picked up a large tray of canapés from the Scotia van that was waiting in the courtyard, then turned and made her way back into the castle, gaining access by tapping the card against the reader at the side of the door. She walked through the ballroom and into the surprisingly small kitchen at the rear. A harassed-looking red-headed chef wearing a Scotia Catering apron nodded at her. 'On the side,' she barked, before busying herself with artfully arranging a selection of tiny, delicate-looking canapés on a silver platter held by a terrified-looking Leanne.

'Okay, take to the vestibule, where Danilo will meet you and escort you down to the General's quarters,' said Grigor, looking nervous and harassed.

'Aye, I'm good,' said Leanne, a tremor in her voice.

'Settle down, stupid girl, just bloody canapés,' said Grigor, balancing a champagne flute on the platter. 'Okay, be very careful.'

Leanne set off into the ballroom with Josie a few steps behind her. Danilo was lurking at the vestibule door, looking at his watch, a scowl on his face. Sensing that this was a one-off opportunity, Josie did something she hadn't done since she was a schoolkid. She flicked her foot forward, just catching the back of Leanne's stiletto heel with the toe of her sneaker-clad foot. The touch was light, and almost undetectable, but it had enough force to knock the tip of Leanne's shoe into the back of her lead foot. She stumbled, and the champagne flute flew forward in a graceful arc before exploding on the vestibule floor, followed by the entire tray and its contents, which hit the marble with a deafening crash. The silence that followed was almost as loud in its intensity.

Josie moved fast. 'Oh you poor thing,' she said, steadying

Leanne with a firm grip on her elbow.

Danilo's face contorted in barely suppressed rage. 'You stupid girl, look what you do, and General Bruzek is waiting. Why you wear such stupid shoe, eh?' he bristled.

Grigor appeared, open-mouthed in shock. 'Oh Leanne, for God's sake. What happened?'

'I'm sorry, I'm sorry, I just tripped,' Leanne stuttered, tears welling in her eyes and smudging her thick make-up. Within seconds, she resembled a panda.

'Grigor, get someone else to do it, quickly. Stupid girl, wearing such shoes for a job. She think General will fuck her, eh? No bonus for you.' Danilo glared at Grigor, his eyes blazing.

Grigor turned to Josie. 'Quick, Mary, run to kitchen, more canapés and more champagne.'

'Fast. General does not wait,' barked Danilo, turning his glare on Josie.

'It wasn't her fault, she just tripped,' said Josie, putting her arm around Leanne's shoulders.

'Never mind that,' snapped Grigor. 'Get tray and champagne, and Leanne, start clearing this mess up.'

Her insides boiling with excitement, Josie turned and jogged back towards the kitchen, where the chef was pulling another tray of canapés from the oven. 'Hi, I need another platter. The last one was dropped.'

'Aye, bloody typical daft wee girly wearing those shite shoes. No surprising, eh? At least you have sensible gutties on.' Quickly and efficiently the chef lined up another selection of the delicious-looking bites on a fresh platter, no trace of panic on her featureless face. Clearly she was used to the heat of a busy kitchen, and a dropped tray was no problem to her.

'Champagne is in the fridge and a new glass is on the side. You know what each of these is?' she said.

'No,' said Josie, looking at the platter.

'Aberdeen Angus beef and horseradish miniature Yorkshire

pudding. Crowdie cheese tartlet. Smoked salmon blini with Beluga caviar. Mini oatcake with Arbroath smokie. Got it?' said the chef, smiling for the first time as she pointed to each canapé.

'Got it,' said Josie, hoping that she had.

She grabbed the champagne bottle from the fridge and quickly filled a single flute, which she put on the tray before setting off towards the vestibule. Danilo and Grigor were waiting for her.

'You're very quick, well done,' said Grigor.

'Sensible footwear.' Josie nodded at her sneaker-clad feet.

'What your name?' said Danilo, his expression softening.

'Mary.'

'Follow me, be very polite and address General Bruzek as "General", okay?'

'Aye.'

'He may ask about the canapés. Make something up if you don't know.' A tight smile formed on his face.

'Chef told me what they are. I think I remember,' said Josie, nodding at the tray.

Danilo narrowed his eyes and appraised Josie with renewed interest. He pulled out a blue lanyard from his pocket and popped it over her head. 'Give red one back at gate when finished. You're now serving VIP guests. Grigor, make sure Leanne wears sensible shoe tomorrow. She a waitress, not a bloody hooker.'

Chapter 50

Macca looked again at the grainy footage that Josie had recorded on her watch camera and paused it as it swept over the external castle door.

'Jesus, the quality isn't perfect, but did Josie somehow banjo that poor girl so she could get into Bruzek's quarters?' said Charlie, his voice full of respect.

'I think she bloody did. She's a marvel. I've never known guts like that under pressure. I've worked with a lot of spies in my time, and she's better than any of them,' said Macca.

'See how she gets on down there, but I agree. What do you make of the doors?'

'Proximity door access systems are a pain in the arse. I can't even pick those bastards. Anything we can do electronically?' Macca looked at Asquith, who was sitting at the scrubbed kitchen table.

'Not without getting hold of a top-end hacker, and I don't know one. We'd need to be able to access the system to disable it remotely, or somehow get a card. I think we may need to be a little more agricultural in our approach.'

'Door ram?' asked Charlie, whose eyes were glued to another screen, watching the feed from the remote camera in its make-shift hide.

'You want to carry one?' asked Macca.

'Well, they're a bit heavy.'

'Aye, and look at the hinges and locks; they look very substantial. That bloody door is thick – I suspect solid oak – so it would be very noisy, and there's nothing more embarrassing than failing to breach a door with multiple bashes. Hopefully Josie can give us more intelligence when she gets back. The ballroom doors look simpler, but I doubt the medals will be there. With any luck she can hold on to the door pass. Even if it gets us through one, it's better than nothing.'

'I've overlaid the GPS position with the blueprints of the castle that your American lady friend supplied. Look.' Asquith turned his laptop around. An architect's drawing of the castle was visible on the screen, overlaid onto a map, with a pulsing blue light visible close to the cliff edge in the main building. 'I'd say that this is the ballroom.' He pointed to the largest of the rooms, which was at the opposite end of the building.

'What room's the tracker in, then?' said Jacko, leaning over, a mug in hand.

'Issue we have is that a fair amount of the new building is underground. The GPS can't tell us what level it's on, but according to the plans, it could either be in the gym, on the lowest level, in a bathroom on the mid lower ground, or in what is described as the master suite, which comprises a huge living space and attached bedroom suite. I think we can be fairly certain he wouldn't have a safe in a gym, or bathroom. What's interesting about this room is that it seems to feature, and I quote, "a seven-metre state-of-the-art viewing facility, with frameless argon-filled triple-glazing and Juliet balcony, which is a unique feat of engineering, being carved into the ancient sandstone".'

'What, so the bastard dug a big fuck-off patio door into the side of a bastard cliff?' Jacko shook his head, his mouth agape.

'Looks like it.'

'What a pretentious prick. I can't bloody stand new money. Zero class.'

'Ostentatious, I grant you. Does it afford us an opportunity?' said Asquith.

'Well, I'm betting the medals are there. It's not like he'd keep them in the shit-house, would he?' said Jacko, scratching his head with a grimace.

'Boys, hold up. Quiet a second,' said Charlie, who had one earbud in his ear with a wire snaking down to the iPad that was open in front of him.

The others turned to face him. 'What?' said Macca.

'Hunter's shop, listen. This is happening live.' Charlie pulled the wire from the iPad and the speaker burst into life.

'. . . This is an outrage. I'm a respected antiques and militaria dealer. If anything that's passed through my hands turns out to be stolen, unbeknownst to me, I can't be held accountable.'

They all immediately recognised Hunter's booming, plummy tones.

A new voice erupted out of the speaker, gruffer and deeper. 'Well, we've just come into possession of significant new evidence, Mr Hunter. You're under arrest on suspicion of handling stolen goods and conspiracy to steal.'

'That's Mark Johnstone. Shit. How the hell have they got to Hunter?'

'I want my solicitor, and I'll be making an official complaint. I would never knowingly handle stolen property.' Hunter's voice was full of bluster, but even through the small speaker, they could all hear the fear in his voice.

'You can have your solicitor, Mr Hunter. However, you need to know that we've also arrested Jimmy Grigson, and we're actively seeking the person we know supplied other medals to him, which we believe to have been passed to you. Grigson is at a police station as we speak.' This voice was female, and self-assured.

'I'll complain in the strongest terms—' began Hunter, but DI Kelly cut him off with a sharp retort.

'We know it all, Mr Hunter. The whole chain of events, from the beating up of Jarman in prison to you receiving the two sets of medals. Your best chance of mitigating the level of trouble you're in is to tell us where those stolen medals are now. Okay?'

The line crackled with static. 'I want my solicitor, and I'll say nothing else.'

'Fine. Let's get out of here.'

There was a tense silence in the farmhouse kitchen. It was Jacko who broke it.

'They've nicked Grigson. Shit, boys, what are we gonna do?'

Chapter 51

Josie followed Danilo's enormous back as he used his blue lanyard and key card to get through the first door, which led to an elegant marble staircase lit by smaller versions of the chandeliers she'd seen in the ballroom. They went down two windowless flights until they came to a couple of large doors in a wide-open space at the bottom of the staircase. A huge mirror hung on the wall, alongside a vast painting of Stonehaven Castle.

The door on the left was unmarked, but the one on the right had a brass plate on it marked *Guest Suites*.

Danilo pressed his key card to the pad on the right-hand door and it clicked open, leading to a small reception room occupied by a large oak desk with a sleek-looking computer monitor on it. The floor was polished marble, and the walls were covered with military-looking prints and paintings.

'My office,' he said as he moved to a further door, which he again used his key card to access. It clicked open and he entered ahead of her.

The sight of the room almost knocked the breath out of her.

It was dominated by an immense full-height window, with the slate-grey North Sea stretching out interminably ahead beyond the glass. While it looked to be frameless, it had a similar proximity pad to the doors, so she assumed it would open, and there was some kind of balcony outside it. As Josie looked harder, she could see a faint horizontal line indicating that there was some type of hidden hinge, probably for access to the balcony, which seemed to run along the entire width of the glass.

'Wow!' she said, taking in the view.

'This isn't Leanne,' said Bruzek, who was sitting in a leather chair to one side of the window. The room seemed to be in the style of a library, with walls of old-looking books, and a chester-field sofa and chair. The flooring was polished parquet, covered with an expensive-looking rug. To the right was a more informal sitting area, with three enormous L-shaped velvet sofas arranged around a vast TV set into the wall. There was not a trace of a wire or cable anywhere. The plain whitewashed walls were covered in art, both modern and old.

'She was clumsy and incompetent, General. This is Mary; she seems smart.'

Bruzek looked at Josie with interest. Her skinny jeans and snug-fitting top showed off her slim body, and his attention seemed to intensify as he gazed.

'Capital. Efficient is essential, Danilo.'

'I need to make a call. Is okay?' said the bodyguard.

'Of course. Mary and I will talk.'

Danilo nodded and left the room.

'Come and tell me about canapés, young lady,' Bruzek said, beckoning her over.

Josie moved forward and proffered the flute of champagne, which he took in his small, pudgy hand, sniffing the straw-coloured liquid. 'Is it the Krug?' he said, his eyebrows raised.

'Yes, General,' she replied. In reality, she had no idea whether it was Krug or not, having not looked closely at the bottle, but seeing as he'd asked the question, it felt sensible to answer in the affirmative. Confirmation bias seemed a good idea right now.

'So, what do we have here, my dear?' he asked with oily charm.

Josie pointed at each small morsel in turn as she described them.

Bruzek picked up the beef canapé and popped it in his mouth, chewing wetly. Josie handed him a small linen napkin, which he used to dab at his thin lips. He then tried the others in turn, in total silence, nodding as he ate.

'All most delicious. My guests will be delighted. You'll be here tomorrow, yes?'

'Yes, General.'

'Excellent. Perform as admirably as you have today, and I'll ensure bonus for you,' he said, nodding.

'I love all your beautiful books, General,' she said, indicating the loaded shelves.

'You like to read?'

'I love to read. I grew up on Harry Potter and never looked back.'

'Reading is for the soul of man, my dear. Please, look at this.' He reached for a tome by his elbow. 'You see, *Harry Potter and the Philosopher's Stone*. First edition. Note that it is written by Joanne Rowling, not J. K. Very few of these exist. Extremely valuable.' He nodded, the loose skin beneath his chin wobbling.

'Wow, incredible.'

'What book you read nowadays?' he said, almost bubbling with enthusiasm.

'I like spy novels, General. Always reading them, particularly Ian Fleming.' Josie smiled, knowing she was on solid ground. She'd studied English at university and had written her dissertation on the Bond novels.'

'You like Fleming. James Bond?'

'Of course, General, classics. Fleming was so far ahead of his time, and the legacy is there for all to see.'

Bruzek seemed gripped with a sudden enthusiasm. 'Well, this is wonderful to hear, Mary. I have the entire set in first edition, but these I keep in my safe. They cost me over four hundred thousand pounds last year.' He looked up, eyes shining, and pointed at one of the bookcases, which was more solid-looking than the others.

'No? Really?' Josie gasped, and her excitement was only partly an act.

'Oh, my dear. To find someone who shares my love of the books, particularly one so young. I must show you.' He almost bounced to his feet, his body quivering with childlike enthusiasm, and reached for the underside of one of the smooth teak shelves. Josie looked at her wristwatch, pointing it towards Bruzek. There was a muffled click, and the bookcase swung open noiselessly.

Suddenly there was another click as the door to the room opened and Danilo reappeared. He cleared his throat and tapped at his watch, looking at his employer with hard eyes.

'Of course. Thank you, Danilo. You must excuse me, my dear, I have an appointment. I'll show you the Flemings another time.'

'See yourself out,' Danilo said, surveying her with a mix of curiosity and suspicion. 'Your pass will work on the doors.'

Josie nodded.

'Give me red lanyard,' he said, holding out his shovel-like hand.

She reached into her pocket and pulled out the pass, sweeping around the room with her watch as she handed it over, hoping that it was transmitting.

Danilo nodded. 'Smart dress tomorrow, yes.'

Josie nodded.

'Maybe no big heels, eh?' he added, a twinkle in his piggy eyes.

She smiled and headed out of the room, her watch extended out as she moved through the office, focusing on the locks and hinges. She stepped up her pace as she ascended the two flights of stairs, finally coming out into the vestibule to be met by a young and beautiful girl. She was very slim, with long dark hair and heavy smoky make-up that made her iridescent blue eyes pop.

Despite the cold weather, she was dressed in a tiny plaid skirt that showed her long, tanned legs, and a sparkling vest top. She wore pink Converse sneakers and white socks on her tiny feet.

She stopped and stared as she came face to face with Josie. Her eyes were full of pain, and her mascara was smudged where she'd clearly shed tears. She stood there statue-like, breathing heavily, a suggestion of a tremble in her narrow, bony shoulders.

'Are you okay?' asked Josie softly.

The girl nodded, but with no conviction, and a solitary tear spilt from her left eye. She swiped it away with the back of her hand, further smudging her make-up. 'No English,' she whispered in a Slav-accented voice.

'*Ceština?*' said Josie in Czech.

'*Slovenské*,' replied the girl.

'You live here?'

The girl's eyes widened in surprise at Josie's command of the language. She shook her head. '*Nie, existujem tu,*' she said, her jaw quivering as she spoke.

The Czech and Slovak languages were closely enough related that Josie could understand what the girl had said. *No, I just exist here.* Together with her desperate face, the meaning was clear.

'Can I help?' she asked.

The girl just shook her head.

'What's your name?'

'Renata,' she said, her voice almost inaudible.

They both jumped as the door to the stairs flew open and Danilo appeared in the doorway that Josie had just exited through, his face red and scowling and his shark-like eyes flat and mean. '*Generál je pre vás pripravený,*' he barked.

The girl yelped and ran straight down back towards Bruzek's quarters.

'You don't speak to other staff at the castle, understand?' the bodyguard said, staring hard at Josie.

'I was just asking if she was okay. She looked unhappy.' Josie

274

spoke defiantly, not taking her eyes from the big man.

'Not your business. You get ready for party, lots of work to do.' He turned away and stomped outside.

Josie stayed where she was, Danilo's barked command to Renata ringing in her ears. *The General is ready for you.*

'You okay, Josie?' said Macca into her earpiece.

She raised her wrist and affected looking at the watch. 'There's something odd going on in this place, boys,' she whispered.

Grigor's voice behind her made her flinch. 'Come on, girl, I don't pay you to stand around. Help me get these canapés unloaded.'

'Sorry, I'm on it,' she said, picking up an insulated box and heading towards the kitchen, her mind reeling at what she'd just witnessed.

Something was very, very wrong at Stonehaven Castle, and it wasn't just stolen medals.

Chapter 52

The whole team sat around the table in the kitchen clutching mugs of steaming tea as they listened to Josie's account of the day. It had been an intense few hours at the castle, setting up the tables, getting all the food and drink in order and erecting the *Thank You People of Stonehaven* banner across the room.

'Once again, girl, you've outdone yourself. You've got the gonads of a gorilla,' said Jacko.

'Thanks, I think,' said Josie with a smile.

'A hidden safe, a very stout door and what looks like a digital lock. I'm hazarding a guess that it's properly fortified so won't go in with a swift kick,' said Macca, looking at the recorded feed from Josie's watch camera.

'I'd say so. There's a switch under one of the shelves, which just pops it open, but then getting through the lock is a different matter.'

'Still, we're in a far better situation than we were. I just hope your confidence isn't writing cheques you can't cash. Don't get over-cocky, girl,' said Macca, eyeing her ruefully.

'I'm all good, but I have to go with what comes up and keep thinking on my feet, right?'

'Aye, you're doing grand, just stay switched on. And don't take any unnecessary risks.'

'I've controlled undercover cops who didn't have ten per cent of your ability, but Macca's right,' added Charlie. 'Don't get too confident, but it does look like there are trafficking victims on site, which shows what scumbags we're dealing with.'

'I can't see any other explanation, can you?' said Josie.

'Well, it's a strong possibility, particularly with the reports from the NCA about the two missing persons, together with Macca's mysterious source of intelligence.'

'I take it we mean the fragrant Ms Laurel Freeman of the CIA?' said Jacko, trying to hide a grin.

'Get tae fuck,' said Macca, glaring at him.

'Is this a new love interest, Macca?' said Josie, her eyes wide with excitement.

'No, it bloody isn't. Now can we get back to the matter at hand. Trafficking victims?' His firm voice indicated that the subject was closed.

'Oh, Macca, I hear she's hot. You could do with a good woman in your life,' said Josie, giggling.

Macca just glared, and then repeated, 'Charlie, trafficking victims?'

'It's a concern, I grant you, but does it change anything? We're here to get the medals back, nothing else. We're not law enforcement. How about this? We do the job, get the medals back, and then once we're clear and safe, we call it in from a burner phone. Come up with something believable and get the cops to raid the place.' Charlie looked around at the others, all of whom nodded their assent.

'Entry to the castle is controlled by key cards, like in hotels, as I described earlier,' said Josie. 'Red lanyard gives restricted access, and blue seems to give unrestricted. Danilo and Teodor have unrestricted passes, as does Bruzek, obviously. A shame they collect them up at the end of the day, but I may be able to hold on to one.'

'Any ideas about the power supply?' said Asquith.

Josie nodded. 'I asked about it, dressed up as "what happens if there's a power cut with it being so remote and exposed", blah, blah. Apparently there's a big diesel generator in a room at the side of the main building.'

'That makes sense. Hold up.' Asquith tapped at his computer and brought up the building plans. 'Here.' He pointed at a small, square building at the north edge of the main building, marked *Plant Room*. 'I was confident that this was where the oil-fired heating and water boiler was sited. It's good for us that it's all in one place, if that's an option. *Is* it an option, Macca?'

'Everything's still an option, but there's only five of us. We need a lot of luck. I can't come up with the final plan until after the party, when Josie's hopefully done the business for us in terms of intelligence.'

'Make your own luck, geezer. We have to be bold, innit?' said Jacko.

'What about Hunter and Grigson?' said Charlie.

'What about them?' asked Macca.

'Does it change anything with them getting nicked?'

'If you mean do we stop – not as far as I'm concerned. It means the cops are on their tail, but as we know, the medals are being moved on Christmas Eve, and Hunter is part of the plan. The police will never get hold of them in time, even if Hunter grasses, which he won't. You've told us how slowly things like this move.'

Charlie raised his eyebrows. 'Probably true. They'll have to deal with the case against those two first, and even if Hunter *does* grass on Bruzek, what then? Cops down south will have to liaise with police up here, and then convince a magistrate that they need to execute a warrant, and get it all done before the twenty-fourth.

I can't see it happening, and that's before we even talk about the fact that Bruzek has his fingers in so many pies that he'd learn of any raid well before it happened. I'd say any police operation up here would be doomed to failure.'

Macca leant forward and rested his elbows on the table, cupping his chin with his palms. 'We carry on as before; in fact this makes it even more urgent. If the bastards want to run with the medals, and whatever else, they've a helicopter on standby ready to fly them to a private jet at Aberdeen. They could be out of the country within an hour. We keep going, but Josie, it's all on you tomorrow. You up for it?'

'Of course.'

'Jacko, anything on the thermal camera?' said Macca.

'More of the same, totally predictable security routine, and I've looked at the recorded footage in the light of what Josie told us about the young girl. There seems to be a minimum of two youngsters that live in that barn there.' He leant over to the blueprint on Asquith's screen and tapped at an oblong building. 'I zoomed in tight on them as they came and went over to the big house a few times. It's not the best footage at that zoom, but it's good enough. Little skinny things, I'd say.'

'Anything in the other barn?'

'No movement from it, and it seems to be always in pitch-blackness, but . . .' Jacko tailed off, as if thinking.

'What?' said Macca, his forehead creased.

'There's definitely something in there. Vague heat signatures on the thermal, and the security man goes in at least once a day. Always carrying a bag of some type.'

'Maybe livestock? Does he keep chickens or something?'

Jacko shrugged.

'Patrols around the perimeter?'

'Hourly on the quad bike. Whoever is on duty also runs the gatehouse after dark, but apart from that, you could mooch about up there and not be seen. Unless there's CCTV.'

'I've not noted any, apart from cameras on the front gate,' said Josie.

'Makes sense. Okay, we carry on regardless, but the stakes are higher. If we don't get them before Christmas Eve, we lose them. That can't happen.' Macca looked up from the table at each person in turn, and they all nodded back.

Chapter 53

Wednesday 22 December 2021

Josie was just pouring herself her first coffee of the day. Her eyes felt gritty, her limbs tired, and a general feeling of exhaustion gripped her. It had been an intense few hours at the castle, but she couldn't help feeling a swell of satisfaction as to what she'd achieved.

The big issue that was worrying her was the girl. The young, skinny, vulnerable-looking Slovak girl, who was clearly a trafficking victim. She felt a surge of anger as she sipped the coffee, determination coursing through her veins. This wasn't just about her dad's medals any more.

Her phone suddenly buzzed on the table. It was Liz, her neighbour from Sandridge and old friend of her parents. She was calling on a WhatsApp voice call.

'Hi, Liz.'

'Hi, Josie. Those two coppers have just been here looking for you, love. Same ones I gave my statement to about what I saw that day. I still feel so terrible about that, love. Meant the bastard got away with bloody murder.' Liz had never got over the fact that her witness statement had led to the manslaughter case being discontinued.

Josie had tipped her the wink that she was going away for a few days, and had asked her to keep an eye out for visitors, particularly police. Liz was smart, and had read between the lines, even if she had no idea what Josie was actually up to.

'Really, what did they say?' she asked, feeling her stomach grip with nerves.

'Not much, but they seemed very keen to get hold of you. They even came around the back, bloody cheek of it. I knew you didn't want them knowing your business, so I said you were out on a long ultra-marathon run. They didn't look happy, I must say.'

'Did they buy it?'

'I think so. I made it look like you were still around,' said Liz.

'How?'

'Coffee pot on the side, radio on, paper on the table and all that. I think they were convinced, so I'd say you're safe. Are you sure you don't want to tell me what this is all about?'

'Best you don't know, Liz. Safe to say it's what my dad would have wanted.'

'You're so like him, love. I've watched you grow up and I know you're a good person, and I hope whatever you're up to, you succeed. You know how much your mum and dad meant to me. They've been wonderful friends.'

'You meant so much to them too. Have you seen Mum?'

'Went in yesterday, but she seemed to think I was a nurse. Got a little snippy with me, but I read her some Danielle Steel and she was all good.'

'Thanks so much, Liz. All being well, I'll be back for Christmas Day.'

'Come for dinner. Can't have you being on your own, and we'd love to have you. The kids will be here, and I've the biggest turkey anyone has ever seen.'

'I'll do that, and thanks again, Liz. I owe you so much.'

'One thing about those coppers, though . . .' Liz left the sentence hanging.

'Go on?' said Josie.

'I stayed eavesdropping out of the window as they were chatting, and DI Kelly got a phone call that seemed to stun her. I think someone's been murdered. They both seemed dumbfounded.'

Josie felt her stomach clench. 'Did they say who?'

'Yes, and I remember because I was shocked by the inspector's potty mouth. She said, "Jesus, Mark, effing Jimmy Grigson has just been found dead in a park in London", and then off they rushed, going like the clappers.'

Chapter 54

Danilo pressed send on the email he'd just composed to his deputy, who was now in Dubai with the other two members of the security detail, preparing for the General's arrival. It had left them a little thin on the ground for this evening's reception, with Teodor having to cover the gate on his own, but it was hardly a risky event, just a few local dignitaries and business owners coming to quaff the General's mid-priced champagne and average-quality canapés. They'd have no problem coping with a drunken shopkeeper, charity boss or garage owner.

His phone began to buzz like a demented wasp on the coffee table in his office next to General Bruzek's quarters, and he looked at the screen to identify the caller on the secure messaging and voice call app he used to communicate with certain contacts.

'Yes,' he said without preamble.

'It's done.' The posh English voice belonged to Charles Overton, the slimy lawyer from London who the General used for sorting legal problems in the capital, both lawfully and unlawfully.

'No problems?'

'None. I used one of my contacts, who contracted a no-mark who doesn't know I exist and certainly doesn't know you. It'll look like a robbery or drug deal gone wrong, and there'll be no leads. Middle of a park with no CCTV, late last night. The stupid idiot decided to buy some cocaine after getting out of the police station. You know the drill.'

'Good. How about Hunter?'

'Hunter is an idiot. Why does the General respect him so much?'

'You know how he is with ex-military types, and he likes Hunter's expertise. What evidence is there linking him to the medals?'

'As long as they don't recover them, there's none, even if they find photographs on his phone. Hunter doesn't even know that idiot burglar Jarman, and vice versa. Jarman's looking at ten years, probably out in five, so he'll keep quiet. Grigson was the link, and all Hunter needs to do with Grigson's sad demise is to claim he was offered the medals and declined, which will explain the photographs on his phone. It'll never cross the prosecution threshold.'

'As long as you're sure,' said Danilo, his forehead creasing. He didn't like this at all.

'It's very important that the medals aren't recovered. Are steps being taken to make sure they're never found? That would be disastrous,' said Overton seriously.

'They won't be. They're currently held securely and are going to Dubai along with the rest of the General's collection. Even if the police did get a tip-off before they go, I'd hear about it immediately. The General is close to many senior police officers in Scotland. Most of them have been to parties at the castle, and shall we say that many availed themselves of all the facilities.' Danilo smirked as he thought of the video footage they had securely stored of police officers, local dignitaries, judges and other VIPs misbehaving at Stonehaven.

'I can imagine,' said Overton, enunciating every syllable.

Danilo sniggered unpleasantly. 'Of course, you've experienced the fleshpots yourself, Charles. The General is always generous at his parties. A shame you'll miss tonight. Are you sure we can't tempt you? The jet is heading south to collect Hunter today.'

'I'll pass. I have family commitments,' said Overton, his voice tight.

'As you wish. Merry Christmas, and send my regards to the lovely Abigail,' said Danilo before hanging up.

The mention of Overton's wife was tactical, of course. He always liked to remind assets he used who exactly held the power, and families always equalled power, particularly when he thought of the video clip that was tucked away of Overton enjoying one of the young Slovakian whores who had passed through the castle a while back. He laughed, a short and crackly sound at the back of his throat, as he reached for a cigar in the humidor on his desk. It was almost time to begin preparations for tonight's festivities and the opportunities they were bound to present.

Weakness always led to opportunities; it was why he and the General had prospered as they had, and Danilo knew that for all his elite military service, it was his ability to manipulate others that was his real skill. He applied a flame to the fragrant cigar with a battered Zippo that bore the crest of his old unit in the 5th Special Forces.

Inhaling the billowing blue smoke, he sat back in his leather recliner and smiled. Tomorrow he'd be sitting by the pool in Dubai, quaffing cocktails and eyeing up the whores who had already been lined up ready for the Christmas party.

'Merry Christmas,' he chuckled.

Chapter 55

'Who was that?' said Macca, as Josie tucked her phone back in her pocket.

'My neighbour Liz. DI Kelly and Charlie's old mate from the Met, Mark Johnstone, have just been at the house looking for me.'

'How did your neighbour have your number? I thought you sent your phone south in the mail?' said Macca.

'I called on my new phone. I thought it wise for her to be kept in the loop if the cops came, and I trust her as much as I trust anyone. She was friends with my folks for years. Anyway, I'm glad I did. She's smart as a whip, that woman. She even used WhatsApp voice call, because she'd seen on some cop show that it was untraceable.'

'Clever.'

'Indeed. She also made it look like I was still at the house, with a pot of coffee and a radio and the like, and she told the police I'd gone out marathon training, which I actually wish I could do. I'm all knotted up and tense.'

'Want a shoulder rub, girl?' said Jacko with a cheeky grin.

'Only if you want me to snap your arm.'

'And I thought you were such a gentle and innocent girl.' Jacko opened his mouth in fake horror.

'Hardly. Anyway, she's a marvel, is Liz. That should keep them well off my case. She said something a bit concerning, though.'

'What?' said Charlie.

'That they rushed off after they got a call, and Liz heard Kelly saying that "fucking Jimmy Grigson has just been found dead in a park in London".'

'Grigson? What? That can't be . . .' Macca paused, mouth agape.

'I'll make a call,' said Charlie, pulling his phone out and walking out of the room.

A silence descended as they waited for him to return. When he did, his grave expression told them everything they needed to know.

'Grigson was found dead in Roundwood Park. Being pegged as a robbery gone wrong, but shit, it's a coincidence, straight after he got nicked and all.'

'These bastards are clearing up. The cops nicked Grigson and then Hunter, and now one of them is dead. Fuck, the stakes are just getting higher every damn second,' said Macca.

'Okay, it's dramatic. But does it change anything?' said Josie, her expression flat.

'What, you're not bothered?' said Jacko.

'About Grigson?'

'Who else?'

'No. Fuck him. He started all this; without him, my dad would still be alive. This changes nothing as far as I'm concerned.'

'Jesus, you're turning into a hard case, Jose.'

Josie just shrugged, her face impassive.

Jacko shook his head. 'Shit, this feels like the cops are closing in.'

'They can't prove anything as long as we keep our heads firmly down and don't do anything stupid,' said Charlie, whose face had grown a little paler since the revelation. 'Even if they do find something out, it'll just be that we're in Scotland, and we have a cover story for that. Lads' fishing trip, phones left at home for a de-stress.'

'They'll never believe that,' said Macca.

'You of all people should know that what they believe doesn't mean jack. It's only what they can prove, and as long as we're disciplined and stay off the radar, we're golden. We can't be linked to the murder, because there *is* no link between us and Grigson, apart from Jacko's meet with him. It could even be a drug deal gone wrong.'

'What time do you need to leave?' said Macca, looking over his spectacles at Josie.

'Soon, I guess. I'm a bit nervous, not gonna lie,' said Josie, looking in the mirror as she brushed her red locks.

'Keeps you sharp. All you need to do is make sure your eyes and ears are open and report anything back to us. We'll be listening.'

'I know. A lot riding on this, though, eh?'

'Aye. You'll be grand. We just need you to try to get eyes on Bruzek's living quarters. If the medals are still there, that's where we'll have to gain entry to, and if they're in a safe, I'll need to be able to blow it. I've managed to get some kit to help, but the more intel I have, the more precise I can make my breaching kit. May have to blow shit up.'

'Are we missing an opportunity here?' said Josie.

'What do you mean?'

'We know that they're flying at ten a.m. on Christmas Eve, right?'

'Aye.'

'And we can be pretty sure that they'll be taking the helicopter. No way is Bruzek gonna behave like a prole.'

'Aye, we know he habitually uses the helo.'

'Well, we also know that Bruzek, Hunter and presumably Danilo will be on the helicopter, and that they'll have the medals, so why don't we wait until they leave and then hold them up?

They won't be armed, will they?'

'Well, not if they're heading for an airport, no. That's a decent point, Josie. Why the hell didn't I think of it?' said Macca.

'Getting old,' said Jacko with a snigger.

'Problem is that Danilo is built like a gorilla and Teodor looks a tough bugger. Plus we can't be sure they won't have guns, and we *don't* have guns,' said Josie.

'Some of that is correct at least,' said Macca.

'Meaning?' said Charlie, his voice full of suspicion.

'I have four Glock 19s hidden away, in case of situations like this.'

'No guns, we agreed no guns,' said Charlie, leaping to his feet, his voice hardening.

'To be fair, we said whatever it takes, and we actually said that if we saw guns we'd re-evaluate,' said Jacko.

'Josie, have you seen guns?' asked Charlie.

'No, no sign.' She shook her head.

'None on the guards we've watched on the camera. So, no guns.' Charlie sat down heavily and jutted his jaw.

'Okay, how about this,' said Macca. 'We give Josie another chance today to see what she can learn. We already know that Bruzek has a strongroom or safe in his quarters, and she's going to be pouring the champagne and dishing out the vol-au-vents tonight. Who knows what might crop up. If we get no other opportunities, we hold them up at the helicopter, and for that we need guns. There's not enough of us to overpower the bastards without firearms, particularly with two of them being ex-Slovak Special Forces. Charlie, at this point you can drop out if you want to, and the rest of us will do it, okay?' Macca looked directly at the ex-cop.

Charlie sighed in despair and dropped his face into his hands. 'I knew hanging with you lot was a bad idea. You know I won't drop out, you utter, utter bastards.' His voice was muffled before he suddenly looked up, eyes blazing. 'Josie, you'd better bloody find a way.'

Josie's hand went to the watch on her wrist. 'I'll try my best,' she said, shoulders squared and jaw firm. At that moment, she'd never looked more like her father.

Chapter 56

DI Kelly felt nervous as she stood next to DS Johnstone by the control tent on the edge of Roundwood Park in Harlesden, opposite a middle-aged detective in an ill-fitting suit. A lanyard around his neck identified him as Detective Superintendent Tim Wilson, and he didn't look happy. His face was pale, his nose bright red and his eyes rheumy. Standing next to him was a slim black woman wearing a windcheater emblazoned with the letters IOPC – the Independent Office for Police Conduct.

'So let me get this straight,' said Wilson. 'You're investigating a complex manslaughter investigation, which you've linked to a couple of fences in the Met area. You nick both of them, and release them under investigation, and now one is dead and the other is being shielded by some high-priced anti-police lawyer. What the hell aren't you telling us, DI Kelly?' His voice with its dark Scottish accent was rough and sounded uncomfortable, and he let out a volley of wet, rattling coughs. 'Sod this bloody cold. I should be at home. So?'

'Nothing, I assure you, sir. We have an inmate who was beaten almost to death, we believe in revenge for the burglary in Sandridge, and also a gang of ex-commandos who we think are hell-bent on recovering the medals. We're simply trying to prevent further bloodshed and vigilante activity.'

'I assume this is all covered in your decision log and risk assessment?' said the IOPC investigator, who had identified herself as Lin Asante.

'Of course,' said Kelly, thinking of the endless blank sheets in her decision log and the empty space on her computer that should have contained the risk assessment she'd been promising herself she'd complete.

'That's good. You'll of course be aware that as the victim was killed within twenty-four hours of his release from detention, it falls to us to supervise this enquiry, yes?'

'Obviously.'

'Excellent, well I look forward to receiving your full report, risk assessment and copies of your decision log. I have to go now, Tim.' Asante turned to Wilson.

'Of course, Lin. I'll make sure all documents come your way as soon as possible,' he said, stifling a further hacking cough.

Asante nodded. 'This will be the fullest investigation into all aspects of this unfortunate case. The public will demand to know how a man possibly at risk could be so senselessly and brutally murdered within hours of his release. I have to say, I'm very concerned about the management of this case, so I'll be sure to study everything you send in great detail.' She turned and strode away.

Wilson wheezed and coughed again, wiping his mouth with a stained handkerchief. 'Fucking all I need just before Christmas. You'd best piss off back to Hertfordshire and get your report written. She's a right cow, that Asante, and will definitely not accept your first answer.' He reached into his jacket for a packet of cigarettes, plucked one out and lit it with a cheap lighter.

Kelly wrinkled her nose at the acrid smoke, but managed to speak politely. 'What are the circumstances, sir?' she said.

'Christ knows. No witnesses, nothing. Looks like a junkie or a dealer called it in – dead body in the park was as far as he went. Pathologist reckons he was dead within four hours of you lot letting him go, stabbed multiple times with a big nasty knife. It stinks to high heaven, and IOPC are going to want to get their teeth into it. Want my advice?' he said, taking a pull on his cigarette and coughing again.

'Sure,' said Kelly, her guts churning.

'Go back to wherever the hell you came from, write this up to within an inch of its life and get all of it to me as soon as is superhumanly possible.'

'We'll do that. Then what?'

'Then piss off for Christmas. Eat turkey, drink Baileys and try and forget about all this crap.'

'Really? Surely we can be of assistance,' said Kelly, feeling the familiar butterflies beginning in her stomach as her temper rose.

'Nope. No chance.' He flicked the half-smoked cigarette onto the damp grass. 'Whatever you do, stay the fucking fuck away from this bastard case. However bad you think whatever these bloody ex-marines are doing is, it's way smaller than what we have here. Am I clear?' he said, his voice firm and wet with phlegm.

'Understood, sir,' said Kelly, nodding.

'That IOPC woman seemed a bit fierce,' said Johnstone as they headed back to their car. 'I hope you've got this all squared away, boss.'

'Yeah, about that. I guess I've some retrospective faffing about to do. Are all the phone data authorities tight? We need that data, urgently.'

'Yeah, all squared. I'm happy as long as you are.'

'Do we still have forward-facing data for associated phones?'

'Yes, until tomorrow, when it expires. We'll need a fresh application after that.'

'Good, check for any updates from the telephone intel folks. I want a full run-down, including any new numbers appearing on wives' or common contacts' call logs. They may have left their phones and got burners. Get the burners and we get them. I'm not having a load of ex-squaddies getting one over on me.'

'Sorry? Didn't we just get told to quit?'

'We did, but he's not my boss, the sleazy bastard.'

'So we're not quitting? Despite the murder?'

'Especially because of the murder. Someone's clearing up, and I'm not having it. I want to know where that bastard Jackson is right now. This all stinks of him.'

'Really? He didn't strike me as that kind of criminal. He's just a commercial burglar, not a murderer.' Johnstone stopped and stared at her.

Kelly felt another surge of anger, and her face began to flush. 'No way. There's more to it; we just aren't seeing it yet. Some bastard is killing people to finish this enquiry, and I'm not putting up with it. We carry on.'

'Despite the IOPC?'

'Despite the IOPC. Come on, let's go.'

Chapter 57

The reception was exactly as Josie had expected for the type of event organised by someone who was really only doing it under duress, as Bruzek clearly was.

The vast ballroom was lavishly decorated, with an enormous tree at the far end, and there were twinkling lights on every available surface and snaking along the walls, suspended over the paintings and artworks.

The ballroom was three-quarters full of people all dressed in their finery, various shades of tartan clashing with evening dresses, and even an occasional fur stole. It was dotted with men in military mess dress adorned with miniature medals, and a senior-looking police officer was in deep conversation with a man Grigor had told them to pay special attention to: the lord provost for the local area, as signified by the gold chain of office around his neck.

A four-piece ceilidh band, consisting of accordion, fiddle, penny whistle and guitar, performed on the small stage, playing low-key tunes as the guests stood in clutches chatting. The scene was one of restrained and yet semi-drunken merriment, thought Josie as she threaded her way through the throng carrying a silver platter loaded with canapés, wearing her best dazzling smile. The rest of the revellers seemed to be local businesspeople, deep in conversation as they sipped from their champagne flutes, which Jamie and Grigor were constantly replenishing from magnum-sized bottles of Laurent-Perrier.

Suddenly there was a hubbub, and Danilo entered the room with Marek Bruzek close behind, looking smaller than ever in the shadow of the huge bodyguard. Josie almost had to suppress a giggle at the sight. Bruzek was wearing a kilt, a cutaway jacket with silver buttons and a bow tie. He had three miniature medals on his chest, none of which she recognised. His brogues were highly polished, and a small knife, which she knew was called a *sgian dubh*, was tucked into his sock top.

He wandered through the crowd, smiling and nodding shyly, limply shaking hands with guests, Danilo always just a few feet away. Reaching the small stage, he sat with a flourish on the Pictish throne and nodded at Professor Henderson, who was standing to one side with a microphone in his hand. Danilo gestured to the band, who ceased playing, and Professor Henderson tapped the microphone. The whole room silenced and turned to face Bruzek, who looked somehow like a gnome on a toadstool, his brogues barely brushing the soft carpet of the stage as the harsh light from the chandeliers reflected in his slick dark hair.

Henderson raised the microphone and spoke, his voice rich with the local Doric accent. 'Ladies and gentlemen, welcome to Stonehaven Castle.' This prompted a smattering of applause. 'Thank you all so much for attending this year's Christmas reception. It's wonderful to see the local community at Stonehaven Castle once more. We have many more plans for the restoration of the site, including the rebuilding of more of the dyke walls and continuing reinforcement of the sea defences. We can also proudly announce that General Bruzek has generously decided that he will fully restore the thirteenth-century chapel, which at present is a ruin at the south edge of the outcrop.' He paused, scanning the room as the crowd gave a warm round of applause.

'My faculty will be working closely with General Bruzek and the team of expert craftsmen, who will be unstinting in their dedication in bringing back to life the ancient chapel. It will be regularly opened to the public, who will be able to experience first-hand how the occupants of Stonehaven Castle worshipped in the past. May I take this opportunity to extend our gratitude to you, General.' There was another smattering of applause, and Bruzek tilted his head regally in recognition.

Professor Henderson stepped forward and with a deferential bow handed the microphone to Bruzek, who stood from his throne and faced the crowd, taking in the uniforms, cocktail dresses and Highland attire with obvious satisfaction. When he spoke, his voice was little more than a whisper, the high pitch and odd delivery making it difficult to understand him. Every guest paused, almost afraid to breathe.

'Lady and gentleman, I want to thank you all for coming to my home to celebrate the festivity season. My desirement to restore Stonehaven to her beautiful self is what drives and motivates me to be able to service my new community. Thanking all of you whose have supported me and my staffs in transporting Stonehaven back into life. Without all of you, it would have been unpossible. So please make sure you have full glass, and let us be making a toast. Stonehaven Castle, happy Christmas.' He raised his flute and smiled widely, his teeth blindingly white in the harsh light.

Everyone in the room followed suit and repeated the toast.

'Thank you. Now, as I am old man, I must retire to my quarters, but please enjoy the rest of the evening.' He handed the microphone back to Henderson and stepped down from the stage, Danilo moving regally ahead of him through the now chattering crowd like Moses parting the Red Sea. Josie had to force herself to stop staring at the contrast of the diminutive figure of Bruzek being led by the broad shoulders of the huge bodyguard.

And then he was gone, and the revellers carried on drinking and chatting and the ceilidh band struck up with a fresh ditty, a sense of bonhomie filling the ballroom once more.

'Josie.' A voice cut through the noise, and she turned to see Grigor at her shoulder.

'Yes?' she said, feeling the flutter of nerves in her belly.

'Change of plan. General Bruzek wants to entertain his male VIP guests to port and cigars in his quarters, like old gentleman club in bloody London.' He rolled his eyes and sighed. 'Get some port glasses from kitchen and take them down, and have chef prepare a selection of cheeses. They're all sick of bloody canapés. You know what port glasses look like?'

'Yes, I'm not an idiot, you know.'

'Good, don't mess up.'

'It's not like I'm gonna trip over my stilettos, is it?' she said, pointing at her black sneakers.

Grigor said nothing, but he narrowed his eyes with disdain, and Josie decided that Leanne might have expressed her suspicions to him about her unfortunate stumble.

'Don't mess up. Important people at VIP reception, and if General flirt with you a little bit, maybe just put up with it, eh?'

'What do you mean?' said Josie, setting her tray down on the table next to her.

'Sometimes with a bit of booze in him, he gets friendly. You want big bonus, you be nice, eh?' Grigor nodded and strode off.

Josie was conflicted. If Bruzek was a sex pest, she might be able to turn that to her advantage, but no way was she willing to lead him on. If he tried anything, she knew that her first reaction, to snap his wrist, wouldn't be the most sensible, bearing in mind the plan for later.

She knew one thing, though. The team and the mission were depending on her. Josie Chapman, daughter of the late Regimental Sergeant Major Frankie Chapman, CGC, DCM.

Her father's words rang in her ears. *Eyes front, shoulders back, my girl. You're a Chapman – never forget that.*

She turned to the door, straightened her spine and set off towards the kitchen.

She would not let him down.

Chapter 58

Josie was standing in General Bruzek's private quarters beside a low teak table that was laden with a large wooden fruit bowl containing a myriad of apples, oranges, peaches, figs and grapes. A heavy crystal decanter of port stood on the table, next to a heavy slate with wedges of various cheeses on it, together with a selection of thin water biscuits and several sharp-looking knives. To her right shoulder was the vast glass wall overlooking the North Sea. Her mind wandered to the blueprints she'd been studying in the farmhouse earlier. The mostly subterranean structure, dug into the soft Aberdeenshire peat, the huge ballroom, the semi-concealed floor-to-ceiling window carved into the granite cliff. Ostentatious though it was, it was still a marvel of construction.

Her face was impassive, despite the initial shock she had felt upon entering the room and seeing Giles Hunter sitting on one of the sofas. He was dressed in a dinner suit, with three miniature medals on his chest and a glass in his hand. The ruby-red port was only a few shades darker than his face. He'd clearly been availing himself of Bruzek's hospitality to the fullest extent. With all the mad events of the last few days, she'd totally forgotten that he was headed for the castle, ready to accompany Bruzek to Dubai the following day. She breathed deeply and evenly. *Calm yourself*, she thought. *You're red-headed Mary McLeish from Arbroath, not Josie Chapman from St Albans.*

The room was full of the acrid stench of cigar smoke as the group of men lounging on the vast acreage of the large sofas puffed away on huge stogies. They all held glasses of the port that Josie had dispensed from the decanter.

'This port is stunning, General. May I ask about it?' said a middle-aged, grey-haired man dressed in tartan trews and a cutaway jacket sporting a small row of dress medals. Josie recognised the insignia as being that of the Black Watch, and the crown and pip on his shoulders signified that the man was a lieutenant colonel.

'Of course you may, Hector. This is very old Taylor Fladgate single harvest, which I procure in London last year. Matured for very long time, my friend,' said Bruzek, raising his glass.

'And expensive, no doubt. Your generosity is legendary, General,' said the lord provost, his chains of office glinting in the light from the huge, modern-looking chandelier.

'What is moneys, my friend, if you can't spend it on the wondrous things you desire?' Bruzek's high-pitched voice was laced with childish enthusiasm. Clearly he was in some awe at the company he was keeping.

'Well, I propose a toast, General, to a merry Christmas and a prosperous new year for all of us,' said the small, wiry, senior-looking police officer Josie had seen in the main hall.

'Of course, Assistant Chief Constable. I'm so gracious for your presence here. Now, I will ask the lovely Mary to bring us over some cheeses. Chef sources them from the best of cheesemongers in Aberdeenshire, and they are the perfect complement for a little more ports. After that, I will treat you to the most specialist and certainly the most expensive whisky you have ever experienced.'

Bruzek giggled, his words slightly slurred, and turned to look at the bookshelf that housed the vault.

Josie's heart leapt. The whisky was kept in the vault; she knew it. There was none on display, and no obvious drinks cabinet, and she hadn't been asked to bring any down. She looked at her watch, sweeping it around the room before moving to the group on the sofas, the decanter in her hand. As she went around filling glasses, she felt invisible to all the men, apart from Bruzek, who eyed her with an unpleasant expression. Hunter just sat back in his seat, his eyes glazed.

Returning to the table, she picked a handful of grapes, and several figs from the fruit bowl, and piled them in the centre of the cheese slate and took it over to the coffee table between the sofas, where she set it down carefully before backing away and retreating to her position.

Bruzek stood and raised his glass. '*Na zdravie*, as we would say in Slovakia, although we would be drinking Slovakian Tatratea, which I don't care for.'

'*Slàinte mhath*, as we say in Scotland,' said the lieutenant colonel, also standing and lifting his glass.

Bruzek smiled seraphically. 'Of course, Hector, *schlàinte mhaths*.'

The rest of them rose and downed their port, laughing. Hunter stumbled as he stood, prompting chuckles from the other men.

'Oh, Giles, it look like you drunks a little too much of my port, eh?' said Bruzek.

'And champagne, and wine, and I suspect gin and tonic,' said Hector with a scornful guffaw.

Hunter just stared glassily at the officer and smiled lopsidedly.

Josie glanced at her watch, which showed that it was 9.30 p.m., and loosened it on her wrist, and tucked it into her palm. As the men were chinking the glasses again, she quickly, and smoothly eased her hand out, and rested it briefly on the fruit bowl, tucking the watch tight in between a couple of apples, the lens pointed straight at the bookshelf where she'd seen Bruzek go to the previous day.

'Mary, my dear young filly, would you return to the ballroom, please. I have important business to discuss with these fine gentlemens,' Bruzek said, oozing insincere and oily charm.

'Of course, General. Shall I pour some more port first?' she asked, reaching for the decanter.

'No thank you, I want to serve guests my beautiful whisky myself. Danilo will instruct you when to come back to clear away.' He folded his arms and puffed out his small chest.

Josie nodded to the group of men and headed out of the room, noting that no swipe was required to exit. Once the door had slammed behind her, she paused in Danilo's office, looking at the large teak desk with the modern computer monitor on it.

'Josie, are . . . out of . . .?' came Macca's distorted voice in her ear. Reception was bad here; she was presumably in a black spot in the bowels of the castle.

She didn't try and answer; there was little point. Instead she moved towards the desk, which had a leather swivel chair pushed up tight against it. Next to the monitor was a framed photograph of the huge bodyguard in khaki uniform, cradling some kind of assault weapon, a red beret perched on his huge head. He looked mean, and nasty, his lopsided grin more of a sneer.

Instinctively her hand was drawn to the desk drawer, which slid open noiselessly when she pulled at the silver handle. Inside was a sheaf of papers all written in Slovak, and a bundle of pens held together with a rubber band.

As she moved the papers to one side, a solitary brass-coloured bullet rolled out from them and onto the wooden drawer base, the noise somehow deafening in the confined space. She sucked in a breath and the hairs on the back of her neck stood up. A bullet. Firearms. The bastards *were* armed.

The sudden squeak of a footfall on the staircase the other side of the door made her flinch, but she didn't panic. She just slid the drawer closed and stepped away from the desk, at the exact moment that the card reader outside beeped. Then the door burst open and Danilo was there, bristling and looming in front of her, a man mountain of muscle, bone and sinew.

'What are you doing?' he snarled, his eyes hard and unrelenting as they seemed to bore into her very soul.

'The General has dismissed me while he talks to his friends. He says you'll call me when it's time to clear up. I'm just on my way to the ballroom,' she said, willing a slight tremor into her voice. Danilo was used to intimidating people, so it seemed a natural thing to do.

He stood there unmoving for a full beat before he nodded and stepped aside to let her pass. Josie breathed a sigh of relief as she left the office, her heart pounding in her chest as she ascended the stairs two at a time. She needed to let the others know.

The vestibule was buzzing with departing guests, all giggling and swaying. Josie went out into the frigid air, pulled out her phone and dialled.

'Macca, they're armed,' she said in a hoarse whisper, cupping her hand over the receiver. 'I looked in Danilo's desk and there was a bullet in there.'

'What are you talking about?'

Josie ignored him. 'I hid the watch camera and mic in the fruit bowl in Bruzek's quarters, it has a direct view of the hidden cupboard in the bookcase. I can hear you, but you can't hear me until I get the watch back, but I thought it might be helpful, bearing in mind I think he's about to go into the safe that I'm sure is behind that shelf.'

A shout from behind her made her jump. It was an angry-sounding Grigor.

'Mary, no phone calls. You here to work, not gossip.'

'I have to go, keep watching.' Josie pocketed her phone. 'Sorry, I'm coming now.'

Chapter 59

Macca and the rest of the team stared with bated breath at the grainy footage from Josie's watch camera, which was focused on the bookshelf.

Voices came through the tinny speakers, a little crackly, but perfectly audible.

'Now that the dolly bird has gone, luscious though she is, General, you said something very interesting about an old whisky, and my taste buds are positively tingling at the prospect,' said a soft Scottish-accented voice.

'Come on, you bastards, do something. Get in there,' said Macca.

'Of course, Hector, a Scottish officer and gentlemans should have only the best whisky. Wait one moment, I keep this one under lock and key, as my insurer was very nervous.'

Bruzek appeared in front of the bookshelf, his kilt almost comically short. He reached underneath one of the shelves and there was a metallic clunk, then the bookcase swung open on well-lubricated hinges. He stepped up to the heavy wooden door behind it, reinforced with criss-cross iron struts, and jabbed at a digital keypad, then pressed his thumb to a glass panel. There was another clunk and the door popped open. Bruzek stepped inside, but the angle and his back didn't allow a clear view; all that was visible was the edges of some picture frames in the brightly lit space. It was, however, clear that it was a decent-sized room.

'Can we see inside?' said Asquith.

'Not properly, but at least we know what we're dealing with. Digital access code and a thumbprint. Shit, that girl is a damn marvel.'

Bruzek turned, cradling a wooden box almost like a newborn baby. He pushed the door closed behind him, followed by the bookshelf, which clunked back into place.

His voice, when he spoke, was akin to that of a proud father. 'Gentlemens, anyone care for a little Macallan 1940 single malt before you depart?' he said, proffering the case with a smile.

'Don't get used to that fucking whisky, shit-for-brains,' said Macca, his voice low and full of menace.

Chapter 60

The reception was thinning out fast, with just a few knots of tartan-clad men and giggling cocktail-dressed women lingering in the ballroom. Grigor and the others were busily clearing away the trays that had been picked clean by the hungry guests. There were empty glasses on every surface, and the floor was littered with crushed pastry, crumbs of oatcake and the occasional sliver of smoked salmon.

'Oh, you've decided to join the plebs, eh, Mary?' said Leanne, a scowl on her face as Josie entered the room and picked up a broom from beside the door.

'He's an old lech. I'd have swapped any time, and I have to go back when that gorilla tells me to bloody clear up. I hope we're all on a decent bonus.' Josie began to sweep the floor.

Grigor was ushering the last few stragglers out of the double doors to where a small fleet of minibuses was waiting to ferry them back across the causeway. When he returned to the ballroom, he clapped his hands.

'Right, we finish up here and get all trays back into van, then we get out of here,' he called, clearly eager to depart.

'I've got to go back and clear up when the General's guests have left,' said Josie.

'Ah, shit, how long?' said Grigor, looking at his watch with a scowl.

'He didn't say. He's sending Danilo when he's ready. He's serving up overly expensive whisky to show off to all the twats in his quarters.' Josie carried on sweeping the parquet.

Grigor swore in Polish, then moved closer and spoke in a hushed voice. 'Look, I need to get the others back to the base before eleven, or I have to pay them until midnight. If you stay behind to clear up General's quarters, I'll pay you till midnight and collect you as soon as you call, okay?' His eyes were pleading, and he was clearly baulking at the prospect of paying his staff to sit and wait for the General to finish with his drunken guests.

'I don't want to hang around. I'm tired, Grigor.'

'Only ten minutes away. I'll come straight away, I promise.' He put his arm around her shoulder, and she brushed him off angrily, grabbing at his sleeve and twisting, her free arm snapping his lanyard away, the safety clasp at the back easily releasing.

Grigor's eyes widened like saucers. 'Steady on, girl.'

'Don't put your hands on me, Grigor,' she spat with venom, tucking the pass up her the back of her sweater.

'Okay, I'm s-sorry. I didn't mean anything.' Grigor seemed genuinely alarmed.

'I don't like to be touched without permission, okay?' she said, glaring at him.

'Fine, I'm sorry, but will you stay?' Grigor suddenly looked worried, and Josie's instinct that the man was a lecherous bastard appeared to be wholly accurate. He'd clearly had his fingers burnt in the past when being rebuffed.

She exhaled, and shook her head. 'All right, but you'll need to tell that brute Danilo before you go, okay? I don't want him giving me hassle for being here. I don't like him.'

'Yes, yes, I'll call him to let him know. When you're finished, call me and walk to gatehouse and I'll meet you there. I don't want to come in again and Teodor will lower gate once we're gone. He's a lazy bugger and will want to put on TV.'

'Fine, you'll tell him I'm staying as well?' Josie folded her arms and pursed her lips, the picture of reluctance.

'Of course. Thank you, you've saved me a lot of money. Despite General being so rich, he doesn't pay as well as you'd think, and I want to end tonight with a bit of profit.' He nodded and clapped his hands again, suddenly animated. 'Come on, you lot, we're going. Get trays on van and we're out of here,' he bellowed.

'Ach, you're a bloody cheapskate, wanting to get us back for eleven. Typical. Don't bother asking me again next year,' said Leanne, scowling as she passed Josie.

'Quiet, girl, you're lucky to still have job after yesterday's effort – never mind next year. Come on, everyone, let's go now, and don't forget to hand in your passes at the gate.'

They all filed out of the ballroom, shoulders slouched, feet shuffling and tired faces yawning. All of a sudden, Josie wanted to join them. Get on that minibus back to Stonehaven, back to the farmhouse and to bed. She was gripped by a longing to be under a duvet and away from playing someone else in a remote castle with dangerous armed criminals.

After the smoky fug in Bruzek's quarters, and then the alcohol fumes of the ballroom, she realised suddenly that she needed some air, so she walked through the ballroom and out into the freezing-cold night, watching with interest as Grigor appeared to be arguing with Teodor, who was standing by the van, a fistful of lanyards in his hand. She strained to hear what the Slovakian was saying, but the words didn't reach her.

There was a whisper in her ear – 'You're doing great, Josie. Stay safe,' – but she didn't respond. With the microphone-enabled watch being down in the General's quarters, she knew there was no point.

Chapter 61

The mood in the cottage was a mixture of elation at the progress Josie had made and concern at what they'd just seen on the grainy image captured by the watch camera, as well as her mention of the bullet.

'She's going well, eh? Shame we can't hear her; the microphone in the watch was a bonus. At least we know what we're dealing with now,' said Macca.

'Door looks substantial. Think you can deal with it?' said Charlie as Asquith replayed the footage of the door being opened.

'Can we make out the digits he pressed?'

'I'm almost certain it's 112233, but I can't be a hundred per cent. Even if it is, we need his thumbprint, and that's a problem, right?'

'You could say that, but I'm prepared for all eventualities. Remember, I was an expert at dynamic explosive entry. I reckon a smallish shaped charge would take that lock clean off and not cause any internal damage. I'll make a few up now.'

'You've got explosives here?' said Jacko.

'Of course. How else were we going to get into a safe, unless you're a safe cracker?'

'Wouldn't have a bastard clue. I wasn't that kind of villain.'

Macca shrugged. 'I can get through it, I reckon, but it'll be noisy when we'd like a sneaky approach.'

'Then we get noisy. As they say, no messing about, in, bang and out,' said Jacko, slapping his palm down on the table.

'I know we're saying this a great deal, but that girl is both reckless and gifted,' said Charlie. 'Her dad was far more careful; maybe she gets the wild streak from her mum?'

'Macey was a real character before the bloody dementia got her,' said Macca. 'Nothing she wouldn't do or try. It's probably why Chappers and her got on so well. Sad, eh?'

He returned his attention to the live feed on the iPad, where lines of people were climbing into minibuses. The stocky guard Josie had told them was called Teodor was seemingly in an intense exchange with the manager from the catering company. There were fingers being pointed and it all seemed a little heated. Very soon, however, the catering staff were aboard their bus, and it joined the queue waiting at the lowered portcullis for the guard to return so they could set off for the mainland.

'What was the barney with the security dude about?' asked Jacko, who was sipping on a large mug of tea. All the team were identically dressed in dark tactical cargo trousers, lightweight boots and sweatshirts.

'Who knows, but neither looked happy. Still, not our problem. What about the bullet Josie mentioned?' said Charlie, his heavy features full of worry.

'It's just a bullet, but it's suggestive of more, obviously,' Macca said thoughtfully. 'I'd say any firearms they have will be out of the way, particularly as there's been cops on site tonight. We've seen no sign on the cameras, and no hint that they'll have them to hand. If we do this right, we'll be gone before they realise.' He stood up and stretched his back, wincing, then looked at each man in turn. 'Anyone having second thoughts?'

The silence that followed was thick and turgid.

'Good. Then we wait for Josie to come back and I'll give the final O group.'

'O group? We're not in the Corps now, Macca,' said Jacko.

'No, but we are planning a covert assault on a fortified castle. Anyone think of a better way of making sure we all know what the plan is?'

Another silence descended on the room.

'Good. Always the plan, boys.'

'I bet you made a fucking model, didn't you?' said Jacko.

'Of course, what do you think I was doing in the garden? I built a replica of the cliffs and castle.' Macca's face was serious.

'What, really?' said Jacko.

'Yes, really. This is now a military operation, and I'm in charge. Unless anyone else in here has thirty years' experience of planning hostile-environment extractions, counter-revolutionary warfare assaults and high-value target incursions?' Macca looked over the top of his reading glasses at the rest of the team, the sarcasm evident in his voice.

'Job's all yours, geezer. Anyone want another wet?'

Chapter 62

A movement caught Josie's eye, and she looked across to the barn where the young girls seemed to live. A flame being applied to a cigarette; clearly Renata was having a late-night smoke. On impulse, she strode towards where the girl was standing, illuminated by the light seeping from the windows.

'Hello?' she said in her best Slovak.

The girl flinched and turned. It wasn't Renata, but another girl, small, skinny and very young.

'You shouldn't talk to me,' she said, her hand trembling as she took a draw on the cigarette.

'It's okay, I'm just on a break. Can I have a cigarette?' Josie smiled.

'You speak my language?' the girl said, handing over the packet and a lighter.

'I speak Czech, but I understand some Slovak. Thank you.' Josie pulled out a cigarette and put one between her lips. She had smoked a little as a youngster, but not for years, and she hoped that she wouldn't have a coughing fit.

She lit the cigarette and took a pull, without inhaling. 'What's your name?' she asked as she handed back the packet.

The girl looked from left to right, quivering in fear. 'If Danilo or Teodor see you, they'll go crazy and I'll be punished. Please leave me,' she said, her voice high-pitched and unsteady.

'I just want to know your name. I'm Mary,' said Josie softly.

'Nina,' the girl said, taking a long pull on her cigarette and looking around her again with wide, hunted eyes, her movements jittery as she shivered in the cold. She was clearly terrified.

'How old are you, Nina?'

'Eighteen,' she said. Josie didn't believe her. She looked younger than eighteen.

'Why are you here? Maybe I can tell someone?'

'No. Don't tell anyone. They'll hurt my family in Slovakia. Now please go.' Tears were brimming in her large, doe-like eyes.

'Nina, are you a prisoner?' said Josie, fury beginning to burn in her chest.

Nina just closed her eyes and began to sob quietly.

'How many of you are in there?'

'Just two. There were more, but they've gone.'

'Just you and Renata?'

Nina's eyes opened, the whites almost iridescent in the half-light. 'You know Renata?'

'We met briefly. It's just you two?'

'There were three, but Petra went. She displeased the General and now she's gone. Away on the helicopter with Danilo and Havel. Maybe she got home, maybe not.'

'Who's Havel?'

'The General's pilot. He's not a nice man, like Danilo. Both of them are very cruel, both—' She stopped abruptly and snapped her mouth shut.

'Nina, what do you mean?' said Josie, her stomach tightening.

'Lots of girls come, and lots go when the General tires of them. Sometimes he lets his friends like Mr Hunter have fun with them

315

before he sends them away, sometimes not. Some make it home, maybe some never do.' She quivered like a leaf.

'Hunter?' Josie's mind jolted.

'Yeah. He's not so nice either. He likes to be rough. He . . .' Nina paused and bit her bottom lip.

'Nina?' Josie stepped forward, but the girl flinched away, her eyes full of fear.

'You should go. You'll get me in so much trouble.' She took a pull on her cigarette, the glow illuminating her face, and she suddenly looked even younger. 'You can't help; no one can,' she said, turning and dashing into the barn and slamming the door.

Josie stood there stunned, her insides boiling, breathing deeply, trying to make sense of what she'd just heard. After a moment, she tossed her cigarette to the soft grass, which was soaking her sneakers, and set off back to the castle, determination gripping her insides like a vice.

'This fucking stops tonight,' she whispered to herself, the latent anger that had been with her ever since the funeral surging into an almost visceral hatred.

The image of her dad came back into focus in her subconscious. *Head up, eyes front, shoulders back. You're a Chapman, my girl.*

Chapter 63

Danilo was coming out of the castle just as Josie approached the main door, a scowl on his face. 'Where you been?' he demanded.

'I had a cigarette,' she said.

'No time to smoke. General's guests are leaving and you need to clear up. Go down now. He wants to retire to his bed and one of his guests is a little drunk and may need escorting to his suite. Giles Hunter always overindulge in free booze. He's sleeping in Stuart suite, so you just escort him through my office to guest wing and then it is first on left through door. His key card will allow access, okay?'

'I'm not a drunk's babysitter, you know. I'm a waitress,' said Josie, her eyes wide with faux concern, though in reality she was sensing an opportunity.

'You'll be fine, he's a big pussy. Just get him through door and leave. I need to secure castle rooms and then I'm going to my bed. If he make trouble, which he won't, I'm in Burns suite on same side as Hunter, okay?'

Josie sighed with apparent exasperation. 'Fine,' she said,

shaking her head.

'Okay, go now. I have to see last of guests away. Stupid drunken idiots had too much of General's expensive whisky, and General gets angry when he's tired and wants to sleep, same as me.' The huge man scowled, clearly irritated at a job way below his pay grade.

Josie nodded and headed into the castle, passing through the doors with her card and descending the staircase. She touched her pass to Danilo's office door and entered before knocking on the door to Bruzek's quarters.

'Come,' came the shout from within. She tapped her card and the door clicked open.

Bruzek was standing, swaying slightly, his hands clasped in front of him, smiling at Josie as she entered. Hunter was slumped on the sofa, his legs splayed, his dinner jacket discarded on the floor and his bow tie hanging down from his open collar. He was snoring gently, his eyes shut. There was a deep red port stain on the front of his shirt and a crumb of cheese in the corner of his mouth.

'This stupid oaf drink too much of my very expensive whisky, and now look. He's skunk as a drunk,' Bruzek slurred, flopping down on the sofa opposite Hunter. He reached for the half-empty bottle of amber liquid on the coffee table and poured a measure into a heavy crystal glass, which he lifted to his lips and drained in one shot.

The table was littered with the detritus of cheese and crumbs from the water biscuits. Plates and knifes were scattered alongside discarded whisky tumblers and port glasses.

'Clear this up, please, Mary my dear. I'm going to retire to my bedroom.' Bruzek pointed to a door at the far end of the huge room, his face suddenly white with fatigue.

'How about Mr Hunter?' she said.

'Escort him to his suite.'

'This really isn't my job, General,' Josie said, folding her arms.

'Please for me do this? I need to sleep very bad; I make sure you get bonus. Here.' He wobbled over to a low table and slid open a small drawer, then took her hand and pressed a fifty-pound note into her palm, with a glassy-eyed smile that was only millimetres away from being a leer. 'Please take this. I won't tell Grigor. Just get Giles to his bed safe, okay, yes?' he said, swaying as he held on to her hand. His palm was limp and damp, so Josie pulled hers away gently.

'Fine. Thank you for the tip.' She smiled, holding up the bank-note.

'Good girl, you impressed me todays.' Bruzek widened his eyes and looked her up and down. 'You very pretty. Maybe when you done, you join me?' he said, smiling widely. His usually dazzling white teeth were stained red by the port, giving him the disturbing look of a vampire. Josie shuddered.

'I'm expected home, General, and Grigor is waiting for me.' Bruzek's face fell, and his expression immediately morphed to acceptance. He nodded, then turned and headed off to his bedroom, some ten metres away, occasionally using the dazzling glass wall for support, his sweaty palms leaving smears as he shuffled along. She watched as he entered the room, noting that there was no key card reader.

The door slammed behind him, and she looked down at Hunter, who continued to snore gently. Quickly she strode over to the bookshelf by the window and retrieved her watch, slipping it over her wrist and fastening it tight.

'Josie, you back with us?' said Macca in her earpiece.

She just tapped the button twice to acknowledge, but didn't speak. Instead, her eyes fell on the card reader by the huge window. She touched her card against it, and there was a click as the locking mechanism was released. Close to the jamb, there was a small recess into the glass big enough for her fingers to grip, and slide the door inwards towards the centre of the vast widow. It ran smoothly, silently and almost invisibly on unseen runners, and she slipped out onto the balcony, the cold, windless air attacking her ears and face. The space was narrow, with just enough depth to stand on, and didn't protrude beyond the rock face, but it stretched the whole length of the room and beyond; she assumed it afforded the same access from Bruzek's bedroom. She gave a low whistle at the feat of engineering: a vast plate-glass window carved into a sheer sandstone cliff a hundred and fifty feet above the North Sea. She suspected it had cost more than her parents had paid for their entire home.

She looked down into the inky blackness but couldn't see the sea below, such was the absence of light. Then she raised her head and looked up. The heavy sandstone was just a couple of feet above her head. She stretched up and touched it, the familiarity of rock against her fingers comforting. Reaching around to the rock face, she felt a fissure, which she slipped her index finger into. Her other hand found a decent grip, and she pulled herself up and looked along the line of the window. At the end there was an opaque glazed barrier, which she was confident led to the balcony of the next suite along.

Suddenly there was a scrape and a thud against the glass behind her, and her blood froze. She released her grip and turned to the source of the sound, her heart in her mouth.

Giles Hunter stood there, swaying slightly, his bloodshot eyes staring at her through the glass, his face pale and full of confusion.

Chapter 64

'What are you doing?' he slurred, suspicion and hostility in his voice as he moved to the open doorway.

Josie didn't miss a beat. 'Just tidying up, Mr Hunter. Come on, I'm to escort you to your suite.' Her voice was calm and level as she re-entered the room, sliding the door almost, but not completely, shut.

'I want another drink.'

'General Bruzek was clear that you were to return to your guest room, Mr Hunter.' Josie spoke gently, but with an undercurrent of firmness.

Hunter's eyes switched from accusatory and confused to pleading and pathetic. 'Please, one more jigger of that very fine Shcotch,' he slurred.

Josie paused, as if considering, and looked at the bottle on the coffee table, next to its open wooden box. She suddenly realised that Hunter being even drunker than he presently was might be of some use. She smiled, widely and knowingly.

'Mr Hunter, you're a naughty man.' She wagged her finger at

him, and he returned her smile.

'Go on, you know you want to. Just one more wee dram, as they say here in Scotland,' he said in an appallingly bad Scottish accent.

Josie went to the coffee table, uncorked the fine malt and poured a liberal measure into the glass that Bruzek had just drunk from. Handing it to Hunter, she pressed her finger to her lips. 'Shh, I won't say anything if you don't.'

His bleary eyes twinkled mischievously as he accepted the glass, raised it and whispered, 'Cheers,' before necking the spirit. 'Shit, that's good Scotch, and forty grand a bottle. I just downed about a thousand quid's worth! Still, who cares? Dubai tomorrow,' he said, managing to giggle and hiccup at the same time.

'Come on, Mr Hunter. Let's get you to your bedroom. It's just down the hall.' Josie took his arm and steered him towards the door.

'Are you propositioning me, young lady?' he said, without resisting.

'I'm on duty. No fraternisation,' she said, keeping gentle pressure on his arm as she steered him through Danilo's office and into the hallway. She used her card to pass through a door with a sign that directed her towards the guest suites, and then supported the staggering antiques dealer towards the first door on the left, marked *Stuart*.

'Home sweet home,' she said, pressing her key card against the reader outside the door. The light blinked but the door didn't open. 'Your key card, Mr Hunter?'

'Oh bugger, hold up.' He began to rifle through his pockets, swaying slightly, before triumphantly pulling out a card on a blue lanyard and handing it to her.

Josie tapped it against the reader and the door unlocked. She pushed it open and held her hand out, indicating that Hunter should enter. 'After you,' she said.

'You're a good girl, whatever your name is,' he slurred, almost tripping over his feet as he stumbled into the suite.

Josie flicked the lights on, revealing a huge room with a battle-field-sized bed and an enormous flat-screen TV recessed into the wall. It was magnificently opulent, even more so than Bruzek's quarters. The vast glazed wall extended halfway along the suite, the glass almost like a mirror as the light was reflected back into the room.

'Bloody fantastic room, eh, girl? Want to try it with me? I bet you've never seen a bed this big, eh?' Hunter guffawed as he kicked off his shoes and removed his bow tie, letting it fall to the floor. Looking up, he caught Josie's reflection in the mirror and froze. His tongue snaked out of his mouth and licked his lips, and a leer crossed his face that Josie didn't like the look of at all.

As Hunter moved closer, she stood her ground, feet planted shoulder-width apart, shoulders square. She had a feeling that a pass from the drunken idiot was almost inevitable, but she felt no fear, despite how much bigger than her he was.

'You're very beautiful,' he whispered, his breath hitting her face like a fetid slap with a mix of whisky and cigar smoke. She grimaced.

'Mr Hunter, don't do anything you'll regret,' she said, her voice icy calm.

'I won't regret *anything*,' he slurred, and reached his hand out to touch her face.

Josie didn't panic; she just took his palm in hers and rotated it, straightening out the elbow joint and pushing him away towards the bed, her foot stuck out so that he stumbled and fell onto the bed in an undignified heap. His eyes closed as he hit the pristine linen, and he was gone, passed out, already snoring.

'Not tonight, or any night, Josephine,' Josie said with a smile.

'All okay?' Macca's voice rang in her ear.

'All good. I'll be leaving very soon, and then we urgently need a debrief,' she said in a whisper into her watch.

'Roger that.'

She walked to the window and pressed her pass against the

reader, which blinked but didn't unlock. Glancing round, she spotted Hunter's key card on the floor, where he had dropped it along with his bow tie. She picked it up and touched it to the window reader. It clicked, and the light flashed green. She slotted her fingers into the recess, which was identical to the one in the General's quarters slid the silent door open and stepped onto the balcony. There was a thick smoked glass barrier between the guest suite and Bruzek's balcony; without hesitating, she climbed onto the handrail, grabbed onto the edge of the barrier and peered around it. The long balcony stretched out in front of her, the General's bedroom as dark as the night itself. She jumped back down and returned to the guest suite, pulling the door shut behind her. It closed with a firm click.

She glanced at the comatose form of Hunter on the bed, his snores loud and rattling, his mouth agape like a fish. Within a few moments she was out in the corridor, pulling the suite door closed behind her and heading back towards Bruzek's quarters. She needed to get back to the others and brief them as soon as possible, as the plan would now radically change. She'd clear up the General's quarters and get out of here, handing her blue lanyard into Teodor, with Grigor's "lost" pass. Together with Hunter's pass they now had two access-all-area cards. She reached into her pocket and pulled out Grigor's red lanyard, switching the card with the one on her own blue lanyard, which she slung around her neck.

Within a few minutes, she'd cleared the plates and glasses, and was depositing them in the empty kitchen when Danilo appeared.

'Gosh, you made me jump. I thought you were going to bed?' said Josie, affecting shock.

'Trouble with drunk locals. They all gone now. Everything okay with General and Hunter?'

'Aye, all fine. The General has gone to bed, and I poured Mr Hunter back into his room.'

'He try anything?' said Danilo.

'Such as?'

'He often try on with girls. Sometimes he even succeed.' A smile crossed his face.

'Not with me. Should I be offended?'

Danilo just shrugged and smiled. 'Where's Grigor?' he said.

'He ran the others back to the town and is coming back for me. He wants me to meet him at the gatehouse so he doesn't have to come in.'

'Grigor is a lazy and stupid man. You could do this yourself next event. General seems to like you. Just need a few staff, and it's easy money, eh?'

'I'll bear that in mind,' said Josie.

A grin stretched over Danilo's face, and he looked almost human for a second. 'Okay, hand pass in to Teodor at gate. He's already pissed with Grigor for losing his, so make sure you have yours, yes?'

Josie held the blue lanyard aloft. 'I have it here. Can I go now?'

'Sure. I go to bed now. Don't worry about doors. Teodor on security duty and he'll make sure everything is locked.' He nodded, and left the kitchen.

Josie headed towards the door in his wake, crossing the ball-room's parquet flooring, now swept clean. In the vestibule, Danilo was keying his way into the living quarters. She reached for her phone and called Grigor.

'Are you finish?' he said.

'Yes, I'm heading for the gate now.'

'Ten or fifteen minutes,' he said.

'See you there.' She hung up and carried on, walking out into the cold night air. Instead of heading straight for the gatehouse, however, she turned left and walked along the building until she got to the end, where the plans had said the plant room was. A small, square building butted onto the end of the main castle. She walked up to the door and tried the wrought-iron handle, and it swung open with a stiff and arthritic creak.

She pulled out her phone, activated the torch and stepped

inside. A boxy generator, about a metre square, sat in the corner. She shone the torch on it; the words *Hyundai, Long Run Diesel Tank* were visible in black transfer on the white housing. It looked new and efficient. She quickly snapped a photograph and sent it to the WhatsApp group.

'You hearing this, guys?' she said into the watch.

'Yes, loud and clear,' replied Macca.

'I've sent a photo of the generator in the plant room, which is unlocked.'

'I'm looking now. Are you heading back? I need to brief you on the plan.'

Josie affected a very poor Mike Tyson impression. 'Everyone has a plan till they get punched in the mouth.'

'Meaning?' said Macca, his voice confused.

'It wasn't a punch in the mouth, but things have changed. We need to alter the plan, and we have to do this tonight.'

Chapter 65

The whole team was waiting in the kitchen at the Airbnb, the tension in the air crackling as Josie relayed what she'd seen and heard at the castle.

'We do it tonight,' she said, after explaining the evening's events. Not a request, not a suggestion, a definitive statement of fact.

A silence descended on the room as the team took it all in, glances exchanged, their faces drawn and tired.

'Maybe a bit more time to plan—' began Asquith, but Josie cut him off.

'No, no more time. Those poor girls have suffered enough, and we won't get a better chance. We have two all-access cards, we leave it any longer they'll inevitably reprogram them. Hunter is shit-faced, Bruzek's been on the Scotch, and the place is lightly guarded with just the man at the gatehouse. I know exactly where those medals are, and how to get to them. I've laid the ground-work, and I can get into Bruzek's suite. We do it tonight.' Josie felt her face begin to redden, but her jaw was tight.

'But—' began Asquith, but this time Macca cut him off.

'She's right, Neil. The occupants are all in their beds, some of them are pissed, the weather is good and Josie's done half the work for us. I think we go tonight. We won't get a better chance. All agree?' He looked around at the team. They all nodded.

'Right, a quick briefing. Josie?'

'Okay. You lot drop me as close to the cliff edge as you can, and I'll descend and get prepared with the ropes and self-belay ready for the ascent. You have all the boat kit ready?'

Macca nodded. 'Aye, boat is all ready, with outboard and the ascent kit. We'll drop you and then head around to the harbour and join you at the foot of the cliff. Are you sure you want to do the climb on your own, with night vision? Maybe wait till we get there, so one of us can safely belay you.'

'Okay,' said Josie flatly. She knew she wasn't going to wait, but she also knew that Macca would moan at her, so it was better he didn't know.

'Right then. We cross the water and join up with you, and we use the expensive bit of climbing kit to get us up the cliff like we practised, yes?'

Everyone nodded.

'Okay, then we monitor the feeds for security patrols and use night vision to approach the objective. Once we're happy, we take the power out, as discussed previously, before we attack the building covertly. Hopefully we'll get access with Josie's cards, then a quiet approach to Bruzek's quarters and breach the safe. I've created a shaped charge that will get through it, no bother. Exfiltration will be the same as infiltration. Fast ropes down to the boat, and off into the night. Any enemy forces, we deal with as discussed. We all agreed?'

Everyone nodded.

'Okay. A final kit check, radios, night vision, and I'll check the breaching explosives. I want to be out of here in twenty. Great job, Josie. Your dad would be proud of you.'

Josie just nodded, her jaw tight and skin tingling. They were doing this, and they were doing it now.

328

Chapter 66

Thursday 23 December 2021

The waves lapped softly against the rough sand of the small beach just along the coastline from Stonehaven harbour.

It was almost two a.m., and the night was moonless. The sky was a deep, velvety black, with just a few twinkling lights coming from the buildings a few hundred metres away.

Macca, Jacko, Charlie and Asquith had parked the Toyota and the Volvo a little way up the track, tucked into a lay-by close to the entrance to the cliff trail that Josie had jogged along just a couple of days ago. They'd hauled the heavy bags down the steep incline that led to the deserted beach, nicely out of sight of any passing motorists or late-night dog walker.

They were all dressed alike, in dark cargo pants, black combat jackets and lightweight military boots. Each man had a rolled-up balaclava on his head and thin climbing gloves on his hands. They all wore climbing harnesses, adorned with karabiners, and each had a discreet wireless earpiece linked to a radio set that was stowed away in a pouch on their harness. The radio was also wirelessly connected to a press-to-talk button secured in their pockets, which could be operated through the fabric. Their climbing harnesses had several sets of zip ties looped around the webbing straps. Macca had a short length of climbing rope wound around his body, together with more karabiners.

'Fuck my old boots, this bastard is heavy,' said Charlie, as he and Asquith appeared on the beach with a heavy black canoe bag, which they deposited with a grunt on the sand.

'A mere fifty kilos. You boys have been in civvy street too long. Now stop dripping and get the bastard inflated. You remember how, I assume?' said Macca.

'Well you made us practise enough times,' said Charlie. 'Why the rope? You look like a Mexican gaucho with his bandoliers around him.'

'Always carry a length of rope on ops. You never know, mate. All ready?'

'Heavy and ready.' Charlie began to unlace the bag, unfolding the thick rubberised material to reveal a matte-black Honwave T38 inflatable dinghy. When Macca had acquired it, it had been white with a smart blue stripe around it, but he'd insisted it had to be black.

Macca was in full military mode now, issuing orders to the others, who busied themselves with the tasks allotted. While Charlie was getting the dinghy ready to launch, Asquith was sitting with four sets of night-vision goggles spread out on a small groundsheet, testing each pair and attaching a spare battery, and Jacko was checking and stowing the coils of rope and climbing equipment, including a stout-looking Pelican case stamped with *Atlas APA-5*.

Charlie attached a small hose to the inflation port on the dinghy and fixed the other end to a small yellow box. He flicked a switch and the pump burst into life, the dinghy beginning to unfurl like a butterfly emerging from its chrysalis and expanding its damp new wings. Meanwhile, Macca was unpacking a long, sleek-looking outboard motor from a tough canvas zip case and slotting a boxy battery into the device.

'What's the life on that thing, Macca?' asked Asquith.

'Long enough to get us there and back. Well that's what I was told, anyway. Much quieter than a petrol one, and less work than paddles on a shitty Gemini. Hurry up, I want to get moving; I don't like being out here. Remember, any bastards pitch up, we're off night fishing. I've even got a couple of rods here, just in case.' He nodded at two canvas cases.

'I just hope they don't think we're a bit commando-looking for that,' said Jacko, who was sitting cross-legged in front of his holdall and Pelican case, a puckish smile on his face.

The whine of the pump suddenly stopped. 'That's it, done,' said Charlie. 'Nice bit of kit, this, Macca. Where'd you find it?'

'Got it off a mate.'

'Would that be the statuesque Ms Freeman?'

'Mind your own bloody business, Charlie.'

'Blimey, she must be on a promise,' said Jacko.

'Piss off, both of you. Now, game faces on and stop talking shit. Neil, night vision all good?'

'Checked and working, with spare batteries. Good kit. I'm assuming the same source as the boat?'

Macca pretended not to have heard the question. 'Jacko?'

'Climbing gear all present and correct.'

'Charlie?'

'I have four oars, you have the motor, and the dinghy is fully inflated. We're good to go, boss.'

Macca's hand went to the radio button in his pocket before he spoke again. 'All personal protective kit, radios and earpieces?'

'Charlie, roger that.'

'Neil, roger that.'

'Jacko, roger that.'

There was a pause, and then a fainter voice crackled in their earpieces. 'Josie, roger that. I'm in position at the foot of the far western edge of the outcrop. Hurry up, the tide's coming in.

Watch for my signal.'

'That's all call signs received. Macca out.' He released the switch and looked at each man in turn. 'Right, we're on. We go in on the motor until we're two hundred metres away and we've seen Josie's signal. Synchronise watches by mine.' He paused and looked at his G-Shock. 'Zero two eighteen. We go tactical now, radio silence all round. We all know the plan, and we have the advantage. We're going in.'

Like a well-oiled machine, they all stood. Charlie and Neil lifted the dinghy and waded into the gently lapping waves, ignoring the icy cold, until the craft floated. The kit was loaded into the rear, then they all climbed in, Jacko up front, Neil and Charlie in the midsection and Macca at the rear.

'Hold up,' Jacko suddenly blurted out.

'What now?' said Macca, his voice hard.

'Gimme a second, I'm breaking my neck for a piss,' said Jacko, stepping back out into the water and heading for the beach.

'Oh for fuck's sake, hurry up,' muttered Macca, shaking his head.

They sat in silence while Jacko relieved himself and then rejoined them, grinning widely. 'I'm good to go now, boys.'

Macca slotted the outboard into position, then twisted the hand grip. A soft whine was all the noise that could be heard, and the dinghy moved off, rising and falling with the gentle swell as they headed for Stonehaven Castle.

Chapter 67

Josie was tied into the cliff, a cam and karabiner securing her into the rock as she turned to look through her night-vision goggles, which bathed the whole seascape in a ghostly green glow.

The others had dropped her close by, and she'd descended the steep hill that led to the rocky beach and hugged the cliff line until she'd reached the outcrop. She had pulled her climbing shoes out of her rucksack and put them on, putting her lightweight boots into her pack. Despite what she'd said to Macca, she had no intention of waiting for him to arrive. She wanted to make a start on the cliff and at least get some of the anchor points in. The tide was turning, and there would soon be no beach at all, which would make getting the others up more difficult, so she wanted to get the top rope in as soon as she could.

She picked up a cam device, pulled the spring-loaded trigger wire and jammed it into a fissure in the rock, securing it tight. She then attached her Wren Industries Silent Partner device to the rope with a clove hitch and secured it to her climbing harness with a karabiner. She was confident that as long as she locked into the face regularly, any fall would be held by the speed-actuated device.

'Macca from Josie, how long?' she said into her radio.

'Twenty minutes,' replied Macca, the whine of the outboard detectable in the background.

As she began to climb, she found that the cliff was actually a little easier than she'd anticipated, despite the weird view through the NVGs making her depth perception a little off-kilter. The handholds were firm and easy to locate and were reasonably sticky. She kept going, relishing the pull and strain on her shoulders and fingers, pausing every few metres play out a little more rope and secure herself in with a cam and karabiner.

Her earpiece crackled. 'Josie, we're five hundred off with direct line of sight,' said Macca.

Josie used the short rope from the harness and locked in to a karabiner. Then she reached into her pocket, pulled out a small penlight and gave three flashes. Scanning the sea from her position about thirty metres up the cliff face, she soon spotted them. A small, dark shape in the dark vastness, bathed in green. 'I see you,' she said into her radio.

'Seen your flash. Jose, are you up the bloody cliff?' said Macca.

'Yeah, about thirty metres. I'm free soloing before you get here. Don't worry, I'm tied in. Pick up the belay when you arrive.'

'Jesus, you're crazy, girl. Can you hear the boat?'

She strained to listen, but could only hear the whispering of the wind. 'No, nothing.'

'Okay, we'll stay on the outboard for a bit longer. Shout if you hear us.'

'Roger that,' she said, turning back to the rock face and resuming her climb. Her fingers were beginning to feel that painful numbness she knew so well, but she pushed on, easily finding the toe- and finger-holds.

After five minutes, Macca's voice sparked up again. 'We're here, and the dinghy's secured. I'm ready to belay. You ready?'

'Wait one.' Josie reached up for a handhold that was just out of reach, extending her toes as far as they'd go, and sighed at the familiar sensation of security as her fingers located the hold. She was pulling herself up when it happened. The rock loosened, and suddenly she was gone, in mid-air, falling. She tensed, waiting for the jolt. As always, it was bigger and more painful than she'd anticipated, as she reached the limit of the safety rope, the air whooshing out of her as it jerked.

'Jose, you okay?' Macca's voice was full of concern.

She relaxed, allowing the safety rope to hold her. 'Belay on?' she said into the radio, her breath escaping her in gasps.

'Belay is on,' said Macca, and relief flooded through her.

She swung back to the rock and located an easy handhold, then unclipped the safety line. 'Climbing,' she said into the radio, and set off again, her confidence flying, knowing that Macca had her.

The rest of the climb was straightforward, and very soon she was pulling herself onto the soft turf of the outcrop. She kept low, on her belly, and whispered into the radio: 'I'm up. Anything on the surveillance feed?'

'Nothing. Guard last did his round twenty minutes ago and is back in the gatehouse,' said Macca.

'Roger that. I'm securing the top rope and then I'll be down to make sure you geriatrics get up without breaking your necks.'

'Hurry up, there's very little beach left.'

Josie scanned the outcrop through her NVGs. The main house and Renata and Nina's barn were in darkness, apart from a couple of twinkling lights above the main door and a light at the top of the building. The gatehouse was lit up like Blackpool Illuminations, and she could just imagine Teodor watching TV in there before his next security round on the quad bike that was parked outside.

The Bell helicopter sat dark and sleek in the middle of the pad, which was fifty metres in front of her, partially obscuring her view of the house. She suddenly wondered if the pilot, Havel, was on the premises, and her thoughts turned to the young girls, hopefully safely sleeping in the barn. She doubted any of the others would be in any fit state to do anything with the amount they'd drunk.

Happy that the coast was clear, she continued to scan around until she saw what she was looking for. A wrought-iron stake had been driven into the ground, presumably as part of a fence or agricultural structure at some point in the past. She crawled over to it, unclipped the rope from her harness and released it from the karabiner, then tied it onto the iron stake with a clove hitch. Without hesitation, she jogged back to the cliff, picked up the slack and secured herself onto the belay device.

'I'm coming down,' she whispered into her radio, before backing out into the abyss and pushing off.

She was down in a matter of seconds, smoothly abseiling and enjoying the feeling of ease after the hard climb.

Macca was waiting for her at the bottom of the cliff, a stern look on his craggy features. 'That was bloody reckless, girl. Free climbing with no belay and bloody NVGs? You could have screwed the whole thing up,' he said, his voice stern.

'Hello, Macca, yes, it was a good climb. Yes, we're ahead of schedule and the tide's nearly bloody in. Now stop moaning. If I'd left it longer, you'd all have been piss-wet through by now.'

'Christ, I'm glad they don't take women in the SBS,' he said, his voice already softening.

'Fine, now let's stop buggering about. Who's going up first?'

'Jacko and Charlie. What's the weight limit on that thing?'

'Six hundred pounds. I know Charlie's let himself go, but it'll be good. Now, just like we practised, hook in and hold on.' Josie stooped down, flicked the Pelican case open and pulled out a hefty-looking black plastic item about the size of a large industrial torch. She opened the rear of the device and fed the top rope through the mechanism at the back.

'This is no good for my poor bloody foot, you know,' said Jacko as he and Charlie attached karabiners from their harnesses to the anchor points on the device and Charlie held the trigger point. 'See you at the top. Are we clear, Neil?'

Asquith took out his phone and checked the feed. 'Still in the gatehouse. Go!'

Charlie pulled the trigger on the device and it began to whirr. Then, as if by magic, both men began to ascend quickly, disappearing from view as the heavy-duty battery-powered device pulled the rope through the internal mechanism with its powerful motor. Within forty seconds, they'd both reached the top.

'Done, unclipping and sending down,' said Charlie over the radio.

Within another minute, the ascender reappeared on the end of a long, thin line.

'You ready?' said Josie to Macca.

'Boat's secure, I'm ready. Neil?'

'As long as I don't end upside down like during the practice, okay?' Even in the dark, Josie could see that Jacko's face was paler than usual.

'Just hold on tight and trust the kit,' said Josie, slapping him on the back.

Macca and Asquith both clipped on, and soon they were zipping up the cliff like a couple of elderly Spider-Men. Josie watched, a mix of nerves and excitement in her belly, as the ascender was lowered again, her fingers touching the cool metal of her dad's watch meditatively, her thoughts on what was next. She knew that it would be dangerous – in fact it could be deadly – and the memory of the brass bullet rolling in the drawer loomed large. She should have been terrified, but she wasn't. She was buzzing.

She clipped on the device and was soon ascending the cliff, the breeze in her face, ready for what came next.

Chapter 68

The five of them lay on the grass behind a low, semi-ruined wall, just waiting. Not talking, not checking kit, not looking at the computer feed. They just lay there tuning in to the environment for ten minutes, getting used to the smells, the sounds and the feel of the outcrop. Macca felt good, in control, and he was breathing easily. It had been many years since he had done anything operational, in the military or the private world, but he was confident. They'd done the preparation and were ready to go.

'How long till the next security round?' He looked at Asquith, his face bug-like because of the NVGs.

Asquith flipped up his goggles and peered at the feed on his phone, shielding the light with his palm. 'Still in the gatehouse, and from what I can see, not moving yet. Last patrol was forty minutes ago.'

'Ready for phase one?' said Macca.

Everyone nodded.

'Right. Josie, take Neil and Charlie to the plant room, hide up and wait for the inevitable, then proceed as per plan. Radio in when you're in position.'

'Roger that,' said Charlie. The three of them stood and set off, circling around the outcrop towards the main house, which sat low, dark and forbidding on the edge of the opposite cliff.

Within a couple of minutes, Macca heard Charlie's voice in his ear. 'All set here.'

'Ready for the fun?' whispered Macca, looking at Jacko.

'I was born ready, geezer. My knees may be knackered, and I constantly need a piss, but it could be worse; I could have terrible bum grapes like you.' He clapped Macca on the shoulder.

Macca just shook his head and sighed before he pulled his phone from his pocket and navigated to a plain-looking app. He opened it up and looked at the three red numbered buttons on the screen.

'Firing now,' he said into the radio, and pressed button 1.

There was a sharp crack audible in the distance, as the small explosive charge that he had earlier strapped to the wooden pole supporting the electricity line that supplied the castle, half a mile from the causeway, was detonated. He could imagine the pole falling, taking the high-voltage wires with it. The castle was suddenly plunged into a darkness as deep and velvety as only the far north of Scotland could provide.

'Jacko, move up towards the gatehouse and watch the guard. Give a warning on the radio when he moves.'

'Roger that.' Jacko stood, and moved off at a steady pace.

Macca stayed put, reaching into his rucksack and bringing out the Glock 19 that he'd tucked away at the cottage. Despite what he'd said to Charlie, there was no way he was doing this job unarmed. He tucked the pistol into the pancake holster at the back of his cargo pants before settling down to wait for what came next. He was sure that the sudden loss of power wouldn't be entirely unexpected in this remote region, but there would be a response, that was for sure.

Jacko's voice came over the radio. 'There's movement at the

gatehouse . . . Your man is leaving, heading on foot towards the plant room. Charlie, Neil and Josie, he'll be with you in two minutes, so stand by.'

Macca flipped down his NVGs and watched as the guard – small, stocky and dressed in dark clothes – appeared the other side of the helicopter, heading for the end of the main house. He was speaking on a radio as he rounded the corner and disappeared from view.

Macca checked his watch; it was almost three a.m. Perfect timing. He stood and headed for the helicopter, reaching into his rucksack once again.

Chapter 69

Charlie, Neil and Josie were tucked behind a wall as Teodor rounded the corner and approached the door to the plant room. Grabbing the handle, he twisted and pulled, but the door didn't move.

It didn't move because Charlie had jammed a sliver of wood underneath it a few moments earlier that had wedged it tightly shut. Teodor shook the handle again, muttering a stifled oath as he did, the noise seeming overly loud in the silence.

Charlie nodded at the other two and rose silently, walking forward quickly. Without hesitation, he looped his arm around Teodor's neck and dragged him backwards away from the door. Teodor's muscles tensed and his hands came up to his throat, but Charlie just tightened the choke, a classic wrestling move that they'd practised back at the cottage. Teodor began to thrash, a strangled rattle coming from his throat as his windpipe was constricted and the blood supply to his brain was slowed. It might have been enough to induce unconsciousness on its own, but they were not taking chances, so Asquith stepped up and jammed his fist into the guard's side. There was a sudden crackle of electricity, and Teodor stiffened as 50,000 volts of low-amperage electricity flowed into his muscles. His whole body locked tight and his eyes opened as wide as saucers. Charlie raised his forearm and jammed it against the man's mouth to stifle his strangled cry. Asquith released the charge from the stun gun, and Teodor suddenly relaxed and slumped, his body spent.

Charlie lowered the twitching, gasping man to the ground, and within seconds Josie had secured his wrists and ankles with thick zip ties and stuffed a gag into his mouth. Asquith pulled out some gaffer tape and wrapped it around Teodor's head, holding the gag in place.

'Get some of that around his ankles and wrists as well,' said Charlie. He reached down and picked up Teodor's radio, which was dark and silent, and handed it to Josie. 'Keep an ear on it, in case they're speaking the lingo.' She nodded and clipped the radio onto her harness.

In a few moments, Teodor was trussed like a turkey, lying on his side and breathing noisily through his nose.

'We'll ditch him behind the wall and tie him to the post at the end, but we need to move fast,' said Charlie, grabbing the man's collar and beginning to drag him along the damp turf to the wall they'd been hiding behind on his arrival.

Once they'd secured the guard, Asquith stood and pulled his rucksack from his back, taking out an adjustable wrench and a spray can. Yanking out the wedge that was securing the door of the plant room, he disappeared inside.

Charlie's hand went to the radio button in his pocket. 'Subject one is secured. Neil is just taking care of the generator.'

'Roger that,' said Macca. 'Move up to position two once done. I'm watching you through NVG. Jacko, all good at gatehouse?'

Jacko's voice came over the net, chirpy as ever. 'Sound as a pound, mate. All quiet in here. Looks like he was watching some questionable porn, so no wonder he was happy staying put. Quad bike is here, keys in the ignition, and the portcullis is down and locked tight. I can't see any way of lifting it without power, over.'

'That's good. Keeps reinforcements out,' said Macca.

'Yeah, and us in,' said Jacko with a chuckle.

'Okay, maintain visual on the front door. We're moving up to effect entry as soon as Neil has disabled the generator.'

On cue, Asquith reappeared carrying a heavy-looking battery, which he took around the rear of the plant room, returning a moment later. 'Disconnected the electrical start battery,' he said in a whisper, his teeth glowing green in the NVG light. 'They'll never get it going again.'

Josie, Charlie and Asquith moved silently, NVGs down, along the building line until they arrived at the main door, where they squatted, backs against the stone wall. Within a minute, Macca had appeared, also with his NVGs down. He nodded, and they all stood. 'Entering now, Jacko – stand by.'

Josie reached into her pocket and took out her all-access pass, which she tapped to the reader. It blinked green, and the door clicked.

'You were correct, battery backup to the locking system,' she whispered.

Asquith nodded. They'd discussed the pros and cons of cutting the power, but the clincher had been when he'd discovered in the fire safety plan Laurel Freeman had supplied that the electronic entry system would have a battery backup in case of power cut and generator failure. Having no power gave them the advantage; as the old adage went, in the land of the blind, the one-eyed man is king. Or in their case, in the pitch-dark, the man with the night-vision aid is king.

'Are we ready?' said Macca.

Everyone nodded.

'Then let's do this.'

One by one, they filed into the building.

Chapter 70

Silently, in the pitch-dark, they descended the stairs, the greenish hue of the night-vision goggles giving the scene a ghostly atmosphere. At the bottom, they stood for a while, listening.

Then Josie heard it: Danilo's gruff, harsh voice and the squeaking of shoes on marble.

'We have company,' she whispered, nodding towards the door to the guest suites.

Macca gestured to Charlie and Asquith and the pair sprang into action, one ready either side of the heavy wooden door. Josie ducked down alongside the stair risers and waited.

The door barely made a noise as it swung open, and her vision suddenly exploded with the onslaught of a torch as Danilo burst through the opening. She flipped up her goggles on the hinge, raised her hand and let go a stream of the pepper spray she was holding. He grunted in pain, and then there was a crackle of electricity as Macca jammed the stun gun into the big man's side. He let out a soft, strangled cry and sank to his knees. There was a dull crack as the big man's head struck the hard floor.

Switching on her flashlight, flooding the lobby with bright light, Josie looked on as Macca, Charlie and Asquith quickly dragged the huge Slovak over to the balustrade of the marble staircase and bound him to it with zip ties. They then followed up with a rag in his mouth, secured with several rounds of gaffer tape, which they also used to reinforce the bonds and to secure his ankles together. There was blood everywhere from a gash on the man's temple; it looked a deep and sticky black, almost like tar, as it spread across the marble floor.

'Is he dead?' she asked.

'No, breathing deeply, but it wouldn't surprise me if the big gorilla has fractured his skull,' said Macca, quickly applying a field dressing to the wound.

'Good, he's an evil bastard,' said Josie.

'We don't want him dying on us, and we also don't want a huge puddle of blood that people might slip on. Why do you want him dead?' said Macca.

'Treats those poor girls like shit. I don't care if he lives or bloody dies, the bastard,' she replied, slightly shocked to realise that she meant it.

'Blimey, girl, you really are like your dad. He could be ruthless when the mood took him. Right, are we ready?'

Everyone nodded.

'Okay, Josie, over to you.'

Josie pressed her key card against the reader. It blinked green, and the door to Danilo's office clicked open. They all moved inside and closed the door silently behind them.

'This is the door to Bruzek's quarters,' she whispered.

They all nodded again, like a load of weird insects with bug eyes.

Josie tapped the card against the reader.

It flashed red and didn't click.

Her stomach flipped; she tapped again.

It flashed red.

Tapped again, still red.

'Shit, it won't open,' she said.

'What? You told us it would work. Why won't it fucking work?' said Macca.

'I don't know. It worked last night.'

'Before midnight?' asked Asquith, looking about the room with his goggles.

'Yes, ten or so.'

'Two possibilities. Either it's the power cut that's prompted it, or possibly the access code changes at midnight, and all temporary cards are wiped. Probably a wise safety move. It's what I'd do if I was writing the security plan for this place. You don't want loads of people having a key card that allows access to the boss's quarters for more than a few hours. Look.' He pointed at Danilo's desk. There was a small pad on it, next to the computer monitor, with a wire snaking down under the desk. 'That's a key card programmer. It's what you see hotel receptionists use when they give you your room card. I'd say there is no permanent access card to Bruzek's place other than his own; the others all have to be programmed each day.'

Something scratched at Josie's mind, something from last night. Then it landed. 'I've an idea. You lot stay here. I can get us in,' she said, feeling the hairs on her neck standing up.

'What the hell are you talking about?' said Macca.

'I left the big window open last night. I can get in via that,' she said.

'How?'

'Easy. Wait here.'

'You should have one of us with you.'

'No, I just need to sneak through Hunter's room, and a bit of a climb will be required, but I can do it.'

'But how will you get into his room?' said Macca.

'Remember, I swiped his card from him when he was pissed last night. It has to work, otherwise what's the point of it? Wait here.'

346

She hurried back to the staircase, where Danilo was still sprawled unconscious on the floor. Moving past him, she keyed her way into the guest corridor, then pulled out Hunter's key card and held her breath. She tapped it against the reader, and the panel flashed green. Relief flooded through her. Silently she pushed the door open and crept in.

Hunter hadn't moved. He was still flat on his back, snoring. Josie crept past him and touched his card to the reader at the window. It flashed green and there was the familiar muted click as the mechanism pulled the bolts back. Slowly she inched the door open just enough for her to be able to slip through, sliding it back into place behind her. Hunter still hadn't moved a muscle.

She pulled off her gloves and pocketed them, then rested her hand against the smoked glass, which was smooth and cold, and slick with condensation. She couldn't get a grip on it, and she suddenly realised that it wasn't a safe option. Instead she reached up to the sandstone above her, searching for a hold on the outside rock face. Finding decent index-finger-sized ridges, she pulled herself up, smoothly and with total control, and stepped onto the guard rail. It was as slippery as ice. Using just the finger-holds, she swung and moved her right hand, reaching for a new grip. The rock was smooth and featureless. She frowned, all her weight resting on just the two fingers of her left hand.

The sound of the now choppy sea was suddenly ominous over a hundred feet below her. She pulled herself higher, and reached up, finding a small fissure in the sandstone the other side of the glass barrier. It was barely enough to grip onto, but she had no choice. She committed to it, and swung her body into the void, thrusting her hips towards Bruzek's balcony. She landed on both feet on the smooth, tiled surface and squatted down reflexively, the breath coming out of her in clouds of vapour as she regained her composure. 'Too bloody close, Josie Chapman,' she muttered to herself.

Silently she inched past Bruzek's bedroom window. She

breathed again, relief flooding through her, when she realised that the door she'd left slightly open hadn't been closed.

Finding the radio button in her pocket, she whispered, 'I'm in, coming through now.'

'Roger that,' came Macca's calm and confident voice in her ear.

Holding her breath, Josie inched the door open and eased herself into the room. As she turned to shut it, there was a flicker above her and the modern chandelier burst into bright, unrelenting light, which overwhelmed the NVGs, rendering her totally blind. She flipped them up and blinked at the stars dancing in her eyes, trying to clear her vision. She reached for her radio button. 'Lights have come on. What's going on?'

'Nothing here, still dark. Get out of there, Jose,' said Macca, his voice full of urgency.

The door to Danilo's office clicked, a heavy industrial sound as the locks engaged. 'Shit, I'm locked in. It must be emergency locks. Fuck, is this a panic room—' she began, but then stopped as there was movement in her peripheral vision.

She turned, but she already knew what she was going to see.

General Marek Bruzek was standing by the sofas, wearing a silk dressing gown and slippers, his hair dishevelled, holding a huge silver revolver in his hand, which was trained on Josie.

Chapter 71

'What the fuck just happened?' whispered Macca as the door they were standing by gave a metallic clunk. He leant against it, but it was immovable. He'd been a door-breaching expert in his time, and he was confident that without a major explosive charge they weren't getting through it; even with a decent-shaped charge, they might get through only to find that Josie was dead. He felt his head spin at the prospect. There were faint sounds coming from within Bruzek's quarters, but they weren't decipherable. One thing was clear from Josie's last transmission, however: she was locked in, with the lights on, and it seemed there was someone in there with her.

'Do we still have access to Josie's watch microphone?' he whispered to Asquith.

Asquith reached into his pocket and pulled out his smartphone. 'Let me check.' He squatted down and swiped and clicked on the screen.

'We need eyes in that room. Shit, I should never have let her go in on her own. How is there light in there?'

'It must be batteries that just serve his quarters – no other possibility. No way could they get power on, and that generator is well disabled,' said Asquith as he continued to fiddle with his phone screen.

'Never mind that now. What are our options?' said Charlie.

'Can she hear us?' asked Macca.

'If the radio is on and she still has the earpiece in, then yes,' replied Asquith.

Macca reached for his presell. 'Josie, can you hear us?'

Nothing.

'Josie, if you can get to your radio button, give us a click.'

Nothing.

'Josie, we're getting you out of there. Be ready to duck when I say, okay?'

Still no answer.

'Right, here's what we're gonna do. Neil and Charlie, stay here. If that door opens, rush them. In fact, here, take this.' Macca reached into the back of his waistband and handed over his Glock.

Charlie's eyes widened, but he said nothing, just accepted the handgun and tucked it in his own waistband, his face grim and hard.

'I'm going for a recce, and I need Jacko.' Macca spoke into the radio. 'Jacko, I'm coming out. Meet me by the front door.' He nodded at the others. 'Any of those fuckers come in here, shoot them.' His eyes blazed for a moment before he turned and stormed out of the room.

Chapter 72

'Who the fuck is you?' said Bruzek, the pistol still levelled at Josie, who just stood there, her hands aloft, saying nothing.

He backed towards the small table where only a few hours ago he'd produced the fifty-pound note for her, opened the drawer and pulled out a radio. The gun barely moved from her chest as he lifted the handset and pressed a switch.

'*Danilo, potrebujem t'a surne v mojej izbe.*' His eyes bored into her.

Josie stood stock-still, desperately wanting to get to her radio to answer Macca's message, or at least open a line so that they could hear, but she just couldn't risk it. She felt slightly faint, and sweat began to bead on her spine. She shivered, the blood icy in her veins. She breathed deeply and evenly, but other than that, she didn't move a muscle.

'*Danilo, opoved*,' Bruzek said.

There was silence from the radio.

'What have you done with him?' he snarled, tightening his grip on the pistol.

Josie just stood there, still not speaking.

'Move and put your back against the door. I assume you didn't come alone, so anyone shoot or blow door, they shoot into you or blow you up too.' He gesticulated with the barrel of the pistol, which looked almost comically big in his tiny hand.

She did as he asked, facing him the whole time, her eyes not leaving his, shuffling her feet until her back was flat against the wooden door, her comrades just a few inches away. She hoped to God they weren't planning on using explosives to take the door off its hinges.

'Take off goggles and balaclava, slowly and easy. Any stupid moves and I shoot you in gut.'

With a sense of dread, Josie did as he ordered. She raised her hand to the goggles and pulled them from her head, dropping them to the marble floor with a clatter.

'Now balaclava.' Bruzek tightened his grip on the pistol and bared his teeth again.

Josie's shoulders sagged. She had no choice, and her skin began to flush hot at the thought of what Bruzek would do once he recognised her, which he surely would. She grabbed the top of the woollen balaclava and pulled it from her head, her dyed red hair flopping over her face as she did.

Bruzek's eyes flared open and his mouth gaped. 'Mary?' he said, before the shock turned rapidly to anger, and then to barely contained fury.

'Not Mary, funnily enough,' and she was astonished to find herself smiling at the little man, despite the cannon-like pistol.

He tightened his grip on the weapon, his face contorting with rage. 'You fuck bitch, you come to my homes and now you come to steal from me, yes?' He moved forward a step, but Josie stayed rooted to the spot. She didn't move a muscle, just held his gaze.

Bruzek stood there, his back to the vast window and the pistol unwavering. 'You think a man of my stature wouldn't have a backup power, eh? I flick switch and battery power kick in from solar windows and doors lock tight. You must think I'm stupid.'

Josie stayed quiet, not taking her eyes from the man.

He raised the radio to his lips and spoke again. '*Danilo, Teodor, reagovat' potrebujem pomoc*. Respond, I need assistance.'

'They're not coming, Bruzek.' Josie's eyes were hard and narrow, and once again she was almost shocked at the absence of any panic. She was scared, she didn't want to die, but she also realised that she wasn't afraid to, either. It was somehow calming.

'You shut up, bitch. You want to see how big a hole this will blow in you, eh? Forty-four Magnum, head clean off, eh?' His eyes were blank and unfathomable, but his face was pale and twisted, and for the first time she wondered if he actually meant it.

A flash of movement caught her eye in the huge window, right at the top, and her heart leapt into her throat, almost like a golf ball was stuck there. A hand appeared, only just visible against the glare caused by the chandelier, and hope surged in her chest. Her earpiece crackled, a hoarse whisper from Macca in her ear. 'Josie, can you hear me? Say something if you can.'

A smile began to stretch across her mouth. 'Big gun, Bruzek. Big gun, tiny cock?' She sniggered, wanting to keep all his attention on her.

'Shut up. You shut up, do you hear me? Shut up,' he said, dropping the radio to the floor and raising his free hand to support the mammoth pistol.

'Oh yes, I hear you. I've been hearing you all along, Macca.' She dropped her hands halfway, desperate to keep Bruzek's eyes on her and not anywhere else.

'Keep your fuck hands up!' he almost shrieked, his face reddening alarmingly.

'Josie, on three, drop to the ground, turn away from the window and cover your head. Say "I'm sorry, Bruzek" to acknowledge.' Macca's voice was urgent in her ear.

Josie planted her feet firmly and raised her hands just a little more before fixing Bruzek with a blank stare. She spoke slowly and robotically, pausing after each word for effect. 'I'm. Sorry. Bruzek.'

'Received, counting now. One. Two. Three.'

Josie dropped like her legs had disappeared and fell with her face away from the window. Gripping the marble floor with her soft-soled boots, she slid a few feet forward until she was behind the nearby sofa and curled into a foetal position. There was a dull crack, followed by a deafening smash as the window shattered inwards with the force of the surgical explosion, followed by a piercing scream as multiple shards of glass were blown into the room.

She glanced up to see Macca diving through the jagged hole in the plate glass, a climbing rope trailing from his harness, and colliding with Bruzek, who hit the glass-strewn floor with a crunch. Macca let out a cry as he landed hard.

Josie sprang to her feet and kicked the pistol away from Bruzek, who was flailing on the floor like a landed fish.

'Macca, are you okay?' she said, her ears ringing from the blast.

'My back,' he said through gritted teeth.

'Blast injuries?

'No, fucking pinged the bastard when I fell. I'm too old for this shit. Check Bruzek.'

The Slovak was trying to sit up, his face slick with blood that was cascading from a laceration in his forehead. A large shard of glass was wedged into his shoulder, and he was gasping and moaning, his face white as alabaster with shock.

'He's screwed. Hold on, I'll help you up; I just need to let the others in.' She ran to the door, praying that it would open. Turning the handle, she held her breath. It swung wide, and Neil, Charlie and Jacko rushed in, Charlie brandishing an automatic pistol. Asquith pulled a piece of wood from his pocket and slotted it under the door, wedging it open.

'It's all good, guys, we're good,' said Macca from his position on the floor.

'Fuck, what happened to you?' said Charlie.

'Pinged my back jumping through the window.' Macca was struggling to get to his feet.

They all surveyed the scene, their faces full of shock. The shattered window, glass littered across the floor, and the white-faced, blood-covered Bruzek with a large shard protruding from his shoulder.

Charlie snorted with laughter, followed by Asquith and then Jacko.

'It's no funny, you bastards, though I think my assaulting days are over.' Macca stood half bent over as he massaged his back, grimacing.

'Jesus, you made a fucking mess,' said Jacko, picking up the big silver handgun, opening the cylinder and letting the six bullets fall to the floor. 'Fuck me, this is a bastard cannon. Does he think he's Clint Eastwood?' He threw the gun on the floor dismissively.

'Yeah, must sweep up before we go,' said Macca, looking at the whimpering Bruzek.

'Not bad for an old bastard, despite your crocked back,' said Charlie with a grin.

'Hurt my damn knee as well. And my wrist is sore and I've a bloody headache. Now let's get that bloody safe open. Is the big silverback secure?' said Macca.

'Yeah, he's awake and spitting venom, but he's not going anywhere,' said Charlie, who was busy zip-tying the Slovak's hands.

Josie went to the bookcase and reached underneath the shelf until she located the switch. She depressed it, and the bookcase jolted and swung open, revealing the reinforced door with the keypad and glass fingerprint pad.

'We need chummy here to get into the safe, don't we?' said Macca.

'Yep, thumbprint and code.'

Bruzek looked up, his face white with alarm and shock. 'I won't help you,' he said, his voice wet and crackly.

'Oh yes you will, dickhead. You definitely will. Try the code,' said Macca.

Josie stepped up to the keypad and tapped in 112233. Charlie's powers of observation had been bang-on. Six stars appeared and the glass pad glowed red.

'Now listen, Bruzek. Here's the choice. Either you walk up there with me and press your thumb to the pad, or I remove your thumb with my Leatherman and press it there myself. Understand?' said Macca, his voice soft but full of menace. Bruzek looked up at the ex-Special Forces man and he knew. His face told the story. He believed every word Macca was saying. He nodded resignedly.

Wincing, Macca pulled him to his feet, the oligarch grunting in pain, and led him to the strongroom door. Without any further complaint, Bruzek reached his zip-tied hands to the pad and pressed his thumb against the glass. The door clicked and popped open.

'Get him over there and make sure he's secure,' said Macca, gesturing.

Charlie led Bruzek to a leather armchair and pushed him into it. He sat heavily with a grunt of pain, the shard of glass wet with blood and glistening in the light. Charlie bent down and quickly zip-tied his ankle to the chair leg.

'Are we ready?' said Macca.

There were nods all round, and Josie reached forward and swung the door open.

They all stared open-mouthed at the four-metre-square space. The valuable-looking paintings on the walls, the medal display, the whisky bottles and the rack full of antique shotguns.

'Holy crap, it's a treasure trove,' said Asquith. 'Will you look at those paintings. That one's a Rembrandt; in fact I recognise it. It's *Storm on the Sea of Galilee*. Stolen about thirty years ago. It's worth bloody millions and the reward for it is massive. Shit, and that one's a Rembrandt too, look. This is huge.'

'We're just here for the medals, Neil,' said Charlie. 'You know that. Once we're clear, we'll call the police and they can find all this shit. We need to get away.'

'Yeah, I guess, but this is going to shake the insurance world to its foundations.'

Josie stepped into the safe and turned to the medal display, set on green baize. The cheap bits of metal and bright ribbons glinted in the harsh light. Her eyes fell on the group at the centre. The Conspicuous Gallantry Cross, the Distinguished Conduct Medal, the Iraq medal with its Mention in Despatches oak leaf, Kosovo, Afghanistan, Sierra Leone, Bosnia, the Bronze Star. Her father's service to his country right there on the wall. As she reached forward and touched them, they felt like they were charged with electricity. She pulled them from the display, tears brimming in her eyes and her heart pounding, and clutched them to her chest.

'Not wanting to interrupt a moment, Jose, but we need to get moving.' Macca's voice was gentle, but it was enough to bring Josie back into the room. She nodded. Looking down, she saw the familiar wooden box with the SBS badge on it. She picked it up and flicked it open. Macca's medal group glinted within, set in the velvet of the case. She passed it to him, and he removed his rucksack and tucked the box inside.

'Fine, take these as well,' she said, handing him her father's medals. He slid them in alongside his own group and shouldered the bag.

'What do we do with chummy here?' said Charlie, pointing at Bruzek.

'Chuck him out of the window?' suggested Josie.

'No, please. I have money, take money, but don't kill me,' Bruzek babbled.

'I'll put field dressings on his wounds and we can leave him where he is,' said Macca. 'Glass shard in his shoulder is holding in the blood, and the cut on his head is superficial. He won't die. Let's get the hell out of here. We've still got to get back down that cliff and into the dinghy.'

Charlie and Asquith nodded and began to pack away their kit.

Bruzek was whimpering in pain, tears streaming down his pale face. 'Oh, stop bloody moaning,' said Macca as he squatted next to him and began to dress the wound on his head.

Once the Slovak had been bandaged up, Macca stood and looked at the others. 'Where's Jacko?

On cue, Jacko emerged from the safe, a long-barrelled shotgun in one hand and a small painting in the other. It was about the size of a piece of A4 paper and seemed to be some type of landscape scene. His face didn't wear its usual puckish grin, but instead was flat and stern.

'Jacko, what the hell are you doing?' said Macca.

'I'm taking this painting and this shotgun.'

Macca strode towards him, scowling. 'Jacko, no. No way. We're not thieves. The medals, just the medals – we agreed, you remember that?'

'I never fucking agreed, Macca, and I'm taking this Cézanne. It's worth ten million quid, and the reward for its return is massive. It's been missing for twenty-two years, and I'm gonna be the one who gets that reward, no arguments.' Jacko's eyes were hard and uncompromising, lacking any of the usual levity that was part of his make-up.

'Why that painting, why not the Rembrandt? It's far more valuable,' said Asquith.

'You really wanna know?' Jacko said, tucking the painting into his rucksack and shouldering it.

'Yes, I really wanna know, and why the shotgun?' added Macca, a trace of concern in his voice.

Jacko broke the shotgun and slotted two red cartridges into the barrels before snapping it shut. 'I'm taking the shotgun because it's an old and valuable Purdey, which I intend selling when I get back down south, and if anyone tries to stop me pissing off with this painting, I'm going to blow them away.'

'Including us?'

'No, not including you. I'm not a bleeding monster. You'll have to shoot me to stop me, though, and then what are you gonna do with my corpse, eh?' He smiled sarcastically.

'Jacko, why? We fought together, and now you're screwing us over.'

His face darkened, and when he spoke, his voice was bitter. 'I did nothing on Harriet. I just got an injury to my foot, was shipped home and then medically discharged. I got no medals, no hero's welcome, nothing, just thank you for your service, Jacko, now piss off. So forgive me if I don't take part in the back-slapping about the medals. I'm off.' He cradled the shotgun; not threateningly, but they could tell from his hard eyes that he meant business.

'But why this painting, Jacko? How do you know so much about it?' said Charlie.

Jacko smiled, his broken teeth like an ancient piano keyboard.

'Because I nicked it. Millennium New Year's Eve, when everyone else was on the piss, I was climbing down a rope ladder at the Ashmolean in Oxford and nicking this painting, *View of Auvers-sur-Oise* by Cézanne, for Giles Hunter, who wanted it for a client. Little did I know the client was dickhead over here.' He jerked his thumb to the quietly mewling Bruzek. 'I did my job but the bastard never paid the middleman, who then never paid me. Well imagine my surprise when the very same bastard turned up on this job. It's why I didn't want to meet him when Macca suggested it. So this is what you call a nicely lucrative bit of payback. Coincidence, eh?'

'But how are you going to get away? You're not coming with us.' Macca folded his arms, his jaw jutting.

'Like I want to do that fucking horrible trip in reverse anyway. Don't you boys worry about me, I'm sorted.' Jacko nodded, and then he was gone.

Chapter 73

Macca, Josie, Charlie and Asquith stood looking at each other in stunned silence. Charlie spoke first. 'I can't believe it. What a treacherous bastard, and I thought he was a mate.' Charlie handed over the Glock to Macca. 'You take this, mate. I'm off guns. It's my ex-cop instinct. I never touched the things since leaving the Corp.'

Macca grinned as he accepted the weapon. 'Not much we can do about it now. He always was a loose cannon, and he'll have to live with the consequences. Let's not sit around griping. We need to get the hell out of here.' Macca tucked the Glock back into his waistband and hoisted his rucksack, then turned towards the door.

Danilo was standing in the doorway, huge and uncompromising, a sub-machine gun in his hands pointing directly at Macca. Hunter hovered nervously behind him, face pale and eyes wide.

'Lucky for me Mr Hunter came out to see what all noise was about. Get your hands up, you bastards.' The bodyguard's face was swollen and bloody, his teeth bared in a snarl.

They all complied silently.

'You fucking will regret coming here. Where is General?'

'Sat comfortably in his chair, mate. Although I'd watch his shoulder, there's a fuck-off piece of glass in it. If that comes out, it could rupture some big old blood vessel.' Macca's voice was surprisingly humorous.

'Shut up!' Danilo roared, so loudly the chandelier quivered. 'This is an Uzi nine millimetre. One press of my finger and you all die. Spray and pray six hundred rounds per minute, so shut fuck up. Now move back towards window, hands on heads.'

'Do it, guys,' said Macca.

They all put their hands on top of their heads and began to shuffle backwards towards the shattered window.

'Now what?' said Macca.

Danilo looked down at Bruzek, who just moaned, 'My shoulder, I need to get to hospital.' His breathing was shallow and his voice almost inaudible.

And then, out of nowhere, Jacko appeared in the room, shotgun in his hands. Hearing the crunch of glass under boot, Danilo began to turn, but it was too late. Jacko had stepped forward and swung the butt of the weapon, the sleek wooden stock crashing into the base of the big Slovakian's neck with a sickening crunch. He fell to the floor like a puppet whose strings had been cut.

'Get the fuck in here, Hunter,' said Jacko, turning to the quivering antiques dealer, who was on his knees, his head in his hands, whimpering.

'Jacko, how . . .' began Josie.

Jacko didn't answer; he just removed the earpiece from his ear and grinned.

'Like the proverbial bad penny, eh?' said Charlie.

'That's me. I wasn't letting this fucking gorilla blow you all away. Now excuse me, I need to leave.'

Macca grinned. 'Don't be a dickhead. You can keep your loot, but come with us, you thieving bastard. We started this job together and we'll finish it together. Come on, let's get these bastards tied up; they can wait here for the cops.'

'Macca, the girls.' Josie spoke urgently. 'They're part of this and I want to make sure they're okay. Can we get the power back on?'

Macca nodded. 'Neil, can you sort power?'

'Roger that,' said Asquith, pulling Danilo over to where Bruzek was sitting and removing some zip ties from his harness.

'Can't I just go?' pleaded Hunter.

Macca pulled his Glock from his waistband and levelled it at the dealer. 'Get the fuck over there before I lose my fast-declining store of patience.'

Within a minute, Bruzek, a compliant Hunter and the still-unconscious Danilo were all secured on the floor, tied to each other with zip ties.

'Right, Josie, once Neil's got the power back on, go and find the girls, but be quick. I want to be away from this place in fifteen. I doubt anyone's called the cops, but I don't want to take the chance. We get away from here, then we call them in, and they'll take care of the girls, okay?

Josie nodded.

'Let's go, folks.'

Chapter 74

It only took Neil a moment to get the generator hooked up, and soon it was chugging away and the castle was bathed in light.

Josie stood outside the barn that the girls lived in and knocked gently on the door. It was opened by a pale-faced Renata, whose eyes widened in alarm at the sight of the black-clad figure at the door.

'Renata, are you and Nina okay?'

'Yes, we're fine. What's been going on? Why was there no power?'

'Look, things have changed. The police are coming and the General and Danilo are going to be arrested. You don't have to be afraid any more. You don't have to do what they say. You're both free to leave.'

'I don't understand. What about the others?'

'What others?' said Josie, her stomach tightening.

'The girls in the other barn. The unfortunates.' Renata's jaw wobbled as she spoke.

'What?' Josie felt her skin go cold.

'There are at least four more girls, but they don't have nice clothes and food. You have to spend time as an unfortunate before you come here to service the desires of the General, Danilo and Havel. If you don't comply, they take you away in the helicopter and throw you in the sea. In here it's bad, but being an unfortunate is much, much worse. We're okay, but please take care of them.' The door closed softly.

Josie stood there, her heart racing. She reached for her radio. 'Macca, we may have an issue. Meet me at the second barn, now, and bring a crowbar.'

The second barn was locked tight and in total darkness, and none of the key cards worked on the pad. Asquith produced a large, heavy chisel he'd found in the plant room and wedged it into the space between the lock and the jamb. It took some effort, but within a minute, the door had sprung open.

The smell hit them immediately. A putrid mix of shit and sweat and terrible food. Josie reached to the side of the room and flicked on the light.

There were four old-fashioned iron-framed beds in the room, covered with filthy bedding, each with a bucket at the end. But it wasn't the smell, or the beds, or the makeshift toilets that made them all almost sick with disgust.

Four emaciated girls lay motionless on the beds, rigid with utter terror. Only their eyes moved from side to side.

Josie was shaking, trying to fight the nausea and cold, bitter rage that was rising in her chest. She heard a noise behind her and turned to see Renata at her shoulder.

'Can I do anything? I'll run and get Nina,' she said. There was no shock or horror in her voice. Of course not, thought Josie. Renata had spent her time in here as an unfortunate, and now she wanted to help them.

'Jesus Christ, what the hell is this?' said Macca, his voice tight with fury.

'They're prisoners, here to be broken before they become sex slaves for Bruzek, Danilo and Havel. Those who don't submit get dropped in the bloody sea.' Josie felt her emotions grip her like a vice.

'Havel's the pilot, right?' said Asquith.

'Yeah, he's not nice, according to the girls.'

'So where is he now?'

'Renata, where's Havel?' said Josie.

'In the guest wing, sleeping. I'll go and get Nina.' Renata turned and headed back to her barn.

Almost on cue, there was a whine from the helicopter pad fifty metres away, and lights began to flash on the rotor.

'Shit, look, there's Bruzek, Hunter and Danilo heading for the helicopter now,' said Macca.

He started towards the aircraft as its blades began to turn, reaching to his waistband as he ran, but a sudden flash followed by gunfire made them all hit the ground hard, hands shielding their heads, bullets kicking up the turf around them.

'The pilot must have found them and released them. The bastards are going to escape. Fire back!' yelled Charlie against the rising note of the engine, which was now at full throttle.

'No point, at this range I've no chance. Let them go.' Macca seemed remarkably calm about it all. He laid his pistol down on the ground and reached for his phone.

'Macca, for fuck's sake, you're the only one with a gun,' bellowed Josie. 'If they leave, they could be on his private jet in fifteen minutes and they'll be gone for ever. Look what they've done. Not just my dad and the medals, but those poor girls, and they're going to get away with it.'

He looked at her and smiled. 'They won't,' he said simply.

'How can you be so sure?'

'Fate is a strange one,' he shouted into her ear as the engine note became almost deafening and the helicopter rose from the ground, gaining height quickly. They watched as it swung out over the edge of the outcrop, then turned and began to head north, the engine note fading as it went.

'Oh, Macca, I can't believe it.' Josie's eyes were wet, her face pale with exhaustion and anger.

He put his hand on her shoulder and winked. Then he raised his phone and stabbed at the screen. There was a sharp crack, and the helicopter bucked in the air, then dipped alarmingly and swerved, totally out of control. A second later, it smashed into the dark surface of the sea with an enormous crash,. There was no flame, just a huge hiss of steam as it began to sink in a tangle of metal.

Josie, Charlie, Jacko and Asquith stared open-mouthed as the tail rotor, still spinning, dipped out of sight.

'What the hell just happened?' said Asquith.

'I fixed a very small explosive device between the control runs and the swash plate on the rotor assembly. It'll have blown out the linkage, guaranteeing a crash. I just wanted to make sure they didn't take off with the medals. I'd planned to blow it up before they got in it, but you know. Plans change.' Macca shrugged, and his eyes twinkled.

No one spoke.

'Even if they recover the wreckage, which I doubt they will, it'll just look like a sheared bolt. They'll never know. We all okay with this?'

There was a pause. A long pause that seemed to fill the cold winter night with even more of a chill.

Josie spoke first. 'Fuck them. Nothing less than they deserved.'

'Me too,' said Asquith.

'Damn straight,' said Charlie.

'You can imagine my feelings,' said Jacko.

Macca nodded. 'Well, shall we get our shit together and piss off then? 'Objective achieved. We need to abseil down and get on that crappy dinghy, so I'd rather do it sooner than later.'

'We could do that, or we could nick their Land Rover. Not like they're gonna need it any more,' said Charlie, holding up a key fob.

'They left it in the ignition?' said Macca.

'No, it was in Bruzek's pocket when I searched him. There's another fob on it that I'm willing to bet is the remote for the portcullis. Failing that, the switch in the gatehouse should be easy to find.'

'Well then, let's use the Land Rover. We need to retrieve the camera and start heading south. Charlie, what will the cops do first?'

'It'll be all about the helicopter crash, but they won't be here for a while. I agree. Let's collect the stuff, get in our cars and piss off home. If I'm not back for Christmas, my missus will go doolally.'

Josie looked over to the barn and saw Nina and Renata standing arm in arm, staring at the bubbles coming up from the sunken helicopter five hundred metres away. She walked across and joined them.

'You both okay?' asked Josie.

'Were Bruzek and Danilo on the helicopter?'

'Yes, along with Havel.'

'Then we're okay. Dead men can't hurt us. We'll go and look after the unfortunates now. Can you send a doctor, maybe?'

'Of course. I'll call for help.'

'It's finally over?' said Renata, her face pale and wan.

'Yes, it's over. Bruzek can never hurt you again.'

Chapter 75

Macca, Josie, Neil, Jacko and Charlie were sitting around the kitchen table, fatigue etched on their faces, their kit piled up, ready to depart. It was almost five a.m., and still there'd been no news on the radio, or on any of their phones.

They'd left Bruzek's Land Rover where they'd parked the Volvo and the Toyota and returned to the farmhouse, the sound of blaring sirens disturbing the still night air. Now, after packing up and cleaning the place, removing all traces of their stay, they were taking a few moments to decompress and debrief over a coffee.

'We all okay with what's just happened?' said Macca, his eyes flitting between the members of the group.

'Which bit? Blowing up a helicopter and its murdering, human-trafficking scumbag rapist passengers and consigning them to the bottom of the North Sea?' said Josie, yawning extravagantly.

'Aye, that's the one.'

'I'm totally cool that Bruzek, Danilo and the pilot are now full fathom five, but I'm wondering about Hunter.'

'Without Hunter, there'd have been no market for your dad's

medals, and therefore Frankie would still be around,' said Charlie.

'Well then, I can live with it. I also got the impression from Nina that Hunter had been helping himself to the girls at the castle as well. So screw him.' Josie banged her palm down on the table and the others all jumped.

'You're turning into a ruthless woman, Jose. I'm proud of you, girl,' said Jacko, who seemed strangely taciturn, unlike the motor-mouthed cockney he usually was.

'Is what it is, Jacko. I don't like bullies, and I don't like scum like Bruzek and his cronies.'

'Well, you did good. You really are a chip off the old block. Now if you'll excuse me, I need a slash.' Jacko stood up and headed out of the room.

There was a long pause, the air of exhaustion palpable as they all sat back with their thoughts, but a sense of satisfaction accompanied the fatigue. In the silence, the large clock ticked rhythmically.

'We should head off, you know,' said Asquith after five minutes had passed.

'Promise to Bev?' said Charlie.

'Definitely. All the family is up, and the turkey cost almost two hundred quid. My life won't be worth living if I'm not there to carve it.'

'Two hundred quid for a bloody turkey? Jesus, what's wrong with a bootiful bit of Bernard Matthews turkey roll and Bisto gravy? That'll be my Christmas dinner.' Macca grinned, his Scottish vowels transforming to a Norfolk burr.

'Philistine. I've also a fillet of beef to prepare, and a large ham I'll need to glaze, so you can appreciate why we need to get on the road quickly. It's a long way back.'

'Aye, let's get weaving.'

'Where's Jacko?' said Charlie. 'He went for a piss ages ago.' He narrowed his eyes.

A sudden engine noise from outside split the silent morning.

They all rushed to the front door, knowing already what they were going to find. The Hilux was heading off along the track, with the shadow of one figure in the driver's seat.

'You little bastard, Jacko,' said Macca, unable to keep the grin from his face.

'I guess he didn't want us all moaning at him about him nicking the painting. Good luck to him.' Charlie actually laughed.

'He was always a wrong 'un,' said Macca, shaking his head.

'When do we think he realised it was Hunter who was the dealer?' said Charlie.

'Do we think he knew from the outset?' asked Josie.

'I can't see how. He didn't need to go through all the rigmarole of getting Jarman squared up in prison and then flogging Macca's medals to Grigson when he could have gone direct to Hunter and cut out the middleman. I suspect he only realised when he saw the photo we took at the hotel, and sensed an opportunity.' Charlie chuckled again. 'What a thieving toerag, eh? Typical Jacko, a decent bloke but eventually he'll always let you down.'

'Well, it took balls to come back and brain Danilo with that Purdey, so BZ to him for that,' said Macca.

'But it's not why we did this, is it?' said Asquith. 'We were just getting the medals back, whatever it took, no mercy, and now Jacko's tainted that.'

'I've thought about it, and I reckon that morally it's all cool,' Josie said, a thoughtful look on her face.

'How d'you work that out?' said Charlie.

'Think about it. Jacko is just going after the reward money, and the public get to see a long-lost painting again. It's almost prophetic, don't you think?'

'Well, at least the painting was the only thing that was stolen,' said Asquith.

'How about the hundred-grand Purdey?' said Charlie.

'Well, that as well. But at least it's just the painting and the shotgun.' Asquith yawned.

Charlie stifled a guffaw. 'Well, almost.'

'Charlie?' said Asquith, narrowing his eyes.

Charlie reached into his bag and pulled out a three-quarters-full bottle of Macallan, holding it aloft with a grin. 'It was just sat there, so I thought it would be remiss to not bring it. I mean, we should toast the success of the operation. Chappers' medals retrieved, Macca's too, and those dirty bastards can never hurt anyone again.' He pulled the cork from the bottle and sniffed. 'A quick nip before we head south?'

'Abso-bloody-lutely,' said Macca, standing up and grabbing four glasses from the cabinet.

Charlie poured a moderate measure of the amber liquid into each glass and slid them across to the others. They all raised the glasses and chinked.

'What are we toasting?' said Josie.

'How about the 11/06? We did a good job, and your old dad would definitely approve,' said Macca.

'The 11/06,' they all parroted and downed the shots.

'Blimey, that's a good drop,' said Macca, puffing his cheeks out.

'I'm not surprised,' said Josie, looking at her phone, a big smile splitting her face.

'Why?' said Macca.

'That's a forty-grand bottle of whisky, and we've just probably drunk about ten grand's worth.'

Chapter 76

Saturday 11 June 2022

Josie, Macca, Charlie and Asquith were sitting around the usual table in the Rose and Crown in Sandridge, pints of beer in front of them and a sombre atmosphere between them. Leo appeared at their table clutching a bottle of port and four small glasses. 'Yo, dudes, I've only got this stuff. You still want it?' he said, holding up a bottle of the deep-red liquid.

'It'll do, Leo, leave it there,' said Josie.

Macca cracked the seal and pulled out the cork, filling the four glasses to the brim. They all took one and raised it high.

'Chappers,' they said in unison.

'I can't believe it's forty years ago, guys,' said Charlie. 'Forty years since we were sat on that bloody hillside getting shot at.'

'Yep, and the 11/06 has grown even smaller. Shame about Jacko. I wonder where the dirty scumbag is now,' said Macca.

'Well, according to the press reports, the insurance company paid a "substantial" reward via a middleman for the safe return of the Cézanne, so I suspect he's somewhere debauched and depraved. This port really is honking, by the way.' Charlie grimaced. 'And to think we left the valuable stuff in that safe. Still, I enjoyed the media circus of all the paintings being rehung in various galleries. Gave me a warm and fuzzy feeling.'

'What did you tell Kelly about the medals?' Macca asked Josie.

'The truth. That they were posted through my door.'

'I bet she loved that. What did she say?' said Asquith.

'She wanted to seize them as evidence. I told her to take a running jump. I'm never letting them out of my sight again. Well, until the money runs out for Mum, anyway.'

'How long will that be?'

'Who knows. Bills keep going up with the cost of living, and I'm not allowed to sell the house. Dad's will made that clear.' She shrugged.

'You know I'll help,' said Asquith.

'You've done more than I could have ever expected, Neil. That's worth way more than money. Another port?'

No one was keen, but Josie poured four more anyway.

'So, Charlie, you reckon we're in the clear?' said Macca.

'I'd say so. We left no trace in Scotland, and the shit that's coming out of that place is off the dial. All sorts of local bigwigs implicated in the abuse, and the latest suggestion is that at least five of those poor girls have disappeared completely. Nasty suspicion that they were thrown out of the helicopter, if the other girls are to be believed.'

'What about the mess we left behind? Bloodstains and exploded windows?'

'Rumours I'm hearing are that the locals think there was a gang raid on the place, and the General fled in the helicopter, wounded, not wanting to get involved with law enforcement as he had more stolen shit in that safe than the British Museum. Air accident investigators have concluded from the black box and some of the wreckage that it was mechanical failure rather than foul play. The systemic abuse of trafficking victims seems to be the headline. I think we're okay—' Charlie stopped, his mouth gaping open and his eyes wide in shock.

'What?' said Macca, looking at Charlie, who was staring at the door.

'That's fucking Mark Johnstone, DI Kelly's deputy. Shit, what's he doing here?'

They all swivelled to look at the new arrival. Johnstone raised his heavy-lidded eyes and surveyed them. His expression was blank and his grey hair bushy and dishevelled.

A silence descended on the table.

Johnstone looked across at Charlie and raised a finger in greeting before turning to the bar and ordering a pint.

'Charlie, why the bloody hell is he here? You said the cops were nowhere with this,' said Asquith.

'I didn't think they were.'

'Charlie?' said Johnstone as he appeared next to them, pint in hand.

'Mark.'

'I heard you'd be here. Spoke to Josie's nice neighbour, and she said you always come to the Rose and Crown on this particular date. Mount Harriet anniversary, right?' He sat and took an exploratory sip.

'What can we do for you, DS Johnstone?' said Josie, her eyes narrowed.

'Just clearing up loose ends, Josie.'

'Loose ends?' Her voice was tight.

'Yeah. One thing always puzzled me, particularly when I was interpreting the phone data. I was concerned about the fact that Hunter, also linked to the medals, was in that helicopter crash in Scotland. What with all that stolen art and the trafficking victims, there were bloody questions being asked in the House and everything, so DI Kelly asked me, "Are there any links with our marines to that area of Scotland?"' He paused to sip his beer.

'Where are you going with this, Mark?' said Charlie.

'Well, we know that Josie was up in that part of the country, but she returned and was at home when the helicopter went down, according to her phone, anyway. And *your* phones suggested the rest of you hadn't left Hertfordshire. Like not at all, which is a bit odd, but I wasn't going to make work for myself. However, the ambitious DI Kelly got very demanding once we realised Hunter was involved, and who got lumbered with reviewing CCTV, eh? Me, that's who.' He slurped at his beer.

'Mark—' began Charlie, but the detective cut him off.

'So I looked at the CCTV, and what did I find?' He took an envelope from his pocket and slid out a black-and-white photo.

It was Josie, at the door to the antique shop, in her Russian wife garb, the fur hat, wool coat and sunglasses. Mark raised his eyebrows.

'That could be anyone,' said Josie.

'That's what I told DI Kelly, but when I looked at the phone data for Hunter, overlaid with yours, what did I find?' He pulled out another still from a CCTV camera. This time it was much clearer. A pin-sharp image of Josie and Charlie in the foyer at the Chesterfield Hotel.

Silence fell, the tension almost crackling.

'Now, I'm sure there's an innocent explanation why you two were impersonating cops to gather CCTV images of Giles Hunter. I just can't think what it is, that's all,' Mark said, looking perplexed, with a touch of a glint in his eyes.

'Are we nicked, then?' said Charlie, his expression resigned. Josie's face was flushing deep red.

Mark just picked up his pint and drained it, smacking his lips in a satisfied fashion.

'What was DI Kelly's view of the CCTV?' said Josie.

Mark sighed and leant back in his chair. 'Do you know when I actually found this out?'

'Obviously not. Why don't you tell us?'

'It was on my last day as a serving cop, so I neglected to tell DI Kelly and accidentally deleted the CCTV from the hotel.

Apparently it's been overwritten on their system now, so unfortunately it's lost for ever.' He grinned widely, ripping the photographs up and stuffing them back into the envelope, which he handed to Josie.

'You bastard, you had me going there.' Charlie chuckled.

Mark laughed. 'Look, I've been a cop for a long time, and I've done some good stuff and some not so good stuff, but the last thing I wanted on my final case was to ruin some decent people. I've deleted it all; you're clear and free. The cops up north are full-on with all the VIP perverts and the fact that half of the world's missing masterpieces were found in that safe. I'm the only one who knows what happened, and even I don't know it all. Anyway, I'd best dash, I just wanted to let you know. DI Kelly has moved onwards and upwards, and no one in Hertfordshire is interested any more. Enjoy your day, lads. You deserve it. You did a good thing.'

'You want another beer?' asked Charlie.

Mark shook his head. 'Nah, I'm good. Don't want to drink and drive, do I? Wouldn't want to break the law.' He turned and ambled off with the air of a satisfied man.

The silence in the bar was long and intense as they all looked at each other.

'Jesus, that was bloody lucky,' said Macca.

'He's a good man, is Mark,' said Charlie.

'It seems so,' said Josie, and silence descended around the table again.

There was a sudden buzzing on the table akin to a demented wasp, and Macca frowned as he looked at his phone. 'It's a video call.'

'Answer it,' said Josie, nodding, her eyes wide.

He swiped at the icon, and when the screen cleared, Jacko was staring at them, his face thin and deeply tanned. His broken and battered teeth had been replaced with neon-white and perfectly straight veneers. The change in him was extraordinary.

'Hello, dickheads, happy 11/06. Forty bloody years, eh?' he chirped, his voice cheery.

Charlie and Asquith stood, and they all crowded around the screen.

'Jacko, you necky bastard,' said Macca, surprised to feel a broad grin spreading across his face.

'Couldn't let the day go without toasting Chappers with me oppos, could I? How are you old buggers doing?'

'We're all good, although the police are still looking for you, mate. Something about phone evidence linking you to Jarman getting a kicking,' said Charlie.

'Well good luck to them in finding me. I'm using my new-found wealth to keep my trotters deep in the trough in South East Asia, and I'm not coming back, that's for sure.'

'What's with the gnashers? You look like an emaciated Simon Cowell.'

'The old ones were never great for trapping the birds, so as I'm flush, I thought I'd indulge. Dentists are skilful over here.'

'How much was your reward, then?' said Macca.

'Well I made a lovely bit of bunce from the shotgun, which tided me over until the insurance company wedged out for the painting. Let's just say I have more than I need to see me out, living at my normal pace, with a bit of spare change.' Jacko's grin grew wider.

'You look skinny as a rail. What happened, food not agreeing?' asked Josie.

'Nah, love the scran, mate. You may remember the overly regular pissing?'

'Yeah, constant stops on the drive up. Why?' said Charlie.

'Fucking cancer, mate. Aggressive ductal prostate cancer, and it's spread. That's why I'm phoning. I suspect I won't make next year's 11/06 meeting.'

A deep, unsettling silence descended on the four of them. No one knew what to say.

'Jacko—' began Josie, but he interrupted immediately.

'Not a word. Not a fucking word, my girl. I've maybe six months left, and I'm behaving disgracefully while my todger is still capable of performing with the aid of the little blue pill, so don't feel sorry for me. I was destined to never make old bones, so I'm good with it. Just do one thing for me, yeah?' he said, the smile wider than ever.

'What?' said Charlie.

'Buy a decent bottle of port next year; the one you just ordered is dog shit. Leo's bringing another one over now. See ya, lads, wouldn't wanna be ya.' He waved, and then he was gone.

They sat there in silence, looking at each other in turn.

'Here we go, guys,' said Leo, arriving with another bottle of port and four fresh glasses and depositing them on the table.

'Who ordered that?' said Josie.

'Some bloke just phoned and asked if you were here. I said you were, and he asked me to serve you up the best bottle of port we had. I found a decent Taylor's that I'd forgotten we had and he paid on a card.'

'Did he have a message for us?'

'Well, yes, but . . .'

'Leo?' said Josie, narrowing her eyes.

'Don't shoot the messenger, but he told me to tell you to shove it up your arses.' He grinned and went back to the bar as they all laughed uproariously.

Macca uncorked the bottle and poured four shots. 'Jacko,' he said, raising his glass.

'Jacko,' they all echoed.

Chapter 77

One year later

S. G. Baldwin's auction house in central London was buzzing with anticipation, bidders lining the seats in the elaborate room. A row of people at the back were attached to phones, with iPads open on their laps.

A green baize board protected by a glass box stood on the table next to the auctioneer, and Frank Chapman's medals were pinned to it, gleaming in the harsh overhead lights. Josie looked at them and felt sick, but she knew she had no choice. The nursing home were starting to make a fuss about payments for her mum, and she could delay no longer.

'Here we go, it's up now. Josie, my offer still stands,' said Asquith.

'Neil, no. No way. No charity. Dad would have gone bloody mad,' she said firmly, her eyes fixed on the medals, fighting the urge to burst into tears with every fibre of her being. Macca put his arm around her shoulders, and pulled her tight, and she leant into her old friend.

'Looking at the buyers, I'm not sure you could afford them,

Neil,' said Macca.

'Yeah, some rich-looking bastards in here,' agreed Charlie.

The auctioneer, a distinguished-looking man wearing a blue suit and pink shirt, banged his gavel on the lectern.

'Ladies and gentlemen, we now come to the final item in today's auction. Lot 29 is a unique and very special group of contemporary medals awarded to the late Regimental Sergeant Major Frank Chapman, Royal Marines. The group comprises the Conspicuous Gallantry Cross, Distinguished Gallantry Medal, GSM Northern Ireland, South Atlantic Medal with rosette, NATO Former Yugoslavia, NATO Kosovo, 1st Gulf War with bar, (Operation Granby), OSM Sierra Leone with rosette, Operation Telic with clasp and Mention in Despatches, OSM Afghanistan, Royal Navy Long Service and Good Conduct Medal, Accumulated Campaign Service Medal with bar, and USA Bronze Star. I know you'll all have studied the catalogue and the citations, and I think I can say that this is one of the most notable groups in modern conflict. The medals have been extensively examined by our resident expert, Mr Mark Smith, and provenance is more than solid. Pre-sale estimate is one hundred and fifty. Who will start me off at a hundred?' He looked around the room expectantly.

Silence. No one wanted to be the first to bid. The auctioneer's experienced eyes scanned the rows, looking for movement.

Suddenly his eyes lit up and he pointed. 'I have one hundred. Do I have one twenty?'

The room was gripped with tension, a low murmur of conversation audible.

'One twenty, I have one twenty. Do I have one thirty? One thirty anyone?'

Silence in the room again, apart from a slight cough from the back.

'Shit, is that it?' said Josie.

'No way, all tactics,' said Asquith, raising his finger.

'I have one thirty. Do I have one forty?' The auctioneer looked around the room. 'I have one forty. Do I have one fifty?'

Asquith raised his finger again.

'Neil, what are you playing at?' said Josie, grabbing his hand and lowering it.

The auctioneer looked confused. 'I have one fifty. Let's make this interesting. How about one seven five, anyone for one seven five?'

'Neil, I promise you I'm gonna choke you out if you bid one more time,' said Josie.

'I have one seven five, back of the room, and I now have an online bid, two hundred thousand pounds,' said the auctioneer, and there was a gasp, followed by more low murmurs. Clearly a curve ball had been thrown in.

'Shit, I couldn't afford that anyway,' said Asquith.

'Thank Christ for that,' said Josie, her face flushed.

'Well, that's stunned the room. Do I have two twenty, anyone for two twenty?' A smile stretched across the auctioneer's face.

Silence.

'Currently at two hundred thousand pounds. Any advance on two hundred thousand?'

Silence.

'Okay, are we all done? At two hundred thousand pounds once . . .'

Silence.

'Twice . . . I have two twenty, two hundred and twenty thousand pounds. Do I have two forty?'

The silence in the room was deafening. Josie held her breath, her heart pounding in her chest.

'Are we all done? At two hundred and twenty thousand pounds . . .' The auctioneer paused, his eyes swivelling around the room, then his gavel rapped briefly on the lectern. 'Sold for two hundred and twenty thousand pounds.'

There was a ripple of applause around the room, and a general hubbub of excited chattering as people headed towards the exit.

'Decent price, Jose. That'll keep your mum for a while,' said Macca, putting his arm around her shoulders again.

'I guess,' said Josie, her face pale but resigned.

'Could have been worse. Neil could have won, and then the fallout from Mrs Asquith would have been cataclysmic.'

'Ain't that the truth,' said Asquith with a shrug.

'I feel sick. Proper sick. Everything we went through to get them back, and now they're gone.' Josie hung her head.

'Difference is, love, they've been sold on your terms, and as your dad wanted. Console yourself with that, maybe?' said Charlie.

'I guess so,' Josie said, shaking her head and cuffing away a stray tear.

A stocky man wearing frameless spectacles and a sharp blue suit approached. 'Hi, I'm Mark Smith,' he said with a warm smile. 'I look after the medal operations at Baldwin's. I just wanted to say congratulations. They went way over my estimate, so I guess you'll be delighted.'

'Thanks, but not as delighted as I'd be if I hadn't had to sell them at all,' said Josie.

'I am aware of the background, Miss Chapman, and I'm so sorry for your loss. Your father was a very brave man, and I don't think I've seen a more impressive contemporary group of medals pass through my hands.'

'Josie Chapman?' came a voice from behind them. Josie turned to see a well-dressed Asian man approaching. His hair was immaculately styled and his suit perfectly fitted.

'Yes,' she said, an eyebrow cocked.

'My name is Hitesh. I'm from Hitesh, Khan and Company, solicitors. We are handling the estate of a Mr James Jackson, who sadly passed away two months ago.'

'Yeah, we heard about that. So sad,' said Josie.

'Indeed.'

'What's this about? We want to go to the pub.'

'Of course. I'm required to tell you that Mr Jackson left an instruction in his will that we were to bid on the medals up to the limit of his available funds, which is what we have done. The medals are now secured, and I'm handing them over to you.' He extended his hand, which held a plain cardboard box.

Josie's stomach clenched tight as she accepted the box. She opened it, her breath held.

Her father's medals looked up at her, glinting in the bright light.

She opened her mouth like a guppy, but couldn't find the words.

'I believe the proceeds of the sale will be transferred direct to your account, Ms Chapman, less auction house fees, of course.'

'But . . .' Josie's mouth gaped again.

'Good day, Ms Chapman. That concludes our business with you. Any questions, please feel free to call me.' Hitesh handed over a business card, then nodded and strode off.

Mark Smith held out his hand and gripped Josie's tightly. His eyes were wet with tears. 'Miss Chapman, I've been in this game a long, long time, and this is a first for me. Congratulations. And now I'd best be off before I make a fool of myself any further.' He smiled and turned away.

Josie just stood there, tears streaming down her face as she brushed her fingers against the medals. Her skin seemed to tingle at the touch. She looked up at Macca, Asquith and Charlie. All three had tears in their eyes.

'God bless you, Jacko,' she said, and the four of them hugged, her father's medals safe, pressed between them.

Epilogue

Josie walked into her mum's room at the Verulam Lodge nursing home. She wasn't surprised to find her slumped asleep in her armchair, a copy of a Danielle Steel novel open in her lap. She bent down and kissed her gently on the cheek. Her mum's eyes opened, and then narrowed as she blinked and focused on her daughter. There was no recognition.

'My goodness, what on earth do you think you're up to, young lady? I'm not one of those, you know.' She pursed her lips and rubbed at her cheek, her eyes full of confusion.

'Hi, Mum,' said Josie, sitting on the chair opposite her with a broad smile. She felt like she was floating on air after the auction, knowing that her mum's future was secure.

Macey reached for her spectacles on a chain around her neck and settled them on her nose, appraising Josie with interest.

'Ah, now I recognise you. Hello, Aggie,' she said. Aggie was her late sister, who had died ten years ago.

Josie didn't correct her. 'How's the book?' she asked.

'It's Danielle Steele, love. She's always good. My Frankie used

384

to read to me, as I struggle to read now, you know. Have you seen Frankie recently? I miss him.' She reached for the glass on the table to her side. It was empty, but she still raised it to her lips to drink.

Josie leapt to her feet and gently took the glass from her mum's hands, refilling it before handing it back to her. 'No Mum, not seen him for a while.'

'A shame. He must be busy, I guess. He was always a busy man, always away on operations. He was a hero, you know. Won medals and all. I miss my Frankie.' Macey's eyes were suddenly damp.

'I know, Mum. Would you like to see his medals again?'

Her eyes opened wide, and a huge grin spread across her face. 'I'd love to,' she said, suddenly animated.

Josie reached into her bag and pulled out the group of shining medals, and her heart leapt as her dear mum's face lit up like a child's on Christmas morning.

Macey's hands shook as she took the medals and stared at them open-mouthed, her eyes shining. Josie could almost see the memories flooding in.

'Oh, they're just so beautiful. I'm so proud of him. What a hero, eh, love?' She gripped them tight to her chest, and at that very moment, Macey Chapman was back, her beautiful smile wide and full of sunshine.

'Yes, Mum. What a hero.' Josie stopped speaking, not because she had nothing more to say, but because her throat was tight and she didn't want her mum to see the tears flowing down her face.

Josie was crossing the car park outside the nursing home when someone called her name.

She turned and saw a man sitting in a parked-up Subaru. He was in his early fifties, lean and tanned, with a shaven head and friendly blue eyes.

'Sorry, did you want something?' she said, not approaching the car. There was something about the man that was familiar, but she was convinced she had not seen him before.

'Josie Chapman?' he said in a well-spoken, unaccented voice.

'Sorry, who are you?' said Josie, tightening her grip on her bag, the medals nestling deep inside.

'Macca sends his regards, Josie. My name is Bas Marchbank and I used to work with our mutual acquaintance many years ago. Could I have a few moments of your time?' He smiled warmly. His face was plain and unremarkable, and he gave off no threatening vibes at all, but she wasn't about to get in the car, certainly not with two hundred grand's worth of medals in her bag.

'What's it about?' she asked guardedly.

The man sighed, picked up a phone from the dash of the car and dialled. 'Speak to her, will you, mate?' he said into the handset, before proffering it to Josie without a word.

Intrigued, she stepped forward and took the phone. 'Hello?'

'How're you doing, hen?' The voice was warm and familiar.

'Macca? What the hell's going on?' Josie felt her breath begin to quicken.

'Bas is an old mate. Well, I say mate, he used to be my boss in the SBS for a while. He's a good man, a hundred per cent legit, and you're safe to chat with him. I think it'll be worth your while, love.'

'Macca, this is odd to say the least. I've just been in to see my mum and he was waiting in the car park.'

'Just have a natter with him. I mean, what's the worst that can happen, eh? Look, gotta run. Speak later.' And with that, he was gone.

'Happy to talk?' said Bas Marchbank.

'If Macca says you're legit, I believe him,' said Josie, moving closer to the car.

'Jump in?' he said, nodding at the passenger seat.

She paused for a moment, then made a snap decision. She rounded the bonnet of the car, opened the door and slumped down into the seat.

'Well?' she said, turning to look at Marchbank, who was

studying her with a half-smile on his face. He looked tough and seasoned, and she could tell he was ex-military, but there was something else about him. His smile was genuine and his eyes were clear, but he looked dangerous. Dangerous, capable and ruthless.

'Macca's right. I was his boss. I was the captain of his squadron.'

'Are you still SBS?'

'Oh no. I moved on a good while ago. I work for the security services now.'

'What do you want from me?' she asked, curiosity burning inside her.

'Macca's told me all about you. He told me what happened before Christmas in London and in Scotland, and I have to say, I'm impressed.'

'Thanks, I guess. But what do you actually want?'

'I want to offer you a job.'

Slang glossary

I thought it would be really useful to include a glossary of the slang that is commonly used by Royal Marines. It is a really important part of the culture of the marines, and I wanted this book to feel as authentic as possible.

I've referred to *Bootneck to English Dictionary*, written by Barry Budden, for accuracy.

ANPR – automatic number plate recognition

Banjo – an egg and bacon roll or sandwich; so called, as when eaten the egg yolk often runs, and the action of the hand brushing it away gives a (sort of) impression that the eater is playing a banjo

Bootneck – a member of the Royal Marines; derives from the strip of leather that used to be used to protect the neck from nefarious sailors with ill intent

Black maskers – gaffer tape, the multi-purpose product used to fix everything from clothing to vehicles

BZ – well done, an appreciation of a job well done

CASEVAC – casualty evacuation

Chinstrapped – to be exhausted. 'I'm totally chinstrapped, mate.' Interchangeable with 'hanging out'

Contact – contact with enemy forces

DMS boots – 'Direct Moulded Sole' boots issued in the 1980s; leaky and impossible to break in

Dripping – complaining

Essence – extremely attractive

Hanging out – someone who is physically exhausted. 'Mate, I'm hanging out after that long yomp.' Also see 'yomp'

Harry ice pigs – very cold. The addition of 'Harry' to anything gives greater emphasis. 'Blimey, it's Harry ice pigs out here.'

Honking – unpleasant, nasty, not nice. 'This scran is totally honking, mate.'

Icers – cold

PMC – private military contractor; mercenary

Proff – to acquire something desirable, either by official or unofficial means

Necky – cheeky, but in an insulting manner. 'You're a necky bugger, you are!'

Rupert – a commissioned officer

SLR – self-loading rifle, which was the standard-issue weapon during the Falklands conflict

Turn-to – to turn up at the prescribed time for duty

Threaders – a feeling of extreme anger, sadness or devastation. Great disappointment. 'I'm totally threaders that my leave has been cancelled.'

Turbo – can be used to accentuate something. 'Mate, that food was turbo essence.' Also see 'essence'

Scran – food

Snurgling – to covertly move up to a tactical position close to the enemy

Spin – police term for 'search'

Solid – unintelligent, or possibly being a bit daft. 'Jacko, we all thought you were solid.'

Wet – a drink of any type. 'Jacko, get the wets in.'

Wooden-top – a slightly derogatory term for a member of the Brigade of Guards, owing to the bearskin headdress worn

Wrap your bangers in – to give up or quit something. 'I've had enough of the Corps. I'm wrapping my bangers in.'

Yomping – to traverse difficult terrain carrying full kit

Cockney rhyming slang

As a number of the characters use slang, I thought a short glossary would help.

Bacardi – Bacardi Breezer = geezer

Bucket – bucket and pail = jail

Blagger – armed robber

Antwacky – antiques

Kettle – kettle and hob = watch (after a fob watch)

George Best – chest

Drum – home; comes from drum and bass, meaning 'place'

'Aris = arse – short for Aristotle; used by cockneys wishing to avoid Chaucerian vulgarity. Aristotle = bottle, which equals bottle and glass = arse. A bit convoluted!

Hendrix – appendix

Blower – telephone

Battle cruiser – boozer

Score – twenty pounds

Monkey – five hundred

Grand – thousand pounds

Claret – blood

Khazi – derived from cockney word 'carsey', meaning privy, which has roots in the nineteenth century

Schmutter – Yiddish for clothing, but in regular use by cockneys

Author's note

I hope you enjoyed this book, which was born out of a conversation with an editor friend of mine, Finn Cotton, in 2022. "You should write a heist book about a group of old codgers, like those blokes that did the Hatton Garden one."

Well, he got me thinking. The idea was hugely appealing. As a society, once you're over the age of about forty, you're almost forgotten as a thriller protagonist. Why is this? The Chinese revere their elders, and really cherish their wisdom and fortitude, but in the West? Not so much. So a story about a group of old chaps in their sixties doing something dodgy? Sounds fun.

I loved the idea, but what, and how, could I bring something new to the novel? There's been loads of heist books over the years, some really brilliant, some less so, but what could I bring to the party that was new?

I knew one thing, as an ex-Met police detective, I didn't want to talk about a load of old villains. I wanted my characters to have right on their side. I wanted them to be the good guys, who the readers would root for with a clear conscience, even if they were skirting around a few laws. So not for money. No personal gain, that didn't seem right.

The ideas were swirling around when I saw a programme on the BBC, called *Falklands War – A soldier's story*. It was the fortieth anniversary of the Falklands conflict. It was a fascinating look back at a few of the soldiers who had been involved in the conflict back in 1982. This was something I couldn't not be fascinated by. Not only had I joined the military a year after the conflict, but I had also spent four long, cold, windswept months on that archipelago in the South Atlantic.

I have no particular personal stories of derring-do about my time there, beyond some daft, funny stories I like to recount at literary festivals. In reality, I mostly wandered about secure areas, patrolling with a snarling German shepherd dog, as a military cop.

However, I was astonished by the harsh, brutal, yet beautiful landscape, unrelenting wind, driving rain, and difficult, peaty terrain, and I remembered thinking, as I looked up at the peaks of Mount Harriet, Mount Longdon and Mount Two Sisters, *How the hell did they manage to win a battle on those hills?* The tales from the programme's contributors, mostly marines and paratroopers, were shocking, inspiring and hugely emotional. There was no celebration of war, no great glories; it was a filthy, dirty and brutal conflict that killed many, and injured many more, some with scars that will never heal.

It catapulted me back in time to 1982, as that naïve kid watching open-mouthed at the TV reports from the terrible events, or poring over the latest accounts from the front. I was sixteen at the time of the conflict, and followed it with almost religious zeal, and was glued to TV reports, and I remember being blown away with what the task force achieved by travelling eight thousand miles to the South Atlantic to retake the islands from a much bigger defensive force.

The veteran's accounts of the dirty, hard and brutal conflict were sometimes difficult to watch, but at the same time I was struck by their selflessness and bravery. They were all around sixty years of age at the time of the documentary, but what really struck me was how formidable they all still seemed to be, as they recounted their memories of those few months in the harsh, unforgiving climate and terrain. There were many battles fought by the marines, paratroopers, guardsmen, and Gurkhas, but one in particular stuck in my mind.

The battle for Mount Harriet, on the 11th of June 1982. The reasons it resonated were twofold. An old colleague from the police had been a member of Lima Company, 42 Commando, during that battle, and over a load of beer one night he told me all about it.

It was shocking and fascinating in equal measure.

Then there was another reason I wanted to write about those men, both during the battle and later during the years that passed. My son, Richard, joined the Royal Marines in 2005, where he remains, almost twenty years later. He has had a tough career, with long months spent in the conflict zones of Iraq and Afghanistan, including the toughest tour with Lima Company, 42 Commando. I somehow just felt like it was meant to be.

So, the 11/06 club was born, with Macca, Charlie, Jacko, and Neil Asquith, and very soon, Josie Chapman, the daughter of a legendary regimental sergeant major, the bravest of men. I now had my cast. I had my characters, all very different, all having lived polar opposite lives, which felt accurate to me. The Royal Marines, more than any branch of the services, attract an incredibly varied type of recruit, so it felt to me like I could bring together these disparate characters for one last caper, and their varied experiences, both inside and outside the marines would make them way bigger than the sum of their parts.

Their bonds, forged by their hard experiences would be what drives them, just like the real veterans who have shared bad and good times. I don't pretend that my books are accurate, but being a veteran myself, I know how I feel about my former comrades.

My brothers in arms. We all shared something that can't be replicated outside of the military.

I hope you enjoyed this book, and look out for more from Josie Chapman, with maybe an appearance from one of the 11/06 in the future.

By the way, some of you may have noticed that Stonehaven Castle bears a striking resemblance, and geographical link, to the wonderful, awe-inspiring Dunnottar Castle, on the Aberdeenshire Coastline. You're correct. It's fundamentally the same place, but the great thing about being an author is that you can play God, and recast people, places and time to suit. Dunnottar Castle is an incredible place, and the chances of a rich oligarch bribing his way to building a home on it is just too ridiculous.

Or is it?

Max Connor (Occasionally known as Neil Lancaster)

Acknowledgements

As always, writing a book is a big old team effort, and this book is no different, so there are people I need to thank.

To Finn, for the idea. It took a while, but I got there.

To all the team at HQ Stories for your huge support in turning my drivel into a cogent story that people won't get angry with. Particular thanks to my editors on this one, George Green, Manpreet Grewal, Jane Selly. PR from Felicia, and marketing from Emma, who get people to know these books exist. All the folks I never get to hear about in sales, analytics, cover design, and the likes.

My agent, Kerr Macrae, for all your sage advice, cheerleading, and bringing this deal in like a ninja!

A big thanks goes to Mark Smith, the chap you see on the *Antiques Roadshow* who is an expert par-excellence in medals. Your advice on coming up with an accurate group of medals that was worth a packet was absolutely vital, and sparked much inspiration for the rest of the book.

To my wonderful wife, Clare. Love you forever.

To my kids, Alec, Richard and Ollie. You guys rock. I don't like to single any one of you out, but in this particular instance I have to mention Richard. This book wouldn't exist without you. I've so much respect, and so much pride in everything you've done, and continue to do.

The apple of my eye, my grandson, "Big Eddie Lancaster".

To all the soldiers, marines, sailors and airmen, all over the world, who are willing to put it all on the line for all of us. My respect is undying for all of you.

To all my writer pals for helping me stay sane, particularly Colin Scott, Tony Kent, and Ed James.

As always, last but definitely not least, all the booksellers, bloggers, reviewers, enthusiasts, and of course readers, thank you. Without you guys, it really, genuinely means nothing.

Dear Reader,

We hope you enjoyed reading this book. If you did, we'd be so appreciative if you left a review. It really helps us and the author to bring more books like this to you.

Here at HQ Digital we are dedicated to publishing fiction that will keep you turning the pages into the early hours. Don't want to miss a thing? To find out more about our books, promotions, discover exclusive content and enter competitions you can keep in touch in the following ways:

JOIN OUR COMMUNITY:

Sign up to our new email newsletter: http://smarturl.it/SignUpHQ

Read our new blog www.hqstories.co.uk

🐦 https://twitter.com/HQStories

📘 www.facebook.com/HQStories

BUDDING WRITER?

We're also looking for authors to join the HQ Digital family!
Find out more here:

https://www.hqstories.co.uk/want-to-write-for-us/

Thanks for reading, from the HQ Digital team